CLASSICS
of
CHILDREN'S
LITERATURE

CLASSICS
of
CHILDREN'S
LITERATURE

Compiled by Leonard Matthews

Exeter Books

NEW YORK

Copyright © 1987 by Martspress Limited

First published in the USA in 1987
by Exeter Books
Distributed by Bookthrift
Exeter is a trademark of Bookthrift Marketing, Inc.
Bookthrift is a registered trademark of Bookthrift Marketing, Inc.
New York, New York

Prepared by
The Hamlyn Publishing Group Limited
Bridge House, Twickenham, Middlesex TW1 3SB, England

ISBN 0-671-09117-4

Printed in Czechoslovakia

CONTENTS

INTRODUCTION

Through the pages of this book you will enter the realm of literature with all its fabulous wealth and splendour.

Here are sagas of high adventure from the ancient days of the Norse and Greek gods, epics of gallantry in the days of old when knights were bold, tales of magic and wonder, as well as poems and ballads whose stirring lines will be long remembered.

Some of the stories are complete in themselves, condensations of the original books. Others are extracts using the authors' own words.

The names of the contributors are legion, famous forever in the annals of the world's literature. Most of them will already be known to you, others possibly less familiar but all of them have enriched the vast treasury of the written word. In your hands now is their gift to you, a veritable garland of golden words. Many happy hours of reading lie ahead of you.

IVANHOE

In his lifetime Sir Walter Scott wrote many tales of high romance. None has proved more popular than Ivanhoe, *based as it was on the deeds of gallant, as well as treacherous, knights and the love of fair ladies. The hero is a Saxon, Wilfred of Ivanhoe, who, banished by his father, had journeyed with King Richard Lionheart on a Crusade to the Holy Land. When the story commences, Ivanhoe has returned to England, disguised as a pilgrim. Unrecognised, he attends a feast given by his father where the most important guest is a Norman Knight Templar, by name Sir Brian de Bois-Guilbert.*

De Bois-Guilbert is on his way to take part in a tournament arranged by Prince John.

Ivanhoe decides to enter the tournament and declares himself to be "the Disinherited Knight". He has long loved the Lady Rowena, his father's ward and is determined to win the contest and name her as the Queen of Love and Beauty. Now follows, in Scott's own words, what happens on the day of the tournament. The narrative opens during an interval in the fighting.

The pause on the tournament was still uninterrupted, excepting by the voices of the heralds exclaiming – "Love of ladies, splintering of lances! stand forth gallant knights, fair eyes look upon your deeds!"

The music also of the challengers breathed from time to time wild bursts expressive of triumph or defiance, while the clowns grudged a holiday which seemed to pass away in inactivity; and old knights and nobles lamented in whispers the decay of martial spirit, spoke of the triumphs of their younger days, but agreed that the land did not now supply dames of such transcendent beauty as had animated the jousts of former times. Prince John began to talk to his attendants about making ready the banquet, and the necessity of adjudging the prize to Brian de Bois-Guilbert, who had, with a single spear, overthrown two knights, and foiled a third.

At length, as the Saracenic music of the challengers concluded one of those long and high flourishes with which they had broken the silence of the lists, it was answered by a solitary trumpet, which breathed a note of defiance from the northern extremity. All eyes were turned to see the new champion which these sounds announced, and no sooner were the barriers opened than he paced into the lists. As far as could be judged of a man sheathed in armour, the new adventurer did not greatly exceed the middle size, and seemed to be rather slender than strongly made. His suit of armour was formed of steel, richly inlaid with gold, and the device on his shield was a young oak-tree pulled up by the roots, with the Spanish word *Desdichado*, signifying Disinherited. He was mounted on a gallant black horse, and as he passed through the lists he gracefully saluted the Prince and the ladies by lowering his lance. The dexterity with which he managed his steed, and something of youthful grace which he displayed in his manner, won him the favour of the multitude, which some of the lower classes expressed by calling out, "Touch Ralph de Vipont's shield – touch the Hospitaller's shield; he has the least sure seat, he is your cheapest bargain."

The champion, moving inward amid these well-meant hints, ascended the platform by the sloping alley which led to it from the lists, and, to the astonishment of all present, riding straight up to the central pavilion, struck with the sharp end of his spear the shield of Brian de Bois-Guilbert until it rung again. All stood astonished at his presumption, but none more than the redoubted Knight whom he had thus defied to mortal combat, and who, little expecting so rude a challenge, was standing carelessly at the door of the pavilion.

"Have you confessed yourself, brother," said the Templar, "and have you heard mass this morning, that you peril your life so frankly?"

"I am fitter to meet death than thou art," answered the Disinherited Knight; for by this name the stranger had recorded himself in the books of the tourney.

"Then take your place in the lists," said Bois-Guilbert, "and look your last upon the sun; for this night thou shalt sleep in paradise."

"Gramercy for thy courtesy," replied the Disinherited Knight, "and to requite it, I advise thee to take a fresh horse and a new lance, for by my honour you will need both."

Having expressed himself thus confidently, he reined his horse backward down the slope which he had ascended, and compelled him in the same manner to move backward through the lists, till he reached the northern extremity, where he remained stationary, in

expectation of his antagonist. This feat of horsemanship again attracted the applause of the multitude.

However, incensed at his adversary for the precautions which he recommended, Brian de Bois-Guilbert did not neglect his advice; for his honour was too nearly concerned, to permit his neglecting any means which might ensure victory over his presumptuous opponent. He changed his horse for a proved and fresh one of great strength and spirit. He chose a new and a tough spear, lest the wood of the former might have been strained in the previous encounters he had sustained. Lastly, he laid aside his shield, which had received some little damage, and received another from his squires. His first had only borne the general device of his rider, representing two knights riding upon one horse, an emblem expressive of the original humility and poverty of the Templars, qualities which they had since exchanged for the arrogance and wealth that finally occasioned their suppression.

Bois-Guilbert's new shield bore a raven in full flight, holding in its claws a skull, and bearing the motto, *Gare le Corbeau.*

When the two champions stood opposed to each other at the two extremities of the lists, the public expectation was strained to the highest pitch. Few augured the possibility that the encounter could terminate well for the Disinherited Knight, yet his courage and gallantry secured the general good wishes of the spectators.

The trumpets had no sooner given the signal, than the champions vanished from their posts with the speed of lightning, and closed in the centre of the lists with the shock of a thunderbolt. The lances burst into shivers up to the very grasp, and it seemed at the moment that both knights had fallen, for the shock had made each horse recoil backwards upon its haunches. The address of the riders recovered their steeds by use of the bridle and spur; and having glared on each other for an instant with eyes which seemed to flash fire through the bars of their visors, each made a demi-volte, and, retiring to the extremity of the lists, received a fresh lance from the attendants.

A loud shout from the spectators, waving of scarfs and handkerchiefs, and general acclamations, attested the interest taken by the spectators in this encounter; the most equal, as well as the best performed, which had graced the day. But no sooner had the knights resumed their station, than the clamour of applause was hushed into a silence, so deep and so dead, that it seemed the multitude were afraid even to breathe.

A few minutes' pause having been allowed, that the combatants and their horses might recover breath, Prince John with his truncheon signed to the trumpets to sound the onset. The champions a second time sprung from their stations, and closed in the centre of the lists, with the same speed, the same dexterity, the same violence, but not the same equal fortune as before.

In this second encounter, the Templar aimed at the centre of his antagonist's shield, and struck it so fair and forcibly, that his spear went to shivers, and the Disinherited Knight reeled in his saddle. On the other hand, that champion had, in the beginning of his career, directed the point of his lance towards Bois-Guilbert's shield, but, changing his aim almost in the moment of encounter, he addressed it to the helmet, a mark more difficult to hit, but which if attained, rendered the shock more irresistible. Fair and true he hit the Norman on the visor, where his lance's point kept hold of the bars. Yet, even at this disadvantage, the Templar sustained his high reputation, and had not the girths of his saddle burst, he might not have been unhorsed. As it chanced, however, saddle, horse, and man, rolled on the ground under a cloud of dust.

To extricate himself from the stirrups and fallen steed, was to the Templar scarce the work of a moment; and, stung with madness, both at his disgrace and at the acclamations with which it was hailed by the spectators, he drew his sword and waved it in defiance of his conqueror. The Disinherited Knight sprung from his steed, and also unsheathed his sword. The marshals of the field, however, spurred their horses between them, and reminded them, that the laws of the tournament did not, on the present occasion, permit this species of encounter.

"We shall meet again, I trust," said the Templar, casting a resentful glance at his antagonist, "and where there are none to separate us."

"If we do not," said the Disinherited Knight, "the fault shall not be mine. On foot or horseback, with spear, with axe, or with sword, I am alike ready to encounter thee."

More and angrier words would have been exchanged, but the marshals, crossing their lances betwixt them, compelled them to sepa-

rate. The Disinherited Knight returned to his first station, and Bois-Guilbert to his tent, where he remained for the rest of the day in an agony of despair.

Without alighting from his horse, the conqueror called for a bowl of wine, and opening the beaver, or lower part of his helmet, announced that he quaffed it, "To all true English hearts, and to the confusion of foreign tyrants." He then commanded his trumpet to sound a defiance to the challengers, and desired a herald to announce to them, that he should make no election, but was willing to encounter them in the order in which they pleased to advance against him.

The gigantic Front-de-Bœuf, armed in sable armour, was the first who took the field. He bore on a white shield a black bull's head, half defaced by the numerous encounters which he had undergone, and bearing the arrogant motto, *Cave adsum*. Over this champion the Disinherited Knight obtained a slight but decisive advantage. Both Knights broke their lances fairly, but Front-de-Bœuf, who lost a stirrup in the encounter, was adjudged to have the disadvantage.

In the stranger's third encounter with Sir Philip Malvoisin, he was equally successful; striking that baron so forcibly on the casque, that the laces of the helmet broke, and Malvoisin, only saved from falling by being unhelmeted, was declared vanquished like his companions.

In his fourth combat with De Grantmesnil, the Disinherited Knight showed as much courtesy as he had hitherto evinced courage and dexterity. De Grantmesnil's horse, which was young and violent, reared and plunged in the course of the career so as to disturb the rider's aim, and the stranger, declining to take the advantage which this accident afforded him, raised his lance, and passing his antagonist without touching him, wheeled his horse and rode back again to his own end of the lists, offering his antagonist, by a herald, the chance of a second encounter. This De Grantmesnil declined, avowing himself vanquished as much by the courtesy as by the address of his opponent.

Ralph de Vipont summed up the list of the stranger's triumphs, being hurled to the ground with such force, that the blood gushed from his nose and his mouth, and he was borne senseless from the lists.

The acclamations of thousands applauded the unanimous award of the Prince and marshals, announcing that day's honours to the Disinherited Knight.

The EAGLE

He clasps the crag with crooked hands:
Close to the sun in lonely lands,
Ringed with the azure world he stands.

The wrinkled sea beneath him crawls;
He watches from his mountain walls,
And like a thunderbolt he falls.

I Remember, I Remember

I remember, I remember,
The house where I was born,
The little window where the sun
Came peeping in at morn;
He never came a wink too soon,
Nor brought too long a day,
But now, I often wish the night
Had borne my breath away!

I remember, I remember,
The roses, red and white,
The violets, and the lily-cups,
Those flowers made of light!
The lilacs where the robin built,
And where my brother set
The laburnum on his birthday, –
The tree is living yet!

I remember, I remember,
Where I was used to swing,
And thought the air must rush as fresh
To swallows on the wing;
My spirit flew in feathers then,
That is so heavy now,
And summer pools could hardly cool
The fever on my brow!

I remember, I remember,
The fir trees dark and high;
I used to think their slender tops
Were close against the sky:
It was a childish ignorance,
But now 'tis little joy
To know I'm farther off from heaven
Than when I was a boy.

The Wind
in the Willows

For a man with the wonderful imagination of Kenneth Grahame, the workaday life of a secretary at the Bank of England may well have proved irksome in the extreme. Was this why, to clear and refresh his brain with laughable fantasies, he sat down to pen the endearing and enduring adventures of Mole, Rat, Otter and Toad? Be that as it may, The Wind in the Willows *is and has been ever since it was written one of the great children's favourites of all time. Here are the opening pages in Kenneth Grahame's own words.*

The River Bank

The Mole had been working very hard all the morning, spring-cleaning his little home. First with brooms, then with dusters; then on ladders and steps and chairs, with a brush and a pail of whitewash; till he had dust in his throat and eyes, and splashes of whitewash all over his black fur, and an aching back and weary arms. Spring was moving in the air above and in the earth below and around him, penetrating even his dark and lowly little house with its spirit of divine discontent and longing. It was small wonder, then, that he suddenly flung down his brush on the floor, said "Bother!" and "O blow!" and also "Hang spring-cleaning!" and bolted out of the house without even waiting to put on his coat. Something up above was calling him imperiously, and he made for the steep little tunnel which answered in his case to the gravelled carriage-drive owned by animals whose residences are nearer to the sun and air. So he scraped and scratched and scrabbled and scrooged, and then he scrooged again and scrabbled and scratched and scraped, working busily with his little paws and muttering to himself, "Up we go! Up we go!" till at last, pop! his snout came out into the sunlight, and he found himself rolling in the warm grass of a great meadow.

"This is fine!" he said to himself. "This is better than whitewashing!" The sunshine struck hot on his fur, soft breezes caressed his heated brow, and after the seclusion of the cellarage he had lived in so long the carol of happy birds fell on his dulled hearing almost like a shout. Jumping off all his four legs at once, in the joy of living and the delight of spring without its cleaning, he pursued his way across the meadow till he reached the hedge on the further side.

"Hold up!" said an elderly rabbit at the gap. "Sixpence for the privilege of passing by the private road!" He was bowled over in an instant by the impatient and contemptuous Mole, who trotted along the side of the hedge chaffing the other rabbits as they peeped hurriedly from their holes to see what the row was about. "Onion sauce! Onion sauce!" he remarked jeeringly, and was gone before they could think of a thoroughly satisfactory reply. Then they all started grumbling at each other. "How *stupid* you are! Why didn't you tell him – " "Well, why didn't *you* say" "You might have reminded him – " and so on, in the usual way: but, of course, it was then much too late, as is always the case.

It all seemed too good to be true. Hither and thither through the meadows he rambled busily, along the hedgerows, across the copses, finding everywhere birds building, flowers budding, leaves thrusting – everything happy, and progressive, and occupied. And instead of having an uneasy conscience pricking him and whispering "Whitewash!" he somehow could only feel how jolly it was to be the only idle dog among all these busy citizens. After all, the best part of a holiday is perhaps not so much to be resting yourself, as to see all the other fellows busy working.

He thought his happiness was complete when, as he meandered aimlessly along, suddenly he stood by the edge of a full-fed river. Never in his life had he seen a river before – this sleek, sinuous, full-bodied animal, chasing and chuckling, gripping things with a gurgle and leaving them with a laugh, to fling itself on fresh playmates that shook themselves free, and were caught and held again. All was a-shake and a-shiver – glints and gleams and sparkles, rustle and swirl, chatter and bubble. The Mole was bewitched, entranced, fascinated. By the side of the river he trotted as one trots, when very small, by the side of a man who holds one spellbound by exciting stories; and when tired at last, he sat on the bank, while the river still chattered on to him, a babbling procession of the best stories in the world, sent from the heart of the earth to be told at last to the insatiable sea.

As he sat on the grass and looked across the river, a dark hole in the bank opposite, just above the water's edge, caught his eye, and dreamily he fell to considering what a nice snug dwelling-place it would make for an animal with few wants and fond of a bijou riverside residence, above flood level and remote from noise and dust. As he gazed, something bright and small seemed to twinkle down in the heart of it, vanished, then twinkled once more like a tiny star. But it could hardly be a star in such an unlikely situation; and it was too glittering and small for a glow-worm. Then, as he looked, it winked at him, and so declared itself to be an eye; and a small face began gradually to grow up round it, like a frame round a picture.

A little brown face, with whiskers.

A grave round face, with the same twinkle in its eye that had first attracted his notice.

Small neat ears and thick silky hair.

It was the Water Rat!

Then the two animals stood and regarded each other cautiously.

"Hullo, Mole!" said the Water Rat.

"Hullo, Rat!" said the Mole.

"Would you like to come over?" inquired the Rat presently.

"Oh, it's all very well to *talk*," said the Mole, rather pettishly, he being new to a river and riverside life and its ways.

The Rat said nothing, but stooped and unfastened a rope and hauled on it; then lightly stepped into a little boat which the Mole had not observed. It was painted blue outside and white within, and was just the size for two animals; and the Mole's whole heart went out to it at once, even though he did not yet fully understand its uses.

The Rat sculled smartly across and made fast. Then he held up his fore-paw as the Mole stepped gingerly down. "Lean on that!" he said. "Now then, step lively!" and the Mole to his surprise and rapture found himself actually seated in the stern of a real boat.

"This has been a wonderful day!" said he, as the Rat shoved off and took to the sculls again. "Do you know, I've never been in a boat before in all my life."

"What?" cried the Rat, open-mouthed: "Never been in a – you never – well, I – what have you been doing, then?"

"Is it so nice as all that?" asked the Mole shyly, though he was quite prepared to believe it as he leant back in his seat and surveyed the cushions, the oars, the rowlocks, and all the fascinating fittings, and felt the boat sway lightly under him.

"Nice? It's the *only* thing," said the Water Rat solemnly, as he leant forward for his stroke. "Believe me, my young friend, there is *nothing* – absolutely nothing – half so much worth doing as simply messing about in boats. Simply messing," he went on dreamily: "messing – about – in – boats; messing –"

"Look ahead, Rat!" cried the Mole suddenly.

It was too late. The boat struck the bank full tilt. The dreamer, the joyous oarsman, lay on his back at the bottom of the boat, his heels in the air.

"– about in boats – or *with* boats," the Rat went on composedly, picking himself up with a pleasant laugh. "In or out of 'em, it doesn't matter. Nothing seems really to matter, that's the charm of it. Whether you get away, or whether you don't; whether you arrive at your destination or whether you reach somewhere else, or whether you never get anywhere at all, you're always busy, and you never do anything in particular; and when you've done it there's always something else to do, and you can do it if you like, but you'd much better not. Look here! If you've really nothing else on hand this morning, supposing we drop down the river together, and have a long day of it?"

The Mole waggled his toes from sheer happiness, spread his chest with a sigh of full contentment, and leaned back blissfully into the soft cushions. "*What* a day I'm having!" he said. "Let us start at once!"

"Hold hard a minute, then!" said the Rat. He looped the painter through a ring in his landing-stage, climbed up into his hole above, and after a short interval reappeared staggering under a fat, wicker luncheon-basket.

"Shove that under your feet," he observed to the Mole, as he passed it down into the boat. Then he untied the painter and took the sculls again.

"What's inside it?" asked the Mole, wriggling with curiosity.

"There's cold chicken inside it," replied the Rat briefly; "cold-tonguecoldhamcoldbeefpickledgherkinssaladfrenchrollscresssandwichespottedmeatgingerbeerlemonadesodawater –"

"O stop, stop," cried the Mole in ecstasies: "This is too much!"

"Do you really think so?" inquired the Rat seriously. "It's only what I always take on these little excursions; and the other animals are always telling me that I'm a mean beast and cut it *very* fine!"

The Mole never heard a word he was saying. Absorbed in the new life he was entering upon, intoxicated with the sparkle, the ripple, the scents and the sounds and the sunlight, he trailed a paw in the water and dreamed long waking dreams. The Water Rat, like the good little fellow he was, sculled steadily on and forbore to disturb him.

"I like your clothes awfully, old chap," he remarked after some half an hour or so had passed. "I'm going to get a black velvet smoking suit myself some day, as soon as I can afford it."

"I beg your pardon," said the Mole, pulling himself together

with an effort. "You must think me very rude; but all this is so new to me. So – this – is – a – River!"

"*The* River," corrected the Rat.

"And you really live by the river? What a jolly life!"

"By it and with it and on it and in it," said the Rat. "It's brother and sister to me, and aunts, and company, and food and drink, and (naturally) washing. It's my world, and I don't want any other. What it hasn't got is not worth having, and what it doesn't know is not worth knowing. Lord! the times we've had together! Whether in winter or summer, spring or autumn, it's always got its fun and its excitements. When the floods are on in February, and my cellars and basement are brimming with drink that's no good to me, and the brown water runs by my best bedroom window; or again when it all drops away and shows patches of mud that smells like plum-cake, and the rushes and weed clog the channels, and I can potter about dry-shod over most of the bed of it and find fresh food to eat, and things careless people have dropped out of boats!"

"But isn't it a bit dull at times?" the Mole ventured to ask. "Just you and the river, and no one else to pass a word with?"

"No one else to – well, I mustn't be hard on you," said the Rat with forbearance. "You're new to it, and of course you don't know. The bank is so crowded nowadays that many people are moving away altogether. O no, it isn't what it used to be, at all. Otters, kingfishers, dabchicks, moorhens, all of them about all day long and always wanting you to *do* something – as if a fellow had no business of his own to attend to!"

"What lies over *there*?" asked the Mole, waving a paw towards a background of woodland that darkly framed the water-meadows on one side of the river.

"That? O, that's just the Wild Wood," said the Rat shortly. "We don't go there very much, we river-bankers."

"Aren't they – aren't they very *nice* people in there?" said the Mole a trifle nervously.

"W-e-ll," replied the Rat, "let me see. The squirrels are all right. *And* the rabbits – some of 'em, but rabbits are a mixed lot. And then there's Badger, of course. He lives right in the heart of it; wouldn't live anywhere else, either, if you paid him to do it. Dear old Badger! Nobody interferes with *him*. They'd better not," he added significantly.

"Why, who *should* interfere with him?" asked the Mole.

"Well, of course – there – are others," explained the Rat in a hesitating sort of way. "Weasels – and stoats – and foxes – and so on. They're all right in a way – I'm very good friends with them – pass the time of day when we meet, and all that – but they break out sometimes, there's no denying it, and then – well, you can't really trust them, and that's the fact."

The Mole knew well that it is quite against animal-etiquette to dwell on possible trouble ahead, or even to allude to it; so he dropped the subject.

"And beyond the Wild Wood again?" he asked: "Where it's all blue and dim, and one sees what may be hills or perhaps they mayn't, and something like the smoke of towns, or is it only cloud-drift?"

"Beyond the Wild Wood comes the Wide World," said the Rat. "And that's something that doesn't matter, either to you or me. I've never been there, and I'm never going, nor you either, if you've got any sense at all. Don't ever refer to it again, please. Now then! Here's our backwater at last, where we're going to lunch."

25

Leaving the main stream, they now passed into what seemed at first sight like a little land-locked lake. Green turf sloped down to either edge, brown snaky tree-roots gleamed below the surface of the quiet water, while ahead of them the silvery shoulder and foamy tumble of a weir, arm-in-arm with a restless dripping mill-wheel, that held up in its turn a grey-gabled mill-house, filled the air with a soothing murmur of sound, dull and smothery, yet with little clear voices speaking up cheerfully out of it at intervals. It was so very beautiful that the Mole could only hold up both fore-paws and gasp, "O my! O my! O my!"

The Rat brought the boat alongside the bank, made her fast, helped the still awkward Mole safely ashore, and swung out the luncheon-basket. The Mole begged as a favour to be allowed to unpack it all by himself; and the Rat was very pleased to indulge him, and to sprawl at full length on the grass and rest, while his excited friend shook out the table-cloth and spread it, took out all the mysterious packets one by one and arranged their contents in due order, still gasping, "O my! O my!" at each fresh revelation. When all was ready, the Rat said, "Now, pitch in, old fellow!" and the Mole was indeed very glad to obey, for he had started his spring-cleaning at a very early hour that morning, as people *will* do, and had not paused for bite or sup; and he had been through a very great deal since that distant time which now seemed so many days ago.

"What are you looking at?" said the Rat presently, when the edge of their hunger was somewhat dulled, and the Mole's eyes were able to wander off the table-cloth a little.

"I am looking," said the Mole, "at a streak of bubbles that I see travelling along the surface of the water. That is a thing that strikes me as funny."

"Bubbles? Oho!" said the Rat, and chirruped cheerily in an inviting sort of way.

A broad glistening muzzle showed itself above the edge of the bank, and the Otter hauled himself out and shook the water from his coat.

"Greedy beggars!" he observed, making for the provender. "Why didn't you invite me, Ratty?"

"This was an impromptu affair," explained the Rat. "By the way – my friend Mr. Mole."

"Proud, I'm sure," said the Otter, and the two animals were friends forthwith.

"Such a rumpus everywhere!" continued the Otter. "All the world seems out on the river today. I came up this backwater to try and get a moment's peace, and then stumble upon you fellows! – At least – I beg pardon – I don't exactly mean that, you know."

There was a rustle behind them, proceeding from a hedge wherein last year's leaves still clung thick, and a stripy head, with

high shoulders behind it, peered forth on them.

"Come on, old Badger!" shouted the Rat.

The Badger trotted forward a pace or two; then grunted, "H'm!

28

Company," and turned his back and disappeared from view.

"That's *just* the sort of fellow he is!" observed the disappointed Rat. "Simply hates Society! Now we shan't see any more of him today. Well, tell us *who's* out on the river?"

"Toad's out, for one," replied the Otter. "In his brand-new wager-boat; new togs, new everything!"

The two animals looked at each other and laughed.

"Once, it was nothing but sailing," said the Rat. "Then he tired of that and took to punting. Nothing would please him but to punt

29

all day and every day, and a nice mess he made of it. Last year it was house-boating, and we all had to go and stay with him in his house-boat, and pretend we liked it. He was going to spend the rest of his life in a house-boat. It's all the same, whatever he takes up; he gets tired of it, and starts on something fresh."

"Such a good fellow, too," remarked the Otter reflectively: "But no stability – especially in a boat!"

From where they sat they could get a glimpse of the main stream across the island that separated them; and just then a wager-boat flashed into view, the rower – a short, stout figure – splashing badly and rolling a good deal, but working his hardest. The Rat stood up and hailed him, but Toad – for it was he – shook his head and settled sternly to his work.

"He'll be out of the boat in a minute if he rolls like that," said the Rat, sitting down again.

"Of course he will," chuckled the Otter. "Did I ever tell you that good story about Toad and the lock-keeper? It happened this way. Toad . . .' An errant May-fly swerved unsteadily athwart the current in the intoxicated fashion affected by young bloods of May-flies seeing life. A swirl of water and a "cloop!" and the May-fly was visible no more. Neither was the Otter.

The Mole looked down. The voice was still in his ears, but the turf whereon he had sprawled was clearly vacant. Not an Otter to be seen, as far as the distant horizon.

So Otter disappears but Mole has not seen the last of that odd fellow, Toad. Tiring of rowing, Toad turns to the joys of a horse-drawn caravan. Swiftly he changes his mind about this when his caravan is wrecked by a passing car. Now nothing will satisfy Toad but the idea of racing everywhere in a fast car. He comes to grief when he takes somebody else's car without permission. Fortunately Mole and Rat are there to help him but while Toad has been away, his home, Toad Hall, has been invaded by a gang of rascally weasels. Badger, Mole, Rat and Toad bravely drive the weasels away and then decide to hold a splendid banquet for all their friends to celebrate their victory. Toad composes a song to sing in honour of his victorious homecoming and here, to end this short version of The Wind in the Willows, *is the last verse of Toad's song:*

Shout – Hooray!
And let each one of the crowd try and shout it very loud,
In honour of an animal of whom you're justly proud,
For it's Toad's – great – day!

Duck's Ditty

All along the backwater,
Through the rushes tall,
Ducks are a-dabbling,
Up tails all!

Ducks' tails, drakes' tails,
Yellow feet a-quiver,
Yellow bills all out of sight
Busy in the river!

Slushy green undergrowth
Where the roach swim,
Here we keep our larder
Cool and full and dim!

Every one for what he likes!
We like to be
Heads down, tails up,
Dabbling free!

High in the blue above
Swifts whirl and call –
We are down a-dabbling,
Up tails all!

OZYMANDIAS

I met a traveller from an antique land
Who said: Two vast and trunkless legs of stone
Stand in the desert. Near them, on the sand,
Half sunk, a shattered visage lies, whose frown
And wrinkled lip and sneer of cold command
Tell that its sculptor well those passions read
Which yet survive, stamped on these lifeless things,
The hand that mocked them and the heart that fed;
And on the pedestal these words appear:
"My name is Ozymandias, king of kings:
Look on my works, ye Mighty, and despair!"
Nothing beside remains. Round the decay
Of that colossal wreck, boundless and bare,
The lone and level sands stretch far away.

Little Women

When Louisa May Alcott, who lived from 1832 to 1888, wrote her celebrated novel Little Women, *she had in mind the story of her own family. The March girls were Louisa's own sisters. Jo was herself. Perhaps this is why the book is so true to life. First published in 1868, it has been a romance of American Civil War-time, particularly appealing ever since to girls and movie producers, never loth to appreciate and film a good story.*

Here is a condensation of the story which still retains much of the atmosphere and emotion of the original book.

Christmas won't be Christmas without any presents," grumbled Jo, lying on the rug.

"It's so dreadful to be poor!" sighed Meg, looking down at her old dress.

"I don't think it's fair for some girls to have lots of pretty things, and other girls nothing at all," added little Amy, with an injured sniff.

"We've got father and mother and each other, anyhow," said Beth contentedly, from her corner.

The four young faces on which the firelight shone brightened at the cheerful words, but darkened again as Jo said sadly:

"We haven't got father, and shall not have him for a long time." She didn't say "perhaps never," but each silently added it, thinking of father far away, where the fighting was.

Nobody spoke for a minute; then Meg said in an altered tone:

"You know the reason mother proposed not having any presents this Christmas was because it's going to be a hard winter for everyone; and she thinks we ought not to spend money for pleasure, when our men are suffering so in the army. We can't do much, but we can make our little sacrifices, and ought to do it gladly. But I am afraid I don't," and Meg shook her head as she thought regretfully of all the pretty things she wanted.

"I'm sure we grub hard enough to earn some fun!" cried Jo, examining the heels of her boots in a gentlemanly manner.

"I know I do, teaching those dreadful children nearly all day," began Meg in the complaining tone again.

"You don't have half such a hard time as I do," said Jo. "How

would you like to be shut up for hours with a nervous, fussy old lady like Aunt March, who keeps you trotting, is never satisfied, and worries you till you're ready to box her ears?"

"I think washing dishes and keeping things tidy is the worst work in the world. It makes me cross, and my hands get so stiff I can't practise good a bit." And Beth looked at her rough hands with a sigh that anyone could hear that time.

"I don't believe any of you suffer as I do!" cried Amy, "for you don't have to go to school with impertinent girls, who plague you if you don't know your lessons, and laugh at your dresses, and label your father if he isn't rich, and insult you when your nose isn't nice."

"If you mean *libel* I'd say so and not talk about labels, as if papa was a pickle bottle," advised Jo, laughing.

"Don't you wish we had the money papa lost when we were little, Jo? Dear me, how happy and good we'd be if we had no worries," said Meg, who could remember better times – before Mr. March lost his property trying to help an unfortunate friend, and the two elder girls left school to earn their living: Meg as nursery governess to the four spoilt King children, and Jo as companion to lame and peppery Aunt March.

"Still, we're a pretty jolly set," Jo rejoined; and was immediately reproved by Amy for using slang and being so boyish.

"Now you're so tall and turn up your hair, you should remember you're a young lady, Jo," said Meg, lecturing in elder-sisterly fashion.

"I'm not! and if turning up my hair made me one, I'll wear it in two tails till I'm twenty," cried Jo, pulling off her net and shaking down a chestnut mane.

As young readers like to know "how people look," we will take this moment to give them a little sketch of the four sisters, who sat knitting away in the December twilight in a room that was comfortable, though shabby and faded, with a pleasant atmosphere of home-peace about it.

Margaret, the eldest, was sixteen and very pretty, with large eyes, plenty of soft brown hair, a sweet mouth and white hands, of which she was rather vain. Fifteen-year-old Jo was very tall, thin and brown, and never seemed to know what to do with her long limbs, which were very much in her way. She had a decided mouth, a comical nose, and sharp grey eyes, which were by turns fierce, funny, or thoughtful. Her long, thick hair was her one beauty; but it was usually bundled into a net, to be out of her way. Round shoulders had Jo, big hands and feet, a fly-away look to her clothes, and the uncomfortable appearance of a girl who was rapidly shooting up into a woman, and didn't like it.

Elizabeth – or Beth, as everyone called her – was a rosy, bright-eyed girl of thirteen, with a shy manner, a timid voice, and a peaceful expression. Her father called her "Little Tranquillity," and the name suited her excellently. Amy, though the youngest, was a most important person, in her own opinion at least. A regular snow maiden, with blue eyes and yellow curls; pale and slender, and always carrying herself like a young lady mindful of her manners.

The clock struck six; and, having swept up the hearth, Beth put a pair of slippers down to warm. Somehow the sight of the old shoes had a good effect upon the girls, for mother was coming, and everyone brightened to welcome her. The four had a dollar each, and they planned how they would spend the money buying surprise gifts for their mother; then Jo called an impromptu rehearsal of the play the girls were getting up for Christmas night – one she herself had written, for Jo had literary ambitions.

"I don't see how you can write and act such splendid things, Jo. You're a regular Shakespeare!" exclaimed Beth, when Amy, who was not gifted with dramatic power, had practised fainting dead away without much success.

"Not quite," replied Jo modestly. "I do think 'The Witch's Curse, an Operatic Tragedy,' is rather a nice thing; but I'd like to try Macbeth, if we only had a trapdoor for Banquo. I always wanted to do the killing part. 'Is that a dagger that I see before me?'" muttered Jo, rolling her eyes and clutching the air.

"No; it's the toasting fork, with mother's shoe on it instead of the bread for supper. Beth's stage-struck!" cried Meg; and the rehearsal ended in a general burst of laughter.

"Glad to find you so merry, my girls," said a cheery voice at the door; and actors and audience turned to welcome a stout, motherly lady, with a "can-I-help-you" look about her which was truly delightful. She wasn't a particularly handsome person, but mothers are always lovely to their children, and the girls thought the grey cloak and unfashionable bonnet covered the most splendid woman in the world.

"Well, dearies, how have you got on today? There was so much to do, getting the boxes ready to go tomorrow, that I didn't come home to dinner."

The girls kissed her and then flew about arranging the tea-table. As they gathered about it Mrs. March said, with a particularly happy face: "I've got a treat for you after supper."

A quick, bright smile went round like a streak of sunshine. They all cried:

"A letter! A letter from father!"

"Yes; a nice long letter. He is well, and sends all sorts of loving messages for Christmas."

"I think it was so splendid of father to go as a chaplain when he was too old to be drafted and not strong enough for a soldier," said Meg warmly.

"Don't I wish I could go as a drummer!" exclaimed Jo.

"When will he come home, Marmee?" asked Beth, with a little quiver in her voice.

"Not for many months, dear, unless he is sick. Now come and hear the letter."

They all drew to the fire, mother in the big chair with Beth at her feet, Meg and Amy perched on either arm of the chair, and Jo leaning on the back, where no one would see any sign of emotion if the letter should happen to be touching.

Very few letters were written in those hard times that were not touching, especially those which fathers sent home. In this one little was said of the hardships endured, the dangers faced, or the home-sickness conquered; it was a cheerful, hopeful letter, full of lively descriptions of camp life, marches and military news; and only at the end did the writer's heart overflow with fatherly love and longing for the little girls at home.

"Give them all my dear love and a kiss. Tell them I think of them by day, pray for them by night, and find my best comfort in their affection at all times. I know they will remember all I said to them, that they will be loving children to you, will do their duty faithfully, fight their bosom enemies bravely, and conquer themselves so beauti-fully that when I come back to them I may be fonder and prouder than ever of my little women."

"We all will!" cried Meg; and the others nodded agreement.

"Look under your pillows Christmas morning, and you will find guide-books to help you," replied Mrs. March.

When the table was cleared by old Hannah, out came the four little work-baskets and the needles flew as the girls made sheets for Aunt March. It was uninteresting sewing, but tonight no one grumbled. They adopted Jo's plan of dividing the long seams into four parts, calling the quarters Europe, Asia, Africa, and America, and in that way got on capitally, especially when they talked about the different countries as they stitched their way through them.

At nine they stopped work and sang, as usual, before they went to bed.

Jo was the first to wake in the grey dawn of Christmas morning. No stockings hung at the fireplace, and for a moment she felt as much disappointed as she did long ago, when her little sock fell down because it was so crammed with goodies. Then she remembered her mother's promise, and slipping her hand under her pillow, drew out a little crimson-covered book. She knew it very well, for it was that beautiful old story of the best life ever lived, and Jo felt that it was a true guide-book for any pilgrim going the long journey. The book was Pilgrim's Progress and the girls had acted the story as they were now acting 'The Witch's Curse'. She woke Meg with a "Merry Christ-mas," and bade her see what was under her pillow. A green-covered book appeared with the same picture inside, and a few words written by their mother, which made their one present very precious in their

eyes. Presently Beth and Amy woke, to rummage and find their little book also – one dove-coloured, the other blue; and all sat looking at and talking about them.

"Where is mother?" asked Meg, as she and Jo ran down half an hour later to thank her for their gifts.

"Goodness only knows. Some poor creeter come a-beggin', and your ma went straight off to see what was needed. There never *was* such a woman for givin' away vittles and drink, clothes and firin'," replied Hannah, who had lived with the family since Meg was born, and was considered by them all more as a friend than a servant.

The bang of the street door sent the girls to the table eager for breakfast. "Merry Christmas, Marmee! Thank you for our books; we read some, and mean to every day," they cried in chorus.

"Merry Christmas, little daughters! I'm glad you began at once, and hope you will keep on. But I want to say one word before we sit down. Not far away from here lies a poor woman with a little new-born baby. Six children are huddled into one bed to keep from freezing, for they have no fire. There is nothing to eat there; and the oldest boy told me they were suffering cold and hunger. My girls, will you give them your breakfast as a Christmas present?"

They were all unusually hungry, having waited nearly an hour, and for a minute no one spoke; then they broke into exclamations of pity and hurried round to pack up the Christmas dainties. They were soon

ready, and all went with their mother to give the food away.

A bare, poor, miserable room it was, with broken windows, no fire, a sick mother, wailing baby, and a group of pale, hungry children trying to keep warm. When the girls saw the happiness and comfort they brought with their food and firing, they were content to have given away their breakfast and to go home to bread and milk.

Afterwards they presented Marmee with the presents they had bought her, and Mrs. March was both surprised and touched. There was a good deal of laughing and kissing and explaining in the loving fashion which makes these home-festivals so long remembered.

The rest of the day was devoted to preparations for the play in the evening. No gentlemen were admitted, so Jo played male parts to her heart's content. The smallness of the company made it necessary for the two principal actors to take several parts apiece; and they certainly deserved some credit for the hard work they did in learning three or four different parts, whisking in and out of various costumes and managing the stage besides.

On Christmas night a dozen girls piled on to the bed, which was the dress circle, and sat before the blue and yellow chintz curtains in a most flattering state of expectancy.

'The Witch's Curse' proved very exciting, and all went swimmingly save for an unrehearsed mishap or two: as when Zara sat in a tower half way up to the ceiling and listened to Roderigo below imploring her to fly. She consented at last, and Roderigo produced a rope ladder with five steps to it, threw up one end, and invited her to descend. She was about to leap gracefully down when, "Alas, alas, for Zara!" she forgot her train. It caught in the window; the tower tottered, fell with a crash, and buried the unhappy lovers in the ruins!

A universal shriek arose as Roderigo's russet boots waved wildly from the wreck. With wonderful presence of mind Don Pedro, the cruel sire, rushed in, dragged his daughter out with a hasty aside: "Don't laugh, act as if it was all right!" and the play gallantly proceeded.

The curtain fell on a triumphant finish, amid tumultuous applause, when the cot-bed on which the "dress circle" was built suddenly shut up and extinguished the enthusiastic audience. Roderigo and Don Pedro flew to the rescue, and all were taken out unhurt, though speechless with laughter. The excitement had hardly subsided when Hannah appeared and requested the ladies to walk down to supper.

This was a surprise, even to the actors, especially when they saw what a fine supper it was.

"Is it fairies?" asked Amy.

"It's Santa Claus," said Beth.

"Both wrong: old Mr. Laurence, next door, the Laurence grandfather, sent it. Hannah told one of his servants about your breakfast party; that pleased him, and as he knew my father years ago, he begged that he might send in this supper for you all," replied Mrs. March smiling.

"That boy put it into his head, I know he did! He's a capital fellow, and I wish we could get acquainted," sighed Jo, as the plates went round.

"What a merry Christmas we've had after all!" said the four girls as they went to bed that night.

As it happened, Jo's wish was fulfilled during the next few days;

41

for Sallie Gardiner invited the two elder March girls to a New Year's party, and there Jo met the "Laurence boy."

Jo, who didn't care much for girls or parties, and had been instructed by Meg to hide a burn and a tear on the back of her dress, stood about carefully against the wall and watched the dancing rather forlornly. Presently she saw a big, red-headed youth approaching her corner, and fearing he meant to engage her, she slipped into a curtained recess, intending to peep and enjoy herself in peace. Unfortu-

nately, another bashful person had chosen the same refuge; for as the curtain fell behind her, she found herself face to face with the "Laurence boy."

"Dear me, I didn't know anyone was here," stammered Jo, preparing to back out as speedily as she had bounced in.

But the boy laughed, and said, pleasantly, though he looked a little startled:

"Don't mind me; stay if you like."

"Sha'n't I disturb you?"

"Not a bit; I only came here because I don't know many people, and felt rather strange at first, you know."

"So did I. Don't go away, please, unless you'd rather."

"How are you, Miss March?" asked the boy, while his black eyes shone with fun.

"Nicely thank you, Mr. Laurence: but I am not Miss March, I'm only Jo," returned the young lady.

"I'm not Mr. Laurence; I'm only Laurie."

"Laurie Laurence; what an odd name."

"My first name is Theodore, but I don't like it; for the fellows called me Dora, so I made them say Laurie instead."

"I hate my name too – so sentimental! I wish everyone would say Jo instead of Josephine."

"Don't you like to dance, Miss Jo?" asked Laurie, looking as if he thought the name suited her.

"I like it well enough if there is plenty of room. In a place like this I'm sure to upset something – tread on people's toes or do something dreadful; so I keep out of mischief and let Meg do the pretty things. Besides, I scorched the back of this frock and the mend shows; so Meg told me to keep still, so that no one would see it. You may laugh if you want to; it is funny, I know."

But Laurie didn't laugh; he only looked down a minute, and the expression of his face puzzled Jo when he said very gently:

"Never mind that; I'll tell you how we can manage. There's a long hall out there, and we can dance grandly and no one will see us. Please come."

Jo thanked him, and gladly went. The hall was empty, and they

had a grand polka. When the music stopped, they sat down on the stairs and talked. Laurie told Jo of the years he had spent abroad, in Paris, and at school in Switzerland; and Jo liked the "Laurence boy" better than ever.

"Curly black hair, brown skin, big black eyes, long nose, nice teeth, little hands and feet, tall as I am; very polite for a boy, and altogether jolly. Wonder how old he is?"

It soon came out that he would be sixteen next month, so that in age he came between Meg and Jo. He took the girls home in his grandfather's carriage that night, and after that he and the March family became the firmest of friends. There wasn't a day Laurie didn't run in and out of the little brown house, and soon the sisters admitted him into all their fun, and grew to know his grandfather very well, too.

"Girls, where are you going?" asked Amy, coming into their room

one Saturday afternoon and finding them getting ready to go out, with an air of secrecy which excited her curiosity.

Meg and Jo had planned to go to the theatre with Laurie, but had said nothing, as they did not want to take Amy; discovering this by teasing them, the little girl began to beseech to go. Meg relented and pleaded for her; but Jo would not give in, for she wanted to enjoy herself with Laurie without having a fidgety child to look after.

Laurie called from below, and the two girls hurried down, leaving Amy to call over the banisters in a threatening tone: "You'll be sorry for this, Jo March! See if you aren't!"

45

"Fiddlesticks!" returned Jo, slamming the door.

When they got home they found Amy reading in the parlour. She assumed an injured air as they came in, and said nothing.

But the next day, as Meg, Beth, and Amy were sitting together late in the afternoon, Jo burst into the room, looking excited, and demanding breathlessly: "Has anyone taken my story?"

Meg and Beth said "No" at once, and looked surprised; Amy poked the fire and said nothing. Jo saw her colour rise, and was down on her in a minute.

"Amy, you've got it!"

"No, I haven't; but you'll never get your silly old story again!" cried Amy, getting excited in her turn. "I burnt it up."

"What! my little book I was so fond of, and worked over, and meant to finish before father got home? Have you really burnt it?" said Jo, turning pale, while her hands clutched Amy nervously.

"Yes, I did! I told you I'd make you pay for being so cross yesterday, and I have, so –"

Amy got no farther, for Jo's hot temper mastered her, and she shook Amy till the teeth chattered in her head, crying, in a passion of grief and anger:

"You wicked, wicked girl! I never can write it again, and I'll never forgive you as long as I live."

Meg flew to rescue Amy, and Beth to pacify Jo; but Jo was quite beside herself, and, with a parting box on her sister's ear, she rushed out of the room up to the old sofa in the garret where she did her writing.

Mrs. March came home and soon brought Amy to a sense of the wrong she had done her sister. Jo's book was the pride of her heart, and Jo was regarded by her family as a literary sprout of great promise. It was only half a dozen little fairy tales, but Jo had worked over them patiently, putting her whole heart into her work, hoping to make something good enough to print. She had just copied them with great care, and had destroyed the old manuscript, so that Amy's bonfire had consumed the loving work of several years. It was a dreadful calamity to Jo, and when Amy begged her forgiveness, she refused it sternly. Even when at bedtime Mrs. March whispered to her not to let the sun go down on her anger, Jo would not relent.

Next day nothing seemed right in the family.

"Everybody is so hateful, I'll ask Laurie to go skating. He is always kind and jolly, and will put me to rights, I know," said Jo to herself; and off she went.

Amy heard the clash of skates, and looked out with an impatient exclamation:

"There! She promised I should go next time, for this is the last ice we shall have. But it's no use to ask such a cross-patch to take me."

"Don't say that; you were naughty, and it's hard to forgive you," said Meg. "Go after them; don't say anything until Jo has got good-natured with Laurie; then just kiss her, or do some kind thing, and I'm sure she'll be friends again."

"I'll try," said Amy, for the advice suited her; and, after a flurry to get ready, she ran after the friends.

It was not far to the river, but both were ready before Amy reached them. Jo saw she was coming, and turned her back; Laurie did not see, for he was carefully skating along the shore, sounding the ice, for a warm spell had preceded the cold snap.

As Laurie turned the bend, he shouted back:

"Keep near the shore; it isn't safe in the middle."

Jo heard, but Amy was just struggling to her feet and did not catch a word.

Laurie had vanished round the bend; Jo was just at the turn, and Amy, far behind, striking out toward the smoother ice in the middle of the river. For a minute Jo stood still, with a strange feeling at her

heart; then she resolved to go on, but something held and turned her round, just in time to see Amy throw up her hands and go down, with the sudden crash of rotten ice, the splash of water, and a cry that made Jo's heart stand still with fear. She tried to call Laurie, but her voice was gone, and for a second she could only stand motionless, staring, with a terror-stricken face, at the little blue hood above the black water. Something rushed swiftly by her, and Laurie's voice cried out:

"Bring a rail; quick, quick!"

How she did it, she never knew; but for the next few minutes she worked as if possessed, obeying Laurie, who was quite self-possessed; and, lying flat, held Amy up by his arm, till Jo dragged a rail from the fence, and together they got the child out more frightened than hurt.

"Now then, we must walk her home as fast as we can; pile our things on her, while I get off these confounded skates!" cried Laurie, wrapping his coat round Amy and tugging away at the straps.

Shivering, dripping, and crying, they got Amy home; and, after an exciting time of it, she fell asleep, rolled in blankets before a hot fire. During the bustle Jo had scarcely spoken; but flown about, looking pale and wild, with her dress torn, and her hands cut and bruised by ice and rails. When Amy was comfortably asleep, the house quiet, and Mrs. March sitting by the bed, she called Jo to her and began to bind up the hurt hands.

"Are you sure she is safe?" whispered Jo, looking remorsefully at the golden head, which might have been swept away from her sight for ever under the treacherous ice.

"Quite safe, dear," replied her mother cheerfully.

"Laurie did it all; I only let her go. It was all my fault," and Jo dropped down beside the bed in a passion of tears and "fessed" to mother all that had happened.

"It's my dreadful temper! I try to cure it; I think I have, and then it works out worse than ever. Oh, mother! what shall I do?" cried poor Jo in despair. "Oh, mother, help me, do help me!"

"I will, my child; I will. Remember this day and resolve you will never know another like it. Jo, dear, you think your temper is the worst in the world; but mine used to be just like it. Even now, I am angry nearly every day, but I have learned not to show it."

"Mother, are you angry when you fold your lips tight and go out of the room sometimes?" asked Jo, feeling nearer and dearer to her mother than ever before.

"Yes, You might try that way of checking the hasty words too, Jo."

Jo's only answer was to hold her mother close. Amy stirred and sighed in her sleep, and Jo leant over her, softly stroking the wet hair.

Suddenly Amy opened her eyes and held out her arms with a smile that went straight to Jo's heart. Neither said a word, but they hugged one another close, and everything was forgiven and forgotten in a kiss.

As spring came on, a new set of amusements became the fashion, and the lengthening days gave long afternoons for walks, gardening, and outdoor fun. Laurie had the bright idea of setting up a post office in the garden hedge; the P.O., as it was called, proved a capital little institution, and flourished wonderfully, for nearly as many queer things passed through it as through the real post office. Tragedies and cravats, poetry and pickles, garden seeds and long letters, music and gingerbread, invitations, scoldings and puppies.

The first of June brought holidays for Meg and Jo and a visit to Laurie from a party of English friends. The long days were full with home duties, river picnics, sketching parties, and castles in the air. All too soon summer was over and autumn came in.

"November is the most disagreeable month in the whole year," said Margaret, standing looking out at the frost-bitten garden.

"That's the reason I was born in it," observed Jo pensively, quite unconscious of the blot on her nose.

Mrs. March came in with Laurie and asked her usual question: "Any letter from father, girls?" looking anxious when they said no. A minute afterwards Hannah came in with a telegram.

Mrs. March snatched it, read the two lines it contained, and dropped back into her chair as white as if the paper had sent a bullet to her heart. Laurie dashed downstairs for water, while Meg and Hannah supported her, and Jo read aloud in a frightened voice:

"Mrs. March, – Your husband is very ill. Come at once. S. Hale. Blank Hospital, Washington."

How very still the room was as they listened breathlessly! How strange the day darkened outside! And how suddenly the whole world seemed to change! Mrs. March was herself again directly; read the message over, and stretched out her arms to her daughters, saying, in a tone they never forgot: "I shall go at once, but it may be too late. Oh, children, children! help me to bear it!"

For several minutes there was nothing but the sound of sobbing in the room, mingled with broken words of comfort, tender assurances of help, and hopeful whispers that died away in tears. Poor Hannah was the first to recover, and with unconscious wisdom she set all the

rest a good example; for with her, work was the panacea for most afflictions.

"The Lord keep the dear man! I won't waste no time a-cryin', but get your things ready right away, mum," she said heartily as she went away to work like three women in one.

"She's right; there's no time for tears now. Be calm, girls, and let me think."

They steadied themselves as she sent them all flying on different errands: Laurie to telegraph that she would come by the next train – the early-morning one; Jo to go to Aunt March's to borrow money for the long, expensive journey; Beth to enlist Mr. Laurence's help; Meg and Amy to aid with the packing and home preparations.

Mr. Laurence came hurrying back with Beth and insisted on sending John Brooke, Laurie's tutor, to Washington with Mrs. March to take care of her and help all he could. There was so much to do that the short afternoon soon wore away; but still Jo did not come. They had grown anxious before she came walking in with a very queer expression

51

of countenance, for there was a mixture of fun and fear, satisfaction and regret in it, which puzzled the family as much as did the roll of bills she laid before her mother, saying, with a little choke in her voice: "That's my contribution towards making father comfortable and bringing him home!"

"Twenty-five dollars! My dear, where did you get it?"

"It's mine, honestly. I only sold what was my own."

As she spoke Jo took off her bonnet, and a general outcry arose, for all her abundant hair was cut short.

"Your hair! Your beautiful hair!" "Oh, Jo, how could you? Your one beauty." "My dear girl, there was no need for this." "She doesn't look like my Jo any more, but I love her dearly for it!"

As everybody exclaimed, and Beth hugged the cropped head tenderly, Jo assumed an indifferent air, which did not deceive anyone a particle, and said, rumpling up the glossy bush, trying to look as if she liked it, "It doesn't affect the fate of the nation, so don't wail, Beth. It will be good for my vanity; I was getting too proud of my wig.

"I hadn't the least idea of selling my hair at first, but as I went along I kept thinking *what* I could do. Then, in a barber's window,

I saw tails of hair with prices marked. It came over me all of a sudden that I had one thing to sell; so, without stopping to think, I walked in and asked them to buy my hair. I took a last look at it while the man got his things, and I confess I felt queer when I saw the dear old hair laid out on the table. I kept just one lock for you, Marmee, to remember past glories by."

Mrs. March carefully folded away the wavy lock. She only said: "Thank you, deary," but something in her face made the girls change the subject and talk as cheerfully as they could about Mr. Brooke's kindness, the prospect of a fine day tomorrow, and the happy times they would have when father came home to be nursed.

In the cold grey dawn next morning the travellers departed, leaving the four girls to Hannah's care and Mr. Laurence's protection. The last thing Mrs. March beheld, as she drove away, was the four young faces, all smiling for the last look, and behind them, like a bodyguard, old Mr. Laurence, faithful Hannah, and devoted Laurie.

What a queer, quiet house it seemed without Marmee, and with anxiety about their father heavy on their hearts! As the days went by, however, news from Washington comforted the girls very much; for, though dangerously ill, the presence of the best and tenderest of nurses had already done him good. Mr. Brooke sent a bulletin every day, which grew more and more cheering as the week passed. Relieved of their anxiety, the girls began to relax their superhuman efforts to be good, and to fall back again into the old ways. Mrs. March had asked them to visit the Hummels – the poor family to whom they had given their Christmas breakfast – regularly; but only faithful Beth remembered to go.

Then fresh trouble came. The Hummel baby died of scarlet fever in Beth's arms, and she took the infection. Amy was sent off, much against her will, to be out of harm's way by staying at Aunt March's; and Jo, who had had the fever long ago, stayed at home to nurse her sister. Hannah insisted that, as Mr. March had had a relapse and his wife could not possibly leave him, nothing should be written to her about this fresh illness.

Beth was much sicker than anyone but Hannah and the doctor suspected. Meg stayed at home, lest she should infect her pupils, and kept house, feeling very guilty when she wrote letters to Washington, in which no mention was made of Beth's illness. Jo devoted herself to the invalid night and day – not a hard task, for Beth bore her pain uncomplainingly as long as she could control herself. But there came a time when she began to talk wildly in delirium, a time when she did not know the familiar faces round her, but called imploringly for her mother. Then Jo grew frightened, Meg begged to be allowed to write the truth, and even Hannah said she "would think of it, though there was no danger *yet*."

How dark the days seemed now, how sad and lonely the house! Beth lay hour after hour tossing to and fro, or sank into a heavy sleep that brought her no refreshment. Dr. Bangs came twice a day. Hannah sat up at night. Meg kept a telegram in her desk all ready to send off at any minute, and Jo never stirred from Beth's side.

The first of December was a wintry day indeed to them. When Dr. Bangs came that morning he looked long at Beth, and said in a low tone to Hannah:

"If Mrs. March *can* leave her husband, she'd better be sent for."

As the tears streamed fast down poor Jo's cheeks, she stretched out her hand in a helpless sort of way, and Laurie took it in his, whispering.

"I'm here, hold on to me, Jo, dear!"

She could not speak, but she did "hold on," and presently felt better. Then Laurie further eased her mind.

"Jo, I got fidgety yesterday, and so did grandpa. We thought Hannah was overdoing the authority business, and your mother ought to know. So I telegraphed yesterday, and Brooke answered she'd come at once. And she'll be here this very night, Jo!"

He was electrified by Jo's joyful cry: "Oh, Laurie! Oh, mother! I *am* so glad!"

Everyone rejoiced but Beth. She lay in a heavy stupor – the once rosy face so changed and wasted. All day she lay so, only rousing now and then to mutter: "Water!" with parched lips. The hours dragged slowly by till night. The doctor had been in to say some change for better or worse would probably take place about midnight, at which time he would return.

The girls never forgot that night, for no sleep came to them as they kept their watch. Downstairs Mr. Laurence marched to and fro in the parlour, and Laurie lay on the rug staring into the fire. Hannah, worn out, was asleep.

Here the clock struck twelve, and Meg and Jo forgot themselves in watching Beth, for they fancied a change passed over her wan face. The house was still as death, and nothing but the wailing of the wind broke the deep hush. Weary Hannah slept on, and no one but the sisters saw the pale shadow which seemed to fall upon the little bed. An hour went by, and nothing happened except Laurie's quiet departure for the station. Another hour, still no one came; and anxious fears of delay in the storm, or accidents by the way, or, worst of all, a great grief at Washington, haunted the poor girls.

It was past two when Jo's excited eyes saw that a great change had taken place. The fever-flush and the look of pain were gone, and the beloved little face looked so pale and so peaceful. At the same moment Hannah started out of her sleep, hurried to the bed, examined Beth closely, and then exclaimed under her breath: "The fever's turned; she's sleepin' nat'ral; she breathes easy. Praise be given! Oh, my goodness me!"

Before the girls could believe the happy truth the doctor came to confirm it. "Yes, my dears; I think the little girl will pull through this time. Keep the house quiet; let her sleep; and when she wakes, give her –"

What they were to give neither heard; for both crept into the dark hall, and, sitting on the stairs, held each other close, rejoicing with hearts too full for words.

"If mother would only come now!" said Jo, as the winter night began to wane.

Never had the sun risen so beautifully, and never had the world seemed so lovely as it did to the heavy eyes of Meg and Jo, as they looked out in the early morning when their long, sad vigil was done.

"It looks like a fairy world," said Meg, smiling to herself.

"Hark!" cried Jo, starting to her feet.

Yes; there was a sound of bells at the door below, a cry from Hannah, and then Laurie's voice, saying in a joyful whisper: "Girls! she's come! She's come!"

I don't think I have any words in which to tell of the meeting between the mother and daughters; so I will merely say that the house was full of genuine happiness, and that when Beth woke from that long, healing sleep, the first object on which her eyes fell was her mother's face.

Like sunshine after storm were the peaceful weeks which followed. The invalids improved rapidly, and Mr. March began to talk of returning early in the new year. Beth was soon able to lie on the study sofa all day, though she was still too feeble to walk.

As Christmas approached, the usual mysteries began to haunt the house, and Jo frequently convulsed the family by proposing utterly impossible or magnificently absurd ceremonies in honour of this unusually merry Christmas. Beth felt uncommonly well that morning, and being dressed in her mother's gift – a soft, crimson merino wrapper – was borne in triumph to the window, to behold the offering of Jo and Laurie. Like elves, they had worked by night, and conjured up a comical surprise. Out in the garden stood a stately snow-maiden, crowned with holly, bearing a basket of fruit and flowers in one hand and a great roll of new music in the other.

How Beth laughed when she saw it; how Laurie ran up and down to bring in the gifts; and what ridiculous speeches Jo made as she presented them.

"I'm so full of happiness that if father was only here I couldn't hold one drop more," said Beth, quite sighing with contentment.

Half an hour afterwards Laurie opened the parlour door and popped in his head very quietly. With a face full of suppressed excitement and a treacherously joyful voice, he said breathlessly: "Here's another Christmas present for the March family."

Before the words were well out of his mouth there appeared a tall man, muffled up to the eyes, leaning on the arm of another tall man. Of course there was a general stampede, and for several minutes everybody seemed to lose their wits as Mr. March became invisible in the embrace of five pairs of loving arms. He had come home with John Brooke to take them all by surprise on Christmas Day.

There seemed no end to the surprises of that wonderful Christmas, for the next day another event happened.

Jo had suspected for some time that Meg was growing up. She didn't seem to take the same interest in their games, and she did, all the time Mrs. March was away, take the very greatest interest in the bulletins which Mr. Brooke sent every day. Once the travellers were home again, she became absent-minded, shy, and silent.

The day after Christmas Mr. Brooke came into the old brown house and found Meg in the parlour alone. Quietly and tenderly he asked her to marry him.

Meg was barely seventeen and hardly knew her own mind she was so young. She faltered: "I don't know"; and at that unpropitious moment Aunt March arrived to see her nephew, and walked unannounced into the parlour. John fled into the adjoining room, and the fierce old lady, guessing very well what had happened, attacked Meg.

"Don't you dream of marrying a poor tutor like that young man, child. If you do, not a penny of my money will you ever have," stormed Aunt March.

Now Aunt March possessed in perfection the art of rousing the spirit of opposition in people, and Meg was angry in a minute.

"I shall marry whom I please, Aunt March, and you can leave your money to whom you like," she retorted.

Strangely enough, directly her John was attacked she realised that she loved him, and when her aunt had departed angrily and John returned, he had an easy victory of it. Poor Jo was inclined to be angry at the breaking up of the family circle by a mere man; but everyone else rejoiced, though Mr. and Mrs. March made a stipulation that, as Meg was so young, the wedding should not be for three years.

So the first curtain falls upon Meg, Jo, Beth and Amy but their adventures were to continue in "Good Wives", the sequel to "Little Women."

The Destruction of Sennacherib

ennacherib was the name of a certain ruthless King of Assyria who lived seven hundred years before Jesus was born. He went to war against Israel and was successful. Twelve years later he decided to attack Israel again and laid siege to the city of Jerusalem. The hand of God has been seen in the retribution that followed.

Without warning a terrible disease broke out amongst the Assyrian warriors, killing many thousands of them. This speedily ended the war. Lord Byron wrote this stirring poem about that awesome event.

The Assyrian came down like a wolf on the fold,
And his cohorts were gleaming in purple and gold;
And the sheen of their spears was like stars on the sea
When the blue wave rolls nightly on deep Galilee.

Like the leaves of the forest when summer is green
That host with their banners at sunset were seen:
Like the leaves of the forest when autumn hath blown
That host on the morrow lay withered and strown!

For the Angel of Death spread his wings on the blast,
And breathed on the face of the foe as he passed;
And the eyes of the sleepers waxed deadly and chill,
And their hearts but once heaved, and for ever grew still!

And there lay the steed with his nostril all wide,
But through it there rolled not the breath of his pride;
And the foam of his gasping lay white on the turf,
And cold as the spray of the rock-beating surf.

And there lay the rider, distorted and pale,
With the dew on his brow and the rust on his mail;
And the tents were all silent, the banners alone,
The lances unlifted, the trumpet unblown.

And the widows of Ashur are loud in their wail,
And the idols are broke in the temple of Baal;
And the might of the Gentile, unsmote by the sword,
Hath melted like snow in the glance of the Lord!

ROOKWOOD

William Harrison Ainsworth, who lived from 1805 to 1882, was a Lancashire author who wrote about 40 novels. Some related stories surrounding certain places and bearing such titles as "The Tower of London," "Windsor Castle" and "Old St. Paul's." Others concerned the criminal activities of such rogues as "Guy Fawkes" and "Jack Sheppard."

One of his best known books, though, is "Rookwood" which concerns the many astonishing adventures of the Rookwood family. Ainsworth wrote in a style that today is known as Gothic. Such romances usually contain tales of witches and demons and ghosts and sundry blood-thirsty, blood-curdling deeds. "Rookwood" is a Gothic story. One of its most thrilling passages is that which recounts in spirited detail the famous Ride to York performed by the notorious highwayman Dick Turpin. That Turpin never made such a ride need not diminish the reader's enjoyment when reading Ainsworth's account of Black Bess's mile-devouring gallop.

The story of the ride is, regrettably, too long to be reprinted in this Treasury but here, in Ainsworth's own words, is the conclusion of Black Bess's heart-killing ordeal. Turpin's pursuers believe that Bess has galloped her last mile – but York is still ahead.

Contrary to all expectation, however, Bess held on, and set pursuit at defiance. Her pace was swift as when she started. But it was unconscious and mechanical action. It wanted the ease, the lightness, the life of her former riding. She seemed screwed up to a task which she must execute. There was no flogging, no gory heel; but the heart was throbbing, tugging at the sides within. Her spirit

spurred her onwards. Her eye was glazing; her chest heaving; her
flank quivering; her crest again fallen. Yet she held on. "She is dying!"
said Dick. "I feel it –" No, she held on.

Fulford is past. The towers and pinnacles of York burst upon him
in all the freshness, the beauty, and the glory of a bright, clear,
autumnal morn. The ancient city seemed to smile a welcome – a
greeting. The noble minster and its serene and massive pinnacles,
crocketed, lantern-like, and beautiful; Saint Mary's lofty spire, All-
Hallows tower, the massive mouldering walls of the adjacent postern,
the grim castle, and Clifford's neighbouring keep – all beamed upon
him, "like a bright-eyed face, that laughs out openly."

"It is done – it is won," cried Dick. "Hurrah, hurrah!" And the sunny air was cleft with his shouts.

Bess was not insensible to her master's exultation. She neighed feebly in answer to his call, and reeled forwards. It was a piteous sight to see her – to mark her staring, protruding eyeball – her shaking flanks; but, while life and limb held together, she held on.

Another mile is past. York is near.

"Hurrah!" shouted Dick; but his voice was hushed. Bess tottered – fell. There was a dreadful gasp – a parting moan – a snort; her eye gazed, for an instant, upon her master, with a dying glare; then grew glassy, rayless, fixed. A shiver ran through her frame. Her heart had burst.

Dick's eyes were blinded, as with rain. His triumph, though achieved, was forgotten, his own safety was disregarded. He stood weeping and swearing, like one beside himself.

"And art thou gone, Bess?" cried he, in a voice of agony, lifting up his courser's head, and kissing her lips, covered with blood-flecked foam. "Gone, gone! and I have killed the best steed that was ever crossed! And for what?" added Dick, beating his brow with his clenched hand – "for what? for what?"

At this moment the deep bell of the minster clock tolled out the hour of six.

"I am answered," gasped Dick; *"it was to hear those strokes!"*

Robinson Crusoe

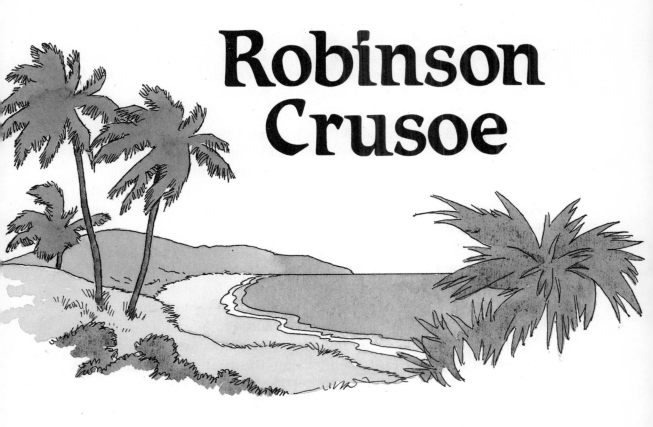

In the year 1703 a certain lowly seaman named Alexander Selkirk signed aboard the Cinque Ports galley as sailing-master. The ship was bound, in company with another craft captained by William Dampier, a buccaneer-cum-explorer, for the west coast of South America. Piracy was their mission. Dampier aimed to attack any Spanish galleon he encountered. During the voyage Selkirk quarrelled repeatedly with his captain, to such an extent that when the Cinque Ports dropped anchor off Juan Fernandez Island he asked to be set ashore. No sooner said than done but Selkirk changed his mind at the last moment and begged to be taken aboard again. His Captain refused and Selkirk was marooned on the island for four years and four months. He managed to survive until relief arrived. Astonishingly, his rescuers were his old shipmates, the buccaneers. Eleven years later there appeared a book entitled The Life and Strange Surprising Adventures of Robinson Crusoe. It was written by a celebrated author named Daniel Defoe. It concerned the experiences of a shipwrecked seaman cast ashore on a lonely island where he contrived to live for the next thirty-five years before being rescued. Naturally it has been assumed that Defoe based his book on the amazing tale of Alexander Selkirk. There is no proof of this but it is a fact that the story of Robinson

Crusoe is still read throughout the world, well over three hundred years since it was first written. One of the best-known adventures of Crusoe is the day he sees a footprint on the shore. Here, in Defoe's own words, is the account of that incident and what followed.

It happened one day about noon going towards my boat, I was exceedingly surprised with the print of a man's naked foot on the shore, which was very plain to be seen in the sand. I stood like one thunderstruck, or as if I had seen an apparition. I listened, I looked round me. I could hear nothing, nor see anything; I went up to a rising ground to look farther; I went up the shore and down the shore, but it was all one, I could see no other impression but that one. I went to it again to see if there were any more, and to observe if it might not be my fancy; but there was no room for that, for there was exactly the very print of a foot, toes, heel, and every part of a foot; how it came thither, I knew not, nor could in the least imagine. But after innumerable fluttering thoughts, like a man perfectly confused and out of myself, I came home to my fortification, not feeling, as we say, the ground I went on, but terrified to the last degree, looking behind me at every two or three steps, mistaking every bush and tree, and fancying every stump at a distance to be a man; nor is it possible to describe how many various shapes affrighted imagination represented things to me in; how many wild ideas were found every moment in my fancy, and what strange unaccountable whimsies came into my thoughts by the way.

When I came to my castle, for so I think I called it ever after this, I fled into it like one pursued; whether I went over by the ladder as first contrived, or went in at the hole in the rock, which I called a door, I cannot remember; no, nor could I remember the next morning; for never frightened hare fled to cover, or fox to earth, with more terror of mind than I to this retreat.

I slept none that night. The farther I was from the occasion of my fright, the greater my apprehensions were. I was so embarrassed with my own frightful ideas of the thing, that I formed nothing but dismal imaginations to myself, even though I was now a great way off it. Sometimes I fancied it must be the Devil; and reason joined in with me upon this supposition: for how should any other thing in human shape come into the place? Where was the vessel that brought them? What marks were there of any other footsteps? And how was it possible a man should come there? But then to think that Satan should take human shape upon him in such a place where there could be no

64

manner of occasion for it, but to leave the print of his foot behind him, and that even for no purpose too, for he could not be sure I should see it; this was an amusement the other way; I considered that the Devil might have found out abundance of other ways to have terrified me than this of the single print of a foot. That as I lived quite on the other side of the island, he would never have been so simple to leave a mark in a place where it was ten thousand to one whether I should ever see it or not, and in the sand too, which the first surge of the sea upon a high wind would have defaced entirely: all this seemed inconsistent with the thing itself, and with all the notions we usually entertain of the subtlety of the Devil.

I presently concluded then, that it must be some more dangerous creature, viz., that it must be some of the savages of the mainland over against me, who had wandered out to sea in their canoes, and either driven by the currents, or by contrary winds, had made the island; and had been on shore, but were gone away again to sea, being as loth, perhaps, to have stayed in this desolate island, as I would have been to have had them.

While these reflections were rolling upon my mind, I was very thankful that I was so happy as not to be thereabouts at that time, or that they did not see my boat, by which they would have concluded that some inhabitants had been in the place, and perhaps have searched farther for me. Then terrible thoughts racked my imagination about their having found my boat, and that there were people here; and that if so, I should certainly have them come again in greater numbers and devour me; that if it should happen so that they should not find me, yet they would find my enclosure, destroy all my corn, carry away all my flock of tame goats, and I should perish at last for mere want.

Thus my fear banished all my religious hope; all that former confidence in God, which was founded upon such wonderful experience as I had had of His goodness, now vanished, as if He that had fed me by miracle hitherto, could not preserve by His power the provision which He had made for me by His goodness.

How strange a chequerwork of Providence is the life of man! and by what secret differing springs are the affections hurried about, as differing circumstances present! Today we love what tomorrow we hate; today we seek what tomorrow we shun; today we desire what tomorrow we fear; nay, even tremble at the apprehensions of. This was exemplified in me at this time in the most lively manner imaginable: for I whose only affliction was, that I seemed banished from human society, that I was alone, circumscribed by the boundless ocean, cut off from mankind, and condemned to what I called silent life; that I was as one whom Heaven thought not worthy to be numbered among the living, or to appear among the rest of His creatures; that to have seen one of my own species would have seemed to me a raising me from death to life, and the greatest blessing that Heaven itself, next to the supreme blessing of salvation, could bestow; that I should now tremble at the very apprehensions of seeing a man, and was ready to sink into the ground at but the shadow or silent appearance of a man's having set his foot in the island.

I then reflected that God, who was not only righteous but Omnipotent, as He had thought fit thus to punish and afflict me so He was able to deliver me; that if He did not think fit to do it, it was my unquestioned duty to resign myself absolutely and entirely to His will; and on the other hand, it was my duty also to hope in Him, pray to Him, and quietly to attend the dictates and directions of His daily Providence.

These thoughts took me up many hours, days, nay, I may say, weeks and months; and one particular effect of my cogitations on this occasion, I cannot omit, viz., one morning early, lying in my bed, and filled with thought about my danger from the appearance of savages, I found it discomposed me very much; upon with those words of the Scripture came into my thoughts, *Call upon Me in the day of trouble, and I will deliver, and thou shalt glorify Me.*

Upon this, rising cheerfully out of my bed, my heart was not only comforted, but I was guided and encouraged to pray earnestly to God for deliverance: when I had done praying, I took up my Bible, and opening it to read, the first words that presented to me, were, *Wait on the Lord, and be of good cheer, and He shall strengthen thy heart; wait, I say, on the Lord.* It is impossible to express the comfort this gave me. In answer, I thankfully laid down the Book, and was no more sad, at least, not on that occasion.

In fact, Crusoe has good cause for the fears that have assailed him for the footprint must have been left by one of a party of cannibals who, unknown to Crusoe, have visited the island with some prisoners. Crusoe later has further proof of this when he comes across some bones and the gruesome remains of the cannibals' feast. When the savages pay a second visit, Crusoe manages to rescue one of their prisoners. He names the man Friday after the day of the poor fellow's rescue. Now Crusoe has at last a human being to talk to and he teaches Friday English. After more brushes with the cannibals, Crusoe and Friday secure the release of two more prisoners, one a Spanish seaman, the other – to the delight of Crusoe's companion – Friday's father.

Then upon a day an English ship anchors close to the shore. The crew has mutinied and the captain and two loyal seamen are set ashore. Crusoe and Friday join forces with the captain and his two faithful crewmen. Together they recover the ship from the control of the mutineers. The way is now clear for Robinson Crusoe to return to his homeland after an absence of thirty-five years.

Brer Rabbit
and the Wonderful Tar-Baby

The jolly adventures of Brer Rabbit, Brer Fox, Brer Bear and Brer Wolf were first given to the world at large by an American newspaper journalist, by name Joel Chandler Harris. Born in the State of Georgia in 1848, he wrote down folk-tales purportedly related by a Negro character, Uncle Remus. They were presented in the quaint dialect of

Negroes then living in the Deep South of the United States. For this reason it is not always easy to understand the various phrases and wording. For instance, "Brer" is short for Brother, a familiar form of address in those times. For that reason this, probably the most popular of the Brer Rabbit stories, culled from the book entitled Uncle Remus, His Songs and his Sayings, *has been rewritten for easy reading.*

ell, folks, you all know, of course, how clever Brer Rabbit was. I expect you think that Brer Fox never *ever* stood a chance of catching him.

But there *was* a time when Brer Fox was smart enough to catch Brer Rabbit and he came mighty close to making him into a rabbit stew, too.

It happened this way.

One day Brer Fox did some mighty hard thinking.

Then Brer Fox got himself some tar.

He mixed the tar with some turpentine and he fixed up a contraption, which he called a Tar-Baby.

Then he took his Tar-Baby and he set her up by the main road.

Then he lay hidden in the bushes to see what would happen.

Well, he didn't have to wait long, because, by and by, along came Brer Rabbit, racing down the road until he spied the Tar-Baby.

And the Tar-Baby, she just sat there, she did and Brer Fox, he just lay low.

"Good morning!" said Brer Rabbit, said he. "Nice weather this morning."

But the Tar-Baby, she didn't say anything and Brer Fox he lay low.

"How are you this morning?" said Brer Rabbit.

But the Tar-Baby, she stayed still and Brer Fox, he lay low.

"You're stuck up, that's what you are," said Brer Rabbit. "And I'm going to cure you of being stuck up, that's what I'm going to do."

Brer Fox, he sort of chuckled way down in his tummy, he did, but the Tar-Baby didn't say anything.

"I'm going to teach you how to talk to respectable folks, if it's the last thing I do," said Brer Rabbit, said he. "If you don't take off that hat and say: 'How-do-you-do?' I'm going to bust you wide open."

But the Tar-Baby, she kept on saying nothing, till presently Brer Rabbit drew back his fist, he did, and – BLIP! – he punched the Tar-Baby on the side of the head.

But his fist stuck and he couldn't pull it loose. The tar held him fast.

70

"If you don't let me loose, I'll hit you again," said Brer Rabbit.

With that he brought round a punch with the other hand – and that hand stuck, too.

"Turn me loose before I really knock the stuffing out of you," said Brer Rabbit.

But the Tar-Baby, she didn't say anything. And Brer Fox he lay low.

Then Brer Rabbit really shouted out that if the Tar-Baby didn't turn him loose, he would butt her with his head.

And he butted her. And his head got stuck.

And *then* Brer Fox strolled out, looking just as innocent as an old lady's pet canary.

"How do you do, Brer Rabbit?" said Brer Fox. "You look sort of stuck up this morning," said he.

And then he rolled on the ground and laughed and laughed.

Because, of course, Brer Fox had intended Brer Rabbit to get stuck on the Tar-Baby from the beginning.

"I expect you will be taking dinner with me *today*, sure enough, Brer Rabbit," laughed Brer Fox. "But *I* am the one who will be doing all the *eating!*"

Of course, he meant that he would make Brer Rabbit into a rabbit stew.

"You just stay there until I collect some brushwood," said Brer Fox, "and then I will make a fire to cook you on."

Well, Brer Rabbit thought mighty quickly and he said: "I don't care what you do with me, Brer Fox, just so long as you don't throw me into the briar patch."

But Brer Fox was busy planning and he said: "It's really too much trouble to light a fire. I will throw you into the river."

"Throw me into as many rivers as you like, but don't throw me into the briar patch, Brer Fox," cried Brer Rabbit.

Then Brer Fox said: "But there aren't any rivers nearby here, so I think I'll tie you up in a sack and take you home."

"Tie me up in as many sacks as you like, Brer Fox, just so long as you don't throw me into the briar patch," shouted Brer Rabbit.

Now Brer Fox began to think. "There must be something mighty horrid about briar patches if Brer Rabbit is so afraid of them. So, as I want to be horrid to Brer Rabbit, I will throw him into a *briar patch*."

So Brer Fox picked Brer Rabbit up by the hind legs and threw him right into the middle of a briar patch.

Now, this was exactly what clever Brer Rabbit wanted.

He knew that in the briar patch were plenty of thorny branches that he could use as combs to clean his fur of all that tar.

Well, Brer Fox watched the briar patch and listened to all the fluttering and scratching that was going on in there.

Then suddenly he heard someone calling him from way up on the hillside.

And there was Brer Rabbit, sitting there as cheekily as anything, just combing the last bits of tar from his fur.

"Rabbits are bred and born in briar patches, you know, Brer Fox," laughed Brer Rabbit. "The thorns that *you* don't like are the rabbits' friends. You *were* stupid to throw me into a briar patch."

And with that Brer Rabbit skipped away home.

And Brer Fox felt mighty silly – mighty silly indeed!

The Last Clipper Race

The dying sun pokes golden finger through rain squalls,
And from gilt tipped royal comes the cry, "Sail-Ho!"
Can it be our rival? In the fo'c'stle
Argument is fierce till a wild howl proclaims
The tea-bell went a half an hour ago.
'Twas not the Beatrice, we are still ahead!

A big and greasy swell rolls all around.
The ship lies stagnant on a sea of glass,
No motion save a gentle roll, a great white hull
Caressed by a lapping cobalt wave.
With creaking, groaning masts and slatting yards,
The figurehead keeps sentry guard below,
White sail above white sail spread in despair
Begging of heaven for wind, mute, still,
A gentle sunset with the harmony
Of Paradise. Then comes the gale loud,
Boisterous, rude, and full of fun.

And so we crossed the line, to find those free
Barefoot days had gone with the flying fish
Into the wake astern. We'd won our race
With white moonrakers set, we'd seen a haze
And the haze was England!

As You Like It

There can be no doubt that William Shakespeare is the world's greatest dramatist. This son of a Stratford-Upon-Avon tradesman won fame during the reign of Queen Elizabeth the First for his historical plays, tragedies and comedies. One of his most popular comedies from the day when it was first staged is As You Like It. *Now there was another writer, born just over two hundred years later, whose works, like Shakespeare's, ranged from grave to gay. His name was Charles Lamb and he is famous in literature for his poems and essays. He decided one day to re-write some of Shakespeare's plays as stories.* As You Like It *must have been an obvious choice and the following is a condensed version of this story taken from Lamb's book* Tales from Shakespeare.

During the time that France was divided into provinces (or dukedoms as they were called), there reigned in one of these provinces an usurper, who had deposed and banished his elder brother, the lawful duke.

The duke, who was thus driven from his dominions, retired with a few faithful followers to the forest of Arden; and here the good duke lived with his loving friends, who had put themselves into a voluntary exile for his sake. Here they lived like the old Robin Hood of England.

The banished duke had an only daughter, named Rosalind, whom the usurper, duke Frederick, when he banished her father, still retained in his court as a companion for his own daughter Celia. A strict friendship subsisted between these ladies, which the disagreement between their fathers did not in the least interrupt, Celia striving by every kindness in her power to make amends to Rosalind for the injustice of her own father in deposing the father of Rosalind; and whenever the thoughts of her father's banishment, and her own dependence on the false usurper, made Rosalind melancholy, Celia's whole care was to comfort and console her.

One day, when Celia was talking in her usual kind manner to Rosalind, saying, "I pray you, Rosalind, my sweet cousin, be merry," a messenger entered from the duke, to tell them that if they wished to see a wrestling match, which was just going to begin, they must come instantly to the court before the palace; and Celia, thinking it would amuse Rosalind, agreed to go and see it.

In those times, wrestling was a favourite sport even in the courts of princes, and before fair ladies and princesses. To this wrestling match, therefore, Celia and Rosalind went. They found that it was likely to prove a very tragical sight; for a large and powerful man, who had been long practised in the art of wrestling, and had slain many men in contests of this kind, was just going to wrestle with a very young man, who, from his extreme youth and inexperience in the art, the beholders all thought would certainly be killed.

When the duke saw Celia and Rosalind, he said, "I pity this young man, I would wish to persuade him from wrestling. Speak to him, ladies, and see if you can move him."

First Celia entreated the young stranger that he would desist from the attempt; and then Rosalind spoke so kindly to him, and with such feeling consideration for the danger he was about to undergo, that instead of being persuaded by her gentle words to forego his purpose, all his thoughts were bent to distinguish himself by his courage in this lovely lady's eyes. He refused the request of Celia and Rosalind in such graceful and modest words, they felt still more concern for him.

And now the wrestling match began. Celia wished the young stranger might not be hurt; but Rosalind pitied him so much, and so deep an interest she took in his danger while he was wrestling, that she might almost be said at that moment to have fallen in love with him.

The kindness shown this unknown youth by these fair and noble ladies gave him courage and strength, so that he performed wonders; and in the end completely conquered his antagonist, who was so much hurt, that for a while he was unable to speak or move.

The duke Frederick was much pleased with the courage and skill shown by this young stranger; and desired to know his name and parentage, meaning to take him under his protection.

The stranger said his name was Orlando, and that he was the youngest son of Sir Rowland de Boys.

Sir Rowland de Boys, the father of Orlando, had been dead some years; but when he was living, he had been a true subject and dear friend of the banished duke: therefore, when Frederick heard Orlando was the son of his banished brother's friend, all his liking for this brave young man was changed into displeasure, and he left the place in very ill humour.

Rosalind was delighted to hear that her new favourite was the son of her father's old friend.

The ladies then went up to him and spoke kind and encouraging words to him; and Rosalind, when they were going away, turned back and taking a chain from off her neck, she said, "Gentleman, wear this for me. I am out of suits with fortune, or I would give you a more valuable present."

When the ladies were alone, Rosalind's talk being still of Orlando, Celia began to perceive her cousin had fallen in love with the handsome young wrestler, and she said to Rosalind, "Is it possible you should fall in love so suddenly?" Rosalind replied, "The duke, my father, loved his father dearly." "But," said Celia, "does it therefore follow that you should love his son dearly? For then I ought to hate him, for my father hated his father; yet I do not hate Orlando."

Frederick being enraged at the sight of Sir Rowland de Boys' son, and having been for some time displeased with his niece, because the people pitied her for her good father's sake, his malice suddenly broke out against her; and while Celia and Rosalind were talking of Orlando, Frederick entered the room, and with looks full of anger ordered Rosalind instantly to leave the palace, and follow her father into banishment; telling Celia, who in vain pleaded for her, that he had only suffered Rosalind to stay upon her account. "I did not then," said Celia, "entreat you to let her stay, for I was too young at that time to value her; but now that I know her worth, and that we so long have learned, played, and ate together, I cannot live out of her

company." Frederick replied, "You are a fool to plead for her. Therefore open not your lips in her favour, for the doom which I have passed upon her is irrevocable."

When Celia found she could not prevail upon her father to let Rosalind remain with her, she generously resolved to accompany her; and leaving her father's palace that night, she went along with her friend to seek Rosalind's father, the banished duke, in the forest of Arden.

Before they set out, Celia considered that it would be unsafe for two young ladies to travel in the rich clothes they then wore; she therefore proposed that they should disguise their rank by dressing themselves like country maids. Rosalind said it would be a still greater protection if one of them was to be dressed like a man; and so it was quickly agreed on between them, that as Rosalind was the tallest, she should wear the dress of a young countryman, and Celia should be habited like a country lass, and that they should say they were brother and sister, and Rosalind said she would be called Ganymede, and Celia chose the name of Aliena.

In this disguise, and taking their money and jewels to defray their expenses, these fair princesses set out on their long travel; for the forest of Arden was a long way off, beyond the boundaries of the duke's dominions.

The lady Rosalind (or Ganymede as she must now be called) with her manly garb seemed to have put on a manly courage. The faithful friendship Celia had shown in accompanying Rosalind so many weary miles, made the new brother, in recompense for this true love, exert a cheerful spirit, as if he were indeed Ganymede, the rustic and stout-hearted brother of the gentle village maiden, Aliena.

It soon appeared that Orlando was also in the forest of Arden: and in this manner this strange event came to pass.

Orlando was the youngest son of Sir Rowland de Boys, who, when he died, left Orlando (being then very young) to the care of his eldest brother Oliver, charging Oliver on his blessing to give his brother a good education, and provide for him as became the dignity of their ancient house. Oliver proved an unworthy brother; and disregarding the commands of his dying father, he never put his brother to school, but kept him at home untaught and entirely neglected. But in his nature and in the noble qualities of his mind Orlando so much resembled his excellent father, that without any advantages of education he seemed like a youth who had been bred with the utmost care; and Oliver so envied the fine person and dignified manners of his untutored brother, that at last he wished to destroy him; and to effect this he set on people to persuade him to wrestle with the famous wrestler, who, as has been before related, had killed so many men.

When, contrary to the wicked hopes he had formed, his brother proved victorious, his envy and malice knew no bounds, and he swore he would burn the chamber where Orlando slept. He was overheard making this vow by one that had been an old and faithful servant to their father, and that loved Orlando because he resembled Sir Rowland. This old man went out to meet him when he returned from the duke's palace. Orlando asked him what was the matter. And then the old man told him how his wicked brother, envying the love all people bore him, and now hearing the fame he had gained by his victory in the duke's palace, intended to destroy him, by setting fire to his chamber that night; and in conclusion, advised him to escape the danger he was in by instant flight; and knowing Orlando had no money, Adam (for that was the good old man's name) had brought out with him his own little hoard, and he said, "I have five hundred crowns, I saved under your father, all this I give to you: let me be your servant; though old I will do the service of a younger man."

Together then this faithful servant and his loved master set out; and Orlando and Adam travelled on, uncertain what course to pursue, till they came to the forest of Arden.

Orlando then searched about to find some food, and he happened to arrive at that part of the forest where the duke was.

The duke inquired who Orlando was; and when he found that he was the son of his old friend, Sir Rowland de Boys, he took him under his protection, and Orlando and his old servant lived with the duke in the forest.

Orlando arrived in the forest not many days after Ganymede and Aliena came there.

Ganymede and Aliena were strangely surprised to find the name of Rosalind carved on the trees, and love-sonnets, fastened to them, all addressed to Rosalind; and while they were wondering how this could be, they met Orlando, and they perceived the chain which Rosalind had given him about his neck.

Orlando little thought that Ganymede was the fair princess Rosalind, who had so won his heart that he passed his whole time in carving her name upon the trees, and writing sonnets in praise of her beauty: but being much pleased with the graceful air of this pretty youth, he entered into conversation with him, and he thought he saw a likeness in Ganymede to his beloved Rosalind, but that he had none of the dignified deportment of that noble lady; for Ganymede assumed the forward manners often seen in youths when they are be- tween boys and men, and with much archness and humour talked to

Orlando of a certain lover, "who," said he, "haunts our forest, and spoils our young trees with carving Rosalind upon their barks, and he hangs odes upon hawthorns, and elegies on brambles, all praising this same Rosalind. If I could find this lover, I would give him some good counsel that would soon cure him of his love."

Many days passed pleasantly on with these young people. Ganymede met the duke one day, and had some talk with him, and the duke asked of what parentage he came. Ganymede answered that he came of as good parentage as he did, which made the duke smile, for he did not suspect the pretty boy came of royal lineage. Then seeing the duke look well and happy, Ganymede was content to put off all further explanation for a few days longer.

One morning, as Orlando was going to visit Ganymede, he saw a man lying asleep on the ground, and a large green snake had twisted itself about his neck. The snake, seeing Orlando approach, glided away among the bushes. Orlando went nearer, and then he discovered a lioness lie crouching, with her head on the ground, with a cat-like watch, waiting until the sleeping man awaked (for it is said that lions will prey on nothing that is dead or sleeping). It seemed as if Orlando was sent by Providence to free the man from the danger of the snake and lioness; but when Orlando looked in the man's face, he perceived that the sleeper who was exposed to this double peril, was

his own brother Oliver who had so cruelly used him, and had threatened to destroy him by fire; and he was almost tempted to leave him a prey to the hungry lioness; but brotherly affection and the gentleness of his nature soon overcame his first anger against his brother; and he drew his sword, and attacked the lioness, and slew her, and thus preserved his brother's life; but before Orlando could conquer the lioness, she had torn one of his arms with her sharp claws.

While Orlando was engaged with the lioness, Oliver awaked, and perceiving that his brother Orlando, whom he had so cruelly treated, was saving him from the fury of a wild beast at the risk of his own life, shame and remorse at once seized him, and he repented of his unworthy conduct, and besought with many tears his brother's pardon for the injuries he had done him. Orlando readily forgave him and from that hour Oliver loved Orlando with a true brotherly affection.

The wound in Orlando's arms having bled very much, he found himself too weak to go to visit Ganymede, and therefore he desired his brother to go and tell Ganymede, "whom," said Orlando, "I in sport do call my Rosalind," of the accident which had befallen him.

Thither then Oliver went, and told to Ganymede and Aliena how Orlando had saved his life: and when he had finished the story of Orlando's bravery, and his own providential escape, he owned to

them that he was Orlando's brother, who had so cruelly used him;
and then he told them of their reconciliation.

The sincere sorrow that Oliver expressed for his offences made
such a lively impression on the kind heart of Aliena, that she instantly
fell in love with him; and Oliver observing how much she pitied the
distress he told her he felt for his fault, he as suddenly fell in love with
her. But while love was thus stealing into the hearts of Aliena and
Oliver, he was no less busy with Ganymede, who hearing of the
danger Orlando had been in, and that he was wounded by the lioness,
fainted.

Oliver made this visit a very long one, and when at last he returned
back to his brother, he had much news to tell him; for besides the
account of Ganymede's fainting at the hearing that Orlando was
wounded, Oliver told him how he had fallen in love with a fair
shepherdess Aliena; and he talked to his brother, as of a thing
almost settled, that he should marry Aliena, saying, that he so well
loved her, that he would live here as a shepherd, and settle his estate
and house at home upon Orlando.

"You have my consent," said Orlando. "Let your wedding be tomorrow, and I will invite the duke and his friends. Go and persuade
your shepherdess to agree to this: she is now alone; for look, here
comes her brother." Oliver went to Aliena; and Ganymede, whom

Orlando had perceived approaching, came to inquire after the health of his wounded friend.

When Orlando and Ganymede began to talk over the sudden love which had taken place between Oliver and Aliena, Orlando said he had advised his brother to persuade his fair shepherdess to be married on the morrow, and then he added how much he could wish to be married on the same day to his Rosalind.

Said Ganymede "Put on your best clothes, and bid the duke and your friends to your wedding; for if you desire to be married tomorrow to Rosalind, she shall be here."

The next morning, Oliver having obtained the consent of Aliena, they came into the presence of the duke, and with them also came Orlando.

They being all assembled to celebrate this double marriage, and as yet only one of the brides appearing, there was much of wondering and conjecture, but they mostly thought that Ganymede was making a jest of Orlando.

While Orlando was answering that he knew not what to think, Ganymede entered, and asked the duke, if he brought his daughter, whether he would consent to her marriage with Orlando. "That I would," said the duke, "if I had kingdoms to give with her." Ganymede then said to Orlando, "And you say you will marry her if I bring her here." "That I would," said Orlando, "if I were king of many kingdoms."

Ganymede and Aliena then went out together, and Ganymede

throwing off his male attire, and being once more dressed in woman's apparel, quickly became Rosalind; and Aliena changing her country garb for her own rich clothes, was with as little trouble transformed into the lady Celia.

While they were gone, the duke said to Orlando, that he thought the shepherd Ganymede very like his daughter Rosalind; and Orlando said, he also had observed the resemblance.

They had not time to wonder how all this would end, for Rosalind and Celia in their own clothes entered, and Rosaland threw herself on her knees before her father, and begged his blessing. Rosalind told him the story of her banishment, and of her dwelling in the forest as a boy, her cousin Celia passing as her sister.

The duke ratified the consent he had already given to the marriage; and Orlando and Rosalind, Oliver and Celia, were married at the same time. And though their wedding could not be celebrated in this wild forest with any of the parade or splendour usual on such occasions, yet a happier wedding-day was never passed: and while they were eating under the cool shade of the pleasant trees, an unexpected messenger arrived to tell the duke the joyful news, that his dukedom was restored to him.

This joyful news, as unexpected as it was welcome, came opportunely to heighten the festivity and rejoicings at the wedding of the princesses. Celia complimented her cousin on this good fortune which had happened to the duke, Rosalind's father, and wished her joy very

sincerely, though she herself was no longer heir to the dukedom, but by this restoration which her father had made, Rosalind was now the heir: so completely was the love of these two cousins unmixed with anything of jealousy or of envy.

The duke had now an opportunity of rewarding those true friends who had stayed with him in his banishment; and these worthy followes, though they had patiently shared his adverse fortune, were very well pleased to return in peace and prosperity to the palace of their lawful duke.

The usurper, enraged at the flight of his daughter Celia, put himself at the head of a large force, and advanced towards the forest, intending to seize his brother, and put him with all his faithful followers to the sword; but, by a wonderful interposition of Providence, this bad brother was converted from his evil intention; for just as he entered the skirts of the wild forest, he was met by an old religious man, a hermit, with whom he had much talk, and who in the end completely turned his heart from his wicked design. Thenceforward he became a true penitent, and resolved, to spend the remainder of his days in a religious house. The first act of his newly-conceived penitence was to send a messenger to his brother (as has been related) to offer to restore to him his dukedom, which he had usurped so long, and with it the lands and revenues of his friends, the followers of his adversity.

Pride and Prejudice

This novel – a comedy of manners, as it is usually described – is doubtless Jane Austen's most popular book. The heroine Elizabeth Bennet, is a most delightful young lady who successfully wins the heart of Mr. Darcy in spite of her early prejudice and dislike of the proud man. This is how the book commences in Jane Austen's own words.

It is a truth universally acknowledged, that a single man in possession of a good fortune must be in want of a wife.

However little known the feelings or views of such a man may be on his first entering a neighbourhood, this truth is so well fixed in the minds of the surrounding families, that he is considered as the rightful property of some one or other of their daughters.

'My dear Mr. Bennet,' said his lady to him one day, 'have you heard that Netherfield Park is let at last?'

Mr. Bennet replied that he had not.

'But it is,' returned she; 'for Mrs. Long has just been here, and she told me all about it.'

Mr. Bennet made no answer.

'Do not you want to know who has taken it?' cried his wife, impatiently.

'*You* want to tell me, and I have no objection to hearing it.'

This was invitation enough.

'Why, my dear, you must know, Mrs. Long says that Netherfield is taken by a young man of large fortune from the north of England; that he came down on Monday in a chaise and four to see the place, and was so much delighted with it that he agreed with Mr. Morris immediately; that he is to take possession before Michaelmas, and some of his servants are to be in the house by the end of next week.'

'What is his name?'

'Bingley.'

'Is he married or single?'

'Oh, single, my dear, to be sure! A single man of large fortune; four or five thousand a year. What a fine thing for our girls!'

'How so? How can it affect them?'

'My dear Mr. Bennet,' replied his wife, 'how can you be so tiresome? You must know that I am thinking of his marrying one of them.'

'Is that his design in settling here?'

'Design? nonsense, how can you talk so! But it is very likely that he *may* fall in love with one of them, and therefore you must visit him as soon as he comes.'

'I see no occasion for that. You and the girls may go, or you may send them by themselves, which perhaps will be still better, for, as you are as handsome as any of them, Mr. Bingley might like you the best of the party.'

'My dear, you flatter me. I certainly *have* had my share of beauty, but I do not pretend to be anything extraordinary now. When a woman has five grown-up daughters, she ought to give over thinking of her own beauty.'

'In such cases, a woman has not often much beauty to think of.'

'But, my dear, you must indeed go and see Mr. Bingley when he comes into the neighbourhood.'

'It is more than I engage for, I assure you.'

'But consider your daughters. Only think what an establishment it would be for one of them. Sir William and Lady Lucas are determined to go, merely on that account; for in general, you know, they visit no newcomers. Indeed you must go, for it will be impossible for *us* to visit him, if you do not.'

'You are over scrupulous, surely. I daresay Mr. Bingley will be very glad to see you; and I will send a few lines by you to assure him

of my hearty consent to his marrying whichever he chooses of the girls; though I must throw in a good word for my little Lizzy.'

'I desire you will do no such thing. Lizzy is not a bit better than the others: and I am sure she is not half so handsome as Jane, nor half so good-humoured as Lydia. But you are always giving *her* the preference.'

'They have none of them much to recommend them,' replied he: 'they are all silly and ignorant like other girls; but Lizzy has something more of quickness than her sisters.'

'Mr. Bennet, how can you abuse your own children in such a way? You take delight in vexing me. You have no compassion on my poor nerves.'

'You mistake me, my dear. I have a high respect for your nerves. They are my old friends. I have heard you mention them with consideration these twenty years at least.'

'Ah, you do not know what I suffer.'

'But I hope you will get over it, and live to see many young men of four thousand a year come into the neighbourhood.'

'It will be no use to us, if twenty such should come, since you will not visit them.'

'Depend upon it, my dear, that when there are twenty, I will visit them all.'

Mr. Bennet was so odd a mixture of quick parts, sarcastic humour, reserve, and caprice, that the experience of three-and-twenty years had been insufficient to make his wife understand his character. *Her*

mind was less difficult to develop. She was a woman of mean under-standing, little information, and uncertain temper. When she was discontented, she fancied herself nervous. The business of her life was to get her daughters married: its solace was visiting and news.

Mr. Bennet was among the earliest of those who waited on Mr. Bingley. He had always intended to visit him, though to the last always assuring his wife that he should not go; and till the evening after the visit was paid she had no knowledge of it. It was then disclosed in the following manner. Observing his second daughter employed in trimming a hat, he suddenly addressed her with, –

'I hope Mr. Bingley will like it, Lizzy.'

'We are not in a way to know *what* Mr. Bingley likes,' said her mother, resentfully, 'since we are not to visit.'

'But you forget, mamma,' said Elizabeth, 'that we shall meet him at the assemblies, and that Mrs. Long has promised to introduce him.'

'I do not believe Mrs. Long will do any such thing. She has two nieces of her own. She is a selfish, hypocritical woman, and I have no opinion of her.'

'No more have I,' said Mr. Bennet; 'and I am glad to find that you do not depend on her serving you.'

Mrs. Bennet deigned not to make any reply; but, unable to contain herself, began scolding one of her daughters.

'Don't keep coughing so, Kitty, for heaven's sake! Have a little compassion on my nerves. You tear them to pieces.'

'Kitty has no discretion in her coughs,' said her father; 'she times them ill.'

'I do not cough for my own amusement,' replied Kitty, fretfully. 'When is your next ball to be, Lizzy?'

'To-morrow fortnight.'

'Ay, so it is,' cried her mother, 'and Mrs. Long does not come back till the day before; so, it will be impossible for her to introduce him, for she will not know him herself.'

'Then, my dear, you may have the advantage of your friend, and introduce Mr. Bingley to *her*.'

'Impossible, Mr. Bennet, impossible, when I am not acquainted with him myself; how can you be so teasing?'

'I honour your circumspection. A fortnight's acquaintance is certainly very little. One cannot know what a man really is by the end of a fortnight. But if *we* do not venture, somebody else will; and after all, Mrs. Long and her nieces must stand their chance; and, therefore, as she will think it an act of kindness, if you decline the office, I will take it on myself.'

The girls stared at their father. Mrs. Bennet said only, 'Nonsense, nonsense!'

'What can be the meaning of that emphatic exclamation?' cried he. 'Do you consider the forms of introduction, and the stress that is laid on them, as nonsense? I cannot quite agree with you *there*. What say you, Mary? for you are a young lady of deep reflection, I know, and read great books, and make extracts.'

Mary wished to say something very sensible, but knew not how.

'While Mary is adjusting her ideas,' he continued, 'let us return to Mr. Bingley.'

'I am sick of Mr. Bingley,' cried his wife.

'I am sorry to hear *that*; but why did not you tell me so before? If I had known as much this morning, I certainly would not have called on him. It is very unlucky; but as I have actually paid the visit, we cannot escape the acquaintance now.'

The astonishment of the ladies was just what he wished; that of Mrs. Bennet perhaps surpassing the rest; though when the first tumult of joy was over, she began to declare that it was what she had expected all the while.

'How good it was in you, my dear Mr. Bennet. But I knew I should persuade you at last. I was sure you loved your girls too well to neglect such an acquaintance. Well, how pleased I am! and it is such a good joke, too, that you should have gone this morning, and never said a word about it till now.'

'Now, Kitty, you may cough as much as you choose,' said Mr. Bennet; and, as he spoke, he left the room, fatigued with the raptures of his wife.

'What an excellent father you have, girls,' said she, when the door was shut. 'I do not know how you will ever make him amends for his kindness; or me either, for that matter. At our time of life, it is not so pleasant, I can tell you, to be making new acquaintance every day; but for your sakes we would do anything. Lydia, my love, though you *are* the youngest, I daresay Mr. Bingley will dance with you at the next ball.'

'Oh,' said Lydia, stoutly, 'I am not afraid; for though I *am* the youngest, I'm the tallest.'

The rest of the evening was spent in conjecturing how soon he would return Mr. Bennet's visit, and determining when they should ask him to dinner.

Not all that Mrs. Bennet, however, with the assistance of her five daughters, could ask on the subject, was sufficient to draw from her husband any satisfactory description of Mr. Bingley. They attacked

him in various ways; with barefaced questions, ingenious suppositions, and distant surmises; but he eluded the skill of them all; and they were at last obliged to accept the second-hand intelligence of their neighbour, Lady Lucas. Her report was highly favourable. Sir William had been delighted with him. He was quite young, wonderfully handsome, extremely agreeable, and, to crown the whole, he meant to be at the next assembly with a large party. Nothing could be more delightful! To be fond of dancing was a certain step towards falling in love; and very lively hopes of Mr. Bingley's heart were entertained.

'If I can but see one of my daughters happily settled at Netherfield,' said Mrs. Bennet to her husband, 'and all the others equally well married, I shall have nothing to wish for.'

In a few days Mr. Bingley returned Mr. Bennet's visit, and sat about ten minutes with him in his library. He had entertained hopes of being admitted to a sight of the young ladies, of whose beauty he had heard much; but he saw only the father. The ladies were somewhat

more fortunate, for they had the advantage of ascertaining, from an upper window, that he wore a blue coat and rode a black horse.

An invitation to dinner was soon afterwards despatched; and already had Mrs. Bennet planned the courses that were to do credit to her housekeeping, when an answer arrived which deferred it all. Mr. Bingley was obliged to be in town the following day, and consequently unable to accept the honour of their invitation, etc. Mrs. Bennet was quite disconcerted. She could not imagine what business he could have in town so soon after his arrival in Hertfordshire; and she began to fear that he might always be flying about from one place to another, and never settled at Netherfield as he ought to be. Lady Lucas quieted her fears a little by starting the idea of his being gone to London only to get a large party for the ball; and a report soon followed that Mr. Bingley was to bring twelve ladies and seven gentlemen with him to the assembly. The girls grieved over such a number of ladies; but were comforted the day before the ball by hearing that, instead of twelve, he had brought only six with him from London, his five sisters and a cousin. And when the party entered the assembly-room, it consisted of only five altogether: Mr. Bingley, his two sisters, the husband of the eldest, and another young man.

Mr. Bingley was good-looking and gentlemanlike: he had a pleasant countenance, and easy, unaffected manners. His sisters were fine women, with an air of decided fashion. His brother-in-law, Mr. Hurst, merely looked the gentleman; but his friend Mr. Darcy soon drew the attention of the room by his fine, tall person, handsome features, noble mien, and the report, which was in general circulation within five minutes after his entrance, of his having ten thousand a year. The gentlemen pronounced him to be a fine figure of a man, the ladies declared he was much handsomer than Mr. Bingley, and he was looked at with great admiration for about half the evening, till his manners gave a disgust which turned the tide of his popularity; for he was discovered to be proud, to be above his company, and above being pleased; and not all his large estate in Derbyshire could then save him from having a most forbidding, disagreeable countenance, and being unworthy to be compared with his friend.

Yes, Mr. Darcy is indeed a very proud and haughty gentleman. In every way he offends Mrs. Bennet and her several daughters. But when one of them elopes with a charming but false rascal, it is Mr. Darcy who dashes to the rescue and returns her to her family. Thus he finally wins the hand of the fair Elizabeth who throughout the story has proved a match for his off-hand manners. So all ends happily.

The Sheep

Lazy sheep, pray tell me why
In the grassy fields you lie,
Eating grass and daisies white,
From the morning till the night?
Everything can something do,
But what kind of use are you?

Nay, my little master, nay,
Do not serve me so, I pray;
Don't you see the wool that grows
On my back to make you clothes?
Cold, and very cold you'd get,
If I did not give you it.

Sure it seems a pleasant thing
To nip the daisies in the spring,
But many chilly nights I pass
On the cold and dewy grass,
Or pick a scanty dinner where
All the common's brown and bare.

Then the farmer comes at last,
When the merry spring is past,
And cuts my woolly coat away
To warm you in the winter's day;
Little master, this is why
In the grassy fields I lie.

Treasure Island

Who has not heard of this, the most exciting story of pirates and buried treasure ever written? It all started when one day the famous poet and author Robert Louis Stevenson amused himself by drawing a map of an imagined treasure island. The idea so fascinated him that later he went on to write his great masterpiece.

Part of the book purports to have been written by young Jim Hawkins, an innkeeper's son and the remainder by Jim's friend, Doctor Livesey. Of course, the best-known character is the rascally one-legged pirate, Long John Silver. He owns a parrot which is always screeching "Pieces of eight! Pieces of eight!" a cry that is to haunt Jim for the rest of his life.

This version of "Treasure Island" commences with the first three chapters of the original book.

CHAPTER ONE

The Old Sea Dog at the "Admiral Benbow"

Squire Trelawney, Dr. Livesey, and the rest of these gentlemen having asked me to write down the whole particulars about Treasure Island, from the beginning to the end, keeping nothing back but the bearings of the island, and that only because there is still treasure not yet lifted, I take up my pen in the year of grace 17 – and go back to the time when my father kept the "Admiral Benbow" inn, and the brown old seaman, with the sabre cut, first took up his lodging under our roof.

I remember him as if it were yesterday, as he came plodding to the inn door, his sea-chest following behind him in a hand-barrow; a tall, strong, heavy, nut-brown man; his tarry pigtail falling over the shoulders of his soiled blue coat; his hands ragged and scarred, with black, broken nails; and the sabre cut across one cheek, a dirty, livid white. I remember him looking round the cove and whistling to himself as he did so, and then breaking out in that old sea-song that he sang so often afterwards:

"Fifteen men on the dead man's chest –
Yo-ho-ho, and a bottle of rum!"

in the high, old tottering voice that seemed to have been tuned and broken at the capstan bars. Then he rapped on the door with a bit of stick like a handspike that he carried, and when my father appeared, called roughly for a glass of rum. This, when it was brought to him, he drank slowly, like a connoisseur, lingering on the taste, and still looking about him at the cliffs and up at our signboard.

"This is a handy cove," says he, at length; "and a pleasant sittyated grog-shop. Much company, mate?"

My father told him no, very little company, the more was the pity.

"Well, then," said he, "this is the berth for me. Here you, matey," he cried to the man who trundled the barrow; "bring up alongside and help up my chest. I'll stay here a bit," he continued. "I'm a plain man; rum and bacon and eggs is what I want, and that head up there for to watch ships off. What you mought call me? You mought call me captain. Oh, I see what you're at – there;" and he threw down three or four gold pieces on the threshold. "You can tell me when I've worked through that," says he, looking as fierce as a commander.

And, indeed, bad as his clothes were, and coarsely as he spoke, he had none of the appearance of a man who sailed before the mast; but seemed like a mate or skipper, accustomed to be obeyed or to strike. The man who came with the barrow told us the mail had set him down the morning before at the "Royal George"; that he had inquired what inns there were along the coast, and hearing ours well spoken of, I suppose, and described as lonely, had chosen it from the others for his place of residence. And that was all we could learn of our guest.

He was a very silent man by custom. All day he hung round the cove, or upon the cliffs, with a brass telescope; all evening he sat in a corner of the parlour next the fire, and drank rum and water very strong. Mostly he would not speak when spoken to; only look up sudden and fierce, and blow through his nose like a fog-horn; and we and the people who came about our house soon learned to let him be. Every day, when he came back from his stroll, he would ask if any seafaring men had gone by along the road? At first we thought it was the want of company of his own kind that made him ask this question; but at last we began to see he was desirous to avoid them. When a seaman put up at the "Admiral Benbow" (as now and then some did, making by the coast road for Bristol), he would look in at him through the curtained door before he entered the parlour; and he was always sure to be as silent as a mouse when any such was present. For me, at least, there was no secret about the matter; for I was, in a way, a sharer in his alarms. He had taken me aside one day, and promised me a silver four-penny on the first of every month if I would only keep my "weather-eye open for a seafaring man with one leg," and let him know the moment he appeared. Often enough, when the first of the month came round, and I applied to him for my wage, he would only blow through his nose at me, and stare me down;

101

but before the week was out he was sure to think better of it, bring me my fourpenny piece, and repeat his orders to look out for "the seafaring man with one leg."

How that personage haunted my dreams, I need scarcely tell you. On stormy nights, when the wind shook the four corners of the house, and the surf roared along the cove and up the cliffs, I would see him in a thousand forms, and with a thousand diabolical expressions. Now the leg would be cut off at the knee, now at the hip; now he was a monstrous kind of a creature, who had never had but the one leg, and that in the middle of his body. To see him leap and run and pursue me over hedge and ditch was the worst of nightmares. And altogether I paid pretty dear for my monthly fourpenny piece, in the shape of these abominable fancies.

But though I was so terrified by the idea of the seafaring man with one leg, I was far less afraid of the captain himself than anybody else who knew him. There were nights when he took a deal more rum and water than his head would carry; and then he would sometimes sit and sing his wicked, old, wild sea-songs, minding nobody; but sometimes he would call for glasses round, and force all the trembling company to listen to his stories or bear a chorus to his singing. Often I have heard the house shaking with *"Yo-ho-ho, and a bottle of rum"*; all the neighbours joining in for dear life, with the fear of death upon them, and each singing louder than the other, to avoid remark. For in these fits he was the most overriding companion ever known; he would slap his hand on the table for silence all round; he would fly up in a passion of anger at a question, or sometimes because none was put, and so he judged the company was not following his story. Nor would he allow anyone to leave the inn till he had drunk himself sleepy and reeled off to bed.

His stories were what frightened people worst of all. Dreadful stories they were; about hanging, and walking the plank, and storms at sea, and the Dry Tortugas, and wild deeds and places on the Spanish Main. By his own account he must have lived his life among some of the wickedest men that God ever allowed upon the sea; and the language in which he told these stories shocked our plain country people almost as much as the crimes that he described. My father was always saying the inn would be ruined, for people would soon cease coming there to be tyrannised over and put down, and sent shivering to their beds; but I really believe his presence did us good. People were frightened at the time, but on looking back they rather liked it; it was a fine excitement in a quiet country life; and there

was even a party of the younger men who pretended to admire him, calling him a "true sea-dog," and a "real old salt," and such like names, and saying there was the sort of man that made England terrible at sea.

In one way, indeed, he bade fair to ruin us; for he kept on staying week after week, and at last month after month, so that all the money had been long exhausted, and still my father never plucked up the heart to insist on having more. If ever he mentioned it, the captain blew through his nose so loudly, that you might say he roared, and stared my poor father out of the room. I have seen him wringing his hands after such a rebuff, and I am sure the annoyance and the terror he lived in must have greatly hastened his early and unhappy death.

All the time he lived with us the captain made no change whatever in his dress but to buy some stockings from a hawker. One of the cocks of his hat having fallen down, he let it hang from that day forth, though it was a great annoyance when it blew. I remember the appearance of his coat, which he patched himself upstairs in his room, and which, before the end, was nothing but patches. He never wrote or received a letter, and he never spoke with any but the neighbours, and with these, for the most part, only when drunk on rum. The great sea-chest none of us had ever seen open.

He was only once crossed, and that was towards the end, when my poor father was far gone in a decline that took him off. Dr. Livesey came late one afternoon to see the patient, took a bit of dinner from my mother, and went into the parlour to smoke a pipe until his horse should come down from the hamlet, for we had no stabling at the old "Benbow." I followed him in, and I remember observing the contrast the neat, bright doctor, with his powder as white as snow, and his bright, black eyes and pleasant manners, made with the coltish country folk, and above all, with that filthy, heavy, bleared scarecrow of a pirate of ours, sitting far gone in rum, with his arms on the table. Suddenly he – the captain, that is – began to pipe up his eternal song:

"Fifteen men on the dead man's chest –
 Yo-ho-ho, and a bottle of rum!
 Drink and the devil had done for the rest –
 Yo-ho-ho, and a bottle of rum!"

At first I had supposed "the dead man's chest" to be that identical big box of his up-stairs in the front room, and the thought had been mingled in my nightmares with that of the one-legged seafaring man. But by this time we had all long ceased to pay any particular notice to the song; it was new, that night, to nobody but Dr. Livesey, and on him I observed it did not produce an agreeable effect, for he looked up for a moment quite angrily before he went on with his talk to old Taylor, the gardener, on a new cure for the rheumatics. In the meantime, the captain gradually brightened up at his own music, and at last flapped his hand upon the table before him in a way we all knew to mean – silence. The voices stopped at once, all but Dr. Livesey's; he went on as before, speaking clear and kind, and drawing briskly at his pipe between every word or two. The captain glared at him for awhile, flapped his hand again, glared still harder, and at last broke out with a villainous, low oath: "Silence there, between decks!"

"Were you addressing me, sir?" says the doctor; and when the ruffian had told him, with another oath, that this was so, "I have only one thing to say to you, sir," replies the doctor, "that if you keep on drinking rum, the world will soon be quit of a very dirty scoundrel!"

The old fellow's fury was awful. He sprang to his feet, drew and opened a sailor's clasp-knife, and, balancing it open on the palm of his hand, threatened to pin the doctor to the wall.

The doctor never so much as moved. He spoke to him, as before, over his shoulder, and in the same tone of voice; rather high, so that all the room might hear, but perfectly calm and steady:

"If you do not put that knife this instant in your pocket, I promise, upon my honour, you shall hang at the next assizes."

Then followed a battle of looks between them; but the captain soon

knuckled under, put up his weapon, and resumed his seat, grumbling like a beaten dog.

"And now, sir," continued the doctor, "since I now know there's such a fellow in my district, you may count I'll have an eye upon you day and night. I'm not a doctor only; I'm a magistrate; and if I catch a breath of complaint against you, if it's only for a piece of incivility like tonight's, I'll take effectual means to have you hunted down and routed out of this. Let that suffice."

Soon after Dr. Livesey's horse came to the door, and he rode away; but the captain held his peace that evening, and for many evenings to come.

CHAPTER TWO
Black Dog appears and disappears

It was not very long after this that there occurred the first of the mysterious events that rid us at last of the captain, though not, as you will see, of his affairs. It was a bitter cold winter, with long, hard frosts and heavy gales; and it was plain from the first that my poor father was little likely to see the spring. He sank daily, and my mother and I had all the inn upon our hands; and were kept busy enough, without paying much regard to our unpleasant guest.

It was one January morning, very early – a pinching, frosty morning – the cove all grey with hoar-frost, the ripple lapping softly on the stones, the sun still low and only touching the hilltops and shining far out to seaward. The captain had risen earlier than usual, and set out down the beach, his cutlass swinging under the broad skirts of the old blue coat, his brass telescope under his arm, his hat tilted back upon his head. I remember his breath hanging like smoke in his wake as he strode off, and the last sound I heard of him, as he turned the big rock, was a loud snort of indignation, as though his mind was still running upon Dr. Livesey.

Well, mother was upstairs with father; and I was laying the break-fast-table, against the captain's return, when the parlour door opened, and a man stepped in on whom I had never set my eyes before. He was a pale, tallowy creature, wanting two fingers of the left hand; and, though he wore a cutlass, he did not look much like a fighter. I had always my eye open for seafaring men, with one leg or two, and I remember this one puzzled me. He was not sailorly, and yet he had a smack of the sea about him too.

I asked him what was for his service, and he said he would take rum; but as I was going out of the room to fetch it he sat down upon a table, and motioned me to draw near. I paused where I was, with my napkin in my hand.

"Come here, sonny," says he. "Come nearer here."

I took a step nearer.

"Is this here table for my mate Bill?" he asked, with a kind of leer.

I told him I did not know his mate Bill; and this was for a person who stayed in our house, whom we called the captain.

"Well," said he, "my mate Bill would be called the captain, as like as not. He has a cut on one cheek, and a mighty pleasant way with him, particularly in drink, has my mate Bill. We'll put it, for argument like, that your captain has a cut on one cheek – and we'll put it, if you like, that that cheek's the right one. Ah, well! I told you. Now, is my mate Bill in this here house?"

I told him he was out walking.

"Which way, sonny? Which way is he gone?"

And when I had pointed out the rock and told him how the captain was likely to return, and how soon, and answered a few other ques-tions, "Ah," said he, "this'll be as good as drink to my mate Bill."

The expression of his face as he said these words was not at all pleasant, and I had my own reasons for thinking that the stranger was mistaken, even supposing he meant what he said. But it was no affair of mine, I thought; and, besides, it was difficult to know what to do. The stranger kept hanging about just inside the inn door, peering round the corner like a cat waiting for a mouse. Once I stepped out myself into the road, but he immediately called me back, and, as I did not obey quick enough for his fancy, a most horrible change came over his tallowy face, and he ordered me in, with an oath that made me jump. As soon as I was back again he returned to his former manner, half fawning, half sneering, patted me on the shoulder, told me I was a good boy, and he had taken quite a fancy to me. "I have a son of my own," he said, "as like you as two blocks, and he's all the pride of my 'art. But the great thing for boys is discipline, sonny – discipline. Now, if you had sailed along of Bill, you wouldn't have stood there to be spoke to twice – not you. That was never Bill's way, nor the way of sich as sailed with him. And here, sure enough, is my mate Bill, with a spyglass under his arm, bless his old 'art, to be sure. You and me'll just go back into the parlour, sonny, and get behind the door, and we'll give Bill a little surprise – bless his 'art I say again."

So saying, the stranger backed along with me into the parlour, and put me behind him in the corner, so that we were both hidden by the open door. I was very uneasy and alarmed, as you may fancy, and it rather added to my fears to observe that the stranger was certainly frightened himself. He cleared the hilt of his cutlass and loosened the blade in the sheath; and all the time we were waiting there he kept swallowing as if he felt what we used to call a lump in the throat.

At last in strode the captain, slammed the door behind him, without looking to the right or left, and marched straight across the room to where his breakfast awaited him.

"Bill," said the stranger, in a voice that I thought he had tried to make bold and big.

The captain spun round on his heel and fronted us; all the brown had gone out of his face, and even his nose was blue; he had the look of a man who sees a ghost, or the evil one, or something worse, if anything can be; and, upon my word, I felt sorry to see him, all in a moment, turn so old and sick.

"Come, Bill, you know me; you know an old shipmate, Bill, surely," said the stranger.

The captain made a sort of gasp.

"Black Dog!" said he.

"And who else?" returned the other, getting more at his ease. "Black Dog as ever was, come for to see his old shipmate Billy, at the 'Admiral Benbow' inn. Ah, Bill, Bill, we have seen a sight of times, us two, since I lost them two talons," holding up his mutilated hand.

"Now, look here," said the captain; "you've run me down; here I am; well, then, speak up: what is it?"

"That's you, Bill," returned Black Dog, "you're in the right of it, Billy. I'll have a glass of rum from this dear child here, as I've took such a liking to; and we'll sit down, if you please, and talk square, like old shipmates."

When I returned with the rum, they were already seated on either side of the captain's breakfast-table – Black Dog next to the door, and sitting sideways, so as to have one eye on his old shipmate, and one, I thought, on his retreat.

He bade me go and leave the door wide open. "None of your keyholes for me, sonny," he said; and I left them together, and retired into the bar.

For a long time, though I certainly did my best to listen, I could hear nothing but a low gabbling; but at last the voices began to grow higher, and I could pick up a word or two, mostly oaths, from the captain,

"No, no, no, no; and an end of it!" he cried once. And again, "if it comes to swinging, swing all, say I."

Then all of a sudden there was a tremendous explosion of oaths and other noises – the chair and table went over in a lump, a clash of steel followed, and then a cry of pain, and the next instant I saw Black Dog in full flight, and the captain hotly pursuing, both with drawn cutlasses, and the former streaming blood from the left shoulder. Just at the door, the captain aimed at the fugitive one last tremendous cut, which would certainly have split him to the chin had it not been intercepted by our big signboard of Admiral Benbow. You may see the notch on the lower side of the frame to this day.

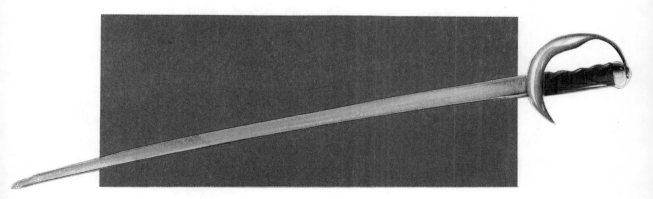

That blow was the last of the battle. Once out upon the road, Black Dog, in spite of his wound, showed a wonderful clean pair of heels, and disappeared over the edge of the hill in half a minute. The captain, for his part, stood staring at the signboard like a bewildered man. Then he passed his hand over his eyes several times, and at last turned back into the house.

"Jim," says he, "rum;" and as he spoke, he reeled a little, and caught himself with one hand against the wall.

"Are you hurt?" cried I.

"Rum," he repeated, "I must get away from here. Rum! rum!"

I ran to fetch it; but I was quite unsteadied by all that had fallen out, and I broke one glass and fouled the tap, and while I was still getting in my own way, I heard a loud fall in the parlour, and, running in, beheld the captain lying full length upon the floor. At the same instant my mother, alarmed by the cries and fighting, came running downstairs to help me. Between us we raised his head. He was breathing very loud and hard; but his eyes were closed, and his face a horrible colour.

"Dear, deary me," cried my mother, "what a disgrace upon the house! And your poor father sick!"

In the meantime, we had no idea what to do to help the captain, nor any other thought but that he had got his death-hurt in the scuffle with the stranger. I got the rum, to be sure, and tried to put it down his throat; but his teeth were tightly shut, and his jaws as strong as iron. It was a happy relief for us when the door opened and Dr. Livesey came in, on his visit to my father.

"Oh, doctor," we cried, "what shall we do? Where is he wounded?"

"Wounded? A fiddle-stick's end!" said the doctor. "No more wounded than you or I. The man has had a stroke, as I warned him. Now, Mrs. Hawkins, just you run upstairs to your husband, and tell him, if possible, nothing about it. For my part, I must do my best to save this fellow's trebly worthless life; and, Jim, you get me a basin."

When I got back with the basin, the doctor had already ripped up the captain's sleeve, and exposed his great sinewy arm. It was tattooed in several places. "Here's luck," "A fair wind," and "Billy Bones his fancy," were very neatly and clearly executed on the forearm; and up near the shoulder there was a sketch of a gallows and a man hanging from it – done, as I thought, with great spirit.

"Prophetic," said the doctor, touching this picture with his finger. "And now, Billy Bones, if that be your name, we'll have a look at the colour of your blood. Jim," he said, "are you afraid of blood?"

"No, sir," said I.

"Well, then," said he, "you hold the basin;" and with that he took his lancet and opened a vein.

A great deal of blood was taken before the captain opened his eyes and looked mistily about him. First he recognised the doctor with an unmistakable frown; then his glance fell upon me, and he looked relieved. But suddenly his colour changed, and he tried to raise himself, crying:

"Where's Black Dog?"

"There is no Black Dog here," said the doctor, "except what you have on your own back. You have been drinking rum; you have had a stroke, precisely as I told you; and I have just, very much against my own will, dragged you head-foremost out of the grave. Now, Mr. Bones –"

"That's not my name," he interrupted.

"Much I care," returned the doctor. "It's the name of a buccaneer of my acquaintance; and I call you by it for the sake of shortness, and what I have to say to you is this: one glass of rum won't kill you, but if you take one you'll take another and another, and I stake my wig if you don't break off short, you'll die – do you understand that? – die, and go to your own place, like the man in the Bible. Come, now, make an effort. I'll help you to your bed for once."

Between us, with much trouble, we managed to hoist him upstairs, and laid him on his bed, where his head fell back on the pillow, as if he were almost fainting.

"Now, mind you," said the doctor, "I clear my conscience – the name of rum for you is death."

And with that he went off to see my father, taking me with him by the arm.

"This is nothing," he said, as soon as he had closed the door. "I have drawn blood enough to keep him quiet awhile; he should lie for a week where he is – that is the best thing for him and you; but another stroke would settle him."

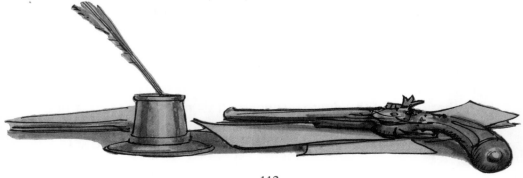

CHAPTER THREE
The Black Spot

bout noon I stopped at the captain's door with some cooling drinks and medicines. He was lying very much as we had left him, only a little higher, and he seemed both weak and excited.

"Jim," he said, "you're the only one here that's worth anything; and you know I've been always good to you. Never a month but I've given you a silver fourpenny for yourself. And now you see, mate, I'm pretty low, and deserted by all; and, Jim, you'll bring me one noggin of rum, now, won't you, matey?"

"The doctor —" I began.

But he broke in, cursing the doctor in a feeble voice, but heartily. "Doctors is all swabs," he said; "and that doctor there, why, what do he know about seafaring men? I been in places hot as pitch, and mates dropping round with Yellow Jack, and the blessed land a-heaving like the sea with earthquakes — what do the doctor know of lands like that? And I lived on rum, I tell you. It's been meat and drink, and man and wife, to me; and if I'm not to have my rum now I'm a poor old hulk on a lee shore, my blood'll be on you, Jim, and that doctor swab"; and he ran on again for awhile with curses. "Look, Jim, how my fingers fidges," he continued, in the pleading tone. "I can't keep 'em still, not I. I haven't had a drop this blessed day. That doctor's a fool, I tell you. If I don't have a drain o' rum, Jim I'll have the horrors; I seen some on 'em already. I seen old Flint in the corner there, behind you; as plain as print, I seen him; and if I get the horrors, I'm a man that has lived rough, and I'll raise Cain. Your doctor hisself said one glass wouldn't hurt me. I'll give you a golden guinea for a noggin, Jim."

He was growing more and more excited, and this alarmed me for my father, who was very low that day, and needed quiet; besides, I was reassured by the doctor's words, now quoted to me, and rather offended by the offer of a bribe.

"I want none of your money," said I, "but what you owe my father. I'll get you one glass, and no more."

When I brought it to him, he seized it greedily, and drank it out.

"Ay, ay," said he, "that's some better, sure enough. And now, matey, did that doctor say how long I was to lie here in this old berth?"

"A week at least," said I.

"Thunder!" he cried. "A week! I can't do that; they'd have the black spot on me by then. The lubbers is going about to get the wind of me this blessed moment; lubbers as couldn't keep what they got, and want to nail what is another's. Is that seamanly behaviour, now, I want to know? But I'm a saving soul. I never wasted good money of mine, nor lost it neither; and I'll trick 'em again. I'm not afraid on 'em. I'll shake out another reef, matey, and daddle 'em again."

As he was thus speaking, he had risen from bed with great difficulty, holding to my shoulder with a grip that almost made me cry out, and moving his legs like so much dead weight. His words, spirited as they were in meaning, contrasted sadly with the weakness of the voice in which they were uttered. He paused when he had got into a sitting position on the edge.

"That doctor's done me," he murmured. "My ears is singing. Lay me back."

Before I could do much to help him he had fallen back again to his former place, where he lay for awhile silent.

"Jim," he said at length, "you saw that seafaring man today?"

"Black Dog?" I asked.

"Ah! Black Dog," says he. "*He's* a bad 'un; but there's worse that put him on. Now, if I can't get away nohow, and they tip me the black spot, mind you, it's my old sea-chest they're after; you get on a horse – you can, can't you? Well, then, you get on a horse, and go to – well, yes, I will! – to that eternal doctor swab, and tell him to pipe all hands – magistrates and sich – and he'll lay 'em aboard at the 'Admiral Benbow' – all old Flint's crew, man and boy, all on 'em that's left. I was first mate, I was, old Flint's first mate, and I'm the on'y one as knows the place. He gave it me at Savannah, when he lay a-dying, like as if I was to now, you see. But you won't peach unless they get the black spot on me, or unless you see that Black Dog again or a seafaring man with one leg, Jim – him above all."

"But what is the black spot, captain?" I asked.

"That's a summons, mate. I'll tell you if they get that. But you keep your weather-eye open, Jim, and I'll share with you equals, upon my honour."

He wandered a little longer, his voice growing weaker; but soon after I had given him his medicine, which he took like a child, with the remark, "If ever a seaman wanted drugs, it's me," he fell at last into a heavy, swoon-like sleep, in which I left him. What I should have done had all gone well I do not know. Probably I should have told the whole story to the doctor; for I was in mortal fear lest the captain should repent of his confessions and make an end of me. But as things fell out, my poor father died quite suddenly that evening, which put all other matters on one side. Our natural distress, the visits of the neighbours, the arranging of the funeral, and all the work of the inn to be carried on in the meanwhile, kept me so busy that I had scarcely time to think of the captain, far less to be afraid of him.

He got downstairs next morning, to be sure, and had his meals as usual, though he ate little, and had more, I am afraid, than his usual supply of rum, for he helped himself out of the bar, scowling and blowing through his nose, and no one dared to cross him. On the night before the funeral he was as drunk as ever; and it was shocking, in that house of mourning, to hear him singing away at his ugly old sea-song; but, weak as he was, we were all in the fear of death for him, and the doctor was suddenly taken up with a case many miles away, and was never near the house after my father's death. I have said the captain was weak; and indeed he seemed rather to grow weaker than regain his strength. He clambered up and down stairs, and went from the parlour to the bar and back again, and sometimes put his nose out of doors to smell the sea, holding on to the walls as he went for support, and breathing hard and fast like a man on a steep mountain. He never particularly addressed me, and it is my belief he had as good as forgotten his confidences; but his temper was more flighty, and, allowing for his bodily weakness, more violent than ever. He had an alarming way now when he was drunk of drawing his cutlass and laying it bare before him on the table. But, with all that, he minded people less, and seemed shut up in his own thoughts and rather wandering. Once, for instance, to our extreme wonder, he piped up to a different air, a kind of country love-song, that he must have learned in his youth before he had begun to follow the sea.

So things passed until, the day after the funeral, and about three o'clock of a bitter, foggy, frosty morning, I was standing at the door for a moment, full of sad thoughts about my father, when I saw someone drawing slowly near along the road. He was plainly blind, for he tapped before him with a stick, and wore a great green shade over his eyes and nose; and he was hunched, as if with age or weakness, and wore a huge, old, tattered sea-cloak with a hood, that made him appear positively deformed. I never saw in my life a more dreadful looking figure. He stopped a little from the inn, and, raising his voice in an odd sing-song, addressed the air in front of him:

"Will any kind friend inform a poor blind man, who has lost the precious sight of his eyes in the gracious defence of his native country, England, and God bless King George! – where or in what part of this country he may now be?"

"You are at the 'Admiral Benbow,' Black Hill Cove, my good man," said I.

"I hear a voice," said he – "a young voice. Will you give me your hand, my kind young friend, and lead me in."

I held out my hand, and the horrible, soft-spoken, eyeless creature gripped it in a moment like a vice. I was so much startled that I struggled to withdraw; but the blind man pulled me close up to him with a single action of his arm.

"Now, boy," he said, "take me in to the captain."

"Sir," said I, "upon my word I dare not."

"Oh," he sneered, "that's it! Take me in straight, or I'll break your arm."

And he gave it, as he spoke, a wrench that made me cry out.

"Sir," said I, "it is for yourself, I mean. The captain is not what he used to be. He sits with a drawn cutlass. Another gentleman –"

"Come, now, march," interrupted he; and I never heard a voice so cruel, and cold, and ugly as that blind man's. It cowed me more than the pain; and I began to obey him at once, walking straight in at the door and towards the parlour, where our sick old buccaneer was sitting, dazed with rum. The blind man clung close to me, holding me in one iron fist, and leaning almost more of his weight on me than I could carry. "Lead me straight up to him, and when I'm in view, cry out, 'Here's a friend for you, Bill.' If you don't I'll do this"; and with that he gave me a twitch that I thought would have made me faint. Between this and that, I was so utterly terrified of the blind beggar that I forgot my terror of the captain, and as I opened the parlour door, cried out the words he had ordered in a trembling voice.

The poor captain raised his eyes, and at one look the rum went out of him, and left him staring sober. The expression of his face was not so much of terror as of mortal sickness. He made a movement to rise, but I do not believe he had enough force left in his body.

"Now, Bill, sit where you are," said the beggar. "If I can't see, I can hear a finger stirring. Business is business. Hold out your left hand. Boy, take his left hand by the wrist, and bring it near to my right."

We both obeyed him to the letter, and I saw him pass something from the hollow of the hand that held his stick into the palm of the captain's, which closed upon it instantly.

"And now that's done," said the blind man; and at the words he suddenly left hold of me, and with incredible accuracy and nimbleness, skipped out of the parlour and into the road, where, as I still stood motionless, I could hear his stick go tap-tap-tapping into the distance.

It was some time before either I or the captain seemed to gather our senses; but at length, and about at the same moment, I released his wrist, which I was still holding, and he drew in his hand and looked sharply into the palm.

"Ten o'clock!" he cried. "Six hours. We'll do them yet;" and he sprang to his feet.

Even as he did so, he reeled, put his hand to his throat, stood swaying for a moment, and then, with a peculiar sound, fell from his whole height face foremost to the floor.

I ran to him at once, calling to my mother. But haste was all in vain. The captain had been struck dead by thundering apoplexy. It is a curious thing to understand, for I had certainly never liked the man, though of late I had begun to pity him, but as soon as I saw that he was dead, I burst into a flood of tears. It was the second death I had known, and the sorrow of the first was still fresh in my heart.

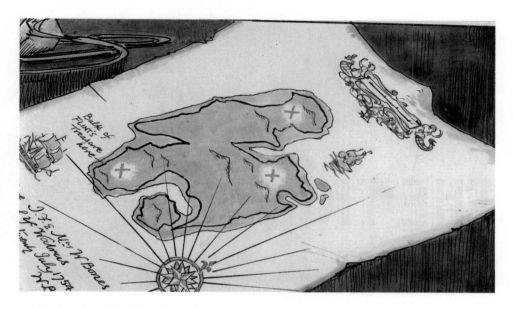

So begins Jim Hawkins' great adventure – a quest for buried treasure destined to carry him from the peace of the English countryside to the perils of the Spanish Main.

Because Billy Bones has not paid for his keep, Jim and his mother open the old pirate's sea-chest hoping to find enough money to settle Bones' account. Gold coins there are in plenty but most exciting of all, they discover a map which locates the spot where Billy Bones' old captain, the pirate Captain Flint, has hidden his ill-gotten plunder.

Jim takes the map to Dr. Livesey, who, together with his friend Squire Trelawney, decides to outfit a ship in the Port of Bristol and venture forth to find the treasure. Jim signs on as cabin boy. On the surface all seems to be going well but the Squire selects, as ship's cook, Long John Silver, a one-legged seaman, "very tall and strong, with a face as big as a ham – plain and pale, but intelligent and smiling."

During the voyage Jim learns that Silver and some members of the crew are, in fact, pirates. They plan to mutiny when the ship arrives at Treasure Island, kill all the honest seamen aboard and seize the treasure for themselves.

As the story unfolds, the ship arrives safely at the island, the mutiny takes place but thereafter it is discovered that the treasure is no longer where Captain Flint buried it. Its actual whereabouts is known only to a nigh-crazy old pirate, Ben Gunn, who was with Captain Flint when the treasure was first buried. Ben has unearthed the vast hoard of riches and hidden it.

How the treasure is finally recovered by Jim and his friends ends one of the most memorable adventure stories ever written.

THE TIGER

Tiger! Tiger! burning bright
In the forests of the night,
What immortal hand or eye
Could frame thy fearful symmetry?

In what distant deeps or skies
Burned the fire of thine eyes?
On what wings dare he aspire?
What the hand dare seize the fire?

And what shoulder, and what art,
Could twist the sinews of thy heart?
And when thy heart began to beat,
What dread hand? And what dread feet?

What the hammer? What the chain?
In what furnace was thy brain?
What the anvil? What dread grasp
Dare its deadly terrors clasp?

When the stars threw down their spears,
And watered heaven with their tears,
Did he smile his work to see?
Did he who made the Lamb make thee?

Tiger! Tiger! burning bright
In the forests of the night,
What immortal hand or eye
Dare frame thy fearful symmetry?

Black Beauty

This famous book is generally hailed as the most popular horse story ever published. It was written by Anna Sewell in 1877. In those days before aircraft and automobiles, horse-drawn carts and carriages were the only means of land transport. Many owners treated their horses badly. Pit-ponies toiled all their lives in coal-mines, never seeing the light of day and losing their sight.

Anna Sewell was horrified at the way "man's best friend" was treated in many quarters and she wrote "Black Beauty" as a stern protest against such cruelty. It still stands today as a monument to a gentle woman's pleading for kindness to dumb animals. Our version starts with the first chapter of the book.

My Early Home

The first place that I can well remember was a large pleasant meadow with a pond of clear water in it. Some shady trees leaned over it, and rushes and water-lilies grew at the deep end. Over the hedge on one side we looked into a ploughed field, and on the other we looked over a gate at our master's house, which stood by the roadside; at the top of the meadow was a plantation of fir trees, and at the bottom a running brook overhung by a steep bank.

Whilst I was young I lived upon my mother's milk, as I could not eat grass. In the day time I ran by her side, and at night I lay down close by her. When it was hot, we used to stand by the pond in the shade of the trees, and when it was cold, we had a nice warm shed near the plantation.

As soon as I was old enough to eat grass, my mother used to go out to work in the day time, and came back in the evening.

There were six young colts in the meadow besides me; they were older than I was; some were nearly as large as grown-up horses. I used to run with them, and had great fun; we used to gallop all together round and round the field, as hard as we could go. Sometimes we had rather rough play, for they would frequently bite and kick as well as gallop.

One day, when there was a good deal of kicking, my mother whinnied to me to come to her, and then she said:

'I wish you to pay attention to what I am going to say to you. The colts who live here are very good colts, but they are cart-horse colts, and, of course, they have not learned manners. You have been well bred and well born; your father has a great name in these parts, and your grandfather won the cup two years at the Newmarket races; your grandmother had the sweetest temper of any horse I ever knew, and I think you have never seen me kick or bite. I hope you will grow up gentle and good, and never learn bad ways; do your work with a good will, lift your feet up well when you trot, and never bite or kick even in play.'

I have never forgotten my mother's advice; I knew she was a wise old horse, and our master thought a great deal of her. Her name was Duchess, but he often called her Pet.

Our master was a good, kind man. He gave us good food, good lodging, and kind words; he spoke as kindly to us as he did to his little children. We were all fond of him, and my mother loved him very much. When she saw him at the gate, she would neigh with joy,

and trot up to him. He would pat and stroke her and say, 'Well, old Pet, and how is your little Darkie?' I was a dull black, so he called me Darkie; then he would give me a piece of bread, which was very good, and sometimes he brought a carrot for my mother. All the horses would come to him, but I think we were his favourites. My mother always took him to the town on a market day in a little gig.

There was a ploughboy, Dick, who sometimes came into our field to pluck blackberries from the hedge. When he had eaten all he wanted, he would have what he called fun with the colts, throwing stones and sticks at them to make them gallop. We did not much mind him, for we could gallop off; but sometimes a stone would hit and hurt us.

One day he was at this game, and did not know that the master was in the next field; but he was there, watching what was going on: over the hedge he jumped in a snap, and catching Dick by the arm, he gave him such a box on the ear as made him roar with the pain and surprise. As soon as we saw the master, we trotted up nearer to see what went on.

'Bad boy!' he said, 'bad boy! to chase the colts. This is not the first time, nor the second, but it shall be the last – there – take your money and go home, I shall not want you on my farm again.' So we never saw Dick any more. Old Daniel, the man who looked after the horses, was just as gentle as our master, so we were well off.

Now follows a condensation of the remainder of this famous book.

Then, when I was nearly two and we were standing in the early morning mist one spring morning, I saw my first hunt. The hare, wild with fright, leapt a stream, closely followed by the dogs and huntsmen. Suddenly, we saw two horses fall. One lay groaning in the grass. Someone ran to our master's house and came back with a gun. There was a loud bang, and then all was still; the black horse moved no more.

My mother was greatly troubled by this, and afterwards would never go near that part of the field.

When I was four, and my bright black coat had grown fine and soft, my master broke me in. Those who have never experienced this cannot imagine how terrible it feels to have a thick piece of steel pushed between one's teeth and tongue and held fast by leather straps, made to come out of the corner of one's mouth.

As a further part of my training, I was put in a field with sheep and cows next to a railway line. I shall never forget the first train that ran by! I thought it dreadful, but the cows went on eating quietly, and hardly raised their heads as the frightful thing went roaring past. Eventually I found that this terrible creature never came into the field or did me any harm. Since then I am as without fear at a railway station as in my own stable.

Eventually I was sold to Squire Gordon. Next to me in my new stable was a little, fat, grey pony called Merrylegs. Next to him was a tall chestnut mare with her ears laid back and an ill-tempered eye. Her name was Ginger, and Merrylegs told me that she had a bad temper, but that this was probably due to faulty upbringing.

The morning after I arrived, John Manly, the coachman, took me for a splendid gallop over the common and back by the watermill and river. I went well, and pleased him, and the next day, after my master had ridden me, there was a discussion between him and his wife as to what I should be called.

Ebony and Blackbird were both suggested. Then she thought of Black Beauty. So I was given my name.

In the stable afterwards, John was telling his assistant, James, about it, when James said:

"If it was not for the past, I should have called him Rob Roy, for I never saw two horses more alike."

"No wonder," said John. "Didn't you know that Farmer Grey's old Duchess was the mother of them both?"

It was always a great treat for us to be turned out into the Home Paddock or the old orchard. The air was so sweet, the turf so cool and soft to our feet, and the freedom so pleasant. Also, it was a good time for talking.

One day, I had a long talk with Ginger about her upbringing and breaking in. Hers, I found, was very different from mine, which accounted for her temper. Instead of the gentle treatment I had, Ginger had been trained by force and flogging. Also, she was high bred and full of spirit, which her owner's son tried to wear out.

Once, this spirit rose against him, and Ginger kicked and plunged and reared as never before. Eventually she threw him and galloped

126

off to the far end of the field, but only after he had punished her cruelly with his whip and spurs. The sun was very hot and the flies swarmed round her and settled on her bleeding flanks, but no one came to catch her. The sun was sinking when, at last, the old master came along with a sieve full of oats and spoke gently and cheerfully to her. She began to eat without fear, she told me, then allowed him to lead her towards the stables. At the door they met the son, at whom Ginger snapped fiercely, and whom the master ordered to stand back, telling him that he had done a bad day's work for her.

Ginger also told me of a second time when she had been forced to lose her temper. This had been when she was in her first place with a fashionable London gentleman, who liked a stylish turn-out and used the bearing-rein.

As Ginger explained, this pulls the head up and will not let it down. Having borne it as long as she could, she became so irritable one day that, just as she was buckled into the carriage, she lashed out. After this she was sold at Tattersall's, and again was badly treated at her new place. By this time she had come to look on all men as natural enemies.

It was late in autumn when I was put in the dog-cart to take my master to town on business. On our return trip night had come and a storm had risen. I was terrified when a huge oak crashed down in front of us and blocked the road. We turned and went the other way by the river. It was here, as my feet touched the bridge, that I felt

sure something was wrong. Neither words nor whip could make me move. Then a man came out yelling that the bridge had given in the middle. I shall never forget my master's gratitude, or the supper he gave me that night!

It was two or three months after this that Ginger and I, with James driving, took my master and mistress to some friends about forty-six miles away. Arriving there, we were led into a long stable with six or eight stalls and two or three horses. Later in the evening a traveller's horse was brought in by an ostler who smoked a large pipe, then James looked in and when he left the door was locked.

Some time later I woke, feeling very uncomfortable. I listened,

and heard a soft rushing sort of noise, and a low crackling and snapping. It was so strange, and I found it so hard to breathe, that I trembled all over.

By now all the other horses were awake, pulling at their halters and stamping. Then a strange ostler arrived and tried to lead us out, but we would not come, so terrified were we. Then I heard James' cheerful voice. I could trust him, so when he came I allowed him to lead me out. He patted me and left me in the yard while he went back for Ginger, and I let out a shrill whinny to give her courage to come.

Smoke was pouring out from the stable door, and I could see flashes

of red light. Something crashed inside, then, at last, James came out with Ginger.

At home again, soon after, John woke me one night and told me that the mistress was ill and we had to fetch a doctor.

For two miles I galloped as fast as I could, and by three we had reached Dr. White's door. His horse, however, had been out all day and was quite done up, so it was agreed I should take him back. By the time I reached the house, my legs shook under me and I could only stand and pant. Unfortunately, Joe did not put my warm cloth on me, and gave me cold water to drink, so that soon I was trembling all over and in great pain. I became very ill, and it even hurt me to breathe, yet I was happy in a way, for I knew that I had saved my mistress's life.

I do not know how long I was ill. Mr. Bond, the horse doctor, came every day. Then once, when Thomas Green came with John to give me some medicine, they stayed a while and talked, and I learned that Joe was heartbroken because he had not taken proper care of me, and Thomas was trying to persuade John to say a kind word to him. Presently John said he would, if I was better in the morning, and Thomas thanked him, saying that he was glad it was only ignorance that had made him so hard on Joe.

This made John flare up, and they had a long argument on ignorance, John saying it was the worst thing in the world and did as much harm as wickedness. They were still arguing when the medicine sent me to sleep, and in the morning I felt better; but I often thought of John's words when later I came to know more of the world.

Then came a sad day. Our mistress was taken ill and had to go away. Our happy days with her and the master had come to an end. Merrylegs was given to the vicar, and Ginger and I were sent to Lord W.'s, a friend of the master. It was a very sad moment for us when John handed us over to our new coachman, Mr. York, then came round to pat and speak to us for the last time. His voice sounded very sad. I held my face close to him – that was all I could do to say good-bye – and then he was gone, and I have never seen him since.

Of course, John had told York all about us, and how we had never worn a bearing-rein, but, unfortunately, our new mistress, a tall, proud-looking woman, insisted on our wearing the rein, and ordered it to be tightened day by day.

Ginger stood this for as long as she could, then one day, when our new mistress was just setting out, she suddenly reared and kicked in a most desperate manner. At last she kicked right over the carriage-pole and fell down, after giving me a severe blow on my near quarter. After that Ginger was never put in the carriage again. I was given a new partner, Max, and together we suffered the great discomfort of

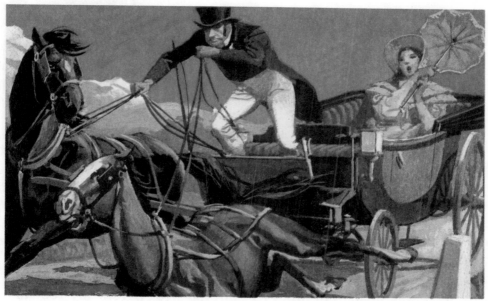

the tight rein, and took our cruel mistress wherever she wanted to go.

Early the next spring, Lord W. and part of his family went up to London, and took York with them. Ginger and I and some other horses were left in charge of the head groom.

I must now say something about Reuben Smith, who was left in charge of the stables when York went to London. Although he was a good groom, I learned from Max that he had a weakness for drink, and had once been discharged. Later he was taken back when he promised never to drink again. This promise he kept until early in April, when we took the brougham into the town to be done up. Reuben took the saddle with him, so that he could leave the brougham, and ride me back.

He told the ostler at the White Lion, where he left me, that he would come back for me at four. But it was nearly nine when he called me in a loud, rough voice. He was drunk, and ignoring a loose nail in one of my shoes, he forced me homewards through the dark at a crazy gallop.

Soon the shoe came off, and my foot was badly cut and the sharp stones hurt it terribly. But still he forced me to gallop. No horse could keep his footing in such circumstances. I fell.

Limping painfully to the side of the road, I saw Reuben lying face down in the road, very still. Hours passed before Ginger came, bringing two men. They picked up Reuben, and led me home limping. Reuben was dead. For weeks I suffered agony from my foot and broken knees; but, I am glad to say, I was cleared of all blame.

As my legs improved, I was turned out into a field for a rest. At first I was lonely. Then Ginger joined me. I was delighted to see her, until I heard that Lord George, a selfish, hard rider, had badly strained her in a steeplechase. So there we were, in the prime of our youth, one ruined by a fool, the other by a drunkard; for, although my knees mended, my appearance was spoiled for the Earl, and I was sold to a man at Bath, who used me for "jobbing".

Most of this work was very unpleasant, as my strange drivers were often inconsiderate or ignorant. Fortunately, I was not there long before a Mr. Barry took a liking to me and bought me.

Although he treated me kindly, Mr. Barry did not know much about horses. So it was, that his groom, Filcher, managed to steal much of my good food. During this time, being improperly fed, I lost a good deal of my energy. Fortunately, my condition finally aroused suspicion, and Filcher was caught and sent to prison for two months.

His successor was little better. I should say he was the laziest, most conceited fellow I ever came near, and, although he spoke smoothly to the master, he did not even bother to clean my stable properly. This gave me bad feet, and my master, disgusted at the trouble he

had had with grooms, decided not to keep a horse any longer. I was sold at a horse-fair to a man called Jeremiah Barker, who was a London cab-driver.

And a very kind man my new master was to me, as were his happy family – Polly, his wife, his boy, Harry, and Dolly, his daughter. Of course, it took me a little time to grow used to the hurry and the crowds of horses, carts, and carriages that filled London's streets. But Jerry was patient, and I soon learned.

Never once did he accept an extra fare if it meant whipping me to a speed beyond my endurance. Nor was I favoured. My companion, a proud horse called Captain, who had carried a cavalry officer in the Crimean War, was treated just as well.

Being a good man who believed it was wrong to work himself or his horses on Sunday, my master even lost one of his best customers for a while, when he politely refused to carry her on a Sunday. In the end, however, she came back to him again.

Only once did we work on Sunday. That was when the mother of one of Jerry's friends, Dinah Brown, was taken dangerously ill, and we took her out to the country to be with her mother. But neither of us minded helping in a case like that.

Then came a sad day. Winter, with its biting cold, and roads one could hardly stand on, had come, when a dreadfully ill and worn-looking horse joined the rank by me. She came up and spoke to me. It was Ginger. She had never recovered from her strain, and she told me that her driver was just burning up her little remaining strength as fast as he could. Even I could not comfort her, and she told me she wished that she were dead.

I never saw her again. But one day I saw a cart with a dead horse pass. The sight was too terrible for me to talk about, but it was a chestnut horse with a long, thin neck, and I saw a white streak down the forehead. I believe it was Ginger. I hope so, for then her troubles would be over.

It was soon after this that a drunken driver lost control of his horses and crashed his cart into us. Poor old Captain was so badly hurt that he was no longer of any use to Jerry. He could have sold Captain for a cart horse, but Jerry was too kind for that. He chose to do without the money, and gently ended proud Captain's days.

Then came New Year's Eve, and some thoughtless young men kept us waiting for hours in the terrible cold. Jerry caught bronchitis. He recovered, but was never again strong enough for his old work. Polly's old mistress, whom we had met on election day, found work for him in the country, and I was sold to a corn-dealer and baker, whose foreman nearly broke me with too heavy loads, and kept me in an unhealthy, dark stable.

However, I escaped serious strain or permanent injury to my sight, and eventually was sold to a large cab-owner.

The bad treatment here was more than I could bear. One day, trying to pull a particularly heavy load up Ludgate Hill, I collapsed and lay where I fell. I was no further use to my selfish owner. Again I was sold, this time to a kind farmer

Here, with kind treatment, I grew strong again, and then he sold me to three ladies, who were also very kind and promised never to sell me again. I was happy, especially as, the first day in my new stables, my groom recognised me, although I had changed so much. It was Joe Green, and I never saw a man so pleased.

So, in this happy home, my story ends. My troubles are all over, and I am at home; and often, before I am quite awake, I fancy I am back in the orchard, standing with my old friends under the apple trees.

THREE MEN IN A BOAT

Certain writers responsible for several books are strangely, renowned for one only. For instance, Richard Blackmore is known today for Lorna Doone *and little else. Likewise Jerome K. Jerome who penned a number of novels and plays is best known as the author of* Three Men In A Boat, *one of the most laughable and interesting of books. It recounts the merry adventures of three friends who decide for the first time ever that they will take a boating holiday on the River Thames. Here, in Jerome's own words, is his account of how George, Harris and J. manage to erect a canvas shelter over their boat on their first night. The story is told in the first person by J., who, one presumes, is Jerome K. Jerome himself. The friends are accompanied by their dog Montmorency.*

We had originally intended to go on to Magna Carta Island, a sweetly pretty part of the river, where it winds through a soft, green valley, and to camp in one of the many picturesque inlets to be found round that tiny shore. But, somehow, we did not feel that we yearned for the picturesque nearly so much now as we had earlier in the day. A bit of water between a coal-barge and a gas-works would have quite satisfied us for that night. We did not want scenery. We wanted to have our supper and go to bed. However, we did pull up to the point – "Picnic Point," it is called – and dropped into a very pleasant nook under a great elm-tree, to the spreading roots of which we fastened the boat.

Then we thought we were going to have supper (we had dispensed with tea, so as to save time), but George said no; that we had better get the canvas up first, before it got quite dark, and while we could see what we were doing. Then, he said, all our work would be done, and we could sit down to eat with an easy mind.

That canvas wanted more putting up than I think any of us had bargained for. It looked so simple in the abstract. You took five iron arches, like gigantic croquet hoops, and fitted them up over the boat, and then stretched the canvas over them, and fastened it down: it would take quite ten minutes, we thought.

That was an under-estimate.

We took up the hoops, and began to drop them into the sockets placed for them. You would not imagine this to be dangerous work; but, looking back now, the wonder to me is that any of us are alive to tell the tale. They were not hoops, they were demons. First they would not fit into their sockets at all, and we had to jump on them, and kick them, and hammer at them with the boat-hook; and, when they were in, it turned out that they were the wrong hoops for those particular sockets, and they had to come out again.

But they would not come out, until two of us had gone and struggled with them for five minutes, when they would jump up suddenly, and try and throw us into the water and drown us. They had hinges in the middle, and, when we were not looking, they nipped us with these hinges in delicate parts of the body; and, while we were wrestling with one side of the hoop, and endeavouring to persuade it to do its duty, the other side would come behind us in a cowardly manner, and hit us over the head.

We got them fixed at last, and then all that was to be done was to arrange the covering over them. George unrolled it, and fastened one end over the nose of the boat. Harris stood in the middle to take it from George and roll it on to me, and I kept by the stern to receive it. It was a long time coming down to me. George did his part all right, but it was new work to Harris, and he bungled it.

How he managed it I do not know, he could not explain himself; but by some mysterious process or other he succeeded, after ten minutes of superhuman effort, in getting himself completely rolled up in it. He was so firmly wrapped round and tucked in and folded over, that he could not get out. He, of course, made frantic struggles for freedom – the birthright of every Englishman – and, in doing so (I learned this afterwards), knocked over George; and then George, swearing at Harris, began to struggle too, and got himself entangled and rolled up.

I knew nothing about all this at the time. I did not understand the business at all myself. I had been told to stand where I was, and wait till the canvas came to me, and Montmorency and I stood there and waited both as good as gold. We could see the canvas being violently jerked and tossed about, pretty considerably; but we supposed this was part of the method, and did not interfere.

We also heard much smothered language coming from underneath

it, and we guessed that they were finding the job rather troublesome, and concluded that we would wait until things had got a little simpler before we joined in.

We waited some time, but matters seemed to get only more and more involved, until, at last, George's head came wriggling out over the side of the boat, and spoke up.

It said:

"Give us a hand here, can't you, you cuckoo; standing there like a stuffed mummy, when you see we are both being suffocated, you dummy!"

I never could withstand an appeal for help, so I went and undid them; not before it was time, either, for Harris was nearly black in the face.

It took us half an hour's hard labour, after that, before it was properly up, and then we cleared the decks, and got out supper. We put the kettle on to boil, up in the nose of the boat, and went down to the stern and pretended to take no notice of it, but set to work to get the other things out.

That is the only way to get a kettle to boil up the river. If it sees that you are waiting for it and are anxious, it will never even sing. You have to go away and begin your meal, as if you were not going to have any tea at all. You must not even look round at it. Then you will soon hear it sputtering away, mad to be made into tea.

It is a good plan, too, if you are in a great hurry, to talk very loudly to each other about how you don't need any tea, and are not going to have any. You get near the kettle, so that it can overhear you, and then you shout out, "I don't want any tea; do you, George?" to which George shouts back, "Oh, no, I don't like tea; we'll have lemonade instead – tea's so indigestible." Upon which the kettle boils over, and puts the stove out.

We adopted this harmless bit of trickery, and the result was that, by the time everything else was ready, the tea was waiting. Then we lit the lantern, and squatted down to supper.

We wanted that supper.

For five-and-thirty minutes not a sound was heard throughout the length and breadth of that boat, save the clank of cutlery and crockery, and the steady grinding of four sets of molars. At the end of five-and-thirty minutes, Harris said, "Ah!" and took his left leg out from under him and put his right one there instead.

Five minutes afterwards, George said, "Ah!" too, and threw his plate out on the bank; and, three minutes later than that, Montmorency gave the first sign of contentment he had exhibited since we had started, and rolled over on his side, and spread his legs out; and then I said, "Ah!" and bent my head back, and bumped it against one of the hoops, but I did not mind it. I did not even swear.

How good one feels when one is full – how satisfied with ourselves and with the world! People who have tried it, tell me that a clear conscience makes you very happy and contented; but a full stomach does the business quite as well, and is cheaper, and more easily obtained. One feels so forgiving and generous after a substantial and well-digested meal – so noble-minded, so kindly-hearted.

KING MIDAS

Many hundreds of years ago, in Macedonia, a country which lies to the north of Greece, there lived a king named Midas. He was a pleasure loving man, fond of good food and rich possessions.

One summer, the army of a god named Dionysus was marching through Macedonia, when an old man called Silenus became separated from it and lost. He wandered about for some time, until at last, he fell exhausted, in the gardens of King Midas.

He was found by the palace guards and taken before the king, who recognized him at once. Silenus had always been a well-known and respected teacher. He had taught Dionysus himself.

"Welcome, dear friend," smiled King Midas.

King Midas knew that Dionysus, also known as Bacchus, was the god of wine and all good fruits of the earth. He knew also that Dionysus was very fond of his old teacher, Silenus.

"If I make Silenus welcome and care for him, until he is well enough to be taken back to rejoin the army of Dionysus, then surely the mighty god will be grateful and reward me," thought King Midas.

"Have no more fears," King Midas then said to Silenus. "You may rest here as long as you wish and then I will personally guide you back to rejoin the great Dionysus."

141

Silenus was lodged in a comfortable room. When he was rested, he was taken to sit with King Midas. Servant girls brought the best food and wine in the land for the two men to enjoy.

"You are very kind, King Midas," said Silenus, who had indeed been frightened at being lost in a strange land.

"Nonsense," smiled the king. "Nothing is too much trouble for a friend of the mighty and powerful Dionysus."

"Please tell me what I may do to thank you for your hospitality," Silenus asked.

"Nothing, nothing," smiled King Midas, calling a servant to pour more wine for Silenus.

Then he went on: "The only thing you might do, when you rejoin your noble master, is to mention to him that you are pleased with the way I was able to help you and that I am a humble admirer of the great god of wine."

"Of course, of course," smiled Silenus. "I will go before Dionysus

the moment I return and tell him that without the help of kind King Midas, I should have perished."

At that, King Midas was very pleased. Every day he dined with Silenus and saw that the old man was given plenty of the best wine, as befitted a follower of Dionysus.

After several days, the old man had regained his strength and together with a party of servants and some guards, Silenus and King Midas made the journey to catch up with Dionysus.

The great god of wine was pleased and happy to see his old teacher safely returned. He had feared that the old man had wandered away and perished in some lonely mountain pass.

Silenus bowed low before his master.

"Indeed I should have perished," he said, "if it had not been for the great kindness of King Midas of Macedonia."

At once the god Dionysus ordered King Midas to be brought before him.

"I am fond of old Silenus and grateful to you for helping him," smiled the god, raising a goblet of wine and looking down at the kneeling figure of Midas. "I should like to grant you a favour. Tell me what you desire."

King Midas had already given this matter much thought and he had his answer ready.

"Great Dionysus," he said, bowing low, "your generosity overwhelms me. The one favour I wish granted, is that everything I touch should turn to gold."

King Midas thought that if he could create gold whenever he wished, then he could buy as many of the good things of life as he wanted for as long as he lived. However, he had forgotten that people who ask favours from the gods, should be very careful how they state their requests.

Dionysus stared at Midas.

"You are quite sure that is what you want?" he asked. "That everything you touch should turn to gold?"

"Yes, yes, please!" replied King Midas, consumed with greed at the thought of so much wealth.

"Very well," smiled Dionysus, "Your wish is granted."

Hurrying out of the presence of the god, King Midas picked up a stone. At once it turned to glittering gold. Midas was delighted. However, his joy soon turned to terror. Not only stones and goblets and chairs and tables turned to gold at his touch, but food and wine and even water.

If he tried to eat the leg of a chicken, the meat turned to hard metal before the unfortunate king could put it into his mouth. Wine became solid in goblets of gold. If the king tried to wash his hands, the water became hard and little beads of gold dripped from the royal fingers.

King Midas realized that if he could not lose the golden touch, very soon he would starve to death. Again he went before Dionysus and this time begged that the gift of the golden touch should be taken away from him.

Smiling a little to himself, Dionysus agreed to grant the request. He told King Midas to go to the well-known River Pactolus, and there bathe himself completely in the waters.

Thankfully, King Midas journeyed to the river and leapt into the water. He splashed and soaked himself from head to toe and was delighted to find that the water remained unchanged as water and the pebbles on the river bed remained unchanged as pebbles.

The golden touch had been taken from him. He could eat and drink and be happy again.

However, it is said that as King Midas lost the curse of the golden touch, the gold ran from his fingers and into the waters of the River Pactolus. Folk do say that those who seek beneath the waters of that river will find the sand bright with gold, even to this day.

None of that concerned Midas as he stepped on to the river bank. He had lost his love of gold and was happy merely to see the flowers stay alive at his touch and the world a normal place again.

The Last Fight of the
REVENGE

The Azores Islands lie in mid Atlantic and it was there in August 1591 that an English squadron under the command of Lord Thomas Howard was sighted by a huge Spanish fleet of fifty three ships. Howard at once set sail with five of his galleons but Sir Richard Grenville, captain of the good ship Revenge, *refused to desert many of his crew who were lying ashore sick. He had them all brought aboard only to find himself trapped by the Spanish fleet. Scorning to surrender, Grenville decided to fight to the death. The battle was immortalised in this ballad by Lord Tennyson.*

At Floòes in the Azorès Sir Richard Grenville lay,
And a pinnace, like a fluttered bird, came flying from far away:
"Spanish ships of war at sea! We have sighted fifty-three!"
Then sware Lord Thomas Howard: "'Fore God I am no coward;
But I cannot meet them here, for my ships are out of gear,
And the half my men are sick. I must fly, but follow quick.
We are six ships of the line; can we fight with fifty-three?"

Then spake Sir Richard Grenville: "I know you are no coward;
You fly them for a moment to fight with them again.
But I've ninety men and more that are lying sick ashore.
I should count myself the coward if I left them, my Lord Howard,
To these Inquisition dogs and the devildoms of Spain."

So Lord Howard passed away with five ships of war that day,
Till he melted like a cloud in the silent summer heaven;
But Sir Richard bore in hand all his sick men from the land
Very carefully and slow,
Men of Bideford in Devon,
And we laid them on the ballast down below;
For we brought them all aboard,
And they blest him in their pain, that they were not left to Spain,
To the thumbscrew and the stake, for the glory of the Lord.

He had only a hundred seamen to work the ship and to fight,
And he sailed away from Florès till the Spaniard came in sight,
With his huge sea-castles heaving upon the weather bow.
"Shall we fight or shall we fly?
Good Sir Richard, tell us now;
For to fight is but to die!
There'll be little of us left by the time this sun is set."
And Sir Richard said again: "We be all good English men;
Let us bang these dogs of Seville, the children of the devil.
For I never turned my back upon Don or devil yet."

Sir Richard spoke and he laughed, and we roared a hurrah, and so
The little *Revenge* ran on, sheer into the heart of the foe,
With her hundred fighters on deck and her ninety sick below;
For half of their fleet to the right and half to the left were seen,
And the little *Revenge* ran on through the long sea-lane between.

Thousands of their soldiers looked down from their decks and laughed,
Thousands of their seamen made mock at the mad little craft
Running on and on, till delayed
By their mountain-like *San Philip*, that of fifteen hundred tons,
And up-shadowing high above us with her yawning tiers of guns,
Took the breath from our sails, and we stayed.

And while now the great *San Philip* hung above us like a cloud
Whence the thunderbolt will fall
Long and loud,
Four galleons drew away
From the Spanish fleet that day,
And two upon the larboard and two upon the starboard lay,
And the battle-thunder broke from them all.

But anon the great *San Philip*, she bethought herself and went,
Having that within her womb that had left her ill content;
And the rest they came aboard us, and they fought us hand to hand,
For a dozen times they came with their pikes and musqueteers,
And a dozen times we shook 'em off us as a dog that shakes his ears
When he leaps from the water to the land.

And the sun went down, and the stars came out far over the summer
    sea,
But never a moment ceased the fight of the one and the fifty-three.
Ship after ship, the whole night long, their high-built galleons came,
Ship after ship, the whole night long, with her battle-thunder and
    flame;
Ship after ship, the whole night long, drew back with her dead and
    her shame,
For some were sunk, and many were shattered, and so could fight
us no more –
God of battles, was ever a battle like this in the world before?

For he said: "Fight on! Fight on!"
Though his vessel was all but a wreck;
And it chanced that, when half of the short summer night was gone,
With a grisly wound to be dressed, he had left the deck,
But a bullet struck him that was dressing it suddenly dead,
And himself, he was wounded again in the side and the head,
And he said: "Fight on! Fight on!"

And the night went down, and the sun smiled out far over the summer
sea,
And the Spanish fleet, with broken sides, lay round us all in a ring;
But they dared not touch us again, for they feared that we still could
sting,
So they watched what the end would be.
And we had not fought them in vain,
But in perilous plight were we,
Seeing forty of our poor hundred were slain,
And half of the rest of us maimed for life
In the crash of the cannonades and the desperate strife;
And the sick men down in the hold were most of them stark and cold,
And the pikes were all broken or bent, and the powder was all of it
spent;
And the masts and the rigging were lying over the side;
But Sir Richard cried in his English pride:

"We have fought such a fight for a day and a night
As may never be fought again!
We have won great glory, my men!
And a day less or more
At sea or shore,
We die – does it matter when?
Sink me the ship, Master Gunner – sink her, split her in twain!
Fall into the hands of God, not into the hands of Spain!"

And the gunner said: "Ay, ay," but the seamen made reply:
"We have children, we have wives,
And the Lord hath spared our lives.
We will make the Spaniard promise, if we yield, to let us go;
We shall live to fight again and to strike another blow."
And the lion there lay dying, and they yielded to the foe.

And the stately Spanish men to their flagship bore him then,
Where they laid him by the mast, old Sir Richard caught at last,
And they praised him to his face with their courtly foreign grace;
But he rose upon their decks, and he cried:
"I have fought for Queen and Faith: like a valiant man and true;
I have only done my duty, as a man is bound to do:
With a joyful spirit I, Sir Richard Grenville, die!"
And he fell upon their decks, and he died.

And they stared at the dead that had been so valiant and true,
And had holden the power and glory of Spain so cheap
That he dared her with one little ship and his English few;
Was he devil or man? He was devil for aught they knew,
But they sank his body with honour down into the deep,
And they manned the *Revenge* with a swarthier, alien crew,
And away she sailed with her loss, and longed for her own;
When a wind from the lands they had ruined awoke from sleep,
And the water began to heave, and the weather to moan,
And ere ever that evening ended, a great gale blew,
And a wave like a wave that is raised by an earthquake grew,
Till it smote on their hulls and their sails and their masts and their flags,
And the whole sea plunged and fell on the shot-shattered navy of
   Spain,
And the little *Revenge* herself went down by the island crags,
To be lost evermore in the main.

Jock of Hazeldean

Why weep ye by the tide, ladie?
Why weep ye by the tide?
I'll wed ye to my youngest son,
And ye sall be his bride:
And ye sall be his bride, ladie,
Sae comely to be seen:
But aye she loot the tears down fa'
For Jock of Hazeldean.

Now let this wilfu' grief be done,
And dry that cheek so pale;
Young Frank is chief of Errington
And lord of Langley-dale;
His step is first in peaceful ha',
His sword in battle keen:
But aye she loot the tears down fa'
For Jock of Hazeldean.

A chain of gold ye sall not lack
Nor braid to bind your hair,
Nor mettled hound, nor managed hawk,
Nor palfrey fresh and fair;
And you the foremost o' them a',
Shall ride our forest-queen:
But aye she loot the tears down fa'
For Jock of Hazeldean.

The kirk was decked at morning-tide,
The tapers glimmered fair;
The priest and bridegroom wait the bride
And dame and knight are there;
They sought her baith by bower and ha';
The ladie was not seen!
She's o'er the Border, and awa'
Wi' Jock of Hazeldean.

The Adventures of Ulysses

Two of the oldest books in the world are the Iliad *and the* Odyssey. *Both were written nearly three thousand years ago by a Greek poet called Homer.*

The Iliad *tells us about the great war between the Greeks and the Trojans. It all began when Paris, Prince of Troy, kidnapped the beautiful Helen, wife of King Menelaus of Sparta in Greece. When Menelaus married Helen, the princes of Greece had all sworn to uphold the cause of Helen if any need arose. The result of the kidnapping was that a huge force of Greeks lay siege to the city of Troy, determined on the recovery of Helen. Odysseus (or Ulysses as he is perhaps better known) was the wisest of all the Greeks. It was he who thought up the idea of the famous wooden horse which brought about the fall of Troy.*

The Odyssey *relates the adventures of Ulysses when, after the ten years siege of Troy, he and his followers set off in their twelve ships, homeward bound to Ithaca where Ulysses was King.*

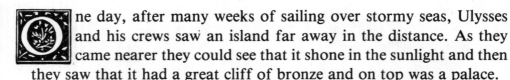

ne day, after many weeks of sailing over stormy seas, Ulysses and his crews saw an island far away in the distance. As they came nearer they could see that it shone in the sunlight and then they saw that it had a great cliff of bronze and on top was a palace.

The sailors anchored and waded ashore and, with Ulysses at their head, they made their way to the great palace, hoping to obtain food and various other provisions for their ships.

They learned that the palace was the home of Aeolus, King of the Winds. Here they were made welcome and Ulysses, King of Ithaca, asked for an audience with the King of the Winds. His request was granted at once.

Ulysses, attended by one of his captains, was ushered into a splendid hall where King Aeolus awaited him. On either side of him stood one of his sons and one of his daughters.

"Welcome, noble Ulysses," smiled the old king and Ulysses was surprised at being greeted by name. "I have heard of the wisest of all the Greeks. Your fame has spread far and wide."

"And I have heard of you, your majesty," replied Ulysses.

Aeolus nodded.

"You are a seaman and who better to know of the powers of Aeolus, king and god of all the winds?" he said. "You will know that I have charge of the gentle breezes that blow the fishermen back to the shore and lord of the raging gales which carry great ships before them and hurl them against the rocks. Hurricanes, storms, gales, breezes—all obey my commands."

"Even so, your majesty," agreed Ulysses with a grin, "and during the last few weeks my ships have been battered by your gales. I therefore request you to allow me and my men to remain on your island for a month for a much needed rest and to carry out repairs to our ships."

"Of course, gallant Ulysses," answered the King of the Winds. He gave orders for a feast to be prepared for the travellers and made arrangements for them to be given food and shelter for a month. During this time Ulysses and Aeolus became firm friends. When the time came for the Greeks to set sail, Aeolus was sad.

"I have enjoyed your visit, Ulysses," he said. "I will remember you kindly and so that you will remember me, I give you this leather bag." He held out a dirty old leather bag and Ulysses stared in surprise. "Do not be surprised," went on Aeolus. "It is the finest gift I can give you. Inside it, tied up, are all the stormy winds which might hinder your return if they were allowed to blow. Tell no man what the bag contains, let no man touch it, for if it is opened, the fierce winds will escape and drive you far from home."

Aeolus then explained to Ulysses that only the warm West Wind, which would blow Ulysses and his ships straight home to the island of Ithaca, had been left out of the bag.

Ulysses and his companions set sail once more on the last stage of their long journey home, and always Ulysses kept the bag at his side. Came the day when the fair island of Ithaca was in sight but as bad luck would have it, Ulysses had fallen asleep where he stood at the wheel. He was worn out after steering his ship for many days and nights. It was his ship which led the little fleet.

Now some of his seamen suspected that the leather bag contained treasure given to Ulysses by King Aeolus. Unable to contain their curiosity, they took the bag and one of them opened it with a knife.

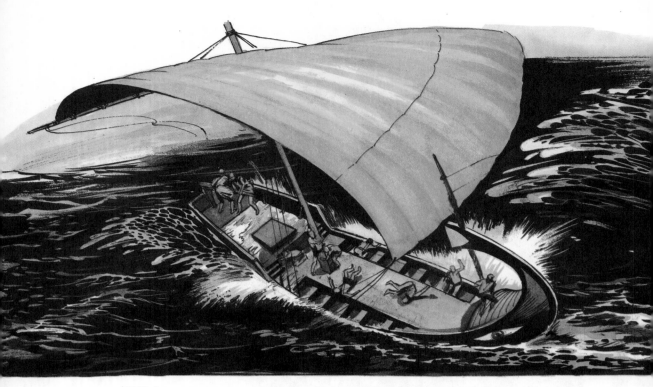

"If there *is* treasure in there," grumbled one of the sailors, "I see no reason why we should not have a share in it. After all, we have shared the captain's perils with him, have we not?"

Before anyone could answer him, a fury of winds burst out of the bag and in a few moments the seas were mountain high. Winds of hurricane force lashed the ships, tearing the sails, snapping the masts and washing men overboard. As the ships were driven along by the howling winds, Ithaca soon disappeared from sight and soon they had been blown into unknown seas.

Ulysses, awakened by the roar of the mighty storms, could hardly stand, for the winds were so strong. He had to cling to the deck until the winds died away and the sea became calmer.

After a while, the ships once more reached the island where King Aeolus lived, but this time the King of the Winds would not allow Ulysses and his men to land. He was afraid there was a curse of the gods on them and they would bring misfortune to him and his people. Instead he drove them away.

"A clever man you might be, Ulysses," he called out, "but surely you must be the most unlucky man living. It is obvious that the gods hate you and they will hate me, too, if I help you."

Ulysses sailed on, not knowing where he was going for seven days and nights, until land was sighted. The ships had reached a harbour with a narrow entrance and steep rocks on either side.

The men in the other ships with Ulysses, pleased to reach the safety of a harbour after the terrible storms, sailed right inside, but Ulysses was more cautious. He did not know whether the people would be friendly or not and therefore he tied his ship to a rock outside the harbour, so that he could leave quickly if the necessity arose. Then he sent three of his men ashore to see who lived there.

They found a young girl drawing water at a well just outside the town and she told them she was the daughter of the king. She led them to her father's palace where, to their horror, they discovered that he was a dreadful giant.

He seized one of the men, meaning to kill him and the other two seamen fled back to the ships as fast as their legs would carry them.

The ships prepared to leave harbour, but all the people ran from the city and lined the tops of the cliffs. As the sailors tried to row away, the screaming people hurled boulders down on them.

Seeing this, Ulysses drew his sword and cut the rope which fastened his ship to the rock. His crew rowed with all their might and they were able to make good their escape. The eleven other ships, however, which had anchored in the harbour itself, were all sunk and the men drowned.

Sad at the death of their friends, Ulysses and his companions rowed away, hoping that in some way they would be able to find their way home to Ithaca once again.

They sailed on and on until at long last they sighted a pleasant island. As they approached, they could see trees and grass growing and knew that there they would find water.

They anchored their boat in a bay and went ashore. Ulysses took his bow and went off in search of game. Luckily he soon spotted a stag and within moments the animal lay dead at his feet. Ulysses called to his men who had meanwhile been searching for water. They came to him smilingly for they had come across a river of clear sparkling water.

The weary seamen feasted royally on roast venison and drank cool water. Then sighing with pleasure, they all rested.

In fact, they rested for three days. Refreshed, Ulysses decided that it was time they found out more about the island and he clambered to the top of a high rock to spy out the land.

There had been no sign of any inhabitants all the time they had been taking it easy on the beach but Ulysses did not want to risk his life or the lives of his men, among people who might be enemies.

From the top of the rock, Ulysses saw smoke rising from the middle of a forest and he knew that there must be some living beings there.

Whether they would be friendly or not, he had no way, of course, of telling.

He returned to his men, having decided to split them into two groups. One group was to explore, the other group to remain on the beach. The first group, led by one of Ulysses' most trusted lieutenants set out for the forest. There they soon came to a beautiful white palace set amongst the trees. To their amazement, tame wolves and lions wandered around outside the palace. When the animals saw the men approaching, they ran to them and wagged their tails and pranced around like friendly dogs.

From inside the palace there came the sound of a sweet voice singing. The sailors were not to know that the lady of the palace was seated at her loom, weaving fine cloth. Neither were they to know that the beautiful woman was a wicked enchantress named Circe.

Ending her song, she rose and left the palace. When the seamen saw this lovely lady, dressed in white robes and rich gleaming jewels, they greeted her heartily. She smiled and won the hearts of all the sailors with the exception of the lieutenant who distrusted her on sight.

Circe invited the sailors to enter her palace and eat. The men went in gladly, but the lieutenant, suspecting some trick, hid behind a tree to see what might happen to the other men.

Through an open door, he watched the beautiful lady call several maidens who spread a great banquet for the men. Then she brought them goblets full of honey and wine and the men, who by this time were very thirsty, drained the wine in great gulps.

At once a very strange thing happened. All the men turned into pigs and Circe drove them all out of the palace into a pigsty. The lieutenant shook with fear and rushed back to Ulysses who was awaiting his return impatiently.

The lieutenant panted out his story and begged his captain and companions to put out to sea at once and get away while they could. Ulysses brushed this suggestion aside for he did not intend to leave his men at the mercy of so ruthless an enchantress.

Clapping his hand to his sword, he declared that he himself would go to the palace of the wicked witch and see for himself what had happened.

"Meanwhile," he warned his men, "you are to remain here and not stir a single step away from the shore until I return."

His men promised to stay where they were and bravely Ulysses set out to pit his quick wits against those of the crafty enchantress who had cast so evil a spell on his loyal companions.

Stepping carefully and keeping his sharp eyes open for any sign of an ambush or treachery, the King of Ithaca made his way towards the forest where stood the magnificent palace of the witch Circe.

He was treading silently along a rocky path when to his amazement he heard a strange voice call to him.

"Greetings, Ulysses, King of Ithaca," said the voice softly.

Ulysses halted in his tracks and looked about him. There, seated gracefully nearby on a rock, was a handsome, slim young man in whose eyes there lurked an odd gleam.

The stranger was wearing a winged helmet and his feet were shod with winged sandals.

"Have no fear, Ulysses," smiled the young man. "Know that I am Hermes, the swift-footed messenger of the gods. They have seen your unhappy plight and are prepared to help you overcome Circe's sorcery."

So saying, Hermes leaped lightly from the rock and stooping, plucked a flower from the ground. The flower was as white as milk, but its root was coal-black. He handed the flower to Ulysses.

"As long as you have this flower," Hermes said to Ulysses, "Circe's magic potion will have no power over you. Take it from her and drink

it. Have no fear. It will not harm you. Then draw your sword and make Circe swear that she will never harm you.''

With this, Hermes turned and on the instant vanished from sight. Clutching the flower, Ulysses sped to Circe's palace. Sure enough, the

enchantress gave him a magic potion which Ulysses drank. Then he threw the goblet to the ground and drew his sword.

"Evil witch," he roared, "your magic cannot harm me. Now promise me that never at any time will you try to use your magic powers

on me. Refuse—and, Circe, you have my word, you will never live to see the sun set." White with rage, Circe bit her lips but fearful of the deadly glance in Ulysses' eyes, she gave her word.

Then she threw herself at Ulysses' feet and begged him to spare her life. Ulysses agreed to do so if she changed his friends back to their proper shapes once more.

This she did and Ulysses and his men were now able to return to their ship and bid farewell to the island of Circe the enchantress, forever. Before they left, however, Circe was so thankful that Ulysses had not slain her that she warned him of some of the dangers that still lay between him and his beloved island of Ithaca.

"Beware especially of the Sirens," Circe said. "They are beautiful maidens who sing so sweetly that sailors cannot bear the thought of going away and leaving them. As the sailors try to land, their ships are wrecked on the rocks that surround the island where the Sirens live. When you have passed the Sirens, you must sail through a channel. Beware of this also, for on each side of the channel there is danger. On one side there lives a monster called Scylla. She has twelve feet and six heads and each head has three rows of fierce teeth. She lies in wait for passing ships and as they sail past, she snatches a sailor from the deck with each one of her heads.

"On the other side of the channel is Charybdis. She sucks in water, making giant whirlpools into which ships are drawn down and never seen again. You must steer your ship between these two great dangers if you are to reach the other end of the channel."

Ulysses thanked Circe for her help and sailed away from her island of peril. For several days, the travellers made their way across the blue sea until one morning Ulysses awoke and noticed that the air was sweetly scented.

He frowned for he knew that the ship was nearing the island where the Sirens dwelt. At once he ordered his crew to gather round and sent some of them to fetch some jars of beeswax that had been given him by Circe before he had taken his leave of her.

Ulysses told them that they must plug their ears with the wax so that they could not hear. His men had been told nothing concerning the Sirens but they agreed.

"And now," he told them, "listen to me very carefully. I want you to tie me to the mast so that I cannot move. The ropes must be strong and tightly knotted about me. I shall be the only one able to hear. I shall not plug my ears, because I must be able to know the moment we are safely past the island of the Sirens."

Naturally the crew wanted to know who the Sirens were and Ulysses repeated all that Circe had told him. When he had finished speaking, not one refused to obey their captain's orders.

"Because your ears will be plugged with wax," Ulysses told them, "you will be unable to hear my commands. If, however, you see me struggling to free myself, take no notice. If I seem to be loosening my ropes you must come and bind me more tightly. When evening draws near and I have stopped struggling you can free me—but not before then."

Every member of the crew then plugged his ears with the soft wax. Then Ulysses was lashed to a spar that was roped to the mast.

Manning the oars, the seamen rowed closer and closer to the island where the lovely Sirens were singing their beautiful and enticing song. Only Ulysses could hear their chanting and as their ship sailed nearer, he struggled and fought to free himself for it was a sound that no man could possibly resist.

Ulysses longed to break loose from his bonds and plunge into the water so that he could swim to where the Sirens sat on the rocks, but the ropes held him fast.

Exerting all his powerful strength, Ulysses strove to free himself and at last the ropes began to give way. One of the crew threw a glance over his shoulder and saw that his captain was almost free. At once he leaped to his feet and bound Ulysses tighter than ever to the mast.

He laughed as Ulysses raved and raged at him for he could not hear a single word. At last, the crew rowed past the island and the singing of the Sirens became fainter and fainter. Not, though, until their magical singing had faded completely did Ulysses cease his struggles. Then his crew loosened the ropes and at a nod from him, took the beeswax from their ears.

They had passed their first danger. Now they must sail through the narrow channel and steer safely past Scylla and Charybdis.

There was no way of avoiding the channel and the very next day they reached it. Ulysses ordered his crew to row as fast as they could through the swirling waters while he stood on deck, dressed in armour and holding two spears, ready to defend his crew against Scylla, the monster.

The water bubbled and roared as the mighty whirlpools endeavoured to drag the ship down into their depths.

They had almost reached the end of the channel when the great whirlpool caused by Charybdis swept them towards the rocks where the monster Scylla lived. Suddenly all six heads flashed down from the rocks and bravely Ulysses attacked them with his spears. It was all to no avail. In spite of Ulysses' courageous efforts, the heads snatched six of his crew-members and bore them away to certain death. There was no more Ulysses could do than to shout to his crew to row for their very lives. The ship sped past the rocks and before the monster could strike again, they had passed out of reach.

The ship sailed on past the whirlpools, and out into the narrow and terrifying channel. The water became calm again and the skies were clear and blue.

Every one of Ulysses' crew was exhausted and it was with thankful hearts that they sank down into the bottom of the boat to rest their tired bodies and put behind them their terrible experiences as the boat drifted on towards Ithaca. Although many dangers still lay ahead of them, they were to arrive safely after all, back to their homes and loved ones. Many of them were not recognised for it had been twenty long years since last they had left their island home. Now, however, they were safe and one of the greatest adventures of all time was over. It is a story that has lived for three thousand years.

Kindness to Animals

Little children, never give
Pain to things that feel and live:
Let the gentle robin come
For the crumbs you save at home, –
As his meat you throw along
He'll repay you with a song;
Never hurt the timid hare
Peeping from her green grass lair,

Let her come and sport and play
On the lawn at close of day;
The little lark goes soaring high
To the bright windows of the sky,
Singing as if 'twere always spring,
And fluttering on an untired wing, –
Oh! let him sing his happy song,
Nor do these gentle creatures wrong.

The Musicians of Bremen

Once there was an old farmer who owned a donkey. For many years the donkey had worked hard, carrying sacks of potatoes and beetroots to market and returning loaded with sacks of grain and flour.

Like the farmer, the donkey was growing old. He was no longer able to work so hard or carry such heavy loads.

"This donkey is useless to me now," said the ungrateful farmer to himself one day. "He is not worth the food he eats and, goodness knows, it costs me more than enough to buy food for him. I will kill him tomorrow."

Now donkeys are supposed to be stupid but this donkey was very wise. He did not like the look in the farmer's eyes when he stared so angrily at him.

"It's time I took myself away from here," the donkey thought and that night, when all was quiet, he left the farm and made off down the road. He decided to spend the rest of his life, earning his living as a wandering musician.

"I have a fine voice even if I am growing old," said the donkey to himself and to prove his words he brayed "Hee-haw! Hee-haw!" several times.

The noise attracted the attention of a dog sitting in the bright moonlight at the side of the road.

"What have you got to be so happy about, donkey?" asked the dog.

"I'm going to the big city of Bremen to earn my living as a strolling musician," replied the donkey. "I am just doing a bit of practising. But what are you doing, friend dog, lying there in the road with your tongue hanging out?"

The dog sighed heavily.

"Ah," muttered the dog, "my story is a sad one. I have served my master faithfully for many years and today I overheard him telling a friend that he was going to kill me because I am getting old and can no longer go hunting with him. So I ran away and now I have nowhere to go. What is to become of me?"

"Come along with me," replied the donkey. "We can travel together and keep each other company."

The dog went with the donkey and farther down the road they came across a cat. The cat looked thin and miserable.

"And what are you doing out so late at night?" asked the donkey. "Why do you look so unhappy?"

"My master wants to get rid of me," answered the cat. "I am no longer so good at catching mice as I used to be. Tomorrow my master intends to drown me."

"Come with us," said the donkey. "We are on our way to Bremen to make our fortune as wandering minstrels."

"I can mew with the best of them," grinned the cat proudly and went along with his new-found friends.

It was dawn when the three animals came to a farm. There, on a fence, sat a cockerel, crowing at the top of his voice.

"You are splitting our eardrums with your crowing," complained the donkey. "Is something wrong?"

"Oh," replied the cockerel, "I am making as much noise as I can while I am alive for later today I shall be dead. I have heard my mistress say that she has guests coming to dinner. She told the cook to kill me and put me in a saucepan."

"Why not come with us?" asked the donkey. "We are going to Bremen to make our fortune as strolling minstrels. Your powerful voice would be a help."

"Yes, yes," crowed the cockerel with delight. The four friends went down the road together, enjoying their new freedom.

The big city of Bremen was a long way off and they decided to spend the night in a wood.

The donkey, the dog and the cat all rested at the foot of a high tree. The cockerel, as was his habit, flew up and perched on the topmost branch. Away in the distance, he saw a light and he called down to his friends.

"It looks as though there is a house over there where we might be able to spend the night more comfortably," he crowed. They all set out and soon found the house. At an open door they all peeped in.

To do so, the dog stood on the donkey's back, the cat climbed up on to the dog's back and the cockerel flew up on to the cat's arched back.

Inside the house they saw several grim wild-looking men seated at a table which was loaded with food.

"We must be very quiet," whispered the dog. "I know those men. I've seen them more than once. They are all robbers."

The donkey could not take his eyes off the food.

"If we could chase them away, out of the house," he muttered, "we could eat all that food and stay in the house for the night."

"But how could we do that?" quietly mewed the cat.

"Let us make a loud noise and scare them away," suggested the dog. "They may be robbers but they are all cowards."

Without more ado, the donkey started to bang on the door with his hooves and loudly he brayed. The dog barked furiously, the cat howled and the cockerel crowed. Then they all leaped through the open doorway and into the room. The robbers were so frightened by the noise and the unexpected attack that they fled in great haste.

The four friends then settled down to eat all the food and lay down to sleep in front of the warm fire. Meanwhile, the robbers reached the safety of some trees and began to recover from their fright. The robber chief glared at his gang.

"What fools we were to run away like that," he said and ordered one of his men to return to the house and see what was happening. The robber tip-toed up to his house, which was in darkness and crept into the room. He saw the cat's eyes gleaming in the dark and thought they were pieces of glowing coals from the fire. He picked up a stick, intending to light it from the fire and make a flaming torch of it but as he did so, the cat sprang at him, scratching his face. The dog bit his leg, the donkey gave him a hearty kick and the cockerel flew at him and pecked at his face with his sharp beak.

The robber rushed from the room, trembling and out of breath. He sped back to his comrades.

"There are witches and demons in the house," he panted. "They attacked me and I only just managed to escape."

From that evening, the robbers did not have the courage to return to their old house and the four friends, who liked the house very much, decided not to become strolling minstrels after all, but to stay there peacefully for the rest of their lives.

The Arab's Farewell
to his Steed

My beautiful! my beautiful! that standest meekly by,
With thy proudly-arched and glossy neck, and dark and fiery eye!
Fret not to roam the desert now with all thy winged speed:
I may not mount on thee again – thou'rt sold, my Arab steed!

Fret not with that impatient hoof, snuff not the breezy wind,
The farther that thou fliest now so far am I behind.
The stranger hath thy bridle rein – thy master hath his gold;
Fleet-limbed and beautiful, farewell! – thou'rt sold, my steed, thou'rt
  sold.

Farewell! Those free, untired limbs full many a mile must roam
To reach the chill and wintry sky which clouds the stranger's home.
Some other hand, less fond, must now thy corn and bed prepare;
The silky mane I braided once must be another's care.

The morning sun shall dawn again, but never more with thee
Shall I gallop o'er the desert paths, where we were wont to be;
Evening shall darken on the earth and o'er the sandy plain
Some other steed, with slower step, shall bear me home again.

Yes, thou must go! The wild, free breeze, the brilliant sun and sky,
Thy master's home – from all of these my exiled one must fly.
Thy proud dark eye will grow less proud, thy step become less fleet,
And vainly shalt thou arch thy neck thy master's hand to meet.

Only in sleep shall I behold that dark eye glancing bright;
Only in sleep shall hear again that step so firm and light;
And when I raise my dreaming arm to check or cheer thy speed,
Then must I, starting, wake to feel – thou'rt sold, my Arab steed.

Ah! rudely then, unseen by me, some cruel hand may chide
Till foam-wreaths lie, like crested waves, along thy panting side;
And the rich blood that's in thee swells in thy indignant pain
Till careless eyes which rest on thee may count each starting vein.

Will they ill-use thee? If I thought – but no, it cannot be,
Thou art so swift, yet easy curbed; so gently, yet so free;
And yet, if haply, when thou'rt gone, my lonely heart should yearn,
Can the hand that casts thee from it now command thee to return?

Return! – alas, my Arab steed! what shall thy master do
When thou, who wast his all of joy, hast vanished from his view?
When the dim distance cheats mine eye, and through the gathering
tears
Thy bright form, for a moment, like the false mirage appears?

Slow and unmounted shall I roam, with weary step alone,
Where with fleet step and joyous bound thou oft hast borne me on;
And, sitting down by that green well, I'll pause and sadly think,
"'Twas here he bowed his glossy neck when last I saw him drink!"
When last I saw thee drink! – Away! The fevered dream is o'er!
I could not live a day and know that we should meet no more!
They tempted me, my beautiful! for hunger's power is strong,
They tempted me, my beautiful! but I have loved too long.

Who said that I had given thee up? Who said that thou wert sold?
'Tis false! 'tis false! my Arab steed! I fling them back their gold!
Thus, thus, I leap upon thy back and scour the distant plains!
Away! who overtakes us now many claim thee for his pains!

Morte D'Arthur

Morte D'Arthur, *(which translated means* The Death of Arthur*) is in fact the entire story of King Arthur and his Knights of the Round Table. It was written in twenty-one books by Sir Thomas Malory who was the member of Parliament for Warwickshire in 1485. The first edition was printed in that year by William Caxton and became at once the accepted expression of chivalry and romance by which writers and artists have been inspired ever since. Here is an edited account of how Arthur first became King of England.*

It befell in the days of Uther Pendragon, when he was king of all England, that there was a mighty duke in Cornwall who waged war against him for a long time. The duke was the Duke of Tintagil. Wishing for peace, King Uther one day sent for this duke and asked him to bring his wife with him when he came. The duke's wife was called Igraine and she was known to be a very wise and fair lady.

The king's messengers returned with the duke's answer. Neither he nor his wife would obey the king's summons. King Uther's rage was wonderful to behold. At once he sent another message to the duke, telling him that he, the king, would set out within forty days and seek him out even though he hid himself in his biggest castle. As soon as he received this warning, the duke fortified two castles of his, one named Tintagil and the other, Terrabil.

He sent his wife Igraine to the castle of Tintagil and barricaded himself in the castle of Terrabil. In great haste came King Uther with a mighty army and laid siege to the castle of Terrabil. There followed much bloodshed and fighting and many people were slain.

The king pretended to accept defeat and commenced to withdraw his forces. The Duke of Tintagil foolishly rode out of his castle, bent on attacking the king's retreating army. At once King Uther ordered his men to turn and attack the duke. In the ensuing battle the duke was killed. Now the king could turn his attention to the castle of Terrabil.

At this moment the king's barons came to him and reasoned that now peace could be drawn up between Igraine and the king. Uther agreed that they should approach Igraine for he, too, was hoping for peace. Now that her husband was dead, the Lady Igraine did not wish to continue the war and so a meeting was arranged.

The barons were pleased that they had managed to bring about this meeting and, moreover, inasmuch as King Uther was unmarried, they wished heartily that he might marry the fair lady. As they were all of the same mind, they went to the king and put the suggestion to him. Uther Pendragon was not averse to this proposal and so, in good time, he and the Lady Igraine were married amid great mirth and joy.

Then upon a day, Queen Igraine told the king that she was expecting a baby. Hearing of this, Merlin the magician came to the king and said "Sir, we have many enemies. When the child is born we must arrange for the baby to be looked after and brought up in secret. Now there is a certain lord of yours, faithful and true to your cause, who owns much land in England and Wales. His name is Sir Ector. Send for him and ask him to do your bidding. Then when the child is born, let it be delivered to me at yonder gate, unchristened."

Merlin's wishes were carried out and Sir Ector came to the king and agreed to raise the child as the king wished. In return, the king granted Sir Ector many rewards. Then when the child, a son, was born, he was delivered to Merlin who carried him to Sir Ector. Merlin arranged for a holy man to christen the baby and he was named Arthur.

Less than two years later King Uther Pendragon fell sick of a great malady. It was then that many enemies of the king rose in revolt and much fighting followed, whereupon Merlin came to the king.

"You must rise from your bed and lead your army in battle," Merlin told the king, "for you shall never have the better of your enemies unless you are there. Only then shall you have the victory."

Obediently, the king rose from his sick bed and at St. Albans, led his forces to a great victory over his enemies. Forthwith he returned to London where he fell passing sick, so that for three days and three nights he was speechless. "Can you not cure the king?" the barons asked Merlin, but the magician shook his head.

"He is sick unto death," he replied. "It is God's will that he should die but tomorrow you must all assemble before the king and I will make him to speak."

So on the morrow all the barons with Merlin stood before the king; then Merlin said aloud to King Uther "Sir, shall your son Arthur be king, after your days, of this realm?"

Then Uther Pendragon turned to Merlin and said in hearing of them all "I give my son God's blessing and mine and rightfully may he claim the crown after my death." So saying, he died and he was buried with all the ceremony due to a king.

The queen, fair Igraine, and all the barons were stricken with sadness. There followed a grievous time for the kingdom, for many lords fought to be king.

Years passed and then one day Merlin went to the Archbishop of Canterbury and asked him to send for all the lords of the realm that they should come to London by Christmas.

"For this reason," said Merlin, "that Jesus, who was born on that night, will of his great mercy show by some miracle who is the rightful king of this realm."

So it was that on Christmas Day in the greatest church of London all the lords prayed for a long time. When the first mass was done, there was seen in the churchyard against the high altar a great stone,

four square, and in the midst thereof was an anvil of steel and therein was stuck a fair sword, naked to the point. On the sword written in letters of gold were these words: "Whoso pulleth out this sword of this stone and anvil is likewise king born of all England." When the people saw this, they marvelled and ran to tell the archbishop, but the archbishop allowed no man to leave the church until the high mass was at an end. Only then did the lords leave the church to behold the stone and the sword.

When they saw the writing, many lords who were desirous of being king attempted to draw the sword but none could move nor pull the sword.

"He is not here," said the archbishop, "who shall draw the sword, but doubt not that God will make him known. Now I suggest that we choose ten knights, to guard this sword."

So it was ordained and then it was announced that any man might attempt to pull the sword. Then to make sure that all the barons should remain in London, it was decreed that a tournament should be held on New Year's Day and that all knights should take part. In this way it was hoped that God would make known who should be king.

Thus it was that on New Year's Day the barons of England rode to the field where the tournament was to be held. It so happened that Sir Ector was riding to the tournament and with him were his son, Sir Kay, and young Arthur. As they rode, Sir Kay suddenly remembered that he had left his sword behind at his lodging and he asked Arthur to ride back and bring it to him.

"That I will," replied Arthur and rode fast to collect the sword but when he arrived at the lodging he found that the hostess and her servants had all gone to the tournament. Arthur was angry and said to himself "I will ride to the churchyard and take the sword that is there stuck in the stone, for my brother Sir Kay shall not be without a sword this day."

When he came to the churchyard Arthur dismounted from his horse and went into the tent which had been erected over the stone. There were no knights there for they were all at the tournament. He gripped the sword lightly and pulled it out of the stone. Then he returned to his horse and rode on his way till he came to his brother Sir Kay. He delivered to him the sword.

As soon as Sir Kay saw the sword he knew full well it was the sword of the stone. So he rode to his father, Sir Ector, and said: "Sir, behold here is the sword of the stone and therefore I must be king of this land."

When Sir Ector saw the sword he rode back to the church with Sir Kay and Arthur and there all three dismounted and entered the church. There he made Sir Kay swear how he had come by the sword. "Sir," replied Sir Kay honestly, "by my brother Arthur, for he brought it to me."

"How came you by this sword?" Sir Ector then asked Arthur. "Sir," replied Arthur, "I will tell you. I returned to our lodging for my brother's sword. I found nobody there who could give me his sword. I was determined my brother should not be swordless so I came here and easily pulled the sword out of the stone."

"Were any knights guarding this stone?" Sir Ector demanded.

"No," answered Arthur.

"Then indeed you must be king of this land," said Sir Ector, "for God will have it so. No other man than he who should be rightly king of this realm could pull the sword from the stone. Now let me see if you can put the sword back as it was and pull it out again."

"That is not difficult," said Arthur and he returned it to the stone. Now Sir Ector tried to pull the sword but he failed. "You try," Sir Ector then said to Sir Kay, who, like his father, tried and failed.

"Now shall you try," said Sir Ector to Arthur who pulled it out easily, whereupon Sir Ector and Sir Kay kneeled before him.

"Alas," said Arthur, "my own dear father and brother, why do you kneel to me?"

"Nay," answered Sir Ector. "I was never your father nor of your blood. You are of a higher blood than I." Then Sir Ector told Arthur how he had taken him and cared for him and how it had all come about. Then Arthur wept when he understood that Sir Ector was not his father.

"Sir," said Sir Ector to Arthur, "will you be my good and gracious lord when you are king?"

"It would be sad indeed if I were not, for in all the world it is you to whom I am most beholden," replied Arthur, "you and your wife, my good lady and mother, who has fostered me and kept me as though I were one of her own. If ever it is God's will that I should be king, I shall not fail you."

"Sir," said Sir Ector, "all I ask is that you make my son, your foster brother, Sir Kay, seneschal of all your lands."

"That shall be done," said Arthur, "and no man but he shall hold that office while he and I live." Thereupon they went to the archbishop and told him how the sword had been drawn and by whom.

At the feast of Pentecost all manner of men attempted to pull the sword, but none could draw it but Arthur; and he pulled it out before all the lords and people who were there, whereupon all the people cried at once: "We will have Arthur for our king, for we all see that it is God's will that he shall be our king. We will slay any who deny this." Then they all kneeled down at once, both rich and poor.

Then Arthur took the sword between his hands and offered it upon the altar. Later the coronation took place and there he swore to be a true king and stand for true justice for all the days of his life.

Then on a day a squire came to Arthur's court. His master had been slain by a knight who lived in the forest. So Arthur and Merlin rode forth and Arthur fought with the knight. Had it not been for Merlin, Arthur would have been killed but Merlin cast a spell over the knight and the knight fell asleep. Then Merlin and Arthur rode away but Arthur had lost his sword.

"No matter," said Merlin, "nearby is a sword that shall be yours." They came to a lake and in the midst of the lake Arthur saw an arm clothed in white samite. In the hand was a fair sword.

"Yonder is the sword that I spoke of," said Merlin and as he spoke they saw a damsel walking close by.

"Who is that?" asked Arthur.

"That is the Lady of the Lake," replied Merlin. "Now speak kindly to this damsel and ask that she will give you her sword."

"Damsel," said Arthur. "I wish that sword were mine."

"Sir Arthur, king," said the damsel, "that sword is mine but you shall have it if you will give me a gift when I ask it of you."

"By my faith," swore Arthur, "I will give you what gift you ask."

"Well," said the damsel, "climb into yonder barge and row yourself to the sword and take it and the scabbard with you. I will ask my gift all in good time."

So Arthur and Merlin went forth in the barge and took the sword and Arthur did many brave deeds with it and called it Excalibur. Later, Merlin told him: "Keep well the scabbard always with you, for while you have the scabbard upon you, you will never lose blood be you never so sore wounded."

In this wise did Arthur come to possess the wondrous sword Excalibur and its scabbard which he was to keep until the day he died.

A Christmas Carol

If the truth be told, the novels of Charles Dickens are not amongst those books which are widely read by children. Even so, he was a wonderful story-teller and it must be admitted that when he penned A Christmas Carol, *he gave to the world a book that is generally acknowledged to be the most famous piece of Christmas fiction ever written. Here is a condensation of that festive masterpiece.*

The tale tells of the adventures that befell an old miser, by name Ebenezer Scrooge upon a certain Christmas Eve many years ago. Scrooge owned a counting house in the City of London. The weather on this particular day was bitterly cold. Even so, Scrooge had only the tiniest of fires in his office. Tiny as his was, though, he allowed his clerk, Bob Cratchit, an even smaller one.

Late that afternoon, Scrooge's happy-go-lucky nephew called on him to wish him a Merry Christmas. Scrooge could only sneer at him. Christmas, said Scrooge, was just a time when everyone spent too much money on rubbishy sentiment. His nephew only smiled and, wishing Scrooge a happy Christmas, went on his way.

After telling Bob Cratchit that he could spend Christmas Day away from the office, Scrooge went home. He lived in a poor building where he was the only tenant. The place had first belonged to Scrooge's partner, Jacob Marley, who had died seven years previously. Marley also had been as much a miserable miser as Scrooge.

Just before bedtime, Scrooge heard a strange sound, that of heavy chains clanking. Then into the room came a ghost – the ghost of Jacob Marley. Around his waist he wore a heavy chain of cash boxes, keys, padlocks, ledgers, deeds and heavy purses. The ghost warned Scrooge that unless he changed his ways, he was doomed after death to know no rest but always to be travelling, cursed by the torture of

ever-lasting regret for the way he had lived. The ghost then went on to tell Scrooge that he still had a chance to turn over a new leaf and that to help him do so, three spirits would be visiting him. These spirits would be the Ghost of Christmas Past, the Ghost of Christmas Present and the Ghost of Christmas Future.

Then Marley's ghost disappeared and Scrooge went to bed. In spite of his fears, the old miser soon fell asleep. He was suddenly awakened by the loud chiming of his clock. Then a figure with a child-like face appeared. Strangely, though, the figure had long white hair and a powerful, well-formed body. He ordered Scrooge to accompany him to past Christmas Days. So it was that Scrooge saw himself at school on the day his sister came to take him home for Christmas. Scrooge had loved his sister and had been broken-hearted when, still a young woman, she had died. The Ghost of Christmas Past then reminded Scrooge that his sister had married and had had a son, the very nephew who had called on Scrooge earlier that day to wish him a Merry Christmas.

Scrooge was then whisked to the days when he was working as an apprentice for a kind old gentleman named Fezziwig. It was Christmas Day when at Fezziwig's jolly party young Scrooge had the time of his life. Later Scrooge was told by the girl he loved that she would not marry him because she had learned that he loved money more than he loved her. Then the spirit took Scrooge back to his bedroom where the miser soon fell asleep again.

A little later the Ghost of Christmas Present arrived. It took Scrooge to the home of Bob Cratchit where a party was in full swing. There Scrooge saw the whole Cratchit family including Tiny Tim, Bob's little son who was a cripple. Scrooge was astonished when Bob proposed a toast to the old miser even though Bob's wife and all his children frowned when Scrooge's name was mentioned. The spirit then whirled Scrooge to the home of his nephew where another merry party was taking place. His nephew also proposed Scrooge's health but this time when Scrooge's name was mentioned, everyone laughed. Suddenly, Scrooge found himself back in his bedroom again.

Now came the turn of the Ghost of Christmas Future. This spirit took Scrooge on a grim mission, to visit his home after he had died. Scrooge watched as a shabby band of thieves stole his belongings, even the shirt in which he was to be buried. The spirit then led Scrooge to the home of Bob Cratchit where misery reigned for Tiny Tim was dead. This was all too much for the old miser. To think that nobody grieved when he was dead, that Tiny Tim would die because Bob

Cratchit could not afford proper medical treatment! Scrooge vowed to be a different man in the future and reached out to seize the hand of the Ghost of Christmas Future only to discover that the spirit had changed into a bedpost.

Scrooge leaped out of bed to find that day had dawned. First he thanked Jacob Marley's ghost for the chance he was being given to be a different man in future. As it was Christmas Day he first arranged for a huge turkey – twice the size of Tiny Tim – to be sent over to the Cratchit home. In the street he met a friend who was collecting money for poor people. Merrily Scrooge handed over a large sum.

Scrooge continued on his way and called on his nephew. He was in time to join in the merry-making. In fact, he was the life and soul of the party. Never had he enjoyed himself so much. Nor did he ever return to his old miserable ways of scrimping and saving, regardless of other people's misfortunes. He increased Bob Cratchit's salary and became a second father to Tiny Tim who did *not* die.

Thereafter, it was always said of Ebenezer Scrooge that he knew how to keep Christmas well. "May that be truly said of us, and all of us! And so, as Tiny Tim observed, God Bless Us, Every One!" With these words did Dickens end his great story *A Christmas Carol*.

Oliver Twist

Charles Dickens' novels teem with long-remembered incidents. One such scene, famous all over the world, occurs in his splendid book Oliver Twist *when little Oliver, born in a workhouse, dares to ask for a second helping of gruel, a thin porridge boiled in water.*

Here is Dickens' own account of the moment when Oliver, who is elected by other starving orphans to try his luck, asks the master of the workhouse "for more."

 council was held; lots were cast who should walk up to the master after supper that evening, and ask for more; and it fell to Oliver Twist.

The evening arrived; the boys took their places. The master, in his cook's uniform, stationed himself at the copper; his pauper assistants ranged themselves behind him; the gruel was served out; and a long grace was said over the short commons. The gruel disappeared; the boys whispered to each other, and winked at Oliver, while his next neighbours nudged him. Child as he was, he was desperate with hunger, and reckless with misery. He rose from the table; and advancing to the master, basin and spoon in hand, said, somewhat alarmed at his own temerity:

"Please, Sir, I want some more."

The master was a fat, healthy man; but he turned very pale. He gazed in stupefied astonishment on the small rebel for some seconds, and then clung for support to the copper. The assistants were paralysed with wonder; the boys with fear.

"What!" said the master at length, in a faint voice.

"Please, Sir," replied Oliver. "I want some more."

The master aimed a blow at Oliver's head with the ladle; pinioned him in his arms; and shrieked aloud for the beadle.

The board were sitting in solemn conclave, when Mr. Bumble rushed into the room in great excitement, and addressing the gentlemen in the high chair, said:

"Mr. Limbkins, I beg your pardon, Sir! Oliver Twist has asked for more!"

There was a general start. Horror was depicted on every countenance.

"For *more*!" said Mr. Limbkins. "Compose yourself, Bumble, and answer me distinctly. Do I understand that he asked for more, after he had eaten the supper allotted by the dietary?"

"He did, Sir," replied Bumble.

"That boy will be hung," said the gentleman in the white waistcoat. "I know that boy will be hung."

Nobody controverted the prophetic gentleman's opinion. An animated discussion took place. Oliver was ordered into instant confinement; and a bill was next morning pasted on the outside of the gate, offering a reward of five pounds to anybody who would take Oliver Twist off the hands of the parish. In other words, five pounds and Oliver Twist were offered to any man or woman who wanted an apprentice to any trade, business, or calling.

"I never was more convinced of anything in my life," said the gentleman in the white waistcoat, as he knocked at the gate and read the bill next morning: "I never was more convinced of anything in my life, than I am, that that boy will come to be hung."

How they brought the good news from Ghent to Aix

What was the good news carried by the three breakneck riders? Robert Browning who wrote the poem never revealed the message. He wrote it as a model of galloping rhyme and rhythm, a superb piece of verse to be found in most of today's anthologies.

I sprang to the stirrup, and Joris, and he;
I galloped, Dirck galloped, we galloped all three;
'Good speed!' cried the watch, as the gate-bolts undrew;
'Speed!' echoed the wall to us galloping through;
Behind shut the postern, the lights sank to rest,
And into the midnight we galloped abreast.

Not a word to each other: we kept the great pace
Neck by neck, stride by stride, never changing our place;
I turned in my saddle and made its girths tight,
Then shortened each stirrup, and set the pique right,
Rebuckled the cheek-strap, chained slacker the bit,
Nor galloped less steadily Roland a whit.

'Twas moonset at starting; but while we drew near
Lokeren, the cocks crew and twilight dawned clear;
At Boom, a great yellow star came out to see;
At Düffeld, 'twas morning as plain as could be;
And from Mecheln church-steeple we heard the half-chime,
So Joris broke silence with, 'Yet there is time!'

At Aerschot, up leaped of a sudden the sun,
And against him the cattle stood black every one,
To stare thro' the mist at us galloping past,
And I saw my stout galloper Roland at last,
With resolute shoulders, each butting away
The haze, as some bluff river headland its spray.

And his low head and crest, just one sharp ear bent back
For my voice, and the other pricked out on his track;
And one eye's black intelligence – ever that glance
O'er its white edge at me, his own master, askance!
And the thick heavy spume-flakes which aye and anon
His fierce lips shook upwards in galloping on.

By Hasselt, Dirck groaned; and cried Joris, 'Stay spur!
Your Roos galloped bravely, the fault's not in her,
We'll remember at Aix' – for one heard the quick wheeze
Of her chest, saw the stretched neck and staggering knees,
And sunk tail, and horrible heave of the flank,
As down on her haunches she shuddered and sank.

So we were left galloping, Joris and I,
Past Looz and past Tongres, no cloud in the sky;
The broad sun above laughed a pitiless laugh,
'Neath our feet broke the brittle bright stubble like chaff;
Till over by Dalhem a dome-spire sprang white,
And 'Gallop,' gasped Joris, 'for Aix is in sight!'

'How they'll greet us!' – and all in a moment his roan
Rolled neck and croup over, lay dead as a stone;
And there was my Roland to bear the whole weight
Of the news which alone could save Aix from her fate,
With his nostrils like pits full of blood to the brim,
And with circles of red for his eye-sockets' rim.

Then I cast loose my buffcoat, each holster let all,
Shook off both my jack-boots, let go belt and all,
Stood up in the stirrup, leaned, patted his ear,
Called my Roland his pet-name, my horse without peer;
Clapped my hands, laughed and sang, any noise, bad or good,
Till at length into Aix Roland galloped and stood.

And all I remember is, friends flocking round
As I sat with his head 'twixt my knees on the ground;
And no voice but was praising this Roland of mine,
As I poured down his throat our last measure of wine,
Which (the burgesses voted by common consent)
Was no more than his due who brought good news from Ghent.

Four Legends from Norway

THE THREE HIDING PLACES

Long, long ago, so the old Norsemen believed, the gods lived in their home of Asgard, far above the Earth. At the end of the world, in Jotenheim, the land of ice and snow, lived the giants who were the enemies of the gods.

One day, one of the giants paid a visit to a peasant, who lived in a little cottage by the sea-shore, with his wife and young son. The peasant was very poor and he had to work hard from dawn to sunset, just to provide enough food for his family to eat, but when he had time to sit by the fire and rest in the evening, his one delight was to play chess.

The giant challenged the peasant to a game of chess and the peasant agreed and asked what stakes they should play for. "Whichever of us wins may take from the other the possession he most desires," replied the giant.

The poor peasant thought for a moment. It seemed a good idea to him, for he had so few possessions that he was sure there was little of his that the giant could want, so he agreed and the game began. They were well matched and the game went on all day and all night, but finally, as dawn was breaking, the giant won.

"Now give me my reward," he said to the peasant. "I will take your son, for, according to our bargain, he is mine."

The horrified peasant begged the giant to change his mind and take something else, but the giant only roared with laughter. Finally, however, he agreed to let the boy stay with them for the night. "If, when I come back tomorrow morning, you have hidden your son so carefully that I cannot find him, you shall keep him," said the giant. Then he left.

195

The parents thought and thought, but it seemed there was nowhere they could hide their child. Finally, very sad, the peasant decided to call on Odin, king of all the gods. Odin heard their pleas and came to the cottage door. When they opened the door he said, "Give me your son and I will hide him for you. Perhaps the giant will not find him." The parents gladly gave Odin their boy and Odin changed him into a grain of wheat which he hid in a wheatfield nearby.

Next morning, the giant came back to the cottage. He looked carefully around and it seemed that he had some magic to aid him, for he went at once to the wheatfield and began to cut it down. He threw aside each armful but the last and from that he plucked a single ear of wheat and began to pick off each grain until he held the one which was really the boy. The peasant and his wife wept in despair and Odin took pity on them, for he blew like a puff of wind so that the grain was tossed from the giant's fingers back to the parents and turned into the boy again. "I have done my best, now you must help yourselves," said Odin.

The giant strode up to the cottage. "That was good, but you must do better than that if you wish to keep your son," he said. "Tomorrow, I shall return and try again." Then he went away.

All that night the parents racked their brains to think of a place to hide their child, but finally they decided to call on the god Honir, who was Odin's brother. Honir knocked on the cottage door and when they opened it he took the boy and turned him into a feather and hid him on the breast of a swan, which swam on the nearby river.

Next morning, the giant returned and looked around. Then he went to the river. He picked the swan off the water, killed it and plucked off its feathers, one by one, until he reached the one which was the boy. Honir, taking pity on the weeping parents, blew like a puff of wind so that the feather flew into the cottage, where it changed into the boy again.

"I have done all I can, now you must help yourselves," said Honir.

The giant went back to the cottage. "That is not good enough," he said. "I will give you one more chance. I will try again tomorrow."

That night, the terrified parents called on Loki, the cunning god of fire. In their fireplace the wood had died down but suddenly it burned up again with a bright flame and in the light of the fire, they saw Loki standing in the room. "Give me your son and I will do my best to see that the giant does not find him this time," he said. Then he changed the boy into the tiny egg of a fish and hid him among the eggs of a haddock which swam far from the shore.

Next morning, the giant returned. He went to the shore and looked carefully around him. Then he hurried away and fetched his boat. As he was climbing into it, Loki called, "Take me fishing with you."

The two got into the boat and set out and in the middle of the sea, the giant baited his hook and caught fish after fish until at last he caught the haddock. He placed it carefully in the boat and rowed back to shore. Then he took his knife, cut it open and took out all the eggs until he came to the one which was the boy.

"What have you there?" asked Loki.

"Only a haddock's egg," replied the giant.

"I don't believe it," said Loki. "No one would take such care to find a single haddock's egg. Let me see it."

The giant held it out for Loki to look at and as he did so, Loki snatched it from his fingers and turned it back into the child. "Run and hide yourself in the cottage," he said to the terrified boy.

The boy ran from the beach to the cottage and rushed inside, banging the door shut behind him. The giant followed, calling to the boy to come out. He wrenched open the door and thrust his head in, but, as Loki had thought, he forgot how small the cottage was and how low the beams were and he struck his head such a blow that he fell senseless to the ground. Loki killed him with one blow of the fishing knife.

Ever after, the grateful parents thought Loki the greatest of the gods, for while the others had given up and gone away, saying "Now you must help yourselves," Loki had stayed with them and tricked the giant to the end.

☞ STORY TWO ☜
THE MAN OF CLAY

Far away in Asgard, which lay far above the Earth, the gods lived, or so the Norsemen of old believed. The gods were strong and fierce, loving adventure and many were the tales that the Norsemen told of them. They were ruled by the great god Odin, father of all the gods.

One day, Odin rode his eight-legged horse out of Asgard and over mountains and plains until he reached Jotenheim, the land of the giants, who were the enemies of the gods. Hrungnir, the strongest of all the giants, whose head was of stone and whose heart was of flint, saw Odin ride past. "Who are you, stranger in the golden helmet?"

he called out.

"I am Odin," came the reply.

"Then that must be your wonderful horse of whom I have heard so many tales," said the giant. "But wonderful though he is, I doubt if he is as swift as my horse."

Hrungnir challenged Odin to a race and Odin agreed. Off they went, galloping across the rocks and plains of Jotenheim and all the time Odin was gaining on Hrungnir. They did not stop until they had reached Asgard and then, for the first time, Hrungnir realised where he was. He turned angrily on Odin. "Is this a trap which I have been led into?" he demanded. "Have you tricked me into coming all the way to Asgard to kill me?"

"It shall never be said of the gods that they tricked one of the giants into coming to their home and killed him there," said Odin. "You are welcome to stay here and feast with us in safety, if you wish."

There was only one god who would never have let a giant into

Asgard. That was Thor, the mighty god of thunder, greatest enemy of the giants. Thor was away from Asgard, seeking adventure and the other gods welcomed Hrungnir as a guest.

He was given a seat at the table and he feasted and drank well, too well, in fact, for the mead which the gods gave him was stronger than the mead he was used to drinking, so that it went to his head and made him boastful and discourteous. He talked more and more loudly of how strong he was, saying that none of the gods could match him for strength and that one day he would return as an enemy and then he would pick up their great palace of Valhalla, which stood in the middle of Asgard and carry it, in one hand, back to Jotenheim.

"I shall destroy you all," he cried. "Only the goddess Sif and the goddess Freya shall be spared, Sif, because she has beautiful golden hair and Freya because she has refilled my glass with mead whenever it has been empty. Those two I will take back to Jotenheim with me and they shall by my wives."

It was at that moment that Thor, the mighty god of thunder, strode into the hall. He was very angry to hear a giant speaking in such a way of his wife, Sif. "Why is a giant here in Asgard as an honoured guest?" cried Thor and Hrungnir answered insolently that he was there at Odin's bidding. So angry was Thor at the insolent answer that he raised his great hammer, to strike the giant to the ground, but the other gods called to him to stop, for the giant was a guest and it would bring great shame on them if they killed an unarmed guest in their hall.

Thor lowered his hammer and the giant suggested that they should meet and fight it out in single combat. They chose the time and the place and Hrungnir rode back to Jotenheim to prepare.

When the giants in Jotenheim heard about the duel to come, they were afraid. They feared that if Thor killed Hrungnir, the strongest of the giants, it would go hard with the weaker ones should they ever annoy him.

"Thor will bring his squire with him," they told Hrungnir. "You, too, must have a squire and he must be so mighty that even the sight of him will fill Thor with fear. In that way, we may be able to defeat him."

However, there was no one in all the land of Jotenheim big enough or fierce enough to act as Hrungnir's squire and strike terror to the heart of the mighty god Thor, so finally, they decided to make a man of clay. When he was finished, he stood nine miles high and three miles broad and they gave him the heart of a mare. Then, his prep-

arations complete, Hrungnir waited for Thor.

They felt him coming, for his mighty stride shook the earth as he moved. At once Hrungnir took up his heavy stone shield and his huge battleaxe, which was made of flint, but the man of clay trembled and was afraid, for he had only a mare's heart and it was weak and timid.

Thor's squire, the young peasant lad named Thialfi, ran on ahead, for he had an idea. When he reached the place where the giant was waiting, he laughed and said, "I thought you were well prepared, but I was wrong,"

"I am well protected," replied the giant. "I have my great stone shield and my battleaxe."

"But what use is your shield when you hold it in front of you?" asked Thialfi. "Thor is coming up out of the ground. You can hear the earth rumble as it splits to let him through. What use is a shield over your heart when the earth is about to open under your feet?"

The foolish giant threw his shield to the ground and stood on it, so that when Thor came in sight he was unprepared. Thor hurled his great hammer and the giant hurled his mighty battleaxe and the two weapons met in mid-air with such a shattering crash that the battleaxe broke in two.

One half of it shattered into a million pieces, which scattered over the Earth. That is why Earth is covered with pieces of flint. The other half of the battleaxe went deep into Thor's brow, so that he fell to the ground.

Thor's mighty hammer struck the giant on the middle of his stone head so that it split in half and the giant fell to the ground, dead.

Then young Thialfi rushed at the giant's huge squire with his sword drawn and although he was nine miles's high, the squire was only made of clay so that, although his mare's heart quivered with fright, he was not able to turn and run away. It needed only one blow to fell him and he hit the ground with such force that the earth trembled.

Then Thialfi saw that Thor was lying pinned to the ground by one of the giant's huge legs, which was across his neck. Try as he might, Thialfi could not move it. He called all the rest of the gods, but they could not free Thor. Then Thor's little son came running up and although he was only a child, he lifted Hrungnir's leg from his father's neck and freed him easily. All the gods marvelled at his strength and said that he would grow to be more powerful than all of them.

Thor returned with the other gods to Asgard, but the flint from Hrungnir's battleaxe remained always in his head. That is why, among the Norsemen, it was always considered a bad thing to throw a flint tool down on the ground, for they feared that by doing so, the flint in Thor's head might be disturbed and it might give the mighty god a headache.

nce upon a time, Aegir, the god of the deep ocean, went to Asgard, the home of the other gods, to a great feast. He had such a good time that, in return, he invited all the gods to his own palace below the waves, for another feast at harvest-time.

"I can offer you plenty of food," he said, "but I am afraid I will not be able to offer as much to drink as you have done here, for I have only a small pot to brew the mead in."

All the gods agreed to drink only a little mead when they visited Aegir – except Thor, the god of thunder. Thor said he did not enjoy a feast unless he could drink as much as he wished and refused to come without more mead.

"But where am I to find a larger pot?" asked Aegir. "Only if I had the pot of old Hymire, the giant, would I be able to brew enough mead for everyone."

"Well," replied Thor, "if that is all you need, you shall have it. I will fetch it for you myself. Who will come with me?"

Tyr, the god of war, who had only one hand, offered to go with Thor, so they set out, Thor taking with him his huge hammer and his belt and gloves, which made him twice as strong when he wore them.

The two gods travelled to Jotenheim, the home of the giants and knocked on the door of Hymir's house, which was in a barren, rocky place near the sea. Jotenheim was a very cold place, always covered in ice and snow, so they were very thankful when Hymir's wife eventually opened the door. She invited them in, but told them to hide behind a row of cooking vessels which hung from a beam, until she had told her husband of their visit, for a glance from his fiery eyes sometimes killed unexpected visitors.

When Hymir came in, with icicles rattling on his beard and hanging from his bushy eyebrows, his wife told him of the two gods from Asgard who had come to visit him. At her words, the giant turned angrily and glared in their direction and his glance made the beam split so that all the cooking pots fell to the floor and broke.

"Nobody from Asgard is welcome in the land of the giants," said Hymir, "but since you are already here, I will treat you as my guests." He then ordered his servants to roast three whole oxen and Thor was so hungry, that he ate the three of them himself.

"Tomorrow," Hymir frowned, "if you stay here, we will dine off what I catch myself in the sea."

Thor agreed. "I shall welcome a day's fishing," he said.

Next morning, Hymir dragged his boat down to the shore.

"Wait on the beach until I return with my catch," he told Thor, "for you are too small a person to go in my great boat and I am fishing for whales."

"I am fishing for something bigger," said Thor, darkly.

"In that case," the giant retorted, "you will need bait." Thor went to where the giant's herd of oxen grazed and killed the finest one for bait. The giant was very angry, but there was nothing he could do about it, because Thor was his guest. As he pushed the boat out, he said to Thor, "Of course, you would be frozen, if you went as far into the icy sea as I do."

"We shall see," replied Thor, jumping in after him.

Hymir rowed out to his fishing grounds and stopped, but Thor seized the oars and rowed even farther, until Hymir protested.

Then Hymir baited his hook and began to fish. Before long, he had caught two large whales.

"There is our supper," he said. "Now let me see you catch a fish."

Thor cast his line into the sea and when he felt something tugging on the end, he pulled.

"What is it, a sprat?" grinned the giant, but he did not laugh when, above the sea by the boat, appeared the head of the mighty sea-serpent which encircled the whole world. The boat rocked violently.

"Quickly, hold the line," shouted Thor, but the giant was afraid and taking out his knife, he cut the line in two, allowing the sea-serpent to sink back into the water. Angrily, Thor struck at the giant, but he missed and in silence, the two of them rowed back to the beach.

That night the giant said, as they sat eating, "You have proved that you can row and fish, but I call no man strong who cannot break my goblet."

Thor picked up the goblet and then smashed it down with all his might against the table top. Although the table top was slighty dented, there was no mark on the goblet. Thor picked up the goblet again and this time flung it against one of the pillars, but the pillar just shattered into fragments. Thor picked up the goblet a third time and dashed it to the floor, but still it would not break.

Then Hymir's wife, who was filling up their glasses, whispered to Thor that the only thing harder than Hymir's goblet was Hymir's own head, so Thor struck the goblet across Hymir's head as hard as he could and the goblet shattered into a thousand pieces.

"I am sorry to lose my goblet, but you have proved your strength," said Hymir. "I will give you a fine gift. What do you want?"

"I would like the big pot, in which you brew your mead," replied Thor, "to take to the god of the ocean, for his feast."

"I was sad to lose the goblet and I shall be even sadder to lose the cauldron," said the giant, "but take it, if you can lift it." He smiled to himself, sure that Thor could not carry such a heavy cauldron.

Thor took the huge pot by its rim and heaved it to his shoulders. Hymir was astonished.

"Come," said Thor to Tyr, "we must leave now," and they walked back over the rocky plains, to Asgard, where they gave the pot to Aegir, god of the ocean, for his feast.

❧ STORY FOUR ❧
THE GOLDEN APPLES

din, king of all the gods, had a son called Bragi. He was a handsome youth and because he sang so sweetly, he was the god of poetry and song.

Bragi did not spend all his time in Asgard, the home of the gods, which lay far above the Earth. He liked to wander far and wide, all over the world.

One day as he sat in a boat on a peaceful river, singing his sweet songs, he saw Idunn, the daughter of one of the dwarfs, coming across the meadow.

The dwarfs were small and ugly. They lived in the dark caves beneath the Earth and they spent all their time mining the gold and precious stones which were hidden in the Earth and working at their forges, making their finely-wrought metalwork.

Idunn's father and brothers were like all the other dwarfs, bent and ugly. They could never come to the surface by day, for a ray of sunlight would have turned them to stone. Only Idunn was different. She was beautiful and gentle and kind-hearted. She could walk about among the trees and flowers in the daylight and come to no harm.

When Bragi saw her, he took her with him in his boat, for he had fallen in love with her at once. He took her back with him to Asgard, the home of the gods, and there they were married. To Idunn was given charge of the golden apples which the gods and goddesses ate to keep them everlastingly young and immortal. Without the golden apples, they would have grown old and died, just like mortals.

Now it happened that Odin and two of the other gods, Loki and Honir, were travelling through the world one day, looking for adventure. At last, tired and weary, they came to a herd of oxen in a valley and they decided to kill an ox, cook and eat it and then rest.

They made a fire of logs and put the ox over the flames, but it would not cook. At last Odin said, "There is some evil power here which wishes us harm."

Loki looked around and nearby he saw an eagle, sitting on a rock, staring at them. "Perhaps it is someone who has taken the shape of a bird," said Loki.

Honir called to the eagle and asked if he was stopping the ox from cooking. "Share your food with me and it will cook," replied the eagle.

"Come and join us," invited Odin. The eagle flew down and fanned the flames with his wings, so that the ox soon cooked, but it insisted on having the first portion for all its hard work and it took more than half of the meat for itself. Then it took a second bite.

Loki, very angry, picked up a stick and dealt the eagle a powerful blow, but he found that he could not lift the stick from its body again, nor could he let go the end he held, so that when the eagle rose into the air, Loki rose with it.

"I am Thiazi, the storm giant," it said. "I have long wished to harm the gods. Now I have you, Loki."

"Let me go and I will give you whatever you ask," said Loki.

"You can go only if you give Idunn and her golden apples into my power, for I wish to have eternal youth," said the eagle.

Loki, despairing of getting free any other way, finally agreed.

Back in Asgard, Loki went to Idunn and told her that he had found a tree, covered with golden apples like hers, in a wood near Asgard.

Idunn would not believe this and wanted to see them for herself, so Loki offered to take her there. "Bring your own apples, so that you can compare them," he said, "for I do not know if these others have magic powers."

Idunn, carrying her casket of golden apples, followed Loki out of Asgard. Soon they reach the dark wood and as they walked among the trees a big eagle, which was really the giant Thiazi in disguise, swooped down from the trees and seized Idunn. The eagle carried her way up, over the trees and back to his home in Jotenheim.

In Asgard, the gods missed Idunn and wondered where she was. Bragi grew sad without his wife and the gods grew tired and jaded without the golden apples to keep their youth.

At last, they held a council, to decide what should be done and one of them told how he had seen Idunn set out with Loki, carrying her casket of apples.

At this, Loki had to admit that Idunn was with the storm giant and the gods were very angry. They threatened Loki with a terrible punishment if he did not bring her back. "I will get Idunn back," replied

Loki, "not because I am afraid of you, but because I am tired of growing old and ugly."

Loki changed himself into a hawk and flew to Thiazi's castle in the country of the giants. He waited until Thiazi left the castle and was pleased to see that he looked no younger than before, so he was sure that Idunn had parted with none of her golden apples.

Then, he flew in through the window and dropping to the floor at Idunn's feet, changed back to his proper shape. "I have come to take you back," he said. "The gods long for a sight of your sweet smile and a taste of your apples."

Idunn did not trust Loki, now, but there seemed no other way of returning to Asgard, so she allowed him to say some magic words over her. At once she was turned into a tiny nut.

Loki changed back into a hawk, picked up the nut in his claws and flew out of the window, but Thiazi saw him and was sure it was one of the gods, come to rescue Idunn. He changed into an eagle and pursued the hawk and being more powerful, he was fast gaining on Loki by the time they reached Asgard.

The gods, watching for Loki's return, saw him flying back, closely pursued by the eagle.

They gathered wood and piled it up before the walls of Asgard and then lit it

The flames rose high into the air and Loki swooped through it, to enter Asgard.

Because he was the god of fire he came through it unharmed, the nut tightly clutched in his claws, but the eagle, flying after him, singed his wings and fell to the ground.

The gods rushed forward and killed the eagle with one blow, while Loki returned once more to his own shape. Then he said the magic words and Idunn appeared before them, her casket of apples clutched in her hands.

The gods were overjoyed to see her again, especially Bragi, who had forgotten to sing while his wife had been lost.

The gods were able to eat the golden apples once again and they quickly became bright and youthful, as they had been before.

Westward Ho!

In his masterpiece Westward Ho! *Charles Kingsley relates the many adventures of Amyas Leigh who lived in the days of Queen Elizabeth I when England was continually quarrelling and often at war with the powerful country of Spain.*

The story tells of the love borne by Amyas, his brother Frank and their treacherous cousin Eustace for Rose Salterne, the lovely daughter of the mayor of Bideford in the county of Devon. At one point in the story Amyas, during an expedition to Ireland under the command of Sir Walter Raleigh, captures Don Guzman de Soto, a Spanish nobleman. He takes De Soto back to Bideford, there to await ransom from Spain. Don Guzman meets and falls in love with Rose Salterne and one day, to the despair and anger of Amyas and Frank, they discover that the Spaniard and the beautiful Rose have disappeared.

Amyas and Frank set out after him, believing that Rose has been kidnapped and taken to La Guayra in Caracas in South America where Don Guzman has been appointed governor. The upshot of all this is that when they arrive in La Guayra they learn that Rose is happily married to Don Guzman and that, moreover, their evil cousin Eustace has already preceded them and warned De Soto and Rose of their coming. Don Guzman orders his men to seize Amyas and Frank. The latter is taken prisoner but Amyas is carried back to his ship, unconscious but safe.

Three years go by, during which time Amyas and his men endure many hardships and narrowly escape death on many occasions. Then one day Amyas learns that his ruthless cousin Eustace has informed the dreaded Spanish Inquisition that Rose and Frank Leigh are English heretics. Both have been executed. Overwhelmed with grief when he learns that the girl he loves and his brother have died at the hands of the Inquisition, Amyas swears vengeance on all Spaniards.

He is only too eager to join the English fleet when it sets sail to fight the invading Spanish Armada in 1588. Don Guzman commands one of the Spanish galleons. The great Spanish fleet is ripped apart by the English sea-hawks. Amyas, sworn to destroy De Soto, singles out the Don's ship and proceeds to track it down. The story now continues in Charles Kingsley's own words.

It was now the sixteenth day of the chase. They had seen, the evening before, St. David's head, and then the Welsh coast round Milford Haven, looming out black and sharp before the blaze of the inland thunderstorm; and it had lightened all round them during the fore part of the night, upon a light south-western breeze.

In vain they had strained their eyes through the darkness, to catch, by the fitful glare of the flashes, the tall masts of the Spaniard. Of one thing at least they were certain, that with the wind as it was, she could not have gone far to the westward; and to attempt to pass them again, and go northward, was more than she dare do. She was probably lying-to-a-head of them, perhaps between them and the land; and when, a little after midnight, the wind chopped up to the west, and blew stiffly till day-break, they felt sure that, unless she had attempted the desperate expedient of running past them, they had her safe in the mouth of the Bristol Channel. Slowly and wearily broke the dawn, on such a day as often follows heavy thunder; a sunless, drizzly day, roofed with low dingy cloud, barred, and netted, and festooned with black, a sign that the storm is only taking breath awhile before it bursts again; while all the narrow horizon is dim and spongy with vapour drifting before a chilly breeze. As the day went on, the breeze died down, and the sea fell to a long glassy foam-flecked roll, while over-head brooded the inky sky, and round them the leaden mist shut out alike the shore and the chase.

Amyas paced the sloppy deck fretfully and fiercely. He knew that the Spaniard could not escape: but he cursed every moment which lingered between him and that one great revenge which blackened all his soul. The men sat sulkily about the deck, and whistled for a wind; the sails flapped idly against the masts; and the ship rolled in the long troughs of the sea, till her yard-arms almost dipped right and left.

"Take care of those guns. You will have something loose next," growled Amyas.

"We will take care of the guns, if the Lord will take care of the wind," said Yeo.

"We shall have plenty before night," said Cary, "and thunder too."

"So much the better," said Amyas. "It may roar till it splits the heavens, if it does but let me get my work done."

"He's not far off, I warrant," said Cary. "One lift of the cloud, and we should see him."

"To windward of us, as likely as not," said Amyas. "The devil fights for him, I believe. To have been on his heels sixteen days, and

221

not sent this through him yet!" And he shook his sword impatiently.

So the morning wore away, without a sign of living thing, not even a passing gull; and the black melancholy of the heaven reflected itself in the black melancholy of Amyas. Was he to lose his prey after all? The thought made him shudder with rage and disappointment. It was intolerable. Anything but that.

"No, God!" he cried, "let me but once feel this in his accursed heart, and then – strike me dead, if Thou wilt!"

"The Lord have mercy on us," cried John Brimblecombe. "What have you said?"

"What is that to you, Sir? There, they are piping to dinner. Go down. I shall not come."

And Jack went down, and talked in a half-terrified whisper, of Amyas's ominous words.

All thought that they portended some bad luck, except old Yeo.

"Well, Sir John," said he, "and why not? What better can the Lord do for a man, than take him home when he has done His work? Our

Captain is wilful and spiteful, and must needs kill his man himself; while for me, I don't care how the Don goes, provided he does go. I owe him no grudge, nor any man. May the Lord give him repentance, and forgive him all his sins: but if I could but see him once safe ashore, as he may be ere nightfall, on the Mortestone or the back of Lundy, I would say, 'Lord, now lettest thou thy servant depart in peace,' even if it were the lightning which was sent to fetch me."

"But, master Yeo, a sudden death?"

"And why not a sudden death, Sir John? Even fools long for a short life and a merry one, and shall not the Lord's people pray for a short death and a merry one? Let it come as it will to old Yeo. Hark! there's the Captain's voice!"

"Here she is!" thundered Amyas from the deck; and in an instant all were scrambling up the hatchway as fast as the frantic rolling of the ship would let them.

Yes. There she was. The cloud had lifted suddenly, and to the south a ragged bore of blue sky let a long stream of sunshine down on her tall masts and stately hull, as she lay rolling some four or five miles to the eastward: but as for land, none was to be seen.

"There she is; and here we are," said Cary: "but where is here? and where is there? How is the tide, master?"

"Running up Channel by this time, Sir."

"What matters the tide?" said Amyas, devouring the ship with terrible and cold blue eyes. "Can't we get at her?"

"Not unless some one jumps out and shoves behind," said Cary. "I shall down again and finish that mackerel, if this roll has not chucked it to the cockroaches under the table."

"Don't jest, Will! I can't stand it," said Amyas, in a voice which quivered so much that Cary looked at him. His whole frame was trembling like an aspen. Cary took his arm, and drew him aside.

"Dear old lad," said he, as they leaned over the bulwarks, "what is this? You are not yourself, and have not been these four days."

"No. I am not Amyas Leigh. I am my brother's avenger. Do not reason with me, Will: when it is over, I shall be merry old Amyas again," and he passed his hand over his brow.

"Do you believe," said he, after a moment, "that men can be possessed by devils?"

"The Bible says so."

"If my cause were not a just one, I should fancy I had a devil in me. My throat and heart are as hot as the pit. Would to God it were done, for done it must be! Now go."

Cary went away with a shudder. As he passed down the hatchway he looked back. Amyas had got the hone out of his pocket, and was whetting away again at his sword-edge, as if there was some dreadful doom on him, to whet, and whet for ever.

The weary day wore on. The strip of blue sky was curtained over again, and all was dismal as before, though it grew sultrier every moment; and now and then a distant mutter shook the air to westward. Nothing could be done to lessen the distance between the ships, for the *Vengeance* had had all her boats carried away but one, and that was much too small to tow her; and while the men went down again to finish dinner, Amyas worked on at his sword, looking up every now and then suddenly at the Spaniard, as if to satisfy himself that it was not a vision which had vanished.

About two Yeo came up to him.

"He is ours safely now, Sir. The tide has been running to the eastward for these two hours."

"Safe as a fox in a trap. Satan himself cannot take him from us!"

"But God may," said Brimblecombe, simply.

"Who spoke to you, Sir? If I thought that He – There comes the thunder at last!"

And as he spoke, an angry growl from the westward heavens seemed to answer his wild words, and rolled and loudened nearer and nearer, till right over their heads it crashed against some cloud-cliff far above, and all was still.

Each man looked in the other's face: but Amyas was unmoved.

"The storm is coming," said he, "and the wind in it. It will be Eastward-ho now, for once, my merry men all!"

"Eastward-ho never brought us luck," said Jack in an undertone to Cary. But by this time all eyes were turned to the North-west, where a black line along the horizon began to define the boundary of sea and air, till now all dim in mist.

"There comes the breeze."

"And there the storm, too."

And with that strangely accelerating pace which some storms seem to possess, the thunder, which had been growling slow and seldom far away, now rang peal on peal along the cloudy floor above their heads.

"Here comes the breeze. Round with the yards, or we shall be taken aback."

The yards creaked round; the sea grew crisp around them; the hot air swept their cheeks, tightened every rope, filled every sail, bent her over. A cheer burst from the men as the helm went up, and they staggered away before the wind right down upon the Spaniard, who lay still becalmed.

"There is more behind, Amyas," said Cary. "Shall we not shorten sail a little?"

"No. Hold on every stitch," said Amyas. "Give me the helm, man. Boatswain, pipe away to clear for fight."

It was done, and in ten minutes the men were all at quarters, while the thunder rolled louder and louder overhead, and the breeze freshened fast.

"The dog has it now. There he goes!" said Cary.

"Right before the wind. He has no liking to face us."

"He is running into the jaws of destruction," said Yeo. "An hour more will send him either right up the Channel, or smack on shore somewhere."

"There! he has put his helm down. I wonder if he sees land?"

"He is like a March hare beat out of his country," said Cary, "and don't know whither to run next."

Cary was right. In ten minutes more the Spaniard fell off again, and went away dead down wind, while the *Vengeance* gained on him fast. After two hours more, the four miles had diminished to one, while the lightning flashed nearer and nearer as the storm came up; and from the vast mouth of a black cloud-arch poured so fierce a breeze that Amyas yielded unwillingly to hints which were growing into open murmurs, and bade shorten sail.

On they rushed with scarcely lessened speed, the black arch following fast, curtained by one flat grey sheet of pouring rain, before which
the water was boiling in a long white line; while every moment, behind
the watery veil, a keen blue spark leapt down into the sea or darted
zigzag through the rain.

"We shall have it now, and with a vengeance; this will try your
tackle, Master," said Cary.

The functionary answered with a shrug, and turned up the collar
of his rough frock, as the first drops flew stinging round his ears.
Another minute, and the squall burst full upon them in rain which
cut like hail – hail which lashed the sea into froth, and wind which
whirled off the heads of the surges, and swept the waters into one
white seething waste. And above them, and behind them, and before
them, the lightning leapt and ran, dazzling and blinding, while the
deep roar of the thunder was changed to sharp ear-piercing cracks.

"Get the arms and ammunition under cover, and then below
with you all," shouted Amyas from the helm.

"And heat the pokers in the galley fire," said Yeo, "to be ready
if the rain puts our linstocks out. I hope you'll let me stay on deck,
Sir, in case –"

"I must have some one, and who better than you? Can you see the
chase?"

No; she was wrapped in the grey whirlwind. She might be within
half a mile of them, for aught they could have seen of her.

And now Amyas and his old liegeman were alone. Neither spoke;
each knew the other's thoughts, and knew that they were his own.
The squall blew fiercer and fiercer, the rain poured heavier and
heavier. Where was the Spaniard?

"If he has laid-to, we may overshoot him, Sir!"

"If he has tried to lay-to, he will not have a sail left in the bolt-ropes,
or perhaps a mast on deck. I know the stiff-neckedness of those
Spanish tubs. Hurrah! there he is, right on our larboard bow!"

There she was indeed, two musket-shots off, staggering away with
canvas split and flying.

"He has been trying to hull, Sir, and caught a buffet," said Yeo,
rubbing his hands. "What shall we do now?"

"Range alongside, if it blow live imps and witches, and try our luck
once more. Pah! how this lightning dazzles!"

On they swept, gaining fast on the Spaniard.

"Call the men up, and to quarters; the rain will be over in ten
minutes."

Yeo ran toward to the gangway; and sprang back again, with a face white and wild –

"Land right a-head! Port your helm, Sir! For the love of God, port your helm!"

Amyas, with the strength of a bull, jammed the helm down, while Yeo shouted to the men below.

She swung round. The masts bent like whips; crack went the fore-sail like a cannon. What matter? Within two hundred yards of them was the Spaniard; in front of her, and above her, a huge dark bank rose through the dense hail, and mingled with the clouds: and at its foot, plainer every moment, pillars and spouts of leaping foam.

"What is it, Morte? Hartland?"

It might be anything for thirty miles.

"Lundy!" said Yeo. "The south end! I see the head of the Shutter in the breakers! Hard a-port yet, and get her close-hauled as you can, and the Lord may have mercy on us still! Look at the Spaniard!"

Yes, look at the Spaniard!

On their left hand, as they broached-to, the wall of granite sloped down from the clouds toward an isolated peak of rock, some two hundred feet in height. Then a hundred yards of roaring breaker upon a sunken shelf, across which the race of the tide poured like a cataract; then, amid a column of salt smoke, the Shutter, like a huge black fang, rose waiting for its prey; and between the Shutter and the land, the great galleon loomed dimly through the storm.

He, too, had seen his danger, and tried to broach-to. But his clumsy mass refused to obey the helm; he struggled a moment, half hid in foam; fell away again, and rushed upon his doom.

"Lost! lost! lost!" cried Amyas madly, and throwing up his hands, let go the tiller. Yeo caught it just in time.

"Sir! Sir! What are you at? We shall clear the rock yet."

"Yes!" shouted Amyas in his frenzy; "But he will not!"

Another minute. The galleon gave a sudden jar, and stopped. Then one long heave and bound, as if to free herself. And then her bows lighted clean upon the Shutter.

An awful silence fell on every English soul. They heard not the roaring of wind and surge; they saw not the blinding flashes of the lightning: but they heard one long ear-piercing wail to every saint in heaven rise from five hundred human throats; they saw the mighty ship heel over from the wind, and sweep headlong down the cataract of the race, plunging her yards into the foam, and showing her whole black side even to her keel, till she rolled clean over, and vanished for ever and ever.

"Shame!" cried Amyas, hurling his sword far into the sea, "to lose my right, my right! when it was in my very grasp! Unmerciful!"

A crack which rent the sky, and made the granite ring and quiver; a bright world of flame, and then a blank of utter darkness, against which stood out, glowing red-hot, every mast, and sail, and rock, and Salvation Yeo as he stood just in front of Amyas, the tiller in his hand. All red-hot, transfigured into fire; and behind, the black night.

★ ★ ★

A whisper, a rustling close beside him, and Brimblecombe's voice said softly, —

"Give him more wine, Will; his eyes are opening."

"Hey day?" said Amyas faintly, "not past the Shutter yet! How long she hangs in the wind!"

"We are long past the Shutter, Sir Amyas," said Brimblecombe.

"Are you mad? Cannot I trust my own eyes?"

There was no answer for awhile.

"We are past the Shutter, indeed," said Cary very gently, "and lying in the cove at Lundy."

"Will you tell me that that is not the Shutter, and that the Devil's-limekiln, and that the cliff – that villain Spaniard only gone – and that Yeo is not standing here by me, and Cary there forward, and – why, by-the-bye, where are you, Jack Brimblecombe, who were talking to me this minute?"

"Oh, Sir Amyas Leigh, dear Sir Amyas Leigh," blubbered poor Jack, "put out your hand, and feel where you are, and pray the Lord to forgive you for your wilfulness!"

A great trembling fell upon Amyas Leigh; half fearfully he put out his hand; he felt that he was in his hammock, with the deck-beams close above his head. The vision which had been left upon his eye-balls vanished like a dream.

"What is this? I must be asleep! What has happened? Where am I?"

"In your cabin, Amyas," said Cary.

"What? And where is Yeo?"

"Yeo is gone where he longed to go, and as he longed to go. The same flash which struck you down, struck him dead."

"Dead? Lightning? Any more hurt? I must go and see. Why, what is this?" and Amyas passed his hand across his eyes. "It is all dark – dark, as I live!" And he passed his hand over his eyes again.

There was another dead silence. Amyas broke it.

"Oh God!" shrieked the great proud sea captain, "Oh, God, I am blind! blind! blind!" And writhing in his great horror, he called to Cary to kill him and put him out of his misery, and then wailed for his mother to come and help him, as if he had been a boy once more; while Brimblecombe and Cary, and the sailors who crowded round the cabin-door, wept as if they too had been boys once more.

Soon his fit of frenzy passed off, and he sank back exhausted.

They lifted him into their remaining boat, rowed him ashore, carried him painfully up the hill to the old castle, and made a bed for him on the floor, in the very room in which Don Guzman and Rose Salterne had plighted their troth to each other, five wild years before.

The story of Westward Ho! *is now nearing its end. One day, Amyas, forever blind, has a vision wherein he sees his beloved Rose with her husband, Don Guzman. He now realises that the two truly loved each other and that the broken-hearted husband De Soto mourned his wife until his death. Amyas fancies that he and Don Guzman meet and ask forgiveness of each other for the wrongs into which their bitter hatred had led them. At last Amyas can live in peace.*

The Donkey

When fishes flew and forests walked
   And figs grew upon thorn,
Some moment when the moon was blood,
   Then surely I was born.

With monstrous head and sickening cry
   And ears like errant wings,
The devil's walking parody
   Of all four-footed things.

The tattered outlaw of the earth,
   Of ancient crooked will;
Starve, scourge, deride me: I am dumb,
   I keep my secret still.

Fools! For I also had my hour;
   One far fierce hour and sweet:
There was a shout about my ears,
   And palms before my feet.

The Children of the New Forest

Captain Frederick Marryat is well-known for his exciting romances of the sea, set against a background of life in the British Navy during the early part of the 19th century. He himself served in the Royal Navy of that time so he certainly knew what he was writing about when he produced novels such as Mr Midshipman Easy, Masterman Ready *and* Peter Simple. *He broke away from such books, on one occasion though, to write the stirring adventures of some Royalist brothers and sisters during the great English Civil War of the 17th Century. Here is a condensation of that book,* The Children of the New Forest.

n the year 1647, King Charles the First of England was being hunted by Oliver Cromwell and his Roundhead troopers. This in a few words is the background to this story.

A short distance from the town of Lymington and adjoining the New Forest, was a property called Arnwood, which belonged to a Cavalier named Colonel Beverley. Colonel Beverley was ever at Prince Rupert's side in battle and at last was killed at the Battle of Naseby. Colonel Beverley had married into the powerful family of the Villiers and had two sons and two daughters. Mrs. Beverley, already worn with anxiety on her husband's account, died a few months afterwards leaving the four children under the charge of an elderly relative until the family of the Villiers could protect them. But the war made this impossible, and the orphans remained at Arnwood under the care of their aunt Miss Judith Villiers and also constantly watched over by Jacob Armitage, a man too old for the Army, who was an old servant of Colonel Beverley and a verderer of the forest.

Jacob Armitage lived in a cottage about a mile and a half from Arnwood, to which mansion he often brought supplies of the venison he had killed. He had promised the Colonel he would always watch over the young Beverleys and be at hand when required.

One day Jacob had gone out into the forest to get venison for Arnwood and was stealthily approaching a fine buck, crawling unperceived through the high fern, when he overheard the conversation of a party of Roundhead troopers, who did not notice his noiseless approach. Among them was James Southwold, who had once been a forest verderer, but had now joined the Roundheads; and to his horror Jacob heard James promise to lead the party to get into Arnwood, where they suspected the runaway king might be concealed. Worse, he heard them planning to set fire to the mansion that night, as a sure means of bringing forth any Royalist fugitives who might be hidden there.

There was no time to be lost. The soldiers had said they should not visit Arnwood before dark, so there were still a few hours left to save the inhabitants. Jacob took the shortest cut he knew across the forest, and at three o'clock on that November afternoon, with less than two hours of daylight remaining, he reached Arnwood.

"I shall have a difficult job with the stiff old lady," thought Jacob as he rang the bell; "I don't believe that she would rise out of her high chair for old Noll and his whole army. But we shall see."

It soon proved that Jacob knew the old lady only too well. When

he broke the news to her, with obstinate Cavalier courage she absolutely refused to take refuge at Lymington. It was beneath the dignity of a Villiers, she said, to be frightened out of her abode by a party of rude soldiers.

The most Jacob could wring from her was permission to take the children to his cottage for the night to keep them out of harm's way. When he told the news to the few servants remaining at Arnwood they were so frightened that they all packed up and fled to Lymington at once, without caring what happened to their mistress and the children.

Jacob found the children playing in the garden. Edward, the eldest boy, was between thirteen and fourteen years old; Humphrey, the second, was twelve; Alice, eleven; and Edith, eight. Jacob drew Edward aside and told him of the danger threatening them. When the boy heard that his aunt refused to leave Arnwood, he at first declined to go either; but Jacob pointed out to him that he could not

manage the younger children without his assistance, and Edward at last reluctantly consented to go for one night. It wanted but a few minutes of twilight when the little party quitted Arnwood and hurried through the thick woods to Jacob's lonely cottage. When the younger children were in bed that night Jacob and Edward, looking across the darkness towards Arnwood, saw the whole sky lighted with the flames the Roundheads had kindled to destroy the house and all within it.

Miss Judith, however, had not perished in the flames. The next day, when Jacob went to Lymington to make inquiries, he learnt that James Southwold, thinking her to be King Charles disguised as an old woman, had carried her off captive on his horse. But she had kicked and struggled so furiously that both she and her captor were thrown and were killed in the fall.

Sorry as he was to hear of the old lady's death, Jacob felt that it made his task easier, for now there was no one alive but himself who knew that the four children had not perished in the fire but were safe in his cottage. Jacob feared that they might be hunted out and killed, on account of their father's side in the war, if it were known they still lived; so when he returned to the cottage he told the young Beverleys that they must now call themselves Armitage, and live a simple forest life with him at the cottage, which was so lonely that few ever passed it. Knowing that he was an old man who could not expect to live very long, he set to work at once teaching his charges how to manage everything, so that they could take care of themselves if deprived of his guardianship. He taught Edward to go out in the forest with him to shoot deer for food and for sale, and showed Alice how to cook and keep the cottage in order. The children learnt readily, and as time passed almost forgot that they had ever had servants to wait on them. Jacob made journeys to Lymington with his pony, White Billy, from time to time, to buy supplies and sell his venison, but he would not allow the boys to go with him until they should be so much grown and changed that no one would recognise them.

They were all so busy that time went rapidly. The winter passed away. The trees began to bud, and in the month of May the forest

began again to look green. Meanwhile the king had been taken prisoner and lodged in Carisbrooke Castle.

While Edward learnt to become expert at the chase and Alice developed into a splendid cook and rearer of poultry, Humphrey showed unusual talent as a farmer and increased their resources and their stock in all kinds of ways. For instance, with much ingenuity and patience he succeeded in catching a cow and her young calf from the herd of cattle that roamed wild in the forest, and the family at the cottage were thenceforth always provided with fresh milk. He also dug a large pitfall in which one day fell a bull. The animal was shot and its flesh fetched a useful sum of money in Lymington.

In the autumn Jacob had selected two puppies from another verderer, Oswald, a faithful friend of his, who lived on the far side of the forest and had promised to call for them when they were three or four months old. When this time had passed and he was now too feeble to go, he consented to Edward going instead in the guise of his grandson. When Edward arrived at Oswald's, he found that the keeper's cottage had been given over to Master Heatherstone, a Roundhead who had been appointed by the Parliament to be Intendant of the New Forest; he was living there with his young daughter, Patience. The Intendant questioned Edward closely, and seemed suspicious that he was of a higher station than grandson to a forester. Edward explained this by saying that he had been brought up at Arnwood with the children of Colonel Beverley. It seemed to Edward that for a Roundhead the Intendant had a good many Cavalier sympathies, and that his bark was worse than his bite.

Edward also saw Oswald, in whom he found a good friend who could be trusted, and Oswald, hearing that Jacob was ill, promised to come over to the cottage to see them before long. Then Edward returned home across the forest with the puppies, full of anxious thought, for he felt that old Jacob could not live much longer. He rejoiced, however, that Humphrey had made the farm so profitable.

On his return he found Jacob very ill in bed. The old man told him that he was dying, and said that after his death Edward would be safe in confiding in Oswald Partridge and making a friend of him. Oswald came to see them the next day, and as he was a keeper and had a right to kill the deer, he and Edward went hunting together. They killed two fine animals, and next morning loaded them into the cart and Edward went with them to convey them to the Intendant. It was so late when they arrived that Edward consented to pass the night there and return home on the following morning.

Phœbe, the Heatherstones' maid, was rather old and rather cross at having a visitor to provide for. She told Edward there was no spare bed in the house, but that there was plenty of good straw in the loft. But when Edward went up the ladder he found there was no door to shut out the wind, which blew piercingly cold, and that there was very little straw, barely enough to lie down upon. He soon grew so chilled that he could not sleep, and went down into the yard to warm himself by walking. As he went to and fro, he saw that a light was still burning in the window of the bedroom above the kitchen, and thought it was Phœbe going to bed.

Suddenly through the white window curtain he perceived a broad light in the room – it increased every moment – and he saw the figure of a female rush past it, and attempt to open the window – the drawing of the curtains showed him that the room was on fire. A moment's thought, and he ran for the ladder by which he had climbed to the loft, and placed it against the window. The flames were less bright, and he could not see the female who had been at the window when he went for the ladder. He ascended quickly, and burst open the casement – the smoke poured out in such volumes that it nearly suffocated him, but he went in; and as soon as he was inside, he stumbled against the body of the person who had attempted to open the window, but who had fallen down senseless. As he raised the body, the fire, which had been smothered from want of air when all the windows and doors were closed, now burst out, and he was scorched before he could get on the ladder again, with the body in his arms; but he succeeded in getting it down safe. Then, for the first time, he discovered that he had brought down the daughter of the Intendant of the forest. There was no time to be lost, so Edward carried her into the stable and left her there, still insensible, upon the straw, in a spare stall, while he hastened to alarm the house.

By this time Edward's continual calls of "Fire! fire!" had aroused the people of the house, and also of the cottages adjacent, and he organised them into a chain to pass water along to extinguish the flames. Before long the fire was out, no more than the furniture of the room being destroyed. Edward's arm was, however, severely burnt and gave him much pain.

Both the Intendant and his daughter felt they could hardly do enough for the young man after the great service he had rendered them, and Edward rode home as early as possible in the morning to escape their thanks. He was met by Humphrey about a mile from the cottage with the news that old Jacob was very near death. Soon after their arrival, when he had given Edward some good advice and blessed all four children, the old man died very peacefully.

At the end of March, on a mild day, Humphrey remembered that he had not examined his pitfall for a good while, and went at daylight to see if any creature was in it. He thought he heard a heavy breathing and once a low groan, which made him very uneasy. He called out, asking if there was anyone there.

A groan was the reply, and now Humphrey was horrified at the idea that somebody had fallen into the pit, and was perishing for want of succour. He ran for the rough ladder he used for getting into the pit, put it into position and descended. At the bottom he found the body of a lad half-clothed lying there. The lad groaned several times and opened his eyes. Humphrey managed to get the poor lad out of the pit.

Humphrey fetched water for the lad to drink, and this seemed to revive him, so that he spoke in a foreign language, which Humphrey could not understand. He hurried back to the cottage for Edward, and together they fed the boy and brought him back. Edward thought he must be some poor beggar lad who had been crossing the forest, but Humphrey guessed him, from his general appearance, to be from one of the bands of gipsies which sometimes roamed the country.

After the boy had been fed he was put to bed, and slept soundly most of that day and the next night. In the morning Humphrey questioned him, and he answered in broken English.

He said his name was Pablo, that he was a gipsy and in company with several others of his race, going down to the sea-coast on one of their usual migrations, and that they had pitched their tents not far from the pitfall. That during the night he had gone out to set some snares for rabbits, and going back to the tents, it being quite dark, he had fallen into the hole. That he had remained there three days and nights, having in vain attempted to get out. His mother was with the party of gipsies to which he belonged; but he had no father. He did not know where to follow the gang, as they had not said where they were going, other than to the sea-coast; that it was no use looking for them; and that he did not care much about leaving them, as he was very unkindly treated. In reply to the question as to whether he would like to remain with them, and work with them on the farm, he replied that he should like it very much if they would be kind to him.

"Well, Pablo, we will try you and do all we can to make you happy," said Edward, "so long as you are well behaved." So the boy stayed with them, and in time became very useful, helping Humphrey with the farm.

One day Edward heard the news that King Charles had been executed by the Parliament. This murder, as he considered it, upset him so much that he wandered out into the forest with his gun, not noticing at all where he was going. At last, night began to fall, and he realised that he was lost and had no idea of the way home. Suddenly he observed, under some trees ahead of him, a spark of fire emitted; he thought it was a glow worm at first; but it was more like the striking of a flint against steel; and as he saw it a second time, he stopped that he might ascertain what it might be before he advanced further.

He approached very cautiously, and arrived at a large tree, behind which he remained to reconnoitre. The people, whoever they might be, were not more than thirty yards from him.

Edward crept noiselessly nearer to them, crawling through the fern on hands and knees until he could hear what they might say. He was cautious because he had been told by Oswald that there were many disbanded soldiers who were now living in the forest. Edward soon heard enough of their conversation to discover that two hours after dark they intended to rob a lonely cottage in the forest, whose tenant, they had found out by prying, had a bag of gold there. There was no one in the cottage but the man with the gold and a young lad, and the two robbers who spoke were confident they could succeed in their ruffianly scheme.

Edward recognised one of them as Benjamin, who had been a

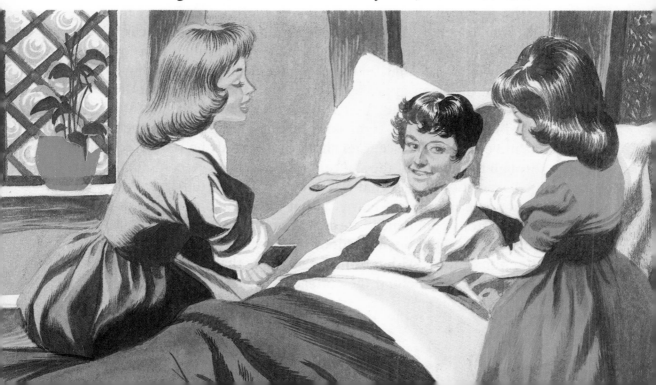

manservant at Arnwood and had fled the night the mansion was burnt down; and the other as Corbould, a villain whom the Intendant had engaged for a time as a verderer, but whom he had had to discharge for his misdeeds.

The two men then rose up and set off, Edward silently following at a little distance. They led him to a cottage which stood in a clearing. All was still and as dark as pitch; the men consulted in a low tone, but the wind was so high that he could not distinguish what they said.

At last one man approached the front door while the other went round the door behind. Edward waited for what was to follow. He heard one man at the front door talking and asking for shelter in a plaintive but loud voice; and shortly afterwards he perceived a light through the chinks of the shutters – for Edward was continually altering his position to see what was going on in the front and at the back. After some minutes of entreaty that they would open the door, the man in front commenced thumping and beating against it, as if he would make them open the door by force; but this was to divert the attention of those within from the attempts that the other robber was making to get in behind the cottage.

Advancing nearer the back, Edward perceived that the fellow had contrived to open the window close to the back door, and was remaining quite close to it with a pistol in his hand, apparently not wishing to run the risk of climbing in. Edward slipped under the eaves of the cottage, not six feet from the man, who remained with his back partly turned towards him. Edward then finding he had obtained this position unperceived, crouched down with his gun ready pointed.

As Edward remained in this position, he heard a shrill voice cry out, "They are getting in behind!" and heard a movement in the cottage. The man near him, who had his pistol in his hand, put his arm through the window and fired inside. A shriek was given, and Edward fired his gun into the body of the man, who immediately fell. Edward lost no time in reloading his gun, during which he heard the bursting open of the front door and the report of firearms; then all was silent for a moment. As soon as his gun was reloaded Edward walked round to the front of the cottage, where he found the man who was called Ben lying across the threshold of the open door. He stepped across the body, and, looking into the room within, perceived a body stretched on the floor, and a young lad weeping over it.

"Don't be alarmed, I am a friend," said Edward, going in to where the body lay; and taking the light which was at the farther end of the chamber, he placed it on the floor, that he might examine the state of the person who was breathing heavily, and badly wounded.

Edward sent the boy for water, and saw that the man was too choked with blood from a wound in the neck to be able to speak, though he was alive and sensible and spoke with his eyes and signs.

When the lad again knelt by his side, weeping bitterly, the man pointed to him and gave such an imploring look that Edward understood that he was asking for protection for the lad.

"I will take him home with me to my family," said Edward, feeling he could not do less than promise, "and he shall have all we have."

The man raised his hand again and a gleam of joy passed over his features. After a minute or two another effusion of blood choked him, and after a short struggle he fell back dead.

Edward wondered what was the best thing to do. He made a tour of the cottage and found Ben lying dead across the threshold of the door and the other robber in a dying condition. Edward gave him water and he expired in a few minutes.

Edward returned into the cottage and noticed that the body of the dead owner, though dressed in rustic clothes, had all the appearance of gentle birth, and he suspected that it was that of a Cavalier in hiding. Soon after dawn, after he had made the boy sleep off the worst of his grief, he took him home to the cottage, where he found the family much alarmed by his absence. The boy told Edward that his father had escaped from prison after having been condemned to death by the Parliament, and for more than a year had been hiding in the lonely cottage which he had bought because of its remote position. On arriving home a great surprise awaited them, for the boy revealed to Alice and Edith that he was in reality a girl, called Clara. Clara's father had had to send her to Lymington whenever supplies were needed, as he dared not go himself, and had made her dress as a boy for greater safety on her solitary expeditions.

Edward sent word to the Intendant, as authority over the forest, of all that had happened, and Mr. Heatherstone came over to see the cottage. He recognised the body of the slain man as that of a Cavalier named Ratcliffe, with whom he had been friendly before they took opposite sides in the civil war; and he insisted that Clara should not remain at the cottage, but should come to live with him and Patience.

The Intendant's opinion of Edward rose higher than ever after his rescue of Clara, and a little later he proposed to the young man that he should come to live with him as secretary, which would enable him to rise above the position of a mere forester and see something of the world. Humphrey, knowing how Edward chafed at the secluded life in the forest, urged him to go; he could manage the farm quite well without Edward now that he had Pablo. Edward, therefore, accepted the offer, and went to live in the Intendant's house. But he often rode across the forest to see his brother and sisters.

Some months went by, and in the late summer Oswald one day said to Edward:

"Have you heard the news, sir?" (for Edward had confided his real name and parentage to the trusty forester). "They say that the King (Charles I's son) is in Scotland and that the Scots have raised an army for him. Perhaps the Intendant did not tell you, for fear you should go straight off to join the King."

This news excited Edward intensely, and he at once resolved to strike a blow for the king. But the Intendant dissuaded him, showing him letters which indicated that the time was not yet ripe and the rising would be unsuccessful; and, sure enough, the next news they had was that the Scottish army had been cut to pieces by Cromwell and that the young king had retreated to the Highlands.

The following winter was a very severe one, and snow lay so deep all over the country that few letters reached the Intendant from London. At last a messenger arrived from the capital with tidings that King Charles had been crowned in Scotland with great solemnity.

The Intendant, who had much secret sympathy with the Cavaliers and had always disapproved of the execution of Charles I, felt he could no longer hold Edward back. But as it would have done him harm with the Parliamentary party had it become known that his secretary had gone straight from his house to join the king, he told Edward that he should send him on a business journey to London. If, after that, Edward decided to go north, he was to send back the manservant who would accompany him, but say no word of his intentions. Thus the Intendant would be aware of what had happened, but could truthfully say, if questioned, that he had not been told of Edward's plan to join the other party.

Edward joyfully agreed, and he went over to the cottage to say good-bye to his family, and set off for London on the following morning. There were tears in the eyes of Patience Heatherstone as she bade him farewell.

Edward arrived safely in London and soon finished the Intendant's business there. A friend of the Intendant's, on whom Mr. Heatherstone had desired him to call, gave him a letter of introduction to two loyalist ladies in Lancashire, and after sending the servant back to the New Forest Edward rode out of London upon the northward

road. As it was late in the day when he started, he did not proceed farther than Barnet, but put up at an inn there for the night.

Edward had made no alteration in the dress which he had worn since he had been received in the house of Mr. Heatherstone. It was plain, although of good materials. He wore a high-crowned hat, and altogether would, from his attire, have been taken for a Roundhead.

When Edward first entered the room there were three persons in it, whose appearance was not very prepossessing. They were dressed in what had once been very gay attire, but which now exhibited tarnished lace, stains of wine, and dust from travelling. They eyed him as he entered with his saddle-bags, and one of them said:

"That's a fine horse you were riding, sir. Has he much speed?"

"He has," replied Edward, as he turned away, and went into the bar to speak with the hostess, and give his property into her care.

"Going north, sir?" inquired the same person when Edward returned.

"Not exactly," replied Edward, walking to the window to avoid further conversation.

The host, who had overheard the conversation, now entered and sent the three men about their business; he then warned Edward to

be careful the next day, as they were known to be highwaymen, though nothing as yet had been proved against them.

Early the next morning Edward rose and went to the stable to see his horse fed. The three men were there, but did not speak to him. Edward returned to the inn, and when he had breakfasted renewed the priming in his pistols. While so occupied he happened to look up, and perceived one of the men with his face against the window, watching him.

"Well, now you see what you have to expect if you try your trade with me," thought Edward. Having replaced his pistols, he paid his reckoning, and went to the stable desiring the ostler to saddle his horse and fix on his saddle-bags. As soon as this was done he mounted and rode off. Before he was well clear of the town the highwaymen cantered past him on three well-bred active horses. "I presume we shall meet again," thought Edward. He had ridden about fifteen miles, when he heard the report of firearms. Soon afterwards a man on horseback, in full speed, galloped towards him. He had a pistol in his hand, and his head turned back. The reason for this was soon evident, as immediately after him appeared the three highwaymen in pursuit. One fired his pistol at the man who fled, and missed him. The man then fired in return, and with true aim, as one of the highwaymen fell. All this was so sudden that Edward had hardly time to draw his pistol and put spurs to his horse before the parties were upon him, and were passing him. Edward fired at the second highwayman as he passed him, and the man fell. The third highwayman, perceiving this, turned his horse and galloped away. The man who had been attacked had pulled up his horse when Edward came to his assistance, and now rode up to him, saying:

"I have to thank you, sir, for your timely aid; for those rascals were too many for me."

"You are not hurt, I trust, sir?" replied Edward.

"No, not the least. They attacked me about half a mile from here. I turned my horse and rode for dear life. They immediately gave chase. The result you saw. Between us we have broken up the gang, for both these fellows seem dead or nearly so."

There was such a gentlemanlike, frank and courteous air about the stranger, whose name was Chaloner, that Edward immediately assented to his proposal of their riding north in company for mutual protection. They soon grew to know each other well, and Edward discovered that Chaloner's purpose in riding north was the same as his own. The bond seemed complete when he found that the two

Lancashire ladies to whom his letter of introduction was addressed were the aunts of Chaloner and that he had his home with them. To Chaloner, Edward revealed that he was the son of Colonel Beverley, a name well known and respected in the royal army.

On reaching Portlake, where the Misses Conynghame lived, both young men were warmly welcomed by Chaloner's aunts and spent the night there. The next day they went to join the army of King Charles, which had advanced south to within a few miles of Portlake. They were received with kindness by the king and given commissions as captains of horses attached to Charles's personal staff. Edward was soon equipped and now attended upon the king.

Unfortunately, the king was defeated soon after in the Battle of Worcester. His forces were routed and the king fled, like his father before him, now a hunted fugitive.

Chaloner and Edward, who had managed to escape even scratches although they had fought valiantly, now determined to make their way towards the New Forest, a proceeding attended with danger, as they were rebels who had fought against the Government. However, luck was on their side. They fell in with Grenville, one of the king's pages, engaged in a skirmish with some Parliamentary troopers, whom they defeated and then dressed themselves in the clothes of the dead Roundheads. In this garb they were able to travel safely across the country and arrived at last at Edward's home.

As the Intendant's secretary, Edward was fairly secure in his own neighbourhood. Chaloner and Grenville, who were not, were hidden

in Clara's unoccupied cottage, until they could find a ship to take them secretly to France, whither the king had now made his way. But before leaving England, Chaloner rendered Edward a service in return for his assistance with the highwaymen. Knowing that Edward and Humphrey felt strongly that now their sisters were growing up they should be educated as gentlewomen, he arranged that they should go to Lancashire to be under the care of his two aunts at Portlake. Edward went with his friends to France.

The rest of Edward's adventures must be told more briefly. On his arrival at Paris he was kindly received by King Charles, who secured for him an appointment in the French army. Chaloner and Grenville, with many other English and Scottish gentlemen, entered the same service, and for some years they were fully engaged in warfare. During these wars Cromwell had been named Protector and had shortly afterwards died.

On the 15th May 1660, the news arrived that Charles had been proclaimed king on the 8th, and a large body of gentlemen went to invite him over. The king was met at Dover by General Monk, and conducted to London, which he entered amidst the acclamations of the people, on the 29th of the same month.

As the procession moved slowly along the Strand, through a countless multitude, the windows of the houses were filled with well-dressed ladies, who waved their white kerchiefs to the king and his suite.

"Look, Edward," said Chaloner, "at those two lovely girls at yon

window. Do you recognise them."

"Indeed I do not."

"Why, they are your sisters; Alice and Edith: and do you not recognise behind them my good aunts Conynghame?"

As they passed, Edward caught the eye of Edith and smiled, and as soon as possible afterwards he and his two friends went to the house of the ladies Conynghame.

After so many years' absence Edward was delighted to find his sisters grown such accomplished and elegant young women. It gave him even more pleasure to learn from them that Patience Heatherstone was still unmarried and one of the beauties of the town. He also heard that the Intendant had been granted the estate of Arnwood by the Parliament, that he had lately rebuilt the house, and that Humphrey was living there in charge of it.

A few days later Edward journeyed down to the New Forest, where he was reunited with Humphrey and went to visit the Intendant.

What was his surprise and joy when Mr. Heatherstone informed him that he had long suspected him of being Edward Beverley, and for this reason had applied to be granted Arnwood, so that it should not fall into other hands. His intention was that Edward should marry Patience, who had admitted to her father that she was fond of him.

About a year after the Restoration there was a fête at Hampton Court, given in honour of three marriages taking place – Edward Beverley to Patience Heatherstone, Chaloner to Alice, and Grenville to Edith; and, as His Majesty himself said, as he gave away the brides, "Could loyalty be better rewarded?"

But our young readers will not be content if they do not hear some particulars about the other personages who have appeared in our little history. Humphrey must take the first place. His love of farming continued. Edward gave him a large farm, rent free; and in a few years Humphrey saved up sufficient to purchase a property for himself. He then married Clara Ratcliffe, who has not appeared lately on the scene, owing to her having been, about two years before the Restoration claimed by an elderly relation, who lived in the country, and whose infirm state of health did not permit him to quit the house. He left his property to Clara, about a year after her marriage to Humphrey. The cottage in the New Forest was held by, and eventually made over to Pablo, who became a very steady character, and in the course of time married a young girl from Arnwood, and had a houseful of young gipsies.

So all ended happily for the one-time Children of the New Forest.

The Charge of the Light Brigade

In the year 1854 Britain, France and Turkey were fighting a great war against Russia in the Crimea, which is a peninsula in South Russia. On October 25th a battle was fought near the small port of Balaklava. During the battle some Turkish guns were captured by the Russians. Lord Raglan, who commanded the British forces, ordered the Light Brigade of cavalry to recapture the guns. Lord Cardigan the commander of the Light Brigade could not see those guns from where he was sitting on his horse. He could, however, see a battery of Russian guns in the valley ahead of him. There were more guns on either side of the valley. Cardigan ordered the Light Brigade to attack. What followed was a disaster.

Half a league, half a league,
Half a league onward,
All in the valley of Death
Rode the six hundred.
'Forward, the Light Brigade!
Charge for the guns!' he said.
Into the valley of Death
Rode the six hundred.

'Forward, the Light Brigade!'
Was there a man dismayed?
Not though the soldier knew
Some one had blundered.
Theirs not to make reply,
Theirs not to reason why,
Theirs but to do and die.
Into the valley of Death
Rode the six hundred.

Cannon to right of them,
Cannon to left of them,
Cannon in front of them
Volleyed and thundered;
Stormed at with shot and shell,
Boldly they rode and well,
Into the jaws of Death,
Into the mouth of Hell
Rode the six hundred

Flashed all the sabres bare,
Flashed as they turned in air
Sabring the gunners there,
Charging an army, while
All the world wondered:
Plunged in the battery-smoke
Right through the line they broke;

Cossack and Russian
Reeled from the sabre-stroke
Shattered and sundered.
Then they rode back, but not,
Not the six hundred.

Cannon to right of them,
Cannon to left of them,

Cannon behind them
Volleyed and thundered;
Stormed at with shot and shell,
While horse and hero fell,
They that had fought so well
Came through the jaws of Death,
Back from the mouth of Hell,
All that was left of them,
Left of six hundred.

When can their glory fade?
O the wild charge they made!
All the world wondered.
Honour the charge they made!
Honour the Light Brigade,
Noble six hundred!

The Three Musketeers

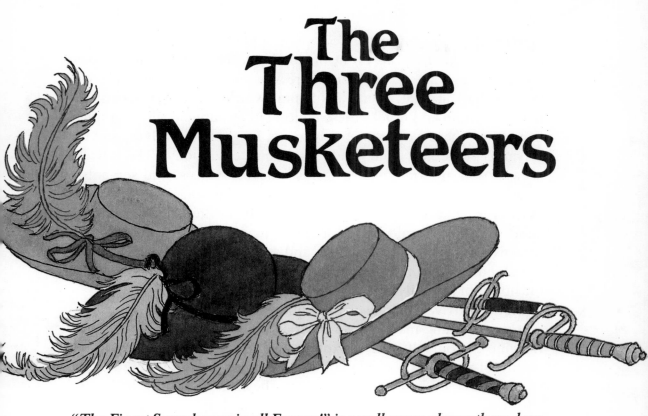

"The Finest Swordsman in all France!" is a well-worn phrase these days, often used when reference is being made to the latest cloak-and-sword romance, film or television serial. Surely, though, it must have been coined on the day that first saw publication of that immortal saga The Three Musketeers *by Alexandre Dumas. Ride now with the young fiery d'Artagnan of Gascony as he leaves home, like so many young men have done before and since, to seek his fortune and make his reputation even in the cannon's mouth. Haughty and proud he is but he soon learns that pride goes before a fall.*

The Three Gifts of Monsieur d'Artagnan the Elder

On the first Monday of April, 1625, the town of Meung, where the author of the *Romance of the Rose* was born, appeared to be in a great state of revolution as if the Huguenots had just made a second Siege of Rochelle of it. Many citizens, seeing the women rushing toward the High Street, and hearing the children crying on the doorsteps, hastened to don their cuirasses, and, supporting their somewhat uncertain courage with a musket or a spear, directed their steps toward the inn of the Jolly Miller, before which was gathered a noisy, and curious group, increasing every minute in numbers.

In those times panics were common, and every few days some city noted in its archives an event of this kind. There were nobles who made war against each other; there was the King, who made war against the Cardinal; there was Spain, which made war against the King. Then, in addition to these concealed or public, official or unofficial wars, there were robbers, beggars, Huguenots, wolves, and the servants of nobles, who made war upon everybody. The citizens always took up arms readily against thieves, wolves, and servants – often against nobles and Huguenots – sometimes against the King – but never against the Cardinal or Spain. It resulted, then, from this 'habit, that on the said first Monday of the month of April 1625, the citizens, on hearing the clamour, and seeing neither the red and yellow standard nor the livery of the Duke de Richelieu, rushed toward the hostel of the Jolly Miller.

On their arrival the cause of this hurly-burly was apparent to all.

It was a young man, whose portrait we can sketch in a few lines. Imagine to yourself Don Quixote at eighteen; Don Quixote without his breast-plate, his coat of mail, and his other pieces of armour; Don Quixote dressed in a woollen doublet, the colour of which had faded into a nameless shade. Imagine to yourself, further, a long, brown face, with high cheek bones (a sign of cunning) and enormously developed jaw muscles, an infallible sign by which a Gascon may always be known, even without his feathered hat. But our young man wore a hat adorned with a feather. He had an open and intelligent eye, and a hooked but finely chiselled nose. Too big for a youth, too small for a grown man, an inexperienced eye might have taken him for a farmer's son upon a journey, had it not been for the long sword, which, dangling from a leather belt, hit against the calves of its owner as he walked, and against the rough side of his steed when he was on horseback.

For our young man had a mount which was noted by all. It was a pony, from twelve to fourteen years old, of a yellow colour, without a hair in its tail, but not without wind-galls on its legs. This pony, though going with its head lower than its knees, rendering a martingale quite unnecessary, managed nevertheless, to travel eight leagues a day. Unfortunately, the good qualities of this steed were so well concealed by its strange-coloured hide and unaccountable gait that, in a quarter of an hour before the gate of Beaugency, it produced an unfavourable feeling that extended to its master.

And this feeling had been the more painful to young d'Artagnan – for so was the Don Quixote of this second Rozinante named, –

because he did not in the least conceal from himself the ridiculous appearance that such a steed gave him, good horseman as he was. He had sighed deeply, therefore, on accepting the gift of the pony from Monsieur d'Artagnan the elder. He was not ignorant of the fact that such a beast was worth the munificent sum of at least twenty whole livres; but the words which had accompanied the present were priceless.

"My son," said the old nobleman – in that pure accent of which King Henry IV could never rid himself – "my son, this horse was born in the house of your father, about thirteen years ago, and has remained in it ever since, which ought to make you love it. Never sell it – allow it to die quietly and honourably of old age; and if you take it to war, take as much care of it as you would of an old servant. At court, provided you have ever the honour to go there," continued Monsieur d'Artagnan the elder, "an honour to which your ancient nobility gives you right, uphold worthily your name of nobleman, which has been worthily borne by your ancestors during five hundred years; uphold it both for your own sake and for those that belong to you. By these I mean your relations and friends. Endure nothing from any one but the Cardinal and the King. It is by his courage, understand me well, by his courage alone, that the nobleman can make his way nowadays. Whoever trembles for a second, perhaps lets the opportunity escape him which, during that exact second, fortune held out to him. You are young; you ought to be brave for two reasons – the first is that you are a Gascon, and the second is that you are my son. Be ever ready for the occasion, and seek adventures. I have taught you how to handle a sword; you have muscles of iron, a wrist of steel: fight on all occasions; fight the more because duels are forbidden, since, in consequence, there is twice as much courage in fighting. I have nothing to give you, my son, but fifteen crowns, my horse, and the advice you have just heard. Your mother will add to them a recipe for a certain balsam, which she had from a gypsy, and which had the miraculous virtue of curing all wounds that do not reach the heart. Take advantage of all, and live happily and long. I have but one word to add, and that is to propose an example to you – not mine, for I myself have never appeared at court, and have only taken part in religious wars as a volunteer. I speak of Captain de Tréville, who was formerly my neighbour, and who had the honour to be as a child the playfellow of our King, Louis XIII, whom God preserve! Sometimes their play became battles, and in these battles the King was not always the stronger. The blows he received gave him a great affection and friendship for Captain de Tréville. Afterward, Captain de Tréville fought with others: on his first journey to Paris, five times; from the death of the late King to the coming-of-age of the young one, without reckoning wars and sieges, seven times; and from that coming-of-age up to the present day, perhaps a hundred times! So that in spite of edicts, warnings and decrees, he is today captain of the Musketeers – that is to say, leader of a legion of Caesars, whom the King holds in great esteem, and whom the Cardinal dreads – he who dreads next to nothing, as

we all know. In addition, Captain de Tréville receives ten thousand crowns a year; he is, therefore, a great noble. He began as you begin; go to him with this letter, and make him your model, that you may do as he has done."

Whereupon Monsieur d'Artagnan the elder hung his own sword round his son, kissed him tenderly on both cheeks, and gave him his blessing.

On leaving the room, the young man found his mother, who was

waiting for him with the famous recipe, of which the counsels we have just repeated would require frequent use. The farewells on this side of the house were longer and more tender than they had been on the other. Not that Monsieur d'Artagnan did not love his son, who was his only offspring, but he was a man, and would have considered it unworthy of a man to give way to his feelings; whereas Madame d'Artagnan was a woman, and, still more, a mother. She wept abundantly, and, let us speak it to the praise of Monsieur d'Artagnan the younger, notwithstanding his efforts to be as firm as a future Musketeer should be, nature prevailed, and he shed many tears, of which he succeeded with great difficulty in concealing half.

That same day the young man set forth on his journey, furnished with the three presents, which consisted, as we have said, of fifteen

crowns, the horse, and the letter for Monsieur de Tréville, the advice being thrown into the bargain.

With such possessions d'Artagnan was, morally and physically, an exact copy of the hero of Cervantes, to whom we compared him so happily when the duty of an historian made it necessary to sketch his portrait. Don Quixote took windmills for giants, and sheep for armies; d'Artagnan took every smile for an insult, and every look as a provocation; whence it resulted that from Tarbes to Meung his fist was constantly doubled, or his hand on the hilt of his sword, and yet the fist did not descend upon any jaw, nor did the sword issue from its scabbard. This was not because the sight of the wretched pony did not excite numerous smiles on the countenances of passers-by, but, as against the side of this pony rattled a sword of respectable length,

261

the said passers-by repressed their laughter, or if laughter prevailed over prudence, they endeavoured to laugh only on one side, like the masks of the ancients. D'Artagnan, then, remained majestic with his sensitive feelings intact till he came to this unlucky city of Meung.

But there, as he alighted from his horse at the gate of the Jolly Miller, without any one, host, waiter, or hostler, coming to hold his stirrup or take his horse, d'Artagnan spied, through an open window on the ground floor, a gentleman, well-made and of good carriage, although of rather a stern countenance, talking with two persons who

appeared to listen to him with respect. D'Artagnan fancied quite naturally, according to his custom, that he must be the object of their conversation, and listened. This time he was only in part mistaken: he himself was not in question, but his horse was. The gentleman appeared to be numbering all its qualities to his listeners, and the listeners, seeming, as I have said, to have great deference for the narrator, every moment burst into fits of laughter. Now, as half a smile was sufficient to awaken the anger of the young man, the effect produced upon him by this loud mirth may be easily imagined.

However, d'Artagnan was desirous of first examining the appearance of this impertinent individual who was laughing at him. He fixed his haughty eye upon the stranger, and perceived a man of from forty to forty-five years of age, with black and piercing eyes, a pale complexion, a strongly marked nose, and a black and well-shaped mustache. He was dressed in a violet doublet, with shoulder-knots of the same colour, but without any ornaments besides the customary slashes through which the shirt appeared. This doublet and hose, though new, looked creased like travelling clothes for a long time packed up in a trunk. D'Artagnan took in these details with the rapidity of a most minute observer, and, doubtless, from an instinctive feeling that this unknown was destined to have a great influence over his future life.

Now, as at the very moment in which d'Artagnan fixed his eyes upon the gentleman in the violet doublet, that gentleman made one of his most knowing and profound remarks respecting the yellow pony, his two listeners laughed even louder than before, and he himself, though contrary to his custom, allowed a pale smile (if we may be allowed to use such an expression) to flit over his countenance. This time there could be no doubt: d'Artagnan was really insulted. Full, then, of this conviction, he pulled his hat down over his eyes, and, endeavouring to copy some of the court airs he had picked up in Gascony among young travelling nobles, he advanced, one hand resting on the hilt of his sword and the other on his hip. Unfortunately, as he advanced, his anger increased at every step, and, instead of the proper and lofty speech he had prepared as a prelude to his challenge, he found nothing at the tip of his tongue but a gross remark, which he accompanied with a furious gesture.

"I say, sir – you, sir, who are hiding yourself behind that shutter! – yes, you, sir, tell me what you are laughing at, and we will laugh together."

The gentleman withdrew his eyes slowly from the nag to its master,

as if he required some time to ascertain whether it could be to him
that such strange reproaches were addressed; then, when he could
not possibly entertain any doubt of the matter, he contracted his
eyebrows slightly, and, with an accent of irony and insolence that it
is impossible to describe, replied to d'Artagnan –

"I am not speaking to you, sir!"

"But I am speaking to you!" shouted the young man, still more
angered by this mixture of insolence and good manners, politeness
and scorn.

The unknown looked at him again with a slight smile, and, retiring
from the window, came out of the hostelry with a slow step, and
placed himself before the horse within two paces of d'Artagnan. His
quiet manner and the ironical expression of his countenance redoubled
the mirth of the persons with whom he had been talking, and who
still remained at the window.

D'Artagnan, seeing him approach, drew his sword a foot out of the scabbard.

"This horse is decidedly, or rather has been in his youth, a buttercup," resumed the unknown, continuing the remarks he had begun, and addressing himself to his friends at the window, without paying the least attention to the fury of d'Artagnan, who, however, placed himself between him and them. "It is a colour very well known in botany, but till the present time very rare among horses."

"There are people who laugh at a horse that would not dare to laugh at its master," cried the young imitator of the terrible Tréville.

"I do not often laugh, sir," replied the unknown, "as you may perceive by my expression; but I claim, nevertheless, the privilege of laughing when I please."

"And I," cried d'Artagnan, "will allow no man to laugh when it displeases me!"

"Indeed, sir," continued the unknown, more calm than ever, "Well! that is perfectly right!" and, turning on his heel, he was about to re-enter the inn by the front gate, under which d'Artagnan, on arriving, had observed a saddled horse.

But d'Artagnan was not of a character to allow a man who had had the insolence to laugh at him to escape him in this way. He drew his sword entirely from the scabbard, and followed him, crying:

"Turn, turn, Master Joker, lest I strike you from behind!"

"Strike me!" said the other, turning sharply round and surveying the young man with as much astonishment as contempt. "Why, my good fellow, you must be mad!" Then, in a quiet tone, as if speaking to himself: "This is annoying. What a God-send this would be for His Majesty, who is seeking everywhere for brave fellows to recruit his Musketeers!"

He had scarcely finished, when d'Artagnan made such a furious lunge at him, that if he had not sprung nimbly backward, he would have jested for the last time. The unknown, perceiving that the matter had gone beyond a joke, then drew his sword, saluted his adversary, and placed himself on his guard. But at the same moment his two friends, accompanied by the inn-keeper, fell upon d'Artagnan with sticks, shovels, and tongs. This caused so rapid and complete a diversion to the attack, that d'Artagnan's adversary, whilst the young man turned round to face this shower of blows, sheathed his sword with the same precision, and from an actor, which he had nearly been, became a spectator of the fight, a part in which he acquitted himself with his usual coldness, muttering nevertheless:

"A plague upon these Gascons! Put him on his orange horse again and let him begone!"

"Not before I have killed you, coward!" cried d'Artagnan, facing his three assailants as well as possible, and never retreating one step before the blows they continued to shower upon him.

"Another Gasconade!" murmured the nobleman. "Upon my honour, these Gascons are incorrigible! Keep up the dance, then, since he will have it so. When he is tired he will tell us perhaps that he has enough of it."

But the unknown did not know the headstrong personage he had to deal with; d'Artagnan was not the man ever to cry for mercy. The fight was consequently prolonged for some seconds; but at length d'Artagnan's sword was struck from his hand by the blow of a stick, and broken in two pieces. At the same moment another blow, full upon his forehead, brought him to the ground, covered with blood and almost fainting.

It was at this moment that people came flocking to the scene of action from all sides. Fearful of consequences, the inn-keeper, with the help of his servants, carried the wounded youth into the kitchen, where some trifling attention was bestowed upon him.

As to the nobleman, he resumed his place at the window, and surveyed the crowd with a certain air of impatience.

That noblemen is, in fact, Count de Rochefort, Cardinal Richelieu's secret agent. While d'Artagnan is unconscious, his letter of introduction to Monsieur de Tréville of the King's Musketeers is taken from him and handed to the Count. Later, in Paris. D'Artagnan manages to secure a meeting with Monsieur de Tréville but during the interview happens to glance through a window and sees Count de Rochefort. D'Artagnan rushes from the room and in his haste offends three valiant Musketeers. The three are known only by their assumed names of Athos, Porthos and Aramis. All, being noblemen, have thus hidden their true identities while serving in the ranks of the Musketeers. Each challenges d'Artagnan to a duel but as Athos and d'Artagnan are about to cross swords, a band of Cardinal's Guards, deadly rivals of the King's Musketeers, appear. Duelling is strictly forbidden. D'Artagnan at once allies himself with the Musketeers and a tremendous battle follows. The Cardinal's Guards are routed and as d'Artagnan now says to his new friends "If I am not yet a Musketeer, I have at least entered upon my apprenticeship, have I not?"

Now ensues one of the greatest adventures in literature. The Queen of France has incautiously given to the English Duke of Buckingham (an admirer of hers but an enemy of France,) some diamond studs, a recent present from the King. The Cardinal hopes to embarrass the Queen by revealing to the King what has happened to his diamonds but d'Artagnan and the Three Musketeers set out for England to bring back the diamonds. D'Artagnan evades all the dangers laid for him by the Cardinal and returns with the diamonds, thus earning the Cardinal's enmity. There now follows a series of exciting adventures ending with d'Artagnan being appointed a lieutenant of the Musketeers by a surprisingly now friendly Cardinal. D'Artagnan is saddened by his three friends deciding the time has come to leave the Musketeers and return to their home. D'Artagnan settles his debt with Count de Rochefort by fighting and wounding him three times. They then make friends and on this note The Three Musketeers *concludes.*

Wuthering Heights

Emily Brontë lived in a grey, bleak parsonage on the Yorkshire moors with her sisters, Anne and Charlotte, her brother Branwell and her father. She was born in 1818, and was only 30 years old when she died.

The sisters were educated abroad, and Emily later became a governess. She was shy and imaginative, and seemed to live in a world of her own. She returned to Yorkshire to keep house for her father (her mother had died in 1821), while her sisters taught.

Emily, Anne and Charlotte were all gifted writers. They wrote under the pen-names of Ellis, Acton and Currer Bell.

Wuthering Heights, a weird, powerful masterpiece, was Emily's only novel. Charlotte said that it was "hewn in a wild workshop, with simple tools, out of homely material".

In an old stone farmhouse, called Wuthering Heights, deep in the Yorkshire moors, lived the Earnshaw family. Mrs. Earnshaw and the two children, Hindley and Cathy, were waiting for Mr. Earnshaw to return from a business trip to Liverpool.

It was late when Cathy's father finally arrived, and he did not bring the expected presents. Instead, wrapped in his overcoat, he carried a dark-skinned, dirty child. He had found the half-starved boy wandering the streets of Liverpool, and intended to bring him up as one of his own family.

Mr. Earnshaw called the child Heathcliff, and from the beginning he was strange and wild. Cathy liked him, and the two spent many happy hours together on the moor. But Hindley was jealous of his father's affection for Heathcliff, and hated the boy.

So the three children grew up, and Hindley went away to college. He did not return until his father died, and then to everyone's astonishment he brought his wife with him. Frances took an immediate dislike to Heathcliff, and Hindley ordered him out of the house. Heathcliff was to work in the fields as a labourer, and eat in the kitchen with the servants.

Heathcliff became bitter and sullen; his only consolation was the gay company of Cathy. Their adventures on the moor continued, until one wild night when they made up their minds to spy on their nearest neighbours, the Lintons of Thrushcross Grange. They were discovered, and during the chase Cathy fell and was bitten by the guard dog. The Lintons took her in, bathed her wounds and made a fuss of her. Heathcliff they turned away.

Hindley Earnshaw blamed Heathcliff for the accident, and forbade him ever to talk to Cathy again.

Cathy stayed with the Lintons for five weeks, and became great friends with the children, Edgar and Isabella. When she came home, it was as a young lady rather than the young savage she had been. Heathcliff was miserable to see the change in Cathy, and although she was still fond of him her new friends promised to be more exciting.

Soon the household at Wuthering Heights was thrilled to hear that Frances was expecting a baby. When the child — a fine boy — was born, he was named Hareton. Unhappily Frances died shortly afterwards, and Hindley, desperate with grief, turned to drink.

   ✳   ✳   ✳

Cathy was by now 15, and growing more beautiful every day. But she had become haughty and headstrong, and thought only of her own pleasure.

One day, during one of his many visits to Wuthering Heights, Edgar Linton asked her to marry him. She did not know what to say. On one hand she was fascinated by Edgar — his handsome looks, his wealth and fine style of living. On the other hand she had always loved Heathcliff.

In the end Cathy decided to marry Edgar. When Heathcliff heard about it, he was heartbroken, and disappeared into a night of storm and rain. Cathy grieved terribly. However, she was young and high-spirited, and soon recovered. Later, she married Edgar and settled down happily at Thrushcross Grange.

Some years passed. At Wuthering Heights, Hindley Earnshaw became a wild drunkard, and treated his son Hareton cruelly in his mad rages. At Thrushcross Grange Cathy was expecting her first baby when both households were astonished by the reappearance of Heathcliff.

He came back as a gentleman with plenty of money – although no one ever found out where the money had come from. It soon became obvious that Heathcliff was determined to have his revenge. Nightly he drank and played cards for money with Hindley Earnshaw. Hindley lost heavily, and mortgaged his lands to pay for his gambling debts.

Meanwhile Heathcliff made himself charming to Edgar Linton's sister, Isabella. The young girl immediately fell madly in love with him, and they ran away to get married. It was only six weeks later that Isabella wrote miserably admitting her mistake. Eventually she left him, and their son was born in London a few months later. She named him Linton.

Driven almost to madness by her unhappiness at Heathcliff's accusation that she had betrayed him in marrying Edgar, Cathy died in childbirth. Her little daughter Catherine was brought up by Edgar.

When young Catherine was 13, her aunt Isabella died. Her son Linton, who was about the same age, came to live at Wuthering Heights, and visited the Grange. He was a frail, peevish boy and when the cousins met, Catherine felt sorry for him. She worked hard to make him smile and petted him like a baby.

Edgar Linton disapproved of the friendship between the cousins, as he never forgave Heathcliff for making his Cathy so unhappy. Catherine was not encouraged to visit Wuthering Heights, so it was several years before the two young people met again. When they did, it was apparent that Heathcliff was in favour of them marrying, as part of his revenge on the Earnshaw family.

Secretly Catherine rode to visit Linton almost every evening, and they became very fond of each other. But Linton, always sickly, grew daily weaker. The fear of displeasing his father, who hated him, did not help.

One day, when Catherine's father was ill and it seemed he had

not long to live, she received his permission to visit her cousin once more. She found Linton in a pitiful state.

Once he had got Catherine inside Wuthering Heights, Heathcliff locked her in a room with Linton, and his evil plan was revealed. He had sent his servants and Hareton Earnshaw away, and kept Catherine locked up all night. In the morning she and Linton were married, Catherine weeping all the while.

Edgar Linton was near to death, but Heathcliff cruelly kept Catherine there. Finally she managed to escape, and fled through the night to the Grange. She was only just in time. Her father died in her arms that night.

Heathcliff forced Catherine to return to Wuthering Heights. Linton was very ill and in spite of her pleading Heathcliff refused to send for a doctor. So Catherine in despair and already grief-stricken at the loss of her father, nursed her husband as well as she could. Poor Linton did not last long. When he died, Catherine sat exhausted by his bed. "He is safe now, and I am free," she cried. "You have left me so long to struggle against death alone, that I feel and see only death."

*　　　*　　　*

Catherine's miserable existence continued. The only person who felt sorry for her was Hareton Earnshaw. He worked in the fields, and Heathcliff had never felt it necessary to have his old enemy's son educated. The young man could neither read nor write, and seemed to Catherine no more than a rough labourer. Hareton had never realised that Wuthering Heights should have been his, if his father had not been cheated by Heathcliff.

Hareton had admired Catherine for a long time, but never dared to tell her so. As for Catherine, she was tired and bitter, and counted him among her enemies.

So things continued for months until Catherine began to feel sorry for Hareton and regretted that she had been unkind to him. She wanted to be friends, but she had a hard time persuading him that she was in earnest. At last Hareton believed that she was not trying to trick him, and Catherine happily set to work to teach him to read.

Heathcliff died soon after, happy for the first time in his life at the thought that he would soon be re-united in heaven with his darling Cathy.

Love grew between Catherine and Hareton, and eventually they were married and went to live at Thrushcross Grange. Wuthering Heights was left with its ghosts, and only the servants to care.

The Four Sweet Months

First, April, she with mellow showers
Opens the way for early flowers;
Then after her comes smiling May,
In a more sweet and rich array;
Next enters June, and brings us more
Gems than those two that went before:
Then, lastly, July comes, and she
More wealth brings in than all
    those three.

The Water Babies

Charles Kingsley, author of Westward Ho! *and* The Heroes, *wrote* The Water Babies *for his youngest son, which is why the book is sub-titled 'A Fairy Tale for a Land-Baby.' Behind the writing of the book also, was Kingsley's outrage at the way during the last century poor children were being ill-treated, even killed, by being forced to work in coal-mines and factories where safety regulations were non-existent. Many little boys and girls were used in other back-breaking and unhealthy jobs down sewers and as chimney-sweeps. Tom, the young hero of* The Water Babies, *is a chimney-sweep.*

It was largely due to the efforts of Charles Kingsley and people like him that children like Tom were finally rescued from such slavery.

Once upon a time there was a little chimney-sweep, and his name was Tom. He lived in a great town in the North Country, where there were plenty of chimneys to sweep, and plenty of money for Tom to earn and his master to spend. He could not read nor write, and did not care to do either; and he never washed himself, for there was no water where he lived.

He cried half his time and laughed the other half. He cried when he had to climb the dark flues, rubbing his poor knees and elbows raw; and when the soot got into his eyes, which it did every day; and when his master beat him, which he did every day; and when he had not enough to eat, which happened every day likewise. And he laughed the other half of the day, when he was playing with the other boys.

One day a smart little groom rode into the court where Tom lived, and said that Mr. Grimes, Tom's master, was to come up next morning to Sir John Harthover's, at the Place, for the chimneys wanted sweeping.

Grimes was so delighted at his new customer that he knocked Tom down out of hand, and drank more beer that night than he usually did in two; and when he got up at four the next morning he knocked Tom down again, which Tom did not mind much, for he was excited at going to so grand a house at Harthover Place.

So he and his master set out. Grimes rode the donkey in front, and Tom and the brushes walked behind, with the roofs all shining grey in the grey dawn.

They passed through the pitmen's village and through the turnpike, and then they were out in the real country, where the road was white instead of black; and at the wall's foot grew long grass and gay flowers, all drenched with dew; and they heard the skylark saying his matins high up in the air.

On they went, and Tom looked and looked, for he had never been so far into the country before. Soon they met up with a poor Irish-woman, trudging along with a bundle at her back. She had a grey shawl over her head and a crimson madder petticoat, and her feet were bare and limped along; but she was a very tall, handsome woman. She took Mr. Grimes's fancy so much that he offered her a lift on the donkey behind him.

But perhaps she did not admire Mr. Grimes's look and voice, for she answered quietly: "No thank you. I'd sooner walk with your little lad here."

So she walked beside Tom and talked to him, till Tom thought he had never met such a pleasant-spoken woman. He asked her where she lived, and she said far away by the sea.

At last, at the bottom of the hill, they came to a spring that rose out of a low cave of rock, at the foot of a limestone crag, and ran away under the road in a flower-bordered stream large enough to turn a mill.

And there Grimes stopped and looked, and Tom looked too. Without a word Grimes got off his donkey and knelt down and began dipping his ugly head into the spring – and very dirty he made it. Tom, who was busily picking flowers, with the Irishwoman to help him, when he saw Grimes actually wash, was most astonished.

"Why, master, I never saw you do that before."

Grimes said he only did it for coolness. He would be ashamed to want washing every week or so, like any smutty collier lad.

"I wish I might go and dip my head in," said poor little Tom. And though Grimes refused him, he ran down to the stream and began washing his face.

Grimes angrily dashed at him with horrid words and began beating him.

"Are you not ashamed of yourself, Thomas Grimes?" cried the Irishwoman; and when he still went on beating Tom she spoke quietly about Vendale and what had happened there one night two years ago. Tom did not know where Vendale was; he only knew that Grimes stopped beating him and got on his donkey again without a word.

"Stop!" said the Irishwoman. "I have one more word for you both, for you will both see me again before all is over. Those that wish to be clean, clean they will be; and those that wish to be foul, foul they will be. Remember."

And she turned away and through a gate into the meadow. But when Grimes ran into the meadow after her the woman was not there, though there was no place to hide in.

And now they had gone three miles and more, and came to Sir John's lodge gates and up the long drive to the big house, which had been built at ninety different times and in nineteen different styles, and looked as if somebody had built a whole street of houses of every imaginable shape, and then stirred them together with a spoon.

Tom and his master went to a little back door, where the ash-boy let them in, yawning horribly; and then in a passage the housekeeper met them, in such a flowered chintz dressing-gown that Tom mistook her for My Lady herself. She turned them into a grand room, all

covered up in sheets of brown paper, and bade them begin; and so, after a whimper or two and a kick from his master, into the grate Tom went and up the chimney.

How many chimneys Tom swept I cannot say; but so many that he got quite tired and fairly lost his way in them in the darkness; and at last, coming down, as he thought, the right chimney, he came down the wrong one, and found himself standing on the hearthrug of a strange room. Tom had never seen the like, because he had never been in gentlefolks' rooms except when they were all covered over ready for sweeping.

This room was all dressed in white – white curtains, white furniture and white walls – with a gay flowered carpet and pictures in gilt frames. The next thing Tom saw, and it puzzled him, was a washing-stand, with ewers and basins, and soap and brushes and towels, and a large bath full of clean water. What a heap of things all for washing!

"She must be a very dirty lady," thought Tom. And then, looking towards the bed, he saw the dirty lady and held his breath with astonishment.

Under the snow-white coverlet, upon the snow-white pillow, lay the most beautiful little girl that Tom had ever seen. Her cheeks were almost as white as the pillow, and her hair was like threads of gold spread all about over the bed. Tom stood staring at her as if she had been a angel out of heaven.

"Are all people like that when they are washed?" he thought. He tried to rub the soot off his own wrist. "Certainly I should be much prettier if I grew at all like her."

And looking round, he suddenly saw, standing close to him, a little ugly, black, ragged figure, with bleared eyes and grinning white teeth. He turned on it angrily. What did such a little black ape want in that sweet young lady's room? And behold, it was himself, reflected in a great mirror, the like of which Tom had never seen before.

And Tom, for the first time in his life, found out that he was dirty;

and burst into tears with shame and anger; and turned to sneak up the chimney again and hide; and upset the fender and threw the fire-irons down, with a noise as of ten thousand tin kettles tied to ten thousand mad dogs' tails.

Up jumped the little white lady in her bed, and, seeing Tom, screamed as shrill as any peacock. In rushed a stout old nurse, and seeing Tom likewise, made up her mind that he had come to rob, plunder, destroy, and burn; and dashed at him, as he lay over the fender, so fast that she caught him by the jacket.

But she did not hold him; he doubled under the good lady's arm, across the room, and out of the window in a moment.

All under the window spread a tree. Down that tree Tom went like a cat, and across the garden lawn and up the park towards the wood, leaving the old nurse to scream murder and fire at the window. And on he ran, followed by a gardener, and a dairymaid, and the steward, and Grimes, and a whole tail of the people at Harthover.

Even the Irishwoman, walking up to the house to beg, threw away her bundle and gave chase to Tom likewise.

All of them ran up the park shouting 'Stop thief!' in the belief that Tom had at least a thousand pounds' worth of jewels in his empty pockets.

And all the while poor Tom paddled along with his little bare feet, like a small black gorilla fleeing to the forest. He made for the woods, and there he scrambled desperately among boughs and brambles, and tough grasses that cut his feet, until he suddenly ran his head against a wall.

This was not pleasant; but Tom was a brave boy and did not mind the hurt a penny. He guessed that over the wall the cover would end, and up it he went, and over like a squirrel.

And there he was, out on the great grousemoors, which the country folk call Harthover Fell – heather and bog and rock stretching away and up, up to the very sky.

Now Tom was a cunning little fellow. He knew that if he backed he might throw the chase off; so he ran along under the wall for nearly half a mile. Whereby all his pursuers took quite the wrong direction, and were soon a mile off. Tom heard their shouts die away, and then he turned bravely away from the wall and up the moor, for now he could go on without being seen.

But the Irishwoman, alone of them all, had seen which way Tom went. She had kept ahead of the chase the whole time. She went quietly over the wall after Tom, and followed him all the while.

Tom went on and on, he hardly knew why; but he liked the great wide strange place, and the cool, fresh, bracing air. He never looked behind to see the Irishwoman following him. And now he began to get a little hungry and very thirsty, for he had come a long way; but he could see nothing to eat anywhere, and still less to drink. Then he saw something to which he determined to go, for that was the place for him.

A deep, deep green and rocky valley, very narrow, and filled with wood; but through the wood, hundreds of feet below him, he could see a clear stream glance – and he was so very thirsty. By the stream he saw the roof of a little cottage, and in the garden of the cottage was a tiny red thing moving, which he saw was a woman in a red petticoat. Perhaps she would give him something to eat. And there were church-bells ringing too. He could get down there in five minutes.

So Tom thought. He did not know that the cottage was more than a mile off, and a good thousand feet below.

However, down he went, like a brave little man, as he was, while the church-bells rang and the river chimed and tinkled far below this song:

Clear and cool, clear and cool,
By laughing shallow and dreaming pool,
Under the crag where the ouzel sings,
And the ivied wall where the church-bell rings.
Undefiled, for the undefiled;
Play by me, bathe in me, mother and child.

Dank and foul, dank and foul,
By the smoky town in its murky cowl,
Darker and darker the farther I go,
Baser and baser the richer I grow:
Who dare sport with the sin-defiled?
Shrink from me, turn from me, mother and child.

Strong and free, strong and free,
The floodgates are open, away to the sea,
To the golden sands and the leaping bar,
And the taintless tide that awaits me afar,
As I lose myself in the infinite main,
Like a soul that has sinned and is pardoned again.

The valley seemed so near, but it took Tom a long weary time, much scrambling, and many bruises, to come down to it. He was dreadfully tired with hunger and thirst and the heat, and he dirtied everything terribly as he went down into Vendale, as the valley was called. There has been a great black smudge down the crag ever since.

And all the while he never saw the Irishwoman coming down behind him.

When at last he reached the cottage he felt so tired and chill and sick that he had hardly strength to peep in. There sat by the empty fireplace the nicest woman that ever was seen; and opposite her sat, on two benches, twelve or fourteen rosy little children, learning their chris-cross-row.

All the children started at Tom's black figure, and at first the old dame spoke to him sharply, saying she wanted no chimney-sweep there; but when she saw that Tom was dropping with hunger and weariness she was very kind to him. She gave him milk and bread and led him away to an outhouse, where she laid him upon soft sweet hay, and bade him sleep till school was over.

But Tom did not fall asleep.

Instead of it he turned and tossed, and felt so hot all over that he longed to get into the river and cool himself; and then he fell half-asleep, and dreamt that he heard the little white lady crying to him: "Oh, you're so dirty; go and be washed"; and then he heard the Irishwoman saying, "Those that wish to be clean, clean they will be." And then he said out loud again and again, "I must be clean. I must be clean."

And all of a sudden he got to the stream on his own legs, between sleep and awake, as children will often get out of bed when they are not quite well. He looked into the clear, clear limestone water, with every pebble at the bottom bright and clean; and he dipped his head in and found it so cool, cool, cool; and he said, "I will be a fish; I will swim in the water; I must be clean, I must be clean."

So he pulled off all his clothes in haste, and tumbled himself as quick as he could into the clear cool stream. And he had not been

in it two minutes before he fell fast asleep, into the quietest, sunniest, cosiest sleep that ever he had in his life.

But before he stepped into the water he never saw the Irishwoman, not behind him this time, but before.

For just before he came to the river side, she had stepped down

into the cool clear water; and her shawl and her petticoat floated off
her, and the green water-weeds floated round her sides, and the white
water-lilies floated round her head, and the fairies of the stream came
up from the bottom and bore her away and down upon their arms;
for she was the Queen of them all; and perhaps of more besides.

When the old dame missed Tom and found his clothes by the
stream, and later, when Sir John Harthover tracked him into Vendale
and heard from her how he had disappeared, they all thought Tom
was dead, and gave up the chase and went quietly home.

But Tom was not dead. When he woke he found himself swimming
about in the stream, being about four inches long. The fairies had
turned him into a water-baby.

They had washed him white all over, and he did not remember
ever having been dirty. Indeed, he did not remember any of his old
troubles, or his master, or Harthover Place, or the little white girl,
when he became a water-baby.

He was very happy in the stream. He had been sadly overworked
in the land world; so now, to make up for that, he had nothing but
holidays for a long, long time to come.

There was plenty of company in his new world – trout and caddises
and many other creatures, not to mention a dragon fly that Tom saw
one day come out of its skin.

One day Tom was sitting on a water lily leaf with him, watching
the gnats dance, when suddenly he heard the strangest noise up the
stream – cooing and grunting and whining. He looked up the water,
and there he saw a sight as strange as the noise – a great ball rolling
over and over down the stream; and yet it was not a ball; for sometimes
it broke up and streamed away in pieces, and then it joined again;
and all the while the noise came out of it louder and louder.

Tom slipped into the water to see for himself what it could be; and when he came near the ball turned out to be four or five beautiful otters, many times larger than he.

But when the biggest of them saw Tom she darted out from the rest, and cried in the water-language sharply enough, "Quick, children, here is something to eat, indeed!" and came at poor Tom, showing such a wicked pair of eyes, and such a set of sharp teeth in a grinning mouth, that Tom slipped in between the water lily roots as fast as he could, and then turned round and made faces at her.

"Come out," said the wicked old otter, "or it will be worse for you."

But Tom looked at her from between two thick roots, and shook them with all his might, making horrible faces all the while.

"Come away, children," said the otter in disgust. "It is not worth eating, after all. It is only a nasty eft, which nothing eats, not even those vulgar pike in the pond."

"I am not an eft," said Tom. "Efts have tails." And he turned his pretty little self quite round, and sure enough, he had no more tail than you.

The otter hastily changed the subject by telling Tom about the salmon, and how they came up the stream from the sea at certain times of year; and then she sailed solemnly away.

But he could not help thinking of what the otter had said about the great river and the broad sea, and he longed to go and see them. Then one stormy night he saw the otter dashing past again with her brood, crying, "Down to the sea, down to the sea!" And after watching them disappear, Tom went too.

And now, down the rushing stream, guided by the bright flashes of the storm; past tall birch-fringed rocks, which shone out one moment as clear as day, and the next were dark as night; on through narrow strids and roaring cataracts, where Tom was deafened and blinded for a moment by the rushing waters; along deep reaches, where the white water lilies tossed and flapped beneath the wind and hail; past sleeping villages; under dark bridge-arches, and away and away to the sea.

And when the daylight came Tom found himself out in the salmon river.

A full hundred yards wide it was, sliding in from broad pool to broad shallow, past green meadows and fair parks, or the smoking chimney of a colliery. Tom liked it; but all his fancy was to get down to the wide, wide sea.

After a while he came to a place where the river spread out into broad, still, shallow reaches, and here he waited and slept too. The next morning he saw one of the things which he had come to look for.

Such fish! Ten times as big as the biggest trout, and a hundred times as big as Tom, sculling up the stream past him as easily as Tom had sculled down. Such fish! Shining silver from head to tail, and here and there a crimson dot, with grand bright eyes, looking round them as proudly as kings.

A well-bred old salmon stopped and spoke to Tom, and told him something which pleased him very much.

"I have met one or two creatures like you before, my little dear," he said. "Only last night, at the river's mouth, one came and warned me of some new stake-nets that had got into the stream."

So there were water-babies in the sea! That made Tom more eager than ever to make his way thither.

After parting from the salmon, Tom went down again for many days. And one clear, still September night he had a very strange adventure.

There were poachers about along the bank. Tom did not know what poachers were, but he saw lights moving above the water and heard voices, and saw two great two-legged creatures, one holding the light and the other a long pole. And then from behind there sprang on these men three other men, and there was a desperate fight.

All of a sudden Tom heard a tremendous splashing, and into the water, close to him, fell one of the men. The others could not find him, and when they had gone away Tom went nearer and swam round the still figure. It was his old master, Grimes. But the next day, when Tom looked again, Grimes had gone.

Then Tom went on down. It was a long and dangerous journey for him; but on and on he went, till at last he reached the sea, and the water turned salt all round him. But he could not find any water-babies, though he sat on the red buoy in the harbour mouth for days – when he was not teasing the sea creatures in a naughty way he had – looking for them.

I hope that you have not forgotten the little white lady all this

while. For it befell in the pleasant short December days that she came to the seaside with her mother, and one day she was out walking along the beach with a friend of the family, the learned Professor Ptthmllnsprts. He was showing her all sorts of curious and wonderful things, but Ellie said she only wanted to see the little children in the water.

"There are none," said the Professor very positively; but Ellie would not believe him. The Professor went on groping with a net in the pools to find more wonderful things, and then, as it befell, he caught poor little Tom. He felt the net very heavy, and lifted it out quickly, with Tom all entangled in the meshes.

"It's a water-baby!" cried Ellie; and, of course, it was.

"Water-fiddlesticks, my dear!" said the Professor, who could not bear to find himself wrong. And while they were arguing about who he was, Tom, who had been terribly frightened, bit his finger and escaped.

"Ah, it is gone," cried Ellie, seeing him dive away, and she jumped down off the rock to try and catch Tom before he slipped into the sea. Too late! She slipped, and fell some six feet, with her head on a sharp rock, and lay quite still.

She was taken home, but she would not waken, except to call out something about the water-baby. And after a week, one moonlight night, the fairies came flying in at the window with a pretty pair of wings for her, and she flew with them over the sea and up through the clouds, and nobody heard or saw anything of her for a very long while.

Meanwhile Tom slipped away off the rocks into the water, and as he was going along he saw a round cage of green withes, and inside it, looking very much ashamed of himself, sat a proud lobster he had met before. He said to Tom in a depressed voice, "I can't get out."

"Where did you get in?"

"Through that round hole at the top."

"Then why don't you get out through it?"

"Because I can't. I've tried four thousand times, but I can't," said the lobster miserably.

Tom felt sorry for him, so he took hold of his claw, and after many struggles he pulled the lobster out. And now happened to Tom a most wonderful thing, for he had not left the lobster five minutes before he came upon a water-baby; a real live water-baby, sitting on the white sand. And when it saw Tom it looked up for a moment and cried, "Why, you are a new baby! Oh, how delightful!"

And it ran to Tom, and they hugged and kissed each other. Tom said, "Oh, where have you been all this while? I have been so lonely, looking for you."

"We have been here all the time. We are always busy helping someone or other. There are hundreds of us about. How was it you did not see us, or hear us when we sing and romp every evening before we go home?"

Tom looked at the baby again, and then he said:

"Well, this is wonderful. I have seen things like you again and again, but I thought you were shells or sea-creatures. I never saw that you were water-babies."

Now was not that very odd? But if you think about it, you will see the reason why.

After that there was no more loneliness for Tom. He helped the baby to repair a great rock that had had its flowers knocked off in a storm, till all the other babies came, laughing and singing, and shouting, and romping, with a noise just like the noise of the ripple. In they came, dozens and dozens of them, all in little white bathing dresses; and they hugged him and kissed him, and danced round him on the sand, and there was no one ever so happy as poor little Tom.

There were water-babies in thousands, more than Tom could count. All the little children who had been untaught or cruelly treated or starved on land, and whom the good fairies had taken pity on, were there, busy cleaning up the rock pools and mending the broken sea-weed, and keeping all under the sea all clean and neat.

But I wish Tom had given up all his naughty tricks and left off tormenting dumb animals now that he had plenty of playfellows to

amuse him. The other children warned him, and said, "Take care what you are at – Mrs. Bedonebyasyoudid is coming." But Tom never heeded them, till one Friday morning early, Mrs. Bedonebyasyoudid came indeed.

A very tremendous lady she was. She had on a black bonnet, and a black shawl, and no crinoline at all; and a pair of large green spectacles, and a great hooked nose, hooked so much that the bridge of it stood quite up above her eyebrows; and under the arm she carried a great birch-rod. Indeed, she was so ugly that Tom was tempted to make faces at her: but did not; for he did not admire the look of the birch-rod.

And she looked at the children one by one, and seemed very much pleased with them, though she never asked them one question about how they were behaving; and then began giving them all sorts of nice sea-things – sea-cakes, sea-apples, sea-oranges, sea-bullseyes, sea-toffee; and to the very best of all she gave sea-ices, made out of sea-cows' cream, which never melt under water.

Now little Tom watched all these sweet things given away till his mouth watered; for he hoped his turn would come at last; and so it did. The lady called him up, and held out her fingers with something

in them, and popped it into his mouth; and lo and behold, it was a nasty, cold, hard pebble.

"You are a very cruel woman," said he, whimpering.

"And you are a very cruel boy, putting pebbles into the sea-anemones' mouths, to make them fancy they have caught a good dinner. As you did to them, so I must do to you. And it is no use trying to hide anything from me, for I always know."

And though her voice was stern the expression on her face was curious and very, very sweet, and there came such a quiet, tender, hopeful smile on it that for a moment she did not look ugly at all.

"You thought me very ugly just now," she said to Tom, guessing his thought, "and I shall be, till people behave themselves as they ought to do. And then I shall grow as handsome as my sister, who is the loveliest fairy in the world, and her name is Mrs. Doasyouwouldbedoneby. So she begins where I end, and I begin where she ends, Now, Tom, every Friday I come down here, and call up all who have ill-used little children, and serve them as they have served the children."

She allowed Tom to stay and watch her do it. He saw careless nursemaids and cruel schoolmasters suffer just the same pains and take just the same horrible physic that they had given to the children in their care. They were beaten and scolded, and had pins stuck into them, and wore tight boots that pinched dreadfully. Their ears were boxed, their heads thumped with rulers, and they were given lines to learn.

Then she said good-bye to Tom, and told him to be a good boy, and then, when her sister came on Sunday, perhaps she would take notice of him and teach him how to behave.

Tom was a very good boy all Saturday, and when Sunday morning came, sure enough, Mrs. Doasyouwouldbedoneby came too, and all the children clapped their hands for joy.

Tom looked at her, and he saw that she had the sweetest, kindest, tenderest, funniest, merriest face he had ever seen, or wanted to see. She was as tall as her sister, but instead of being gnarly and horny like her, she was the most soft, cuddly and delicious creature who ever nursed a baby. When the children saw her they all caught hold of her, and pulled her down till she sat on a stone, and then they all climbed and clung round her, cuddling and kissing. But she pushed some of them away and gave Tom the very best place in her arms, because he was a new baby.

"Don't go away," said little Tom. "This is so nice. I never had anyone to cuddle me before."

The fairy sang them all a beautiful song, and before she went away she made him promise that he would never torment the sea-beasts again.

Tom kept his word, because she was so pretty and cuddled him so delightfully; but he was not so true to Mrs. Bedonebyasyoudid, for he watched her on her visits to find out where she kept the sweet things she gave the babies; and when he had discovered them in a beautiful mother-of-pearl cabinet away in a deep crack of the rocks, he stole and ate a great many.

And all the while, close behind him, stood Mrs. Bedonebyasyoudid.

But when she came again on the Friday she said nothing, but gave him his share like all the rest; and he could not bear the sweets, but took them in spite of himself.

And when Mrs. Doasyouwouldbedoneby came on Sunday she said:

"I should like to cuddle you, Tom, but I cannot. You are so horny and prickly." And Tom looked at himself; and he was all over prickles, just like a sea-egg. Nobody would play with him all that week, and he was so miserable that when the ugly fairy came he burst out crying and confessed what he had done.

She did not scold.

"I will forgive you, my little man," she said. "I always forgive every one the moment they tell me the truth of their own accord. And I think it is time for you to go to school. So I shall fetch you a school-mistress, who will teach you how to get rid of your prickles."

When the fairy brought her, she was the most beautiful little girl that ever was seen. She looked at Tom and Tom looked at her, and she taught Tom every day in the week. Only on Sundays she always went away home, and the kind fairy took her place. And before she had taught Tom many Sundays, his prickles had vanished quite away.

'Dear me!" said the little girl. "Why, I know you now. You are the very same little chimney-sweep who came into my bedroom."

"And you are the little white lady whom I saw in bed!"cried Tom.

They told each other all their adventures since then. And then they both set to work at their lessons again, and liked them so well that they went on till seven full years were past and gone.

But all the while Tom had one thing on his mind – where little Ellie went when she went home on Sundays. To a very beautiful place, she said, but she could not describe it. That only made Tom more anxious to go there, and he asked Mrs. Bedonebyasyoudid if he might.

"Those who go there," she said gravely, "must go first where they do not like, and help somebody they do not like. Ellie did this when she came to teach you against her will and you were all over ugly prickles." And Mrs. Doasyouwouldbedoneby gave him just the same answer in just the same words.

In the end Tom was so cross with Ellie because she could not explain to him where she went on Sunday that the fairy sent her away home, and Tom missed her terribly.

Mrs. Bedonebyasyoudid took the sobbing boy on her knee, and told him how he had been in the nursery long enough, and must go out now and see the world, if he intended ever to be a man; and how he must go all alone by himself, and gain his own experience. Then she fetched Ellie back for a moment to say good-bye to Tom.

"And now," he said bravely, "I am ready to be off, if it is to the world's end."

"But you must go farther than the world's end," said the fairy,"and find Mr. Grimes, for he is at the Other-End-of-Nowhere. You must go to Shiny Wall, and through the white gate that never was opened; and then you will come to Peacepool, and Mother Carey's Haven, where the good whales go when they die. And there Mother Carey will tell you the way to the Other-End-of-Nowhere, and there you will find Mr. Grimes."

Then Tom shook hands with Ellie and set off.

Tom did not know the way to Shiny Wall, but the fairy had said he must find out for himself. So he asked all the beasts in the sea and all the birds in the air, but none of them knew. For why? He was still too far down south.

So he swam northward, day after day, till at last he met the King of the Herrings, with a sprat in his mouth for a cigar, and asked him the way to Shiny Wall. So he bolted his sprat head foremost and said:

"If I were you, young gentleman, I should go to the All-alone-stone and ask the last of the Gairfowl."

Tom asked his way to her, and the King of the Herrings told him very kindly. And away Tom went for seven days and seven nights due north-west, till he came to a great codbank. And there he saw the last of the Gairfowl, standing up on the All-alone-stone, all alone. And a very grand old lady she was, full three feet high, and bolt upright, like some old Highland chieftainess.

Tom came up to her very humbly, made his bow, and asked if she knew the way to Shiny Wall.

She was a very talkative old lady, was the Gairfowl, and told him long stories which he would rather not have waited to hear; and in the end, getting impatient, he asked her his question again.

"Oh, you must go, my little dear – you must go. Let me see – I am sure – that is – really, my poor old brains are getting quite puzzled. Do you know, my little dear, I am afraid, if you want to know, you must ask some of those vulgar birds about, for I have quite forgotten."

And the poor old Gairfowl began to cry tears of pure oil; and Tom was quite sorry for her; and for himself too, for he was at his wits' end whom to ask.

But by there came a flock of petrels, who are Mother Carey's own chickens. They flitted along like a flock of black swallows, and hopped and skipped from wave to wave, lifting up their little feet behind them so daintily, and whistling to each other so tenderly, that Tom fell in love with them at once, and called them to know the way to Shiny Wall.

"Shiny Wall? Do you want Shiny Wall? Then come with us, and we will show you. We are Mother Carey's own chickens, and she sends us out over all the seas, to show the good birds the way home."

Tom was delighted, and swam off to them, after he had made his bow to the Gairfowl. And he swam with them north-eastward through a great storm, and they found a poor little dog that was saved from a wrecked ship; and the dog followed Tom the whole way to the Other-End-of-Nowhere.

Presently they handed Tom over to a whole flock of molly-mocks, jolly birds who promised to take him to Mother Carey. At last they came to the edge of the great ice-pack, and could see Shiny Wall looming beyond it. The great floes of ice looked terribly dangerous, and many wrecks lay among them; but the good mollys took Tom and his dog up, and flew with them safe over the pack, and set them down at the foot of Shiny Wall.

Tom dived under the great white gate that never was opened yet,

and went on in black darkness at the bottom of the sea for a whole week; but at last he got out in the light to the top of the water, and saw the pool where the good whales go. And a very large pool it was, miles and miles across, guarded by the ice-fairies who drive away the storms and clouds from Peacepool and the happy, sleepy whales that lie there.

Tom swam up to the nearest whale and asked the way to Mother Carey.

"There she sits in the middle," said the whale, and pointed to one peaked iceberg. "That's Mother Carey, making old beasts into new all the year round."

Tom went on to the iceberg, wondering. And when he came near to it, it took the form of the grandest old lady he had ever seen, sitting on a white marble throne. And from the foot of the throne there swam away millions of newborn creatures – Mother Carey's children, whom she makes out of the sea-water all day long.

Tom told her his errand and asked the way to the Other-End-of-Nowhere.

"Your dog knows the way well enough. And, of course, as the dog will always go behind you, you must go the whole way backwards. If you look behind you and keep your eyes on the dog, you will see the way before you as plainly as if you saw it in a looking-glass."

And so it happened to Tom. He found it much slower work to go backwards than to go forwards, but he was such a little dogged brick of an English boy that he never turned his head round once all the way from Peacepool to the Other-End-of-Nowhere.

If I were to tell you of the nine hundred and ninety wonderful things that befell Tom on the remainder of his journey, this story would never end. So I will only say that at last, after innumerable adventures, he came to a queer big building, where he had a strange fancy that he might find Mr. Grimes. There he met three or four people who, when they came nearer, were nothing else than policemen's truncheons, running along without arms or legs.

One of them led him to the great iron door of the prison, and there they inquired for Mr. Grimes, from a tremendous old brass blunderbuss, who was the porter.

"Grimes is up chimney No. 345," said the blunderbuss. And so he was; for Tom was conducted along the leads by another truncheon, who said that Grimes was the most hardhearted fellow in his charge, till they came to chimney No. 345.

Out of the top of it, his head and shoulders just showing, stuck poor Mr. Grimes, so sooty and bleared and ugly that Tom could hardly bear to look at him. And in his mouth was a pipe; but it was not alight, though he was pulling at it with all his might.

"Attention, Mr. Grimes," said the truncheon; "here is a gentleman come to see you."

But Mr. Grimes only said bad words.

"Keep a civil tongue, and attend!" said the truncheon; and popped up just like Punch, hitting Grimes a great crack over the head with itself. He tried to get his hands out and rub the place, but he could not, for they were stuck fast in the chimney. Now he was forced to attend.

"Hey!" he said, "why, it's Tom! I suppose you have come here to laugh at me, you spiteful little atomy?"

Tom assured him he had not, but only wanted to help him.

"Can't I help you get out of this chimney?" he asked.

"No," interposed the truncheon. "He has come to the place where everybody must help themselves. His heart is so cold that it freezes other folks' kindness."

"Oh yes," said Grimes, "of course it's me. Did I ask to be set to sweep your foul chimneys? Did I ask to have lighted straw put under me to make me go up? Did I ask to stick fast in the very first chimney of all, because it was so shamefully clogged up with soot?"

"No," answered a solemn voice behind. "No more did Tom, when you behaved to him in the very same way."

It was Mrs. Bedonebyasyoudid.

"Oh, ma'am," said Tom, "don't think about me. That's all past and gone. But may I not help poor Mr. Grimes? Mayn't I try and get some of these bricks away, that he may move his arms?"

"You may try, of course," she said.

So Tom pulled and tugged at the bricks, but he could not move one. And then he tried to wipe Mr. Grimes's face, but the soot would not come off.

"You had best leave me alone," said Grimes. "You are a good-

natured, forgiving little chap, but you'd best be off. The hail's coming on soon, and it will beat the eyes out of your little head. It falls every evening here, and knocks me about like small shot."

"That hail will never come any more," said the strange lady. "I have told you before what it was. It was your mother's tears for you, her graceless son, who ran away years ago from her little school in Vendale. But she is gone to heaven now, and will weep no more for you."

Grimes began crying and blubbering like a great baby.

"My poor old mother! It's too late now. Foul I would be and foul I am, as an Irishwoman said to me once. It's all my own fault; but it's too late." And he cried so bitterly that Tom began crying too.

"Never too late," said the fairy, in such a strange, soft, new voice that Tom looked up at her; and she was so beautiful for the moment that Tom half fancied she was her sister.

No more was it too late. For, as poor Grimes cried and blubbered on, his own tears did what his mother's could not do, and Tom's could not do, and nobody's on earth could do for him; for they washed the soot off his face and off his clothes; and then they washed the mortar away from between the bricks, and the chimney crumbled down, and Grimes began to get out of it.

Up jumped the truncheon, and was going to hit him on the crown a tremendous thump, and drive him down like a cork into a bottle. But the strange lady put it aside.

Grimes looked up at her, and Tom looked up too; for suddenly

she was the Irishwoman who met them the day that they went together to Harthover.

"Take him away," said she to the truncheon. "Get him to sweep out the crater of Etna; but mind, if that crater gets choked again, and there is an earthquake in consequence, bring him to me and I shall investigate the case very severely."

So the truncheon marched off Mr. Grimes, and for aught I know he is sweeping the crater of Etna to this very day.

As for Tom, the fairy blindfolded him and took him home by the back stairs, which were very much shorter than the way he had come. And when she took the bandage away, there on a rock sat Ellie, looking for them.

"Oh, Miss Ellie," said he, "how you are grown!"

"Oh, Tom!" said she, "how you are grown too!"

And no wonder. They were both quite grown up – he into a tall man and she into a beautiful woman. They stood staring at each other for ever so long.

At last they heard the fairy say: "Attention, children. Are you never going to look at me again?"

They looked, and both of them cried out at once, "Oh, who are you, after all?"

"You are our dear Mrs. Doasyouwouldbedoneby,"

"No, you are good Mrs. Bedonebyasyoudid; but you are grown quite beautiful now!"

"To you," said the fairy. "But look again."

"You are Mother Carey," said Tom, in a very low, solemn voice.

"But you are grown quite young again."

"To you," said the fairy. "Look again."

"You are the Irishwoman who met me the day I went to Harthover!"

And when they looked she was neither of them, and yet all of them at once.

She turned to Ellie.

"You may take him home with you now on Sunday, Ellie. He has won his spurs in the great battle, and become fit to go with you and be a man; because he has done the thing he did not like."

And Tom's dog, you ask?

Oh, you may see him any clear night in July; for the old dog-star was so worn out by the last three hot summers that there have been no dog-days since; so that they had to take him down and put Tom's dog up in his place. Therefore, as new brooms sweep clean, we may hope for some warm weather this year. And that is the end of my story.

A SEA-SONG

A wet sheet and a flowing sea,
   A wind that follows fast
And fills the white and rustling sail
   And bends the gallant mast;
And bends the gallant mast, my boys,
   While like the eagle free
Away the good ship flies, and leaves
   Old England on the lee.

O for a soft and gentle wind!
   I heard a fair one cry:
But give to me the snoring breeze
   And white waves heaving high;
And white waves heaving high, my lads,
   The good ship tight and free –
The world of waters is our home,
   And merry men are we.

There's tempest in yon hornèd moon,
   And lightning in yon cloud;
But hark the music, mariners!
   The wind is piping loud;
The wind is piping loud, my boys,
   The lightning flashes free –
While the hollow oak our palace is,
   Our heritage the sea.

The Man who wrote 'Don Quixote'

It seemed as though Miguel de Cervantes, the author of Don Quixote, was born under an unlucky star. He first saw light of day in 1547, the son of a poor surgeon. Miguel was a young man when, in search of adventure, he went to fight for his country against the Turks.

After five years of hard fighting, Miguel was given leave. His commanding officer gave him letters to the king, recommending Miguel for promotion. Unfortunately, he had scarcely put out to sea before his ship was captured by pirates. These vultures of the seas, upon reading the officer's letter to the king, thought that Miguel must be a very rich and important man. They demanded a huge ransom for his release. Meanwhile he was chained to an oar in a pirate ship and treated as a slave.

There followed five years of incredible hardship and brutality before Miguel was finally released when his family, gathering together every peseta they owned, at last managed to pay his ransom.

He was now thirty-three years of age. The rest of his life was spent in poverty, always in trouble for one reason or another, always fighting gallantly against his many misfortunes. He was fifty-five when, contemptuous of all the then very popular romances of brave knights in armour rescuing beautiful damsels in distress and fighting gigantic dragons and terrible ogres, he wrote the delightful adventures of Don Quixote.

Miguel set the world laughing with his great book but his bad luck never forsook him. He made little money out of his masterpiece and died in 1616, living on charity. No one knows where he lies buried but his hero, Don Quixote, will live forever.

DON QUIXOTE

In a certain village in La Mancha, in Spain, there lived in the sixteenth century one of those old-fashioned gentlemen, who are never without a lance upon a rack, an old shield, a lean horse and a greyhound. His family consisted of a housekeeper, a niece, and a man that served in the house and in the field, and could saddle a horse and handle the pruning hook. The master himself was nigh fifty years of age, hale and strong, lean-bodied and thin-faced, an early riser, and a lover of hunting. His surname was Quixada, that is, lantern-jaws.

When our gentleman had nothing to do, which was almost all the year round, he passed his time in reading books of knight-errantry, which he did with such application and delight that he left off his country sports, and even the care of his estate. He even sold many of his acres to purchase books of that kind. He used to dispute with the curate which was the best knight, and with the barber and others. In fact, he gave himself up to reading romances about knighthood, reading on all day till it was night, and at night till it was day.

His imagination became crowded with enchantments, quarrels, battles, challenges, wounds, complaints, love passages and abundance of absurd possibilities, so that all the fables and fantastical tales which he read seemed to him to be now as true as authentic histories.

Having lost his reason, there came to him the oddest fancy that ever entered into a madman's brain, to turn knight-errant and roam through the world, armed head to toe, and mounted on his steed in quest of adventures, thus imitating the lives of those knights about whom he had read.

The first thing he did was to scour a suit of armour that had belonged to his great-grandfather. Then he made himself a helmet, and covered it with thin plates of iron to make it sword-proof. He next went to view his horse, whose bones stuck out but who appeared to him to be a finer horse than that of any of the knights he had read about. He thought for four days what to call his horse, and decided on the name, Rozinante. Then, having chosen a name for his horse, he began to think of one for himself. After long thought he at last decided to call himself Don Quixote.

Don Quixote saw that nothing more was wanted but a lady on whom he might bestow the empire of his heart. Near the place where he lived dwelt a good-looking country girl. Her name was Aldonza Lorenzo, and it was she whom he chose as the lady of his heart, the lady for whom he would seek adventure and knightly honour. But as with himself and his steed, he must needs find her a new name which would sound like the name of a lady of quality or a princess, and at last he resolved to call her Dulcinea del Toboso.

One morning, early, in the middle of July, with all the secrecy imaginable, Don Quixote armed himself, mounted Rozinante, and sallied out into the fields, wonderfully pleased to see how easily he had succeeded in the beginning of his enterprise. He had not gone far when a terrible thought alarmed him, that the honour of knighthood had not yet been conferred upon him, and therefore, according to the laws of chivalry, he determined that he would be dubbed a knight by the first he should meet, after the example of several whom he had read about. He rode calmly on, leaving it to his horse to go which way he pleased, firmly believing that in this consisted the very spirit of adventure.

He travelled almost all that day without meeting any adventure, and towards the evening he and his horse being heartily tired and almost famished, Don Quixote looked about him, in hopes to discover some castle, or at least some shepherd's cottage, there to repose and refresh himself. And at last near the road on which he was travelling, he espied an inn, a most welcome sight to his longing eyes. By the inn door stood two young women.

No sooner had Don Quixote seen the inn than he imagined it to be a castle, and the two country girls to be lovely dames taking the air at the castle gate. It chanced at that moment that a swineherd, who was in a field close by tending a drove of hogs, blew his horn, as was his custom, to call them together. Don Quixote immediately imagined that this was the sound of a trumpet to announce to the castle inmates the arrival of a knight, and with great joy in his breast at being so recognised, he rode up to the inn.

The two girls would have fled, but Don Quixote lifted up his vizor and in a gentle voice spoke to them.

"Fly not, ladies, nor fear any discourtesy; for the order of knighthood, which I profess, forbids my offering any injury to anyone, much less to damsels of such exalted rank as your appearance denotes you to be."

Naturally the two girls stared at Don Quixote in astonishment and could not help laughing at the extraordinary figure he presented.

"Modesty is akin to beauty," he cried, feeling offended. "And excessive laughter, proceeding from a slight cause, is folly. I have no wish but to do you service."

This language, which they did not understand, only made them laugh the more, and increased the displeasure Don Quixote felt. He would probably have shown it in a less civil way if the innkeeper had not appeared. Don Quixote looked upon him as the governor of the

castle and addressed him as Signor Castellano. The innkeeper civilly
asked Don Quixote to alight, and soon the latter was sitting down to
supper with the rest of the people in the inn. He talked to all of them
in the language of chivalry, calling the ladies the ladies of the castle,
and telling them stories of knighthood, much to their astonishment,
for they were, after all, only ignorant country folk.

As soon as he had finished his supper, to the astonishment of the
innkeeper, he knelt at the latter's feet and cried:

"I will never rise from this place, most valorous knight, till you have graciously granted me a boon, that you will be pleased to bestow the honour of knighthood upon me. This night I will watch my armour in the chapel of your castle, and on the morrow I shall be duly qualified to seek out adventures in every corner of the universe, to help the distressed, according to the laws of chivalry and the missions of knights-errant."

The innkeeper quickly perceived that Don Quixote was mad, and to ease the mind of his visitor agreed to fall in with his wishes and knight him. And in the morning he saddled his Rozinante and sallied forth, convinced now that he was a true knight, and fit for any adventure which might befall him.

Our knight had not gone above two miles when he discovered a

company of people riding towards him, who proved to be merchants of Toledo, going to buy silks. They were six in all, besides four servants on horseback, and three muleteers on foot. The knight no sooner perceived them but he imagined this to be some new adventure; so fixing himself in his stirrups, couching his lance, and covering his breast with his shield, he posted himself in the middle of the road. As soon as they came within hearing he cried haughtily: "Hold! Let no man hope to pass further, unless he acknowledge and confess there is not in the universe a more beautiful damsel than the empress of La Mancha, the peerless Dulcinea del Toboso."

The merchants laughed at him, and this made Don Quixote angry. With his lance couched he ran full tilt on Rozinante at one of the merchants, and if it had not been that his steed stumbled and threw its rider, the merchant might have paid dearly for his raillery. So encumbered was Don Quixote with his lance and shield and his spurs and the weight of his rusty armour, that he was unable to get up for a while. One of the servants snatched at the lance, and having broken it in pieces, beat the fallen knight vigorously and then left him in the road and went on after the rest of the company, who had laughed till their sides ached at Don Quixote's predicament and discomfort.

It was not until a countryman came by that our knight was able to get on his feet. He was so bruised and battered that he could only obtain relief by taking off his helmet and armour and placing them on the back of Rozinante, while he rode on the donkey belonging to the countryman who trudged by his side in amazement at the extravagant words which Don Quixote used to explain his adventure.

Bruised and battered and sore, Don Quixote returned to his own village at nightfall and was there met by the curate and barber. The newly returned knight was put to bed, all the time telling in terms of chivalry his adventures. The curate and barber were certain that he had been driven mad by constantly reading his books on knight-errantry, and they resolved, with the consent of the unhappy man's niece, that the best thing to do was to burn all the books on which he had spent so much money that he had become almost poverty-stricken. And that night all the books which had caused so much trouble to the brain of Don Quixote were burned in the yard of his house.

The priest warned all those who knew about this to tell Don Quixote, when he had recovered from his beating and bruises, that an evil sorcerer had carried away all his books.

"Would it not be better now to stay at home," asked his niece, "than to ramble round the world?"

"My dear niece," answered Don Quixote, "how little dost thee know of the matter!"

Despite all the entreaties of his friends and his niece, Don Quixote decided to set out again on his adventures. And this time he resolved to take with him a companion as his squire. For this purpose he picked on a countryman of weak intellect, whose name was Sancho Panza, and by dint of many fair promises, induced him to follow him. And one night, fifteen days after his first return, Don Quixote and Sancho Panza, on their steeds, stole off out of the village in search of fresh adventures.

By break of day they were far from the village and they jogged along, while Don Quixote discoursed on famous knights and deeds of chivalry. As he was thus discoursing they came to a wide plain, and on it were some thirty to forty windmills.

"Fortune," cried Don Quixote, as soon as he saw the windmills, "directs our affairs better than we could have wished; look yonder, Sancho, there are at least thirty outrageous giants, whom I intend to encounter; and having deprived them of life, we will begin to enrich ourselves with their spoils; for they are lawful prizes – and the extirpation of that cursed brood will be an acceptable service to heaven."

"What giants?" quoth Sancho Panza.

"Those whom thou seest yonder," answered Don Quixote, "with their long-extended arms."

"Pray look better, sir," quoth Sancho. "Those things yonder are not giants, but windmills, and the arms are their sails, which being whirled about by the wind, make the mill go."

"'Tis a sign," cried Don Quixote, "thou art but little acquainted with adventures! I tell thee they are giants; and therefore if thou art afraid, go aside and say thy prayers, for I am resolved to engage in combat with them all."

This said, he clapped spurs to his horse, without giving ear to his squire, who bawled out to him, and assured him that they were windmills, and not giants. But he was so fully possessed with an idea to the contrary, that he did not so much as hear his squire, nor was he sensible of what they were, although he was already very near them.

"Stand, cowards!" he cried as loudly as he could. "Stand your ground, ignoble creatures, and fly not basely from a single knight, who dares encounter you all."

At the same time the wind rising, the mill sails began to move, which, when Don Quixote spied, he cried: "Base miscreants, though you move your arms you shall pay for your arrogance."

He most devoutly recommended himself to his Lady Dulcinea, imploring her assistance in this perilous adventure, and so covering himself with his shield and couching his lance, he rushed with Rozinante's utmost speed upon the first windmill he could come at and, running his lance into the sail, the wind whirled it about with such swiftness that the rapidity of the motion presently broke the lance into shivers and hurled away both knight and horse along with it, till down they fell, rolling a good way off. Sancho Panza ran as fast as he could to help his master, whom he found lying and not able to stir.

"Did I not give your worship fair warning?" he cried. "Did not I tell you they were windmills, and that nobody could think otherwise, unless he had also windmills in his head?"

"Peace, friend Sancho," replied Don Quixote. "I am truly persuaded that the sorcerer, who carried away my books, has transformed these giants into windmills, to deprive me of the honour of the victory; such is his wicked malice against me; but in the end he shall not prevail against the edge of my sword."

"So let it be," replied Sancho.

And heaving him up again upon his legs, once more the knight mounted poor Rozinante, who was half-disjointed with his fall.

The two continued on their way, and that night they passed under some trees, from one of which Don Quixote tore a withered branch, which he used for a fresh lance, after fixing on it the spear of his broken lance. The following afternoon, as they were riding along and talking, they spied coming towards them two monks mounted on two handsome mules. After them came a coach, with four or five men on horseback and two muleteers on foot.

Scarce had the Don perceived the monks, who were not of the same company, though they went the same way, then he cried to his squire: "Either I am deceived, or this will prove the most famous adventure that ever was known, for without all question those two black things that move towards us must be wicked wizards that are carrying away by force some princess in that coach, and 'tis my duty to prevent so great an injury."

In the coach, of a truth, was a lady who was going to Seville.

"I fear me this will prove a worse job than the windmills," quoth Sancho. "These are monks, and the coach must belong to some travel-ler. Take warning, sir, and do not be led away a second time."

"I have already told thee, Sancho," replied Don Quixote, "thou art miserably ignorant in matters of adventures; what I say is true, and thou shalt find it so presently."

This said, he spurred on his horse, and posted himself in the middle of the road. And when the two monks came within hearing, he immediately cried out in a loud and haughty tone: "Release those high-born princesses whom you are violently carrying away in the coach, or else prepare to meet with instant death, as the just punish-ment for your deeds."

The monks stopped, no less astonished at the figure than the expres-sions of Don Quixote.

"Sir Knight," they cried, "we are no such persons as you are pleased to term us, but religious men that travel about our own affairs, and are wholly ignorant whether or no there are any princesses carried away by force in that coach."

"I am not to be deceived," replied Don Quixote. "I know you well enough, you villains."

Immediately, without waiting their reply, he set spurs to Rozinante, and ran so furiously, with his lance couched, against the first monk, that if he had not wisely flung himself on the ground, the knight would certainly have laid him dead, or greviously wounded. The other, observing this, clapped his heels to his mule's flanks, and sped over the plain as if he had been running a race with the wind.

Sancho no sooner saw the monk fall, but he leapt off his steed, and running to him, began to strip him immediately; but the two muleteers, who waited on the monks, came up to him, and asked what he was doing. Sancho told them that the property of the fallen man belonged to him as lawful plunder, being the spoils won in battle by his lord and master, Don Quixote.

The fellows seeing Don Quixote at a good distance away by the side of the coach, both fell upon poor Sancho, threw him down, tore his beard from his chin, trampled on him, and left him in the road without breath or motion. In the meanwhile the monk, scared out of his wits and as pale as a ghost, got upon his mule as fast as he could, and spurred after his friend, who stayed for him at a distance, and they both rode away, not wishing to see the end of the adventure.

Don Quixote was all this while talking with the lady in the coach.

"Lady," cried he, "that you may not be at a loss for the name of your deliverer, know I am called Don Quixote de la Mancha, by profession a knight-errant and adventurer, champion of that peerless beauty, Donna Dulcinea del Toboso; nor do I desire any other recompense for the service I have done you, but that you return to Toboso to present yourself to that lady, and let her know what I have done to purchase your deliverance."

As Don Quixote refused to let the coach continue unless the lady within it gave that promise, one of her escort drew his sword and attacked Don Quixote. There ensued a furious battle, and remarkable to relate, the knight soon had the other at his mercy. In his blind rage he would have killed him had not the lady in the coach prayed Don Quixote to spare his life, which he did on her giving a solemn promise she would go to Toboso and see the fair Donna Dulcinea. And not till then did Don Quixote ride on, well satisfied by his adventure, but followed by a very dissatisfied and bruised Sancho Panza.

The knight and his squire went on their way and a little while after perceived a great and thick cloud of dust coming towards them. Upon which Don Quixote cried: "This is the day, Sancho, that shall manifest the good fortune in store for me. Seest thou that cloud of dust, Sancho? It is raised by a mighty army of several nations, who are on the march this way."

"If so, there must be two armies," said Sancho, "for here, on this side, arises just such another cloud of dust."

Don Quixote turned, and seeing that it really was so, he rejoiced exceedingly, taking if for granted there were two armies coming to engage in the midst of that spacious plain, for at all hours and moments his imagination was full of the battles, enchantments, adventures, combats and challenges detailed in his favourite books.

Now the cloud of dust he saw was raised by two great flocks of sheep going the same road from different parts, and as the dust concealed them until they came near, and Don Quixote affirmed so positively that they were armies, Sancho began to believe it, and said: "Sir, what then must we do?"

"What," replied Don Quixote, "but favour and assist the weaker side?"

But Sancho could now hear the bleating of the sheep and lambs and pointed out to his mad master that they were two flocks approaching, and not two armies.

"Thy fears, Sancho," said Don Quixote, "prevent thee from hearing or seeing aright, and if thou art so much afraid, retire and leave me alone. For, with my single arm, I shall ensure victory to that side which I favour with my assistance."

With these words he rushed into the midst of the sheep, as courageously and intrepidly as if in good earnest he was engaging his mortal

enemies. The herdsmen and shepherds called out to him to stop, and
seeing that he took no notice, began to hurl stones at him. One struck
him with such violence that he believed himself either slain or sorely
wounded, and another hit him on the mouth and knocked several
teeth out, and he fell from his horse to the ground. The shepherds
believed they had killed him and in haste gathered their scattered
flock together, and their dead sheep, which amounted to seven, and
marched off without further inquiry.

Sancho Panza, who had remained in the background, now ran
forward.

"Did I not beg you, Signor Don Quixote," he cried, "to come back?
For those you went to attack were a flock of sheep, and not an army
of men."

"How easily," replied Don Quixote, "can that thief of a sorcerer, my enemy, transform things or make them invisible!"

"Sir," said Sancho, "you would make a better preacher than a knight-errant. Let us begone hence, and endeavour to get a lodging for the night."

Night overtook them without their finding a lodging; and the worst of it was, they were famished with hunger, as Sancho had lost the wallets containing their provisions. The night was very dark and suddenly advancing towards them they saw a great number of lights, Sancho was frightened, but Don Quixote cried: "I beseech thee, Sancho, to be of good courage; for experience shall give thee sufficient proof of mine."

"I will, if it please God," answered Sancho, but when he saw a great number of persons clothed in white approaching, his teeth began to chatter. It was, as a matter of fact, a procession of mourners, but Don Quixote's lively imagination instantly believed the bier was a litter whereon was carried some knight sorely wounded or slain, whom it was his duty to avenge.

"Ho, halt," he cried, as the procession approached, "and give me an account of who ye are."

"We are in haste," answered one of the mourners, "and we cannot stay."

He tried to pass, but Don Quixote seized the bridle of the mule he was riding. The mule shied and threw its rider to the ground and a servant came up and began to abuse Don Quixote. The latter, in his madness, immediately started attacking the mourners, who, being unarmed and hampered by their mourning garments, fled in all directions. On one of the mules following the procession Sancho Panza meanwhile had discovered a store of food, and so famished was he that he took a quantity of it for himself and his master, who, he was now convinced, was a man of great valour.

One of the servants, in the procession, who had been unable to fly, asked in trembling tones, of Sancho, who his master was.

"He is Don Quixote de la Mancha, otherwise called the Knight of the Rueful Countenance," replied Sancho.

And from that day forward Don Quixote always added that title to his name.

One day when Don Quixote and Sancho Panza were travelling along the road, they saw coming towards them about a dozen men on foot, strung, like beads in a row, by the necks, in a great iron chain, and all handcuffed. There came also with them two men on horseback and two men on foot, those on horseback armed with firelocks and those on foot with pikes and swords.

"This is a chain of galley slaves," cried Sancho. "Persons forced by the king to the galleys."

"How, forcèd do you say?" quoth Don Quixote. "Is it possible the king should force anybody?"

"They are condemned by their crimes and forced to serve the king," cried Sancho.

"Then," said his master, "here the execution of my office takes place, which is to aid all who are in need of help."

After some argument with one of the guards, Don Quixote attacked him so suddenly that he was knocked from his horse and in the confusion which followed, the galley slaves released themselves from their chain and overwhelmed the remaining three guards. Don Quixote was immensely pleased with his exploit and he commanded the released men to make the best speed they could to Toboso, and there relate to the Lady Dulcinea del Toboso how they had been rescued by Don Quixote de la Mancha, the Knight of the Rueful Countenance.

"This we cannot possibly do," declared one of the released men. "We must scatter in different directions or we shall be recaptured."

This so enraged Don Quixote that he threatened to chain them again, and the galley slaves thereupon rained a shower of stones upon him and then fled.

"Sancho," cried Don Quixote. "I have always heard it said that to do good to the vulgar is to throw water into the sea."

The two met with many more extraordinary adventures, but at last there came the final adventure of all.

In this adventure, a friend, disguised as a Knight of the White Moon, challenged Don Quixote to mortal combat. It was hoped that if Don Quixote could be defeated in combat with another supposed knight, that he would return home and there be looked after by his friends.

The Knight of the White Moon had no difficulty in overthrowing the Knight of the Rueful Countenance, and as he lay upon the ground expecting to be killed, he heard the Knight of the White Moon say: "Return home for a year and I am satisfied."

Don Quixote was very dejected at his defeat, never thinking that it had been by a friend of his from his own village, who had inflicted it out of kindness, knowing that Don Quixote would keep his word and return home and be looked after. Nothing that Sancho could say could cheer him up and he grew more and more melancholy every day.

"I shall only retire for a year, Sancho," he said at last, "and then resume my honourable profession."

Shortly after he and the faithful Sancho Panza had returned to their native village, Don Quixote, who was getting old, was seized with a violent fever. During the time he was ill his good friends, the curate and barber and others in the village visited him regularly, for they loved the old man in spite of his eccentricities. One day, he woke up after a sound sleep, and cried out in a loud voice: "Praised be the Almighty! My mind is now clear of the shadows which the continual reading of those books of knight-errantry had cast over my understanding. Send for my honest friend the curate, and the barber. I intend to make my confession and my will. My end approaches."

With them came Sancho Panza, to whom Don Quixote left all he could to make up for what the squire had suffered.

"Pardon me, my friend," he said, "that I have brought upon thee the scandal of madness, by drawing thee into my own errors, and persuading thee that there have been, and still are, knights-errant in the world."

"Woe is me," cried Sancho, all in tears. "Do not die this time, but even take my counsel, and live on many years."

But three days later after he had made his will and recovered his sanity, Don Quixote died.

My Love
is like a
Red Red Rose

My love is like a red red rose
That's newly sprung in June:
My love is like the melodie
That's sweetly play'd in tune.

So fair art thou, my bonnie lass,
So deep in love am I:
And I will love thee still, my dear,
Till a' the seas gang dry.

Till a' the seas gang dry, my dear,
And the rocks melt wi' the sun:
And I will love thee still, my dear,
While the sands o' life shall run.

And fare theè weel, my only love,
And fare thee weel awhile!
And I will come again, my love,
Tho' it were ten thousand mile.

PERSEUS

This story of Perseus, hero of one of the most famous Greek legends, appears in Charles Kingsley's book entitled The Heroes. *Here is a condensation of the tale using Kingsley's own words.*

Once upon a time there were two princes who were twins. Their names were Acrisius and Proetus and they lived in the pleasant vale of Argos, in Hellas. They had fruitful meadows and vineyards, sheep and oxen and great herds of horses, yet they were wretched because they were jealous of each other.

When they grew up, each tried to take the other's share of the kingdom. So first Acrisius drove out Proetus; and he went across the seas and brought home a foreign princess for his wife and foreign warriors to help him, who were called Cyclopes; and drove out Acrisius in his turn. They fought a long while until the quarrel was settled.

Acrisius took Argos and one half of the land and Proetus took Tiryns and the other half. Proetus and his Cyclopes built around

332

Tiryns great walls of unhewn stone.

But there came a prophet to that hard-hearted Acrisius and said: "Because you have sinned against your kindred, by your kindred you shall be punished. Your daughter Danae shall bear a son and by that son's hands you shall die. So the Gods, have ordained, and it will surely come to pass."

At that Acrisius was very much afraid. He had been cruel to his family and instead of repenting and being kind to them, he went on to be more cruel than ever.

He shut up Danae in a cavern underground, lined with brass, so that no one might come near her. So he fancied himself more cunning than the Gods; but you will see presently if he escaped them.

In time Danae bore a son; so beautiful a babe that any but King Acrisius would have had pity on it. But he had no pity; for he took Danae and her babe down to the seashore and put them into a great chest and thrust them out into the sea.

The north-west wind blew freshly out of the blue mountains, down the pleasant vale of Argos and away and out to sea. And out to sea before it floated the mother and her babe, while all who watched them wept, save that cruel father, King Acrisius.

For two days and two nights the chest floated on. After a while, Danae was awakened suddenly, for the chest was jarring and grinding and the air was full of sound. Over her head were mighty cliffs, all red in the setting sun; around her, rocks and breakers and flying flakes of foam. Terrified, she shrieked aloud for help.

Over the rocks came a tall stately man, carrying a trident for spearing fish and over his shoulder was a casting-net. Danae could see that he was no common man by his stature and walk, and by the two servants who came behind him, carrying baskets for his fish.

Laying aside his trident and skilfully casting his net over the chest, he drew it safe upon a ledge. Taking Danae's hand he asked: "What strange chance has brought you to this island in so frail a ship? Surely you are a king's daughter, and this boy more than mortal?"

As he spoke he pointed to the babe, for its face shone like the morning star. But Danae held down her head and cried.

"Tell me to what land I have come," she sobbed.

"This isle is called Seriphos," he replied. "I am the brother of Polydectes the king; men call me Dictys the netter." Danae then told him her sad story.

When she had finished, Dictys said "I have no children. You shall be a daughter to me and my wife and this babe shall be our grandchild."

So Danae was comforted and went home with Dictys, the good fisherman, to live with him and his wife till fifteen years were past.

The babe grew to be a tall lad and a sailor and went on many voyages after merchandise to the islands round. His mother called him Perseus; but all the people in Seriphos said that he was not the son of mortal man and called him the son of Zeus, the king of the Immortals. For though he was but fifteen, he was taller by a head than any man in the island; and he was the most skilful of all in

running and wrestling and boxing, and in throwing the quoit and the javelin, and in rowing with the oar and in playing on the harp, and in all which befits a man. He was brave and truthful, gentle and courteous, for Dictys had trained him well.

Dictys' brother, Polydectes, was king of the island but, unlike Dictys, was greedy, cunning and cruel. When he saw Danae, at first he wanted to marry her, but Danae refused, caring for no one except Perseus.

While Perseus was away at sea, Polydectes took Danae away from Dictys, saying: "If you will not be my wife, you shall be my slave."

So Danae had to fetch water from the well, grind in the mill, and wear a heavy chain because she refused to marry him.

Unaware of what had happened to his mother, Perseus had arrived on the island of Samos. While the ship was loading, he fell asleep and had a strange dream.

It was quite the strangest dream that Perseus had ever had in his life. There came to him a lady. On her head was a helmet and in her hand a spear. Over her shoulder hung a goat-skin, which bore up a mighty shield of brass polished like a mirror.

Her clear grey eyes looked through him, as if she knew all that he had ever thought or longed for.

"Perseus, you must do an errand for me," she told him.

Trembling, Perseus asked "Who are you and how do you know my name?"

"I am Pallas Athene: I know all men's hearts and from the souls of clay, I turn away. But to the manful I give a might more than man's. These are the heroes, the sons of the Immortals. I drive them forth that they might fight the enemies of Gods and men. Tell me, Perseus, which of these two sorts of men seem to you more blest?"

Perseus answered boldly: "Better to die on the chance of winning a noble name than to live at ease like the sheep and die unloved and unrenowned."

The strange lady laughed and held up her shield. "See here, Perseus; dare you face such a monster as this and slay it, that I may place its head on this shield?"

In the mirror of the shield there appeared a face, and as Perseus looked on it his blood ran cold. It was the face of a beautiful woman; but her cheeks were pale as death, and her brows were knit with everlasting pain, and her lips were thin and bitter like a snake's; and instead of hair, vipers wreathed about her temples, and shot out their forked tongues; while round her head were folded wings like an eagle's, and upon her bosom claws of brass. Then he said: "If there

336

is anything so fierce and foul on the earth, it were a noble deed to
kill it. Where can I find the monster? Tell me, so that I may go and
seek it out."

"Not yet; you are too young and unskilled," replied the strange
lady, "for this is Medusa the Gorgon, mother of a monstrous brood.
Return home and do the work that awaits you there before I can
think you worthy to go in search of the Gorgon."

Then slowly the vision began to fade and he stirred in his sleep.

Perseus awoke from his dream, but day and night he saw before
him that dreadful woman with vipers writhing around her head. So
he returned home to Seriphos and was furious to learn that Polydectes
had made his mother a slave.

He went in search of his mother and found her at a stone hand-mill,
weeping. He kissed her and bade her follow him, but before they
could leave, an enraged Polydectes arrived.

Perseus flew on him as the mastiff flies on the boar.

"Villain and tyrant!" he cried. "Is this your respect for the Gods,
and thy mercy to strangers and widows? You shall die!"

Because he had no sword he caught up the stone hand-mill, and
lifted it to dash out Polydectes' brains, while his mother clung to him,

shrieking: "Oh, my son, we are strangers and helpless in the land: if you kill the king the people will fall on us and we shall both die."

Dictys, who had come in, entreated: "Remember he is my brother. I trained you as my own son. Spare him for my sake."

Perseus lowered his hand; and Polydectes, who had been trembling like a coward, because he knew he was in the wrong, let Perseus and his mother pass.

Perseus took his mother to the temple of Athene, for there she would be safe, and not even Polydectes would dare to drag her away from the altar. Daily, Perseus, Dictys and his wife visited her. Polydectes, not being able to get what he wanted by force, cast about in his wicked heart how he might get it by cunning.

Now he was sure that he could never get back Danae so long as Perseus was on the island; so he made a plot to rid himself of him. First he pretended to have forgiven Perseus, and to have forgotten Danae; so that for a while; all went as smoothly as ever.

Next he proclaimed a great feast, so that all who were invited, including Perseus, might do him homage as their king. As was the custom, each guest brought a present – except Perseus – who, being but a poor sailor, had nothing to bring. Too ashamed to go before

the king without a gift, he stood at the door watching the rich men go in, proudly carrying their presents.

His face grew very red as they pointed to him and whispered: "What has that foundling to give?"

This was what Polydectes wanted. He had Perseus brought in and asked scornfully before them all "Where is your present?"

As Perseus blushed and stammered, everyone laughed and openly jeered.

Perseus grew mad with shame and, hardly knowing, what he said, he boasted: "I'll bring a nobler gift than all of yours!"

When asked what it would be, he rashly answered, "The head of the Gorgon!" At which Polydectes laughed loudest of all.

"You have promised to bring me the Gorgon's head? Then never appear again on this island without it," cried Polydectes, glad to be so easily rid of Perseus.

Down to the cliffs went Perseus and prayed: "Pallas Athene, was my dream true? Shall I slay the Gorgon?" Three times he called on her before a small white cloud, as bright as silver, came out of the endless blue.

As it parted, Pallas Athene appeared and beside her was a young man whose eyes were like sparks of fire. He had a scimitar of diamond, all of one clear precious stone, and on his feet were golden sandals, from the heels of which grew living wings.

They looked upon Perseus keenly, and yet they never moved their
eyes; and they came up the cliff towards him more swiftly than the
sea-gull, and yet they never moved their feet, nor did the breeze stir
the robes about their limbs. Perseus fell down and worshipped, for
he knew that they were more than man.

But Athene stood before him and spoke gently, and bid him have
no fear. Then –

"Think well before you attempt to brave Medusa the Gorgon," she
said. "This deed requires a seven-year journey from which you cannot
turn back. If your heart fails you, you must die in the Unshapen
Land, where no man will ever find your bones."

But even this prospect could not deter Perseus, who begged the
Goddess to tell him where he could find the Gorgon.

"You must go northward," she said, "to the country of the Hyper-boreans, till you find the three Grey Sisters, who have but one eye and one tooth between them. Ask them the way to the Nymphs, who dance about the golden tree to the west. They will tell you the way to the Gorgon that you may slay her, my enemy, the mother of monstrous beasts, she whose scales are of iron and brass."

Then Athene went on "Her eyes are so terrible that whosoever looks on them is turned to stone. But bring me Medusa's head."

"How am I to escape her eyes?" asked Perseus. "Will she not freeze me too into stone?"

"You shall take this polished shield," said Athene, "and when you come near her look not at her herself, but at her image in the brass; so you may strike her safely. And when you have struck off her head, wrap it, with your face turned away, in the folds of the goat-skin on which the shield hangs. So you will bring it safely back to me, and win yourself renown, and a place among the heroes who feast with the Immortals upon the peak where no winds blow."

Then Perseus said "But how shall I cross the seas without a ship? And who will show me the way? And when I find her, how shall I slay her, if her scales be iron and brass?"

Then the young man spoke: "These sandals of mine will bear you across the seas, and over hill and dale like a bird, as they bear me all day long; for I am Hermes, the messenger of the Immortals who dwell on Mount Olympus. This sword will kill the Gorgon, for it is divine, and needs no second stroke. Put them on, Perseus, and go!"

So Perseus girded on the sandals and the sword.

And Athene cried "Now leap from the cliff and be gone. Leap and trust in the armour of the Immortals."

Perseus leaped and instead of falling, he floated and stood, and ran along the sky; and the sandals led him northward. The winged sandals bore him each day a seven-days' journey till he reached the Unshapen Land and the edge of everlasting night. There he found the three Grey Sisters on a log of driftwood by the shore of the freezing sea. Their hair was frosted and they sat passing their one eye from one to the other.

Perseus told them: "The rulers of Olympus have sent me to you to ask the way to the Gorgon."

One sister asked: "Who is this rash and insolent man who pushes unbidden into our world?"

Said another: "Give me the eye that I may see him."

And another said: "Give me the tooth that I may bite him."

When Perseus saw what he was up against, he watched closely as they groped for the eye between themselves. He held out his hand until one of them, thinking it was the hand of her sister, gave him the eye. Perseus sprang back and laughed.

"Cruel and proud old women, I have your eye; and I will throw it into the sea unless you tell me the path to the Gorgon," he cried.

The sisters wept, chattered and scolded, but in vain.

At last they told him.

"Go southward to Atlas the Giant, who holds heaven and earth apart. Ask his daughters, the Hesperides, the way from there." Only then did Perseus give them back their eye.

At once they fell asleep and were turned into icebergs. Now, forever they float, weeping whenever they meet the sun and the warm south wind. But Perseus flew on into the sun, leaving the snow and ice behind.

At last he saw far away a mighty mountain, rose-red in the setting sun. When he landed, he found valleys and waterfalls; trees, strange ferns and flowers – but no sign of man. Hearing sweet voices singing, he knew he had come to the garden of the Nymphs.

These were the daughters of the Evening Star, who sang and danced around the charmed tree, which bent under its golden fruit. When they saw Perseus, they stopped and asked: "Are you Heracles the mighty, come to rob our garden and carry off our golden fruit?"

Then Perseus explained why he had come. But the Nymphs did not know the way to the Gorgon and took him to see their uncle, the Giant Atlas, who told them: "This youth can never come near the Gorgon unless he has the hat of darkness, whose wearer cannot be seen."

Then cried Perseus, "Where is that hat, that I may find it?"

But the giant smiled. "No living mortal can find that hat, for it lies in the depths of Hades, in the regions of the dead. But my nieces are immortal, and they will fetch it for you, if you will promise me one thing and keep your faith."

Then Perseus promised; and the giant said, "When you come back with the head of Medusa, you shall show me the beautiful horror, that I may lose my feeling and my breathing, and become a stone for ever; for it is weary labour for me to hold the heavens and the earth apart."

Perseus promised and the eldest of the Nymphs went down, and into a dark cavern among the cliffs, out of which came smoke and thunder, for it was one of the mouths of Hell.

And Perseus and the Nymphs sat down seven days, and waited trembling, till the Nymph came up again; and her face was pale, and her eyes dazzled with the light, for she had been long in the dreary darkness; but in her hand was the magic hat.

Then all the Nymphs kissed Perseus, but he was only impatient to be gone. And at last they put the hat upon his head, and he vanished from their sight.

Perseus went on boldly, past many an ugly sight, far away into the heart of the Unshapen Land, beyond the streams of Ocean, to the isles where no ship cruises, where is neither night nor day, where nothing is in its right place, and nothing has a name; till he heard the rustle of the Gorgons' wings and saw the glitter of their brazen talons;

and then he knew it was time to halt, lest Medusa should turn him into stone.

He remembered Athene's words. He rose aloft in the air and held the mirror of the shield above his head, and looked up into it that he might see all that was below him.

And he saw the three Gorgons sleeping, as huge as elephants. He knew that they could not see him, because the hat of darkness hid him; and yet he trembled as he sank down near them, so terrible were those brazen claws.

Two of the Gorgons were sleeping heavily; but Medusa tossed to and fro restlessly, and as she tossed Perseus pitied her, she looked so fair and sad. Her plumage was like the rainbow, and her face was like the face of a nymph, only her eyebrows were knit, and her lips clenched, and her long neck gleamed so white in the mirror that Perseus had not the heart to strike, and said "Ah, that it had been either of her sisters!"

But as he looked, from among her tresses the vipers' heads awoke and peeped up with their bright dry eyes, and showed their fangs and hissed; and Medusa, as she tossed, threw back her wings and showed

her brazen claws; and Perseus saw that, for all her beauty, she was as foul and venomous as the rest.

Looking steadfastly into the mirror, Perseus boldly struck once at the Medusa with the sword of Hermes. Then without looking at it, he wrapped the head in the goatskin Athene had provided and sprang into the air aloft.

Then Medusa's sisters awoke and took to the air with a fearful howl, flapping their wings like eagles. Perseus trembled and cried aloud: "Bear me well now, brave sandals, for the hounds of death are at my heels."

On rushed the two foul sisters while the wind rattled hoarse in their wings.

And well the brave sandals bore Perseus, aloft through cloud and sunshine, across the shoreless sea; and fast followed the hounds of death, as the roar of their wings came down the wind; but the sandals were too swift, even for Gorgons, and by nightfall they were far behind, two black specks in the southern sky, till the sun sank and he saw them no more.

Then he came again to Atlas, and the garden of the Nymphs; and when the giant heard him coming, he groaned, and said, "Fulfil thy promise to me." Then Perseus held up to him the Gorgon's head,

and he had rest from all his toil; for he became a crag of stone, which sleeps forever far above the clouds.

Then Perseus thanked the Nymphs, and asked them, "By what road shall I go homeward again?"

And they wept and cried, "Go home no more, but stay and play with us, the lonely maidens."

But he refused, and they told him his road, and said, "Take with you this magic fruit, which, if you eat once, you will not hunger for seven days. For you must go eastward and eastward ever, over waste and desert, with shingle, and rock, and sand."

Then they kissed Perseus, and wept over him, and he went on, away and out over the sea. He flitted on, across the desert: over rock-ledges, and banks of shingle, and level wastes of sand. But now came down a mighty wind, and swept him back toward the desert. Seven days he strove against the storms. If he had not been of the Immortals, he would have perished; but his life was strong within him, because it was more than man's.

In desperation, he prayed aloud to the Goddess Athene, crying: "I have brought the Gorgon's head at thy bidding; wilt thou leave me here to die of drought; dost thou now desert me?"

Miraculously he suddenly heard the sound of running water and saw before him a streamlet that sparkled and wandered among rocks and date trees and grass. With joy he ate, drank and finally slept.

When he awoke, he felt sure the Gods willed him to undertake another act of bravery. So he flew on to the hills, which heaved like a bubbling cauldron before the wrath of King Poseidon, shaker of the earth.

Chained to the rocks below, he saw a beautiful girl whose blue-black hair streamed in the breeze. Now and then she looked up and cried aloud, but did not see Perseus because he wore the hat of darkness which made him invisible to her.

She was frightened when Perseus, after lifting his hat of darkness, flashed into her sight. Then she said: "I am the victim of the Sea-Gods, who will slay you if you dare to set me free."

But Perseus said "I carry the weapons of the Immortals. Let the Sea-Gods measure their strength against mine!"

"I am Andromeda," said the girl, as Perseus cut through her chains. "I am here for sea-monster's food because my mother once boasted I was fairer than Altergatis, the Queen of the Fishes, who was so angry she sent the floods. Afterwards a monster was bred of the slime who must now devour me."

But Perseus only laughed and said: "I have fought with worse than a sea-monster. Led by the Lords of Olympus, I slew the Gorgon. With their help, I will slay this monster, with that same Gorgon's head. Hide your eyes when I leave, lest the sight of it turns you to stone."

But terrified, Andromeda pointed out to sea and shrieked. "There he comes, with the sunrise as promised. Now I must die! Go!"

"Promise me," said Perseus, "that if I slay this beast, you will be my wife, and come back with me to my kingdom of Argos, for I am a king's heir." This Andromeda promised.

As Perseus took to the air he saw below him the monster and heard the water gurgling in and out of his wide jaws. At the sight of Andromeda, the beast shot forward to take his prey.

Then down from the height of the air fell Perseus like a shooting star; down to the crests of the waves, while Andromeda hid her face as he shouted; and then there was silence for a while.

At last she looked up trembling, and saw Perseus springing toward her; and instead of the monster a long black rock, with the sea rippling quietly round it.

Who then so proud as Perseus, as he leapt back to the rock, and lifted his fair Andromeda in his arms and flew to where her father King Cepheus and his Queen were awaiting their daughter's end.

They received their daughter back again as one alive from the dead. Then King Cepheus said "Hero of the Hellens, stay with me and be my son-in-law, and I will give you half my kingdom."

"I will be your son-in-law," said Perseus, "but of your kingdom I will have none, for I long after the pleasant land of Greece, and my mother waits for me at home."

They made a great wedding-feast, which lasted seven whole days, and who so happy as Perseus and Andromeda?

A year later, Perseus and Andromeda set sail for Perseus' island home of Seriphos. On landing he was greeted by his mother, Danae,

and Dictys, his foster-father. Then Perseus went up to Polydectes' hall to fulfil his promise. Polydectes sat at the table-head with all his nobles feasting and drinking the blood-red wine.

After seven years, Perseus stood like a wild bull in his pride but Polydectes knew him and cried aloud "Ah, foundling! Have you found it more easy to promise than to fulfil?"

Said Perseus "Those whom the Gods help, fulfil their promises. Behold, the Gorgon's head!" As the king and his guests tried to rise, they turned to stone.

Perseus then sailed in search of his grandfather, King Acrisius. He found Acrisius in exile in the country of a wild people called the Pelasgi. All kinds of games were being held in the town of Larissa.

Perseus did not tell his name, but went up to the games unknown; for he said, "If I carry away the prize in the games, my grandfather's heart will be softened toward me."

So he threw off his helmet, and his cuirass and stood among the youths of Larissa, while all wondered at him, and said, "Who is this young stranger who stands like a wild bull in his pride?"

And when the games began they wondered still more; for Perseus was the best man at all the running, and leaping, and wrestling, and throwing the javelin; and he won four crown coins; and took them, and then said to himself, "There is a fifth crown yet to be won for hurling the quoits: I will win that, and lay all the crowns upon the knees of my grandfather."

Then he took the quoits and hurled them, five fathoms beyond all the others. But a gust of wind came and carried a quoit aside, and far beyond the rest; and it fell on the foot of Acrisius, and he swooned away with the pain.

Perseus ran up to him; but when they lifted the old man up he was dead, for his life was slow and feeble.

Then Perseus wept a long while for his grandfather. At last he rose and called to all the people aloud, and said: "The Gods are true, and what they have ordained must be. I am Perseus, the grandson of this dead man, the far-famed slayer of the Gorgon."

Then he told them how the prophecy had declared that he should kill his grandfather, and all the story of his life. Then Perseus went to the temple, and was purified from the guilt of the death, because he had done it unknowingly.

Then he went home to Argos, and reigned there well with fair Andromeda; and they had four sons and three daughters, and died in a good old age.

The Prince
and the Pauper

The famous American humorist Samuel Langhorne Clemens is better known by his pen-name of Mark Twain. He spent his boyhood in a little town on the banks of the River Mississippi and it was this early experience that provided the background to his well-known stories of Tom Sawyer *and* Huckleberry Finn. *Mark Twain turned his genius easily to tales of Old England and two of these books are very popular, both having been filmed on more than one occasion. They are* A Connecticut Yankee at the Court of King Arthur *and* The Prince and the Pauper. *The latter tale is about two look-alikes – one, the young Prince Edward of Wales, the other a poor urchin, Tom Canty. Here are the first three chapters as written by Mark Twain.*

CHAPTER ONE

The Birth of the Prince and the Pauper

In the ancient city of London, on a certain autumn day in the second quarter of the sixteenth century, a boy was born to a poor family of the name of Canty, who did not want him. On the same day another English child was born to a rich family of the name of Tudor, who did want him. All England wanted him too. England had so longed for him, and hoped for him, and prayed God for him, that, now that he was really come, the people went nearly mad for joy. Mere acquaintances hugged and kissed each other and cried. Everybody took a holiday, and high and low, rich and poor, feasted and danced and sang, and got very mellow: and they kept this up for days and nights together. By day, London was a sight to see, with gay banners waving from every balcony and house-top, and splendid pageants marching along. By night, it was again a sight to see, with its great bonfires at every corner, and its troops of revellers making merry around them. There was no talk in all England but of the new baby, Edward Tudor, Prince of Wales, who lay lapped in silks and satins, unconscious of all this fuss, and not knowing that great lords and ladies were tending him and watching over him – and not caring, either. But there was no talk about the other baby, Tom Canty, lapped in his poor rags, except among the family of paupers whom he had just come to trouble with his presence.

CHAPTER TWO

Tom's Early Life

Let us skip a number of years.

London was fifteen hundred years old, and was a great town – for that day. It had a hundred thousand inhabitants – some think double as many. The streets were very narrow, and crooked, and dirty, especially in the part where Tom Canty lived, which was not far from London Bridge. The houses were of wood, with the second storey projecting over the first, and the third sticking its elbows out beyond the second. The higher the houses grew, the broader they grew. They

were skeletons of strong criss-cross beams, with solid material between, coated with plaster. The beams were painted red or blue or black, according to the owner's taste, and this gave the houses a very picturesque look. The windows were small, glazed with little diamond-shape panes, and they opened outward, on hinges, like doors.

The house which Tom's father lived in was up a foul little pocket called Offal Court, out of Pudding Lane. It was small, decayed, and rickety, but it was packed full of wretchedly poor families. Canty's tribe occupied a room on the third floor. The mother and father had a sort of bedstead in the corner; but Tom, his grandmother, and his two sisters, Bet and Nan, were not restricted – they had all the floor to themselves, and might sleep where they chose. There were the remains of a blanket or two, and some bundles of ancient and dirty straw, but these could not rightly be called beds, for they were not organized; they were kicked into a general pile, mornings, and selections made from the mass at night, for service.

Bet and Nan were fifteen years old – twins. They were good-hearted girls, unclean, clothed in rags, and profoundly ignorant. Their mother was like them. But the father and the grandmother were a couple of fiends. They got drunk whenever they could; then they fought each other or anybody else who came in the way; they cursed and swore always, drunk or sober; John Canty was a thief, and his mother a beggar. They made beggars of the children, but failed to make thieves of them. Among, but not of, the dreadful rabble that inhabited the house was a good old priest whom the king had turned out of house and home with a pension of a few farthings, and he used to get the children aside and teach them right ways secretly. Father Andrew also taught Tom a little Latin, and how to read and write; and would have done the same with the girls, but they were afraid of the jeers of their friends, who could not have endured such a queer accomplishment in them.

All Offal Court was just such another hive as Canty's house. Drunkenness, riot, and brawling were the order there, every night and nearly all night long. Broken heads were as common as hunger in that place. Yet little Tom was not unhappy. He had a hard time of it, but did not know it. It was the sort of time that all the Offal Court boys had, therefore he supposed it was the correct and comfortable thing. When he came home empty-handed at night, he knew his father would curse him and thrash him first, and that when he was done the awful grandmother would do it all over again and improve on it; and that away in the night his starving mother would slip to him stealthily

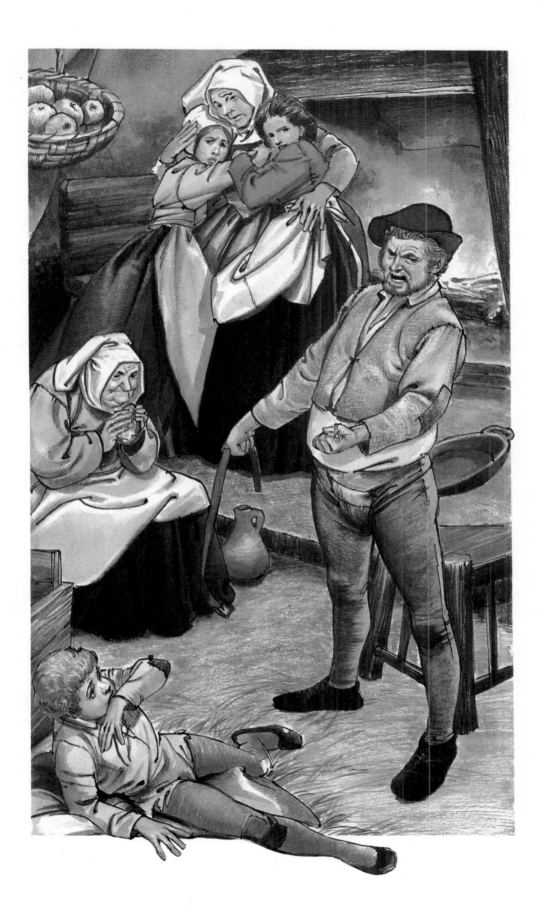

with any miserable scrap or crust she had been able to save for him by going hungry herself, notwithstanding she was often caught in that sort of treason and soundly beaten for it by her husband.

No, Tom's life went along well enough, especially in summer. He only begged just enough to save himself, for the laws against mendicancy were stringent, and the penalties heavy; so he put in a good deal of his time listening to good Father Andrew's charming old tales and legends about giants and fairies, dwarfs, and genii, and enchanted castles, and gorgeous kings and princes. His head grew to be full of these wonderful things, and many a night as he lay in the dark on his scant and offensive straw, tired, hungry, smarting from a thrashing, he unleashed his imagination and soon forgot his aches and pains in delicious picturings to himself of the charmed life of a petted prince in a regal palace. One desire came in time to haunt him day and night, it was to see a real prince, with his own eyes. He spoke of it once to some of his Offal Court comrades; but they jeered him and scoffed him so unmercifully that he was glad to keep his dream to himself after that.

He often read the priest's old books and got him to explain and enlarge upon them. His dreamings and readings worked certain changes in him, by and by. His dream-people were so fine that he grew to lament his shabby clothing and his dirt, and to wish to be clean and better clad. He went on playing in the mud just the same, and enjoying it, too; but instead of splashing around in the Thames solely for the fun of it, he began to find an added value in it because of the washings and cleansings it afforded.

Tom could always find something going on around the Maypole in Cheapside, and at the fairs; and now and then he and the rest of London had a chance to see a military parade when some famous unfortunate was carried prisoner to the Tower, by land or boat. One summer's day he saw poor Anne Askew and three men burned at the stake in Smithfield, and heard an ex-bishop preach a sermon to them which did not interest him. Yes, Tom's life was varied and pleasant enough, on the whole.

By and by Tom's reading and dreaming about princely life wrought such a strong effect upon him that he began to *act* the prince, unconsciously. His speech and manners became curiously ceremonious and courtly, to the vast admiration and amusement of his intimates. But Tom's influence among these young people began to grow, now, day by day; and in time he came to be looked up to, by them, with a sort of wondering awe, as a superior being. He seemed to know so much!

and he could do and say such marvellous things! and withal, he was so deep and wise! Tom's remarks, and Tom's performances, were reported by the boys to their elders; and these, also, presently began to discuss Tom Canty, and to regard him as a most gifted and extra-ordinary creature. Full-grown people brought their perplexities to Tom for solution, and were often astonished at the wit and wisdom of his decisions. In fact he was become a hero to all who knew him except his own family – these, only, saw nothing in him.

Privately, after a while, Tom organized a royal court! He was the prince; his special comrades were guards, chamberlains, equerries, lords and ladies in waiting, and the royal family. Daily the mock prince was received with elaborate ceremonials borrowed by Tom from his romantic readings; daily the great affairs of the mimic king-dom were discussed in the royal council, and daily his mimic highness issued decrees to his imaginary armies, navies, and viceroyalties.

After which, he would go forth in his rags and beg a few farthings, eat his poor crust, take his customary cuffs and abuse, and then stretch himself upon his handful of foul straw, and resume his empty grand-eurs in his dreams.

And still his desire to look just once upon a real prince, in the flesh, grew upon him, day by day, and week by week, until at last it absorbed all other desires, and became the one passion of his life.

One January day, on his usual begging tour, he tramped despon-dently up and down the region round about Mincing Lane and Little East Cheap, hour after hour, barefooted and cold, looking in at cook-shop windows and longing for the dreadful pork-pies and other deadly inventions displayed there – for to him these were dainties fit for the angels; that is, judging by the smell, they were – for it had never been his good luck to own and eat one. There was a cold drizzle of rain; the atmosphere was murky; it was a melancholy day. At night Tom reached home so wet and tired and hungry that it was not possible for his father and grandmother to observe his forlorn cond-ition and not be moved – after their fashion; wherefore they gave him a cuffing at once and sent him to bed. For a long time his pain and hunger, and the swearing and fighting going on in the building, kept him awake; but at last his thoughts drifted away to far, romantic lands, and he fell asleep in the company of jewelled and gilded prin-celings who lived in vast palaces, and had servants salaaming before them or flying to execute their orders. And then, as usual, he dreamed that *he* was a princeling himself.

All night long the glories of his royal estate shone upon him; he

moved among great lords and ladies, in a blaze of light, breathing perfumes, drinking in delicious music, and answering the reverent obeisances of the glittering throng as it parted to make way for him, with here a smile, and there a nod of his princely head.

And when he awoke in the morning and looked upon the wretchedness about him, his dream had had its usual effect – it had intensified the sordidness of his surroundings a thousandfold. Then came bitterness, and heartbreak, and tears.

CHAPTER THREE
Tom's Meeting with the Prince

om got up hungry, and sauntered hungry away, but with his thoughts busy with the shadowy splendours of his night's dreams. He wandered here and there in the city, hardly noticing where he was going, or what was happening around him. People jostled him and some gave him rough speech; but it was all lost on the musing boy. By and by he found himself at Temple Bar, the farthest from home he had ever travelled in that direction. He stopped and considered a moment, then fell into his imaginings again, and passed on outside the walls of London. The Strand had ceased to be a country road then, and regarded itself as a street, but by a strained construction; for, though there was a tolerably compact row of houses on one side of it, there were only some scattering of great buildings on the other, these being palaces of rich nobles, with ample and beautiful grounds stretching to the river – grounds that are now closely packed with

grim acres of brick and stone.

Tom discovered Charing Village presently, and rested himself at the beautiful cross built there by a bereaved king of earlier days; then idled down a quiet, lovely road, past the great cardinal's stately palace, toward a far more mighty and majestic palace beyond – Westminster. Tom stared in glad wonder at the vast pile of masonry, the widespreading wings, the frowning bastions and turrets, the huge stone gateway, with its gilded bars and its magnificent array of colossal granite lions, and the other signs and symbols of English royalty. Was the desire of his soul to be satisfied at last? Here, indeed, was a king's palace. Might he not hope to see a prince now – a prince of flesh and blood, if Heaven were willing?

At each side of the gilded gate stood a living statue, that is to say, an erect and stately and motionless man-at-arms, clad from head to heel in shining steel armour. At a respectful distance were many country-folk, and people from the city, waiting for any chance glimpse of royalty that might offer. Splendid carriages, with splendid people in them and splendid servants outside, were arriving and departing by several other noble gateways that pierced the royal enclosure.

Poor little Tom, in his rags, approached, and was moving slowly and timidly past the sentinels, with a beating heart and a rising hope, when all at once he caught sight through the golden bars of a spectacle that almost made him shout for joy. Within was a comely boy, tanned and brown with sturdy outdoor sports and exercises, whose clothing was all of lovely silks and satins, shining with jewels; at his hip a little jewelled sword and dagger; dainty buskins on his feet, with red heels; and on his head a jaunty crimson cap, with drooping plumes fastened with a great sparkling gem. Several gorgeous gentlemen stood near – his servants, without a doubt. Oh! he was a prince – a prince, a living prince, a real prince – without the shadow of a question; and the prayer of the pauper boy's heart was answered at last.

Tom's breath came quick and short with excitement, and his eyes grew big with wonder and delight. Everything gave way in his mind instantly to one desire: that was to get close to the prince, and have a good, devouring look at him. Before he knew what he was about, he had his face against the gate-bars. The next instant one of the soldiers snatched him rudely away, and sent him spinning among the gaping crowd of country gawks and London idlers. The soldier said:

"Mind thy manners, thou young beggar!"

The crowd jeered and laughed; but the young prince sprang to the gate with his face flushed, and his eyes flashing with indignation, and cried out:

"How dar'st thou use a poor lad like that! How dar'st thou use the king my father's meanest subject so! Open the gates, and let him in!"

You should have seen that fickle crowd snatch off their hats then. You should have heard them cheer, and shout, "Long live the Prince of Wales!"

The soldiers presented arms with their halberds, opened the gates, and presented again as the little Prince of Poverty passed in, in his fluttering rags, to join hands with the Prince of Limitless Plenty.

Edward Tudor said:

"Thou lookest tired and hungry: thou'st been treated ill. Come with me."

Half a dozen attendants sprang forward to – I don't know what; interfere, no doubt. But they were waved aside with a royal gesture, and they stopped stock still where they were, like so many statues. Edward took Tom to a rich apartment in the palace, which he called his cabinet. By his command a repast was brought such as Tom had

never encountered before except in books. The prince, with princely delicacy and breeding, sent away the servants, so that his humble guest might not be embarrassed by their critical presence; then he sat near by, and asked questions while Tom ate.

"What is thy name, lad?"

"Tom Canty, an it please thee sir."

"'Tis an odd one. Where dost live?"

"In the city, please thee, sir. Offal Court, out of Pudding Lane."

"Offal Court! Truly, 'tis another odd one. Hast parents?"

"Parents have I, sir, and a granddam likewise that is but indifferently precious to me, God forgive me if it be offence to say it – also twin sisters, Nan and Bet."

"Then is thy granddam not overkind to thee, I take it?"

"Neither to any other is she, so please your worship. She hath a wicked heart, and worketh evil all her days."

"Doth she mistreat thee?"

"There be times that she stayeth her hand, being asleep or overcome with drink; but when she hath her judgment clear again, she maketh it up to me with goodly beatings."

A fierce look came into the little prince's eyes, and he cried out:

"What! Beatings?"

"Oh, indeed, yes, please you, sir."

"*Beatings*! – and thou so frail and little. Hark ye: before the night come, she shall hie her to the Tower. The king my father –"

"In sooth, you forget, sir, her low degree. The Tower is for the great alone."

"True, indeed. I had not thought of that. I will consider of her punishment. Is thy father kind to thee?"

"Not more than Grammer Canty, sir."

"Fathers be alike, mayhap. Mine hath not a doll's temper. He smiteth with a heavy hand, yet spareth me: he spareth me not always with his tongue, though, sooth to say. How doth thy mother use thee?"

"She is good, sir, and giveth me neither sorrow nor pain of any sort. And Nan and Bet are like to her in this."

"How old be these?"

"Fifteen, an it please you, sir."

"The Lady Elizabeth, my sister, is fourteen, and the Lady Jane Grey, my cousin, is of mine own age, and comely and gracious withal; but my sister the Lady Mary, with her gloomy mien and – Look you: do thy sisters forbid their servants to smile, lest the sin destroy their souls?"

"They? Oh, dost think, sir, that *they* have servants?"

The little prince contemplated the little pauper gravely a moment, then said:

"And prithee, why not? Who helpeth them undress at night? who attireth them when they rise?"

"None, sir. Wouldst have them take off their garment, and sleep without – like the beasts?"

"Their garment! Have they but one?"

"Ah, good your worship, what would they do with more? Truly they have not two bodies each."

"It is a quaint and marvellous thought! Thy pardon, I had not meant to laugh. But thy good Nan and thy Bet shall have raiment and lackeys enow, and that soon, too: my cofferer shall look to it. No, thank me not; 'tis nothing. Thou speakest well; thou hast an easy grace in it. Art learned?"

"I know not if I am or nor, sir. The good priest that is called Father Andrew taught me, of his kindness, from his books."

"Know'st thou the Latin?"

"But scantly, sir, I doubt."

"Learn it, lad: 'tis hard only at first. The Greek is harder; but neither these nor any tongues else, I think, are hard to the Lady Elizabeth and my cousin. Thou shouldst hear those damsels at it! But tell me of thy Offal Court. Hast thou a pleasant life there?"

"In truth, yes, so please you, sir, save when one is hungry. There be Punch-and-Judy shows, and monkeys – oh, such antic creatures! and so bravely dressed! – and there be plays wherein they that play do shout and fight till all are slain, and 'tis so fine to see, and costeth but a farthing – albeit 'tis main hard to get the farthing please your worship."

"Tell me more."

"We lads of Offal Court do strive against each other with the cudgel, like to the fashion of the 'prentices, sometimes."

The prince's eyes flashed. Said he:

"Marry, that would I not mislike. Tell me more."

"We strive in races, sir, to see who of us shall be fleetest."

"That would I like also. Speak on."

"In summer, sir we wade and swim in the canals and in the river, and each doth duck his neighbour, and spatter him with water, and dive and shout and tumble and –"

"'Twould be worth my father's kingdom but to enjoy it once! Prithee go on."

"We dance and sing about the Maypole in Cheapside; we play in the sand, each covering his neighbour up; and times we make mud pastry – oh, the lovely mud, it hath not its like for delightfulness in all the world! – we do fairly wallow in the mud, sir, saving your worship's presence."

"Oh, prithee, say no more, 'tis glorious! If that I could but clothe me in raiment like to thine, and strip my feet, and revel in the mud once, just once, with none to rebuke me or forbid, meseemeth I could forego the crown!"

"And if that I could clothe me once, sweet sir, as thou art clad – just once –"

"Oho, wouldst like it? Then so shall it be. Doff thy rags, and don these splendours, lad! It is a brief happiness, but will be not less keen for that. We will have it while we may, and change again before any come to molest."

A few minutes later the little Prince of Wales was garlanded with Tom's fluttering odds and ends, and the little Prince of Pauperdom was tricked out in the gaudy plumage of royalty. The two went and stood side by side before a great mirror, and lo, a miracle: there did not seem to have been any change made! They stared at each other, then at the glass, then at each other again. At last the puzzled princeling said:

"What dost thou make of this?"

"Ah, good your worship, require me not to answer. It is not meet that one of my degree should utter the thing."

"Then will *I* utter it. Thou hast the same hair, the same eyes, the same voice and manner, the same form and stature, the same face and countenance, that I bear. Fared we forth naked, there is none could say which was you, and which the Prince of Wales. And, now that I am clothed as thou wert clothed, it seemeth I should be able

the more nearly to feel as thou didst when the brute soldier – Hark ye, is not this a bruise upon your hand?"

"Yes; but it is a slight thing, and your worship knoweth that the poor man-at-arms –"

"Peace! It was a shameful thing and a cruel!" cried the little prince, stamping his bare foot. "If the king – Stir not a step till I come again! It is a command!"

In a moment he had snatched up and put away an article of national importance that lay upon a table, and was out at the door and flying through the palace grounds in his bannered rags, with a hot face and glowing eyes. As soon as he reached the great gate, he seized the bars, and tried to shake them, shouting:

"Open! Unbar the gates!"

The soldier that had maltreated Tom obeyed promptly; and as the prince burst through the portal, half smothered with royal wrath, the soldier fetched him a sounding box on the ear that sent him whirling to the roadway, and said:

"Take that, thou beggar's spawn, for what thou got'st me from his Highness!"

The crowd roared with laughter. The prince picked himself out of the mud, and made fiercely at the sentry, shouting:

"I am the Prince of Wales, my person is sacred; and thou shalt hang for laying thy hand upon me!"

The soldier brought his halberd to a present-arms and said mockingly:

"I salute your gracious Highness." Then angrily, "Be off, thou crazy rubbish!"

Here the jeering crowd closed around the poor little prince, and hustled him far down the road, hooting him, and shouting, "Way for his royal Highness! way for the Prince of Wales!"

Many adventures and misadventures lie ahead for both Tom and Edward, with the young prince having by far the worse time, as one would expect. He falls in and out of the hands of wicked John Canty, his one piece of good fortune being the friendship he forms with gallant swordsman Miles Hendon, the disinherited son of a baronet. Comes the day when the prince's father King Henry VIII dies and Edward, now King of England, is to be crowned. Tom Canty, well-nigh worried out of his wits with having to impersonate the real king, is on his way to Westminster for the coronation. The crown is just about to be placed on his head when Prince Edward steps forth from the crowd to claim his rightful inheritance. He proves his claim by revealing where he has hidden the Great Seal of England. Thus all ends happily with Tom returning to his old home with the young king's promise that he and his family will be honoured for the rest of their lives. Miles Hendon is created an earl while evil John Canty disappears and of him no more is ever heard.

Breathes There
The Man

Breathes there the man with soul so dead
Who never to himself hath said,
   This is my own, my native land!
Whose heart hath ne'er within him burned,
As home his footsteps he hath turned
   From wandering on a foreign strand?
If such there breathe, go, mark him well;
For him no minstrel raptures swell;
High though his titles, proud his name,
Boundless his wealth as wish can claim,
Despite those titles, power, and pelf,
The wretch, concentred all in self,
Living, shall forfeit fair renown,
And, doubly dying, shall go down
To the vile dust from whence he sprung,
Unwept, unhonoured, and unsung.

The Inchcape Rock

Off the east coast of Scotland at the entrance of the Firth of Tay and eleven miles from the city of Arbroath (Aberbrothok in the following poem) lies the dangerous Inchcape Rock. It is just below the surface of the sea, sometimes three metres below, at other times barely covered. It is not surprising, therefore, to learn that many ships have been wrecked on the Rock. It is said that the first bell was secured to the Rock by a certain Abbot of Arbroath and, moreover, that the Rock is haunted by the ghost of the Abbot and sundry other phantoms. A lighthouse was erected in 1811 to warn off unwary mariners. Robert Southey, the celebrated poet and friend of those other two pre-eminent poets Samuel Taylor Coleridge and William Wordsworth, was moved by the weird legends surrounding the Inchcape Rock to write these memorable lines.

No stir in the air, no stir in the sea,
The ship was as still as she could be;
Her sails from heaven received no motion,
Her keel was steady in the ocean.

Without either sign or sound of their shock,
The waves flowed over the Inchcape Rock;
So little they rose, so little they fell,
They did not move the Inchcape Bell.

The good old Abbot of Aberbrothok
Had placed that bell on the Inchcape Rock;
On a buoy in the storm it floated and swung
And over the waves its warning rung.

When the rock was hid by the surges' swell
The mariners heard the warning bell;
And then they knew the perilous rock,
And blest the Abbot of Aberbrothok.

The sun in heaven was shining gay,
All things were joyful on that day;
The sea birds screamed as they wheeled round,
And there was joyance in their sound.

The buoy of the Inchcape Rock was seen,
A darker speck on the ocean green;
Sir Ralph, the Rover, walked his deck,
And he fixed his eye on the darker speck.

He felt the cheering power of spring,
It made him whistle, it made him sing;
His heart was mirthful to excess,
But the Rover's mirth was wickedness.

His eye was on the Inchcape float;
Quoth he, "My men, put out the boat,
And row me to the Inchcape Rock,
And I'll plague the priest of Aberbrothok."

The boat is lowered, the boatmen row,
And to the Inchcape Rock they go;
Sir Ralph bent over from the boat,
And he cut the bell from the Inchcape float.

Down sank the bell, with a gurgling sound,
The bubbles rose and burst around;
Quoth Sir Ralph, "The next who come to the rock
Won't bless the Abbot of Aberbrothok."

Sir Ralph the Rover sailed away,
He scoured the seas for many a day;
And now, grown rich with plundered store,
He steers his course for Scotland's shore.

So thick a haze o'erspreads the sky
They cannot see the sun on high;
The wind hath blown a gale all day,
At evening it hath died away.

On the deck the Rover takes his stand,
So dark it is, they see no land.
Quoth Sir Ralph, "It will be lighter soon,
For there is the dawn of the rising moon."

"Canst hear," said one, "the breakers roar?
For methinks we should be near the shore;
Now where we are I cannot tell,
But I wish I could hear the Inchcape Bell."

They hear no sound, the swell is strong;
Though the wind hath fallen, they drift along,
Till the vessel strikes with a shivering shock,
Oh, Christ, it is the Inchcape Rock!

Sir Ralph, the Rover, tore his hair,
He curst himself in his despair;
The waves rush in on every side,
The ship is sinking beneath the tide.

But even in his dying fear
One dreadful sound could the Rover hear;
A sound as if with the Inchcape Bell
The fiends below were ringing his knell.

GOOD WIVES

The June roses over the porch were awake bright and early on the morning of Meg March's wedding to John Brooke. Quite flushed with excitement, they swung in the wind and the sunshine.

Meg looked very like a rose herself; for all that was best and sweetest in heart and soul seemed to bloom into her face that day, making it fair and tender, with a charm more beautiful than beauty. Neither silk, lace, nor orange flowers would she have. "I don't want to look strange or fixed up today," she said.

So she made her wedding gown herself, sewing into it the tender hopes and innocent romances of a girlish heart. Her sisters braided up her pretty hair, and the only ornaments she wore were the lilies of the valley, which "her John" liked best of all the flowers that grew.

Aunt March and a flock of cousins arrived, and "the party came in," as Beth used to say when a child. There was no bridal procession, but a sudden silence fell upon the room as Mr. March and the young pair took their places. Mother and sisters gathered close, as if loath to give up Meg; the fatherly voice broke more than once, which only seemed to make the service more beautiful and solemn; the bridegroom's hand trembled visibly, and no one heard his replies; but Meg looked straight up in her husband's eyes, and said, "I will!" with such tender trust in her own voice that her mother's heart rejoiced, and Aunt March sniffed audibly.

The minute she was fairly married, Meg cried, "The first kiss for Marmee!" and, turning, gave it with her heart on her lips. Everyone said something brilliant or tried to, which did just as well, for laughter is ready when hearts are light. There was a plentiful lunch of cake and fruit dressed with flowers. Then people strolled about through the house and garden.

The little new home was not far away, and the only bridal journey Meg had was the quiet walk with John from the old home to the new.

"Thank you all for my happy wedding day," she said, clinging to them all in turn as she said good-bye.

While Meg started housekeeping for her John, Beth helped at home as usual, and Amy divided her time between lessons in art and some rather comic attempts to impress the world with her importance, fortune suddenly smiled upon Jo and dropped a good luck penny in her path. For some time past the *Spread Eagle* had been paying her a dollar a column for her "rubbish," as Jo called her stories, but now a larger opportunity came her way.

Jo's writing came upon her in fits. Every few weeks she would shut herself up in her room, put on her scribbling suit, and fall "into a vortex," as she expressed it, writing away at her novel with all her heart and soul, for till that was finished she could find no peace. Her "scribbling suit" consisted of a black woollen pinafore on which she could wipe her pen at will, and a cap of the same material, adorned with a cheerful red bow into which she bundled her hair when the decks were cleared for action. This cap was a beacon to the inquiring eyes of her family, who during these periods kept their distance, merely popping in their heads semi occasionally to ask with interest, "Does genius burn, Jo?" They did not always venture even to ask this question, but took an observation of the cap and judged accordingly. If this expressive article of dress was drawn low upon the forehead, it was a sign that hard work was going on; in exciting moments it was pushed rakishly askew, and when despair seized the author it was plucked wholly off and cast upon the floor. At such times the intruder silently withdrew; and not until the red bow was seen gaily erect upon the gifted brow did anyone dare address Jo.

While the writing fit was on, sleep forsook her eyes, meals stood untasted, Laurie coaxed in vain for her to come out. Then in a week or two she emerged from her "vortex," hungry, sleepy, cross or despondent.

She was just recovering from one of these attacks when, at a lecture, she noticed a studious-looking lad absorbed in a pictorial newspaper. Jo examined the work of art nearest her, idly wondering what unfortuitous combination of circumstances needed the melodramatic illustration of an Indian in full war costume tumbling over a precipice with a wolf at his throat, while two infuriated young gentlemen, with unnaturally small feet and big eyes, were stabbing each other close by, and a dishevelled female was flying away in the background with her mouth wide open. Pausing to turn a page, the lad saw her looking, and, with boyish good nature, offered half his paper, saying bluntly, "Want to read it? That's a first-rate story."

Jo accepted it with a smile, for she had never outgrown her liking for lads, and soon found herself involved in the usual labyrinth of love, mystery and murder.

"Prime, isn't it?" asked the boy. "She makes a good living out of such stories, they say", and he pointed to the name of the writer, a woman.

Here the lecture began, but Jo heard very little of it, for she was deep in daydreams. The next day she fell to work to turn out a story on the same lines as the one she had read, to compete for a hundred-dollar prize which the newspaper was offering. She sent off the manuscript, without a word to anyone at home, and kept her secret for six long weeks.

She was just beginning to give up all hope, when a letter arrived which almost took her breath away; for on opening it a cheque for

a hundred dollars fell into her lap. For a minute she stared at it, then she read her letter and began to cry.

"Now Beth and Marmee must go to the seaside. That's what I tried for, and that's why I succeeded. Won't it be fun to see you come home plump and rosy again? Hurrah for Dr. Jo, who always cures her patients!"

To the seaside they went, after much discussion, and though Beth didn't come home as plump and rosy as could be desired, she was much better, while Mrs. March declared she felt ten years younger; so Jo was satisfied with the investment of her prize money, and fell to work with a cheery spirit, bent on earning more of those delightful cheques. She did earn several that year, and began to feel herself a power in the house; for by the magic of her pen, her "rubbish" turned into comforts for them all. "The Duke's Daughter" paid the butcher's bill, "A Phantom Hand" put down a new carpet, and the "Curse of the Coventrys" proved the blessing of the Marches in the way of groceries and gowns.

Little notice was taken of Jo's stories, but they found a market; and encouraged by this fact she wrote a novel. She submitted it with fear and trembling to three publishers, and at last disposed of it on condition she would cut it down one-third and omit all the parts she particularly admired.

Well, it was printed, and she got three hundred dollars for it; likewise plenty of praise and blame, both so much greater than she expected that it took her some time to recover from her bewilderment.

A year had rolled round since Meg's wedding, and at midsummer there came to her a new experience – the deepest and tenderest of a woman's life.

Laurie came sneaking into the kitchen of the Dovecote – as they all called the Brookes' little home – one Saturday, with an excited face, and was received with a clash of cymbals; for Hannah clapped her hands with a saucepan in one and the cover in the other.

"How's the little mamma? Where is everybody? Why didn't you tell me before I came home from college?" began Laurie in a loud whisper.

Just then Jo appeared, proudly bearing a flannel bundle laid forth upon a large pillow. Jo's face was very sober, but her eyes twinkled, and there was an odd sound in her voice of repressed emotion of some sort.

"Shut your eyes and hold out your arms," she said invitingly.

Laurie backed precipitately into a corner, and put his hands behind him with an imploring gesture: "No, thank you, I'd rather not. I shall drop it or smash it, as sure as fate."

"Then you shan't see your nevvy," said Jo decidedly, turning as if to go.

"I will, I will! only you must be responsible for damages"; and, obeying orders, Laurie heroically shut his eyes while something was put into his arms. A peal of laughter from Jo, Amy, Mrs. March, Hannah, and John caused him to open them the next minute, to find himself invested with two babies instead of one.

No wonder they laughed, for the expression on his face was droll enough to convulse a Quaker, as he stood and stared wildly from the unconscious innocents to the hilarious spectators, with such dismay that Jo sat down on the floor and screamed.

"Twins, by Jupiter!" was all he said for a minute; then, turning to the women with an appealing look that was comically piteous, he added, "Take 'em quick, somebody! I'm going to laugh, and I shall drop 'em."

John rescued his babies, and marched up and down with one on

each arm, as if already initiated into the mysteries of baby-tending, while Laurie laughed till the tears ran down his cheeks.

"It's the best joke of the season, isn't it? I wouldn't have you told, for I set my heart on surprising you, and I flatter myself I've done it," said Jo, when she got her breath.

"Boy and girl. Aren't they beauties?" said the proud papa.

"The boy's to be named John Laurence, and the girl Margaret, after mother and grandmother. We shall call her Daisy, so as not to have two Megs, and I suppose the mannie will be Jack, unless we find a better name," said Amy, with aunt-like interest.

"Name him Demijohn, and call him Demi for short," said Laurie.

"Daisy and Demi, just the thing! I *knew* Teddy would do it!" cried Jo.

Teddy certainly had done it that time, for the babies were Daisy and Demi to the end of the chapter.

A few days later Amy insisted on Jo going out to pay calls with her. There was nothing the older sister hated more than to dress in her best, behave with dignity and make polite conversation; so by the time they finished their round of visits with one to Aunt March

and Jo had made various blunders *en route*, she was feeling perverse and bad tempered.

They found Aunt Carrol with the old lady, both absorbed in some very interesting subject; but they dropped it as the girls came in, with a conscious look that betrayed that they had been talking about their nieces. Jo looked and felt cross; but Amy, who had virtuously done her duty and pleased everyone all the afternoon, was in a most angelic frame of mind, and both the aunts looked at her with affectionate approval. This was increased when Amy sweetly promised to help with a charity fair, while Jo ungraciously refused, because the Chesters, who were at the head of it, patronised her.

A week later a letter came from Aunt Carrol, and Mrs. March's face was illuminated to such a degree when she read it that Jo and Beth, who were with her, demanded what the glad tidings were.

"Aunt Carrol is going abroad next month and wants –"

"Me to go with her," burst in Jo rapturously.

"No, dear, not you; it's Amy."

"Oh, my tongue, my abominable tongue, why can't I learn to keep it quiet?" groaned Jo, remembering words which had been her undoing.

The young lady herself received the news as tidings of great joy, and began to pack her colours and pencils at once, leaving such trifles as clothes, money and passports to those less absorbed in visions of art than herself.

"It isn't a mere pleasure trip to me, girls," she said impressively. "It will decide my career; for if I have any genius, I shall find it out in Rome, and will do something to prove it."

The house was in a ferment till Amy was off. Jo bore up very well till the last flutter of blue ribbon vanished, then retired to her refuge, the garret, and cried till she couldn't cry any more. Amy likewise bore up stoutly till the gangway was about to be withdrawn; then she clung to Laurie, the last lingerer, saying with a sob: "Oh, take care of them for me!"

"I will, dear, I will; and if anything happens I'll come and comfort you," whispered Laurie, little dreaming that he would be called upon to keep his word.

As the weeks and months went by, Amy wrote bright letters, first from London, later from Paris and Heidelberg. Meanwhile, at home, quiet Beth, who never sought for attention as Amy did, occupied the thoughts of her mother and Jo. She seemed sad and depressed, unlike her usual cheerful self, and those who loved her could not get her to tell what was the matter.

One night Jo was just dropping off to sleep when the sound of a stifled sob made her fly to Beth's bedside with the anxious inquiry: "Is it the old pain, my precious?"

"No, it's a new one; and there's no cure." There Beth's voice gave way, and clinging to her sister she cried so despairingly that Jo was frightened. Jo comforted and petted her, but she did not tell her trouble.

That winter Jo was restless; her writing ceased to absorb her. Presently she suggested to her mother that she should go to New York for a few months.

"You know Mrs. Kirke wrote to you for some respectable young person to teach her children and sew when she's busy with her boardinghouse. My writing will be all the better for the change, and besides" – Jo looked up and Jo looked down, with sudden colour in her cheeks – "I'm afraid – Laurie is getting too fond of me."

"Then you don't care for him in the way it is evident he begins to care for you?" And Mrs. March looked anxious as she put the question.

"Mercy, no! I love the dear boy, as I always have, and am immensely proud of him; but as for anything more, it's out of the question."

"I'm glad of that, Jo."

"Why, please?"

"Because, dear, I don't think you suited to one another. As friends you are very happy, and your frequent quarrels soon blow over; but I fear you would both rebel if you were mated for life. You are too much alike and too fond of freedom, not to mention hot tempers and strong wills, to get on happily together, in a relationship which needs infinite patience and forebearance, as well as love."

"That's just the feeling I had, though I couldn't express it. I'm glad you think he is only beginning to care for me. It would trouble me sadly to make him unhappy."

It was soon arranged that Jo should go to New York for a time; Mrs. Kirke gladly accepted her. When Laurie said "Good-bye" he whispered significantly, "It won't do·a bit of good, Jo. My eye is on you; so mind what you do, or I'll come and bring you home."

"New York, *November*

"Dear Marmee and Beth, – I'm going to write you a regular volume, for I've got heaps to tell. Mrs. Kirke welcomed me so kindly I felt at home at once, even in that big house full of strangers. She gave me a funny little sky-parlour, all she had; but the fine view atones for the many stairs. The two little girls are pretty children – rather spoilt, I fancy.

"As I went downstairs the first time I saw something I liked. The flights are very long in this tall house, and as I stood waiting at the head of the third one for a little servant girl to lumber up, I saw a gentleman come along behind her, take the heavy hod of coal out of her hand, carry it all the way up, put it down at a door near by, and walk away, saying with a kind nod and a foreign accent – 'It goes better so. The little back is too young to haf such heaviness.'

"Wasn't it good of him? I like such things, for, as father says, trifles show character. When I mentioned it to Mrs. K. that evening, she laughed, and said: 'That must have been Professor Bhaer; he's always doing things of that sort.'

"Mrs. K. told me he was from Berlin; very learned and good, but poor as a church mouse, and gives lessons to support himself and two little orphan nephews whom he is educating here, according to the wishes of his sister, who married an American. Not a very romantic story, but it interested me, and I was glad to hear that Mrs. K. lends him her parlour for some of his scholars. There is a glass door between it and the nursery, and I mean to peep at him, and then I'll tell you how he looks. He's almost forty, so it's no harm, Marmee.

"Good night and more tomorrow."

"*Tuesday Eve.*

"After lunch the girl took the children for a walk, and I went to my needlework. Suddenly I heard someone humming in the next room like a big bumble-bee. I couldn't resist the temptation, and lifting one end of the curtain before the glass door I peeped in. Professor Bhaer was there arranging his books. He has brown hair tumbled all over his head, a bushy beard, the kindest eyes I ever saw, and a splendid big voice. He looked like a gentleman, though two buttons were off his coat, and there was a patch on one shoe.

"When a tap came at the door, he called out in a loud, brisk tone: 'Herein!' and a morsel of a child entered, and ran to kiss and play with him, while he stroked her pretty hair with a fatherly look. Another knock, and the appearance of two young ladies for German lessons sent me back to my work."

Jo soon became acquainted with the professor. She found him trying to darn his socks, clumsily enough, one day, and offered to do his mending for him. In return he gave her German lessons, and they spent many pleasant hours together. Though very happy in the social atmosphere about her, and very busy with the daily work that earned her bread, Jo still found time for literary labours, and turned out many stories.

It was a pleasant winter and a long one, for she did not leave Mrs. Kirke until June.

"Going home? Ah, you are happy that you haf a home to go in," said Professor Bhaer when she bade him good-bye.

"Now, sir, you won't forget to come and see us, if you travel our way, will you?" she said.

"Shall I come?" he asked, looking down at her with an eager expression which she did not see.

"Yes, come next month; Laurie graduates then, and you'd enjoy Commencement as something new."

"That is your best friend, of whom you speak?" he said in an altered tone.

"Yes, my boy Teddy; I'm very proud of him and should like you to see him."

Jo looked up then, quite unconscious of anything but her own pleasure in the prospect of showing them to one another. Something in Mr. Bhaer's face suddenly recalled the fact that she might find Laurie more than a "best friend," and simply because she particularly wished not to look as if anything was the matter, she involuntarily began to blush; and the more she tried not to the redder she became.

That night the professor sat long before his fire, with a tired, homesick look on his face. Once when he remembered Jo he leant his head on his hands a minute and then roamed about the room as

if in search of something he could not find. Next morning early he saw Jo off at the station.

Whatever his motive might have been, Laurie studied to some purpose that year, for he graduated with honour; and a day or two afterwards he begged Jo to marry him.

Jo never had a harder task in her life than to refuse her boy when he pleaded so hard. Not till months afterwards did she understand how she had the strength of mind to hold fast to the resolution she had made when she decided that she did not love Laurie and never could. It was very difficult to do, but she did it, knowing that delay was both useless and cruel.

Laurie took it terribly to heart, and his grandfather arranged for them both to go abroad to Europe to give him something fresh to think of and stop him continually seeing Jo. Before the blighted being recovered spirit enough to rebel they were off.

When the parting came, he affected high spirits. He put his arms round Jo as she stood on the step above him, and just for a moment the gaiety fled. He looked up at her with a face that made his short appeal both eloquent and pathetic.

"Oh, Jo, can't you:"

"Teddy, dear, I wish I could!"

That was all, except a little pause; then Laurie straightened himself up, said "It's all right, never mind," and went away without another word. Ah, but it wasn't all right, and Jo *did* mind; for while the curly head lay on her arm a minute after her hard answer, she felt as if she had stabbed her dearest friend; but when he left her without a look behind him she knew that the boy Laurie never would come again.

Once the travellers had gone, she had leisure to notice the change in Beth. No one spoke of it or seemed aware of it, but to eyes sharpened by absence it was very plain; and a heavy weight fell on Jo as she saw her sister's face. There was a strange, transparent look about it, as of the immortal shining through the frail flesh with an indescribably pathetic beauty.

Jo took Beth for a holiday to the seaside, where they excited much interest in those around them, who watched with sympathetic eyes the strong sister and the feeble one, always together, as if they felt instinctively that a long separation was not far away.

They often felt it, yet neither spoke of it till one day when Beth lay on the shore with her head in Jo's lap. It came to Jo then more bitterly than ever that Beth was slowly drifting away from her, and her arms instinctively tightened their hold upon the dearest treasure she possessed. There was hardly any need for Beth to say: "Jo, dear, I'm glad you know it. I've tried to tell you, but I couldn't. I've known it for a good while, dear, and now I'm getting used to it. I gave up hope in the autumn, before you went away."

Jo could not speak; she leaned down to kiss the tranquil face, and with that silent kiss she dedicated herself soul and body to Beth.

She had dreaded telling them at home; but there was no need. Beth's secret was plain now. Tired with her short journey, she went at once to bed. When Jo went downstairs her father stood leaning

his head on the mantelpiece and did not turn as she came in; but her mother stretched out her arms as if for help, and Jo went to comfort her without a word.

On Christmas Day Laurie was in the sunshine at Nice, strolling along the promenade. The quick trot of ponies' feet made him look up as a little carriage containing a single lady came rapidly down the street. He stared a minute, then his whole face woke up and, waving his hat like a boy, he hurried to meet her.

"Oh, Laurie, is it really you? I thought you'd never come!" cried Amy.

"I was detained by the way, but I promised to spend Christmas with you, and here I am. Grandfather has settled in Paris for the winter. He has friends there, and I come and go."

As she drove him along, Amy watched Laurie and felt a new sort of shyness steal over her; for he was changed from a merry-faced boy

into a moody looking man, greatly improved, but tired and spiritless. When he complimented her on her appearance she blushed with pleasure, but was disappointed, too, at missing the old Laurie.

That night there was a Christmas party at the hotel where the Carrols and Amy were staying, and, of course, Laurie came. Amy prinked that evening and looked her best, and Laurie received some charming new impressions of her as a young lady who had been polished and brought out by her foreign travels.

Laurie had gone to Nice intending to stay a week and remained a month. Amy never would pet him as her sisters had done at home, but she was very glad to see him now, and quite clung to him, feeling that he was the representative of the dear family for whom she longed more than she would confess. They were much together, riding, walking and dawdling, all the while half consciously making discoveries and forming opinions about each other. Amy rose daily in the estimation of her friend, but he sunk in hers.

Laurie made no effort of any kind, but just let himself drift comfortably along, trying to forget, and feeling that all women owed him a kind word because one had been cold to him, though he rather dreaded the keen blue eyes that watched him with such half-sorrowful, half-scornful surprise.

One day Amy was going to Valrosa to sketch, and Laurie went with her.

"Laurie, when are you going to your grandfather?" she asked presently as she settled herself on a rustic seat. "He expects you, and you really ought to go."

"Very soon."

"Then why don't you do it?"

"Natural depravity, I suppose."

"Natural indolence, you mean. It's really dreadful!" said Amy severely, and she proceeded to lecture him on his lazy, drifting ways.

"Flo and I have got a new name for you; it's 'Lazy Laurence.' And if you want to know what I honestly think of you – well, I despise you," she wound up.

In a minute a hand came down over the page so that she could not draw, and Laurie's voice said, with a droll imitation of a penitent child:

"I will be good, oh, I will be good!"

That night he went back to his grandfather in Paris. Amy had done him good.

When the first bitterness was over, the family put away their grief and vied with each other in making that last year a happy one. The pleasantest room in the house was set apart for Beth, and here they all gathered round her day by day, like a cherished household saint in its shrine. The first few months were very happy ones.

But by and by Beth said her needle was "so heavy" and put it down for ever; talking wearied her, faces troubled her and pain claimed her for its own.

Jo never left her for an hour since Beth had said, "I feel stronger when you are near." All day she haunted the room, jealous of any other nurse, and at night she slept on a couch close by.

So the spring days came and went, the sky grew clearer, the earth greener, the flowers were up fair and early, and the birds came back in time to say good-bye to Beth.

As Beth had hoped, the "tide went out easily"; and in the dark hour before the dawn, on the bosom where she had drawn her first breath, she quietly drew her last, with no farewell but one loving look, one little sigh.

Amy's lecture did Laurie good. Turning it over in his mind often afterwards, he presently brought himself to admit that he *had* been lazy and selfish. After staying a time with his grandfather, he went off to Vienna, where he had musical friends, determined both to practise his playing very hard and to compose music. Laurie thought that the task of forgetting Jo would absorb all his powers for years; but to his great surprise he discovered it grew easier every day. These hearts of ours are curious and contrary things, and his *wouldn't* ache. Instead of trying to forget, he found himself trying to remember. Meanwhile he corresponded regularly with Amy.

While these changes were going on abroad trouble had come at home; but the letter telling that Beth was failing never reached Amy, and when the next found her, at Vevey in Switzerland, the grass was green above her sister. Amy bore it very well, but her heart was very heavy; she longed to be at home, and every day looked wistfully across the lake, waiting for Laurie to come and comfort her.

He did come as soon as possible, and first saw her sitting in the hotel garden, leaning her head on her hand, thinking of Beth. She looked up and saw him; then, dropping everything, she ran to him, exclaiming in a tone of unmistakable love and longing:

"Oh, Laurie, Laurie, I knew you'd come to me!"

I think everything was said and settled then: for as they stood together quite silent for a moment, Amy felt that no one could comfort and sustain her so well as Laurie, and Laurie decided that Amy was the only woman in the world who could fill Jo's place and make him happy. But actually it was not till a week or two later, rowing on the lake at midday, that they became engaged.

Jo was alone in the twilight, lying on the old sofa, looking at the fire and thinking. Her face looked tired, grave and rather sad. Tomorrow was her birthday. Almost twenty-five, and she was thinking how fast the years went by, and how little she seemed to have accomplished.

The months since Beth's death had been very hard ones for her, when her heart ached with a ceaseless longing for her sister, when the everyday duties seemed a weariness now there was no Beth to serve and she could not write at all. Now she was thinking how little the future appeared to offer, how dull it would be compared with Amy's – for the news of the younger sister's engagement had been received some time.

"An old maid, that's what I am to be, with a pen for a spouse, a family of stories for children, and twenty years hence a morsel of fame, perhaps."

Jo must have fallen asleep, for suddenly Laurie's ghost seemed to stand before her – a substantial life-like ghost that suddenly stopped and kissed her. She flew up, crying joyfully:

"Oh, my Teddy! Oh, my Teddy! Where's Amy?"

"Your mother has got her down at Meg's. We stopped there by the way, and there was no getting my wife out of their clutches."

"You've gone and got married?" cried Jo.

"Yes, please, but I never will again"; and he went down upon his knees, with a penitent clasping of hands, and a face full of mischief, mirth and triumph.

Then he sobered down and explained that the Carrols had decided to stay abroad another winter, while Mr. Laurence wanted to come home. Laurie couldn't let the old gentleman travel alone, nor would he leave Amy, so they had settled matters by getting married quietly in Paris before sailing for America.

Then Amy's voice was heard calling: "Where is she? Where's my dear old Jo?" In trooped the whole family, and everyone was hugged and kissed all over again. No one could forget Beth, but it was a happy homecoming all the same. They were all there, even the twins, and Jo was the only one who felt partnerless. Suddenly there was a knock at the porch door, and there stood a tall bearded gentleman, beaming on her from the darkness like the midnight sun.

"Oh, Mr. Bhaer, I am so glad to see you!" cried Jo. She positively clutched him in, shut the door behind him, and bereft him of his hat. "Father, mother, this is my friend, Professor Bhaer," she said, with a face and tone of such irrepressible pride and pleasure that she might as well have blown a trumpet.

Everyone gave Mr. Bhaer a cordial welcome for Jo's sake, and soon liked him for his own; while Jo's own stealthy glances at him now and then refreshed her like sips of water over a dusty walk. Poor Jo, how she did glorify that plain man as she sat knitting away so quietly, yet letting nothing escape her.

"Dear old fellow! He couldn't have got himself up with more care if he'd been going awooing," said Jo to herself, and then blushed furiously.

Nobody knew where the evening went, for Hannah skilfully abstracted the babies at an early hour, and the others sat round the fire, talking away, regardless of time. At last Meg, thinking of her children, made a move to go.

Professor Bhaer stared at Amy putting on her bonnet, for she had been introduced simply as "my sister," and no one had called her by her new name since he came. He forgot himself still further when Laurie said in his most gracious manner at parting: "My wife and I are very glad to meet you, sir. Please remember that there is always a welcome waiting for you over the way."

Then the professor thanked him so heartily, and looked so suddenly

illuminated with satisfaction, that Laurie thought him the most delightfully demonstrative old fellow he ever met.

"I, too, shall go; but I shall gladly come again, if you will gif me
leave, dear madam, for a little business in the city will keep me here
some days."

He spoke to Mrs. March, but he looked at Jo, and the mother's
voice gave as cordial an assent as did the daughter's eyes.

For a fortnight Mr. B'haer came and went with lover-like regularity.
It was amazing how often Jo met him on her evening strolls and how
blooming she looked after them. Then Mr. Bhaer stayed away for
three whole days and made no sign, and Jo became pensive at first,
and then – alas, for romance! – very cross.

"It's nothing to me, of course; but I should think he would have
come and bid us good-bye, like a gentleman," she said to herself, as
she put on her things for the customary walk, one dull afternoon.

She quite forgot the umbrella her mother reminded her to take, and though she had gone out to buy needles and ribbon, she somehow found herself among the counting-houses and banks in the business part of the town, where gentlemen do congregate, loitering about as if waiting for someone.

A drop of rain on her cheek recalled her thoughts from baffled hopes to ruined ribbons. Now she remembered the little umbrella which she had forgotten; but regret was unavailing, and nothing could be done but borrow one or submit to a drenching. She looked up at

394

the lowering sky, down at the crimson bow already flecked with black, forward along the muddy street, then one long, lingering look behind, at a certain grimy warehouse, with "Hoffman, Swartz and Co." over the door, and said to herself, with a sternly reproachful air: "It serves me right! What business had I to put on all my best things and come philandering down here, hoping to see the professor? Jo, I'm ashamed of you! No, you shall not go there to borrow an umbrella, or find out where he is, from his friends. You shall trudge away and do your errands in the rain, and if you catch your death and ruin your bonnet, it's no more than you deserve. Now then!"

With that she rushed across the street so impetuously that she narrowly escaped annihilation from a passing truck, and precipitated herself into the arms of a stately old gentleman, who said: "I beg pardon, ma'am," and looked mortally offended. Somewhat daunted, Jo righted herself, spread her handkerchief over the devoted ribbons, and, putting temptation behind her, hurried on, with increasing dampness about the ankles and much clashing of umbrellas overhead. The fact that a somewhat dilapidated blue one remained stationary above the unprotected bonnet attracted her attention, and, looking up, she saw Mr. Bhaer looking down.

"I feel to know the strong-minded lady who goes so bravely under

many horse-noses, and so fast through much mud. What do you down here, my friend?"

"I'm shopping."

Mr. Bhaer smiled, as he glanced from the pickle factory on one side to the wholesale hide and leather concern on the other; but he only said politely: "You haf no umbrella. May I go also and take for you the bundles?"

"Yes, thank you."

Jo's cheeks were as red as her ribbon; but she didn't care, for in a minute she found herself walking away arm-in-arm with her professor, feeling as if the sun had suddenly burst out with uncommon brilliancy, that the world was all right again, and that one thoroughly happy woman was paddling through the wet that day.

"We thought you had gone," said Jo. "We rather missed you – father and mother especially."

"And you?"

"I'm always glad to see you, sir."

In her anxiety to keep her voice quite calm Jo made it rather cool,

and the frosty little monosyllable at the end seemed to chill the professor, for his smile vanished as he said gravely: "I thank you, and come one time more before I go."

"You are going, then."

"I haf no longer any business here; it is done."

"Successfully, I hope?" said Jo, for the bitterness of disappointment was in that short reply of his.

"I ought to think so, for I haf a way opened to me by which I can make my bread and gif my nephews much help. My friends find for me a place in a college, where I teach and earn enough to make the way smooth for Franz and Emil. But you and I will not meet often, I fear; this place is at the West."

"So far away!" And Jo left her skirts to their fate, as if it didn't matter now what became of her clothes or herself.

"Now shall we go home?" he asked.

"Yes; it's late, and I'm so tired." Jo's voice was more pathetic than she knew, for now the sun seemed to have gone in as suddenly as it came out, the world grew muddy and miserable again, and for the first time she discovered that her feet were cold, her head ached, and that her heart was colder than the former, fuller of pain than the latter. Mr. Bhaer was going away; he only cared for her as a friend; it was all a mistake, and the sooner it was over the better. With this idea in her head she hailed an approaching omnibus in haste.

"This is not our omniboos," said the professor, waving the loaded vehicle away.

"I beg your pardon, I didn't see the name distinctly. Never mind, I can walk. I'm used to plodding in the mud," returned Jo, winking hard, because she would have died rather than openly wipe her eyes.

Mr. Bhaer saw the drops on her cheeks; the sight seemed to touch him very much, for, suddenly stooping down, he asked in a tone that meant a great deal: "Heart's dearest, why do you cry?"

That undignified creature answered with an irrepressible sob: "Because you are going away."

"Ach, mein Gott, that is so good!" cried Mr. Bhaer, managing to clasp his hands in spite of the umbrella and the bundles. "Jo, I haf nothing but much love to gif you; I came to see if you could care for it, and I waited to be sure that I was something more than a friend. Am I? Can you make a little place in your heart for old Fritz?" he added, all in one breath.

"Oh, yes!" said Jo; and he was quite satisfied, for she folded both hands over his arm, and looked up at him with an expression that plainly showed how happy she would be to walk through life beside him, even though she had no better shelter than the old umbrella, if he carried it.

"Haf you patience to wait a long time, Jo? I must go away and do my work alone. I must help my boys first, because, even for you, I may not break my word to Minna. Can you forgif that, and be happy while we hope and wait?"

"Yes, I know I can, for we love one another."

"Ah, thou gifest me such hope and courage, and I haf nothing to gif back but a full heart and these empty hands," cried the professor.

Jo never, never would learn to be proper, for when he said that as they stood upon the steps, she just put both hands into his, whispering tenderly: "Not empty now," and, stooping down, kissed her Friedrich under the umbrella. It was dreadful, but she would have done it if the flock of draggle-tailed sparrows on the hedge had been human beings, for she was very far gone indeed, and quite regardless of everything but her own happiness. Though it came in such a very simple guise, that was the crowning moment of both their lives, when, turning from the night and storm and loneliness to the household light and warmth and peace waiting to receive them, with a glad "Welcome home!" Jo led her lover in and shut the door.

Gay Robin
is seen no more

Gay Robin is seen no more:
He is gone with the snow,
For winter is o'er
And Robin will go.
In need he was fed, and now he is fled
Away to his secret nest.
No more will he stand
Begging for crumbs,
No longer he comes
Beseeching our hand
And showing his breast
At window and door:
Gay Robin is seen no more

Blithe Robin is heard no more:
He gave us his song
When summer was o'er
And winter was long:
He sang for his bread, and now he is fled
Away to his secret nest,
And there in the green
Early and late
Alone to his mate
He pipeth unseen
And swelleth his breast;
For us it o'er:
Blithe Robin is heard no more.

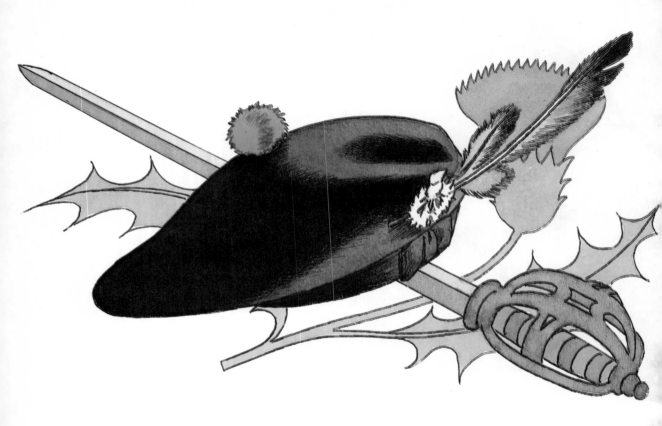

KIDNAPPED

Robert Louis Stevenson is justly renowned for his novels and poems.
Kidnapped, *like his other thrilling novels, is packed with thrills and
action from cover to cover. It tells of the adventures of young David
Balfour and the story is related in the first person.*

*It features a stolen inheritance and the kidnapping of David by an
evil seaman named Captain Hoseason.*

*David forms a lasting friendship with Alan Breck, a hunted High-
lander and the range of the book runs from battle and sudden death on
the high seas to murder in the Scottish Highlands. But first David meets
his rascally uncle Ebenezer Balfour of Shaws.*

*The book begins as David sets out to meet his uncle. There now fol-
lows in Stevenson's words the opening scenes of this exciting story.*

CHAPTER ONE
I set off upon my journey to the House of Shaws

I will begin the story of my adventures with a certain morning early in the month of June, the year of grace 1751, when I took the key for the last time out of the door of my father's house. The sun began to shine upon the summit of the hills as I went down the road; and by the time I had come as far as the manse, the blackbirds were whistling in the garden lilacs, and the mist that hung around the valley in the time of the dawn was beginning to arise and die away.

Mr. Campbell, the minister of Essendean, was waiting for me by the garden gate, good man! He asked me if I had breakfasted; and hearing that I lacked for nothing, he took my hand in both of his and clapped it kindly under his arm.

"Well, Davie, lad," said he, "I will go with you as far as the ford, to set you on the way."

And we began to walk forward in silence.

"Are ye sorry to leave Essendean?" said he, after awhile.

"Why, sir," said I, "if I knew where I was going, or what was likely to become of me, I would tell you candidly Essendean is a good place indeed, and I have been very happy there; but then I have never been anywhere else. My father and mother, since they are both dead, I shall be no nearer to in Essendean than in the Kingdom of Hungary; and, to speak truth, if I thought I had a chance to better myself where I was going I would go with a good will."

"Ay?" said Mr. Campbell. "Very well, Davie. Then it behoves me to tell your fortune; or so far as I may. When your mother was gone, and your father (the worthy, Christian man) began to sicken for his end, he gave me in charge a certain letter, which he said was your inheritance. 'So soon,' says he, 'as I am gone, and the house is redd up and the gear disposed of' (all which, Davie, hath been done), 'give my boy this letter into his hand, and start him off to the house of Shaws, not far from Cramond. That is the place I came from,' he said, 'and it's where it befits that my boy should return. He is a steady lad,' your father said, 'and a canny goer; and I doubt not he will come safe, and be well liked where he goes.'"

"The house of Shaws!" I cried. "What had my poor father to do with the house of Shaws?"

"Nay," said Mr. Campbell, "who can tell that for a surety? But the name of that family, Davie, boy, is the name you bear – Balfours of Shaws: an ancient, honest, reputable house, peradventure in these latter days decayed. Your father, too, was a man of learning as befitted his position; no man more plausibly conducted school; nor had he the manner or the speech of a common dominie; but (as ye will yourself remember) I took aye a pleasure to have him to the manse to meet the gentry; and those of my own house, Campbell of Kilrennet, Campbell of Dunswire, Campbell of Minch, and others, all well-kenned gentlemen, had pleasure in his society. Lastly, to put all the elements of this affair before you, here is the testamentary letter itself, superscrived by the own hand of our departed brother."

He gave me the letter, which was addressed in these words: "To the hands of Ebenezer Balfour, Esquire, of Shaws, in his house of Shaws, these will be delivered by my son, David Balfour." My heart was beating hard at this great prospect now suddenly opening before a lad of seventeen years of age, the son of a poor country dominie in the Forest of Ettrick.

"Mr. Campbell," I stammered, "and if you were in my shoes, would you go?"

"Of a surety," said the minister, "that would I, and without pause. A pretty lad like you should get to Cramond (which is near in by Edinburgh) in two days of walk. If the worst came to the worst, and your high relations (as I cannot but suppose them to be somewhat of your blood) should put you to the door, ye can but walk the two days back again and risp at the manse door. But I would rather hope that ye shall be well received, as your poor father forecast for you, and for anything that I ken come to be a great man in time. And here, Davie, laddie," he resumed, "it lies near upon my conscience to improve this parting, and set you on the right guard against the dangers of the world."

Here he cast about for a comfortable seat, lighted on a big boulder under a birch by the trackside, sat down upon it with a very long, serious upper lip, and the sun now shining in upon us between two peaks, put his pocket-handkerchief over his cocked hat to shelter him. There, then, with uplifted forefinger, he first put me on my guard against a considerable number of heresies, to which I had no temptation, and urged upon me to be instant in my prayers and reading of the Bible. That done, he drew a picture of the great house that I was bound to, and how I should conduct myself with its inhabitants.

"Be soople, Davie, in things immaterial," said he. "Bear ye this in mind, that, though gentle born, ye have had a country rearing. Dinnae

shame us, Davie, dinnae shame us! In yon great, muckle house, with all these domestics, upper and under, show yourself as nice, as circumspect, as quick at the conception, and as slow of speech as any. As for the laird – remember he's the laird; I say no more: honour to whom honour. It's a pleasure to obey a laird: or should be, to the young."

"Well, sir," said I, "it may be; and I'll promise you I'll try to make it so."

"Why, very well said," replied Mr. Campbell, heartily. "And now to come to the material, or (to make a quibble) to the immaterial. I have here a little packet which contains four things." He tugged it, as he spoke, and with some great difficulty, from the skirt pocket of his coat. "Of these four things, the first is your legal due: the little pickle money for your father's books and plenishing, which I have bought (as I have explained from the first) in the design of re-selling at a profit to the incoming dominie. The other three are gifties that Mrs. Campbell and myself would be blithe of your acceptance. The first, which is round, will likely please ye best at the first off-go; but, O Davie, laddie, it's but a drop of water in the sea; it'll help you but a step, and vanish like the morning. The second, which is flat and square and written upon, will stand by you through life, like a good staff for the road, and a good pillow to your head in sickness. And as for the last, which is cubical, that'll see you, it's my prayerful wish, into a better land."

With that he got upon his feet, took off his hat, and prayed a little while aloud, and in affecting terms, for a young man setting out into the world; then suddenly took me in his arms and embraced me very hard; then held me at arm's length, looking at me with his face all working with sorrow; and then whipped about, and crying good-bye to me, set off backward by the way that we had come at a sort of jogging run. It might have been laughable to another; but I was in no mind to laugh. I watched him as long as he was in sight; and he never stopped hurrying, nor once looked back. Then it came in upon my mind that this was all his sorrow at my departure; and my conscience smote me hard and fast, because I, for my part, was overjoyed to get away out of that quiet country-side, and go to a great, busy house, among rich and respected gentlefolk of my own name and blood.

"Davie, Davie," I thought, "was ever seen such black ingratitude? Can you forget old favours and old friends at the mere whistle of a name? Fie, fie; think shame!"

And I sat down on the boulder the good man had just left, and opened the parcel to see the nature of my gifts. That which he had called cubical, I had never had much doubt of; sure enough it was a little Bible, to carry in a plaid-neuk. That which he had called round,

I found to be a shilling piece; and the third, which was to help me so wonderfully both in health and sickness all the days of my life, was a little piece of coarse yellow paper, written upon thus in red ink:

"TO MAKE LILLY OF THE VALLEY WATER – Take the flowers of lilly of the valley and distil them in sack, and drink a spooneful or two as there is occasion. It restores speech to those that have the dumb palsey. It is good against the Gout; it comforts the heart and strengthens the memory; and the flowers, put into a Glasse, close stopt, and set into ane hill of ants for a month, then take it out, and you will find a liquor which comes from the flowers, which keep in a vial; it is good, ill or well, and whether man or woman."

And then, in the minister's own hand, was added:

"Likewise for sprains, rub it in; and for the cholic, a great spoonful in the hour."

To be sure, I laughed over this; but it was rather tremulous laughter; and I was glad to get my bundle on my staff's end and set out over the ford and up the hill upon the farther side; till, just as I came on the green drove-road running wide through the heather, I took my last look of Kirk Essendean, the trees about the manse, and the big rowans in the kirkyard where my father and my mother lay.

CHAPTER TWO
I come to my journey's end

On the forenoon of the second day, coming to the top of a hill, I saw all the country fall away before me down to the sea; and in the midst of this descent, on a long ridge, the city of Edinburgh smoking like a kiln. There was a flag upon the castle, and ships moving or lying anchored in the firth; both of which, for as far away as they were, I could distinguish clearly; and both brought my country heart into my mouth.

Presently after, I came by a house where a shepherd lived, and got a rough direction for the neighbourhood of Cramond; and so, from one to another, worked my way to the westward of the capital by Colinton, till I came out upon the Glasgow road. And there, to my great pleasure and wonder, I beheld a regiment marching to the fifes, every foot in time; an old red-faced general on a grey horse at the one end, and at the other the company of Grenadiers, with their Pope's-hats. The pride of life seemed to mount into my brain at the sight of the red coats and the hearing of that merry music.

A little farther on, and I was told I was in Cramond parish, and began to substitute in my inquiries the name of the house of Shaws. It was a word that seemed to surprise those of whom I sought my way. At first I thought the plainness of my appearance, in my country habit, and that all dusty from the road, consorted ill with the greatness of the place to which I was bound. But after two, or maybe three, had given me the same look and the same answer, I began to take it in my head there was something strange about the Shaws itself.

The better to set this fear at rest, I changed the form of my inquiries; and spying an honest fellow coming along a lane on the shaft of his cart, I asked him if he had ever heard tell of a house they called the house of Shaws.

He stopped his cart and looked at me, like the others.

"Ay," said he. "What for?"

"It's a great house?" I asked.

"Doubtless," says he. "The house is a big, muckle house."

"Ay," said I, "but the folk that are in it?"

"Folk?" cried he. "Are ye daft? There's nae folk there – to call folk."

"What?" says I; "not Mr. Ebenezer?"

"Ou, ay," says the man; "there's the laird, to be sure, if it's him you're wanting. What'll like be your business, mannie?"

"I was led to think that I would get a situation," I said, looking as modest as I could.

"What?" cries the carter, in so sharp a note that his very horse started; and then, "Well, mannie," he added, "it's nane of my affairs; but ye seem a decent-spoken lad; and if ye'll take a word from me, ye'll keep clear of the Shaws."

The next person I came across was a dapper little man in a beautiful white wig, whom I saw to be a barber on his rounds; and knowing well that barbers were great gossips, I asked him plainly what sort of a man was Mr. Balfour of the Shaws."

"Hoot, hoot, hoot," said the barber; "nae kind of a man, nae kind of a man at all"; and began to ask me very shrewdly what my business was; but I was more than a match for him at that, and he went on to his next customer no wiser than he came.

I cannot well describe the blow this dealt to my illusions. The more indistinct the accusations were, the less I liked them, for they left the wider field to fancy. What kind of a great house was this, that all the parish should start and stare to be asked the way to it? or what sort of a gentleman, that his ill-fame should be thus current on the wayside? If an hour's walking would have brought me back to Essendean, I had left my adventure then and there, and returned to Mr. Campbell's. But when I had come so far a way already, mere shame would not suffer me to desist till I had put the matter to the touch of proof; I was bound, out of mere self-respect, to carry it through; and little as I liked the sound of what I heard, and slow as I began to travel, I still kept asking my way and still kept advancing.

It was drawing on to sundown when I met a stout, dark, sour-looking woman coming trudging down a hill; and she, when I had put my usual question, turned sharp about, accompanied me back to the summit she had just left, and pointed to a great bulk of building standing very bare upon a green in the bottom of the next valley. The country was pleasant round about, running in low hills, pleasantly watered and wooded, and the crops, to my eyes, wonderfully good; but the house itself appeared to be a kind of ruin; no road led up to it; no smoke arose from any of the chimneys; nor was there any semblance of a garden. My heart sank. "That!" I cried.

The woman's face lit up with a malignant anger. "That is the house of Shaws!" she cried, "blood built it; blood stopped the building of it, blood shall bring it down. See here!" she cried again – "I spit upon the ground, and crack my thumb at it! Black be its fall! If ye see the laird, tell him what ye hear; tell him this makes the twelve hunner and nineteen time that Jennet Clouston has called down the curse on him and his house, byre and stable, man, guest, and master, wife, miss, or bairn – black, black be their fall!"

And the woman, whose voice had risen to a kind of eldritch sing-song, turned with a skip, and was gone. I stood where she left me, with my hair on end. In those days folk still believed in witches and trembled at a curse; and this one, falling so pat, like a wayside omen, to arrest me ere I carried out my purpose, took the pith out of my legs.

I sat me down and stared at the house of Shaws. The more I looked, the pleasanter that country-side appeared; being all set with hawthorn bushes full of flowers; the fields dotted with sheep; a fine flight of

rooks in the sky; and every sign of a kind soil and climate; and yet the barrack in the midst of it went sore against my fancy.

Country folk went by from the fields as I sat there on the side of the ditch, but I lacked the spirit to give them a good-e'en. At last the sun went down, and then, right up against the yellow sky, I saw a scroll of smoke go mounting, not much thicker, as it seemed to me, than the smoke of a candle; but still there it was, and meant a fire, and warmth, and cookery, and some living inhabitant that must have lit it; and this comforted my heart.

So I set forward by a little faint track in the grass that led in my direction. It was very faint indeed to be the only way to a place of habitation; yet I saw no other. Presently it brought me to stone uprights, with an unroofed lodge beside them, and coats of arms upon the top. A main entrance it was plainly meant to be, but never finished; instead of gates of wrought iron, a pair of hurdles were tied across with a straw rope; and as there were no park walls, nor any sign of avenue, the track that I was following passed on the right hand of the pillars, and went wandering on toward the house.

The nearer I got to that, the drearier it appeared. It seemed like the one wing of a house that had never been finished. What should have been the inner end stood open on the upper floors, and showed against the sky with steps and stairs of uncompleted masonry. Many of the windows were unglazed, and bats flew in and out like doves out of a dove-cote.

The night had begun to fall as I got close; and in three of the lower windows, which were very high up and narrow, and well barred, the changing light of a little fire began to glimmer.

Was this the palace I had been coming to? Was it within these walls that I was to seek new friends and begin great fortunes? Why, in my father's house on Essen-Waterside, the fire and the bright lights would show a mile away, and the door open to a beggar's knock!

I came forward cautiously, and giving ear as I came, heard someone rattling with dishes, and a little dry, eager cough that came in fits; but there was no sound of speech, and not a dog barked.

The door, as well as I could see it in the dim light, was a great piece of wood all studded with nails; and I lifted my hand with a faint heart under my jacket, and knocked once. Then I stood and waited. The house had fallen into a dead silence; a whole minute passed away, and nothing stirred but the bats overhead. I knocked again, and hearkened again. By this time my ears had grown so accustomed to the quiet, that I could hear the ticking of the clock inside as it slowly counted out the seconds; but whoever was in the house kept deadly still, and must have held his breath.

I was in two minds whether to run away; but anger got the upper hand, and I began instead to rain kicks and buffets on the door, and to shout out aloud for Mr. Balfour. I was in full career, when I heard

the cough right overhead, and jumping back and looking up, beheld a man's head in a tall nightcap, and the bell mouth of a blunderbuss, at one of the first-storey windows.

"It's loaded," said a voice.

"I have come here with a letter," I said, "to Mr. Ebenezer Balfour of Shaws. Is he here?"

"From whom is it?" asked the man with the blunderbuss.

"That is neither here nor there," said I, for I was growing very wroth.

"Well", was the reply, "ye can put it down upon the doorstep, and be off with ye."

"I will do no such thing," I cried. "I will deliver it into Mr. Balfour's hands, as it was meant I should. It is a letter of introduction."

"A what?" cried the voice, sharply.

I repeated what I had said.

"Who are ye, yourself?" was the next question, after a considerable pause.

"I am not ashamed of my name," said I. "They call me David Balfour."

At that, I made sure the man started, for I heard the blunderbuss rattle on the window-sill; and it was after quite a long pause, and with a curious change of voice, that the next question followed:

"Is your father dead?"

I was so much surprised at this, that I could find no voice to answer, but stood staring.

"Ay," the man resumed, "he'll be dead, no doubt; and that'll be what brings ye chapping to my door." Another pause, and then defiantly, "Well, man," he said, "I'll let ye in"; and he disappeared from the window.

CHAPTER THREE
I make acquaintance of my uncle

resently there came a great rattling of chains and bolts, and the door was cautiously opened and shut to again behind me as soon as I had passed.

"Go into the kitchen and touch naething," said the voice; and while the person of the house set himself to replacing the defences of the door, I groped my way forward and entered the kitchen.

The fire had burned up fairly bright, and showed me the barest room I think I ever put my eyes on. Half-a-dozen dishes stood upon the shelves; the table was laid for supper with a bowl of porridge, a horn spoon, and a cup of small beer. Besides what I have named, there was not another thing in that great, stone-vaulted, empty chamber but lock-fast chests arranged along the wall and a corner cupboard with a padlock.

As soon as the last chain was up, the man rejoined me. He was a mean, stooping, narrow-shouldered, clayfaced creature; and his age might have been anything between fifty and seventy. His nightcap was of flannel, and so was the nightgown that he wore, instead of coat and waistcoat, over his ragged shirt. He was long unshaved; but what most distressed and even daunted me, he would neither take his eyes away from me nor look me fairly in the face. What he was, whether by trade or birth, was more than I could fathom; but he seemed most like an old, unprofitable serving-man, who should have been left in charge of that big house upon board wages.

"Are ye sharp-set?" he asked, glancing at about the level of my knee. "Ye can eat that drop parritch?"

I said I feared it was his own supper.

"O," said he, "I can do fine wanting it. I'll take the ale, though, for it slockens my cough." He drank the cup about half out, still keeping an eye upon me as he drank; and then suddenly held out his hand. "Let's see the letter," said he.

I told him the letter was for Mr. Balfour; not for him.

"And who do ye think I am?" says he. "Give me Alexander's letter!"

"You know my father's name?"

"It would be strange if I didnae," he returned, "for he was my born brother; and little as ye seem to like either me or my house, or my good parritch, I'm your born uncle, Davie, my man, and you my born nephew. So give us the letter, and sit down and fill your kyte."

If I had been some years younger, what with shame, weariness, and disappointment, I believe I had burst into tears. As it was, I could find no words, neither black nor white, but handed him the letter, and sat down to the porridge with as little appetite for meat as ever a young man had.

Meanwhile, my uncle, stooping over the fire, turned the letter over and over in his hands.

"Do ye ken what's in it?" he asked, suddenly.

"You see for yourself, sir," said I, "that the seal has not been broken."

"Ay," said he, "but what brought you here?"

"To give the letter," said I.

"No," says he, cunningly, "but ye'll have had some hopes, nae doubt?"

"I confess, sir," said I, "when I was told that I had kinsfolk well-to-do, I did indeed indulge the hope that they might help me in my life. But I am no beggar; I look for no favours at your hands, and I want none that are not freely given. For as poor as I appear, I have friends of my own that will be blithe to help me."

"Hoot-toot!" said Uncle Ebenezer, "dinnae fly up in the snuff at me. We'll agree fine yet. And, Davie, my man, if you're done with that bit parritch, I could just take a sup of it myself. Ay," he continued, as soon as he had ousted me from the stool and spoon, "they're fine, halesome food – they're grand food, parritch." He murmured a little grace to himself and fell to. "Your father was very fond of his meat, I mind; he was a hearty, if not a great eater; but as for me, I could never do mair than pyke at food." He took a pull at the small beer, which probably reminded him of hospitable duties, for his next speech ran thus: "If ye're dry ye'll find water behind the door."

To this I returned no answer, standing stiffly on my two feet, and looking down upon my uncle with a mighty angry heart. He, on his part, continued to eat like a man under some pressure of time, and to throw out little darting glances now at my shoes and now at my home-spun stockings. Once only, when he had ventured to look a little higher, our eyes met; and no thief taken with a hand in a man's pocket could have shown more lively signals of distress. This set me in a muse, whether his timidity arose from too long a disuse of any human company; and whether perhaps, upon a little trial, it might pass off, and my uncle change into an altogether different man. From this I was awakened by his sharp voice.

"Your father's been long dead?" he asked.

"Three weeks, sir," said I.

"He was a secret man, Alexander – a secret, silent man," he continued. "He never said muckle when he was young. He'll never have spoken muckle of me?"

"I never knew, sir, till you told it me yourself, that he had any brother."

"Dear me, dear me!" said Ebenezer. "Nor yet of Shaws, I dare say?"

"Not so much as the name, sir," said I.

"To think o'that!" said he. "A strange nature of a man!" For all that, he seemed singularly satisfied, but whether with himself, or me, or with this conduct of my father's, was more than I could read. Certainly, however, he seemed to be outgrowing that distaste, or ill-will, that he had conceived at first against my person; for presently he jumped up, came across the room behind me, and hit me a smack upon the shoulder. "We'll agree fine yet!" he cried. "I'm just as glad I let you in. And now come awa' to your bed."

To my surprise, he lit no lamp or candle, but set forth into the dark passage, groped his way, breathing deeply, up a flight of steps, and paused before a door, which he unlocked. I was close upon his heels, having stumbled after him as best I might; and then he bade me go in, for that was my chamber. I did as he bid, but paused after a few steps, and begged a light to go to bed with.

"Hoot-toot!" said Uncle Ebenezer, "there's a fine moon."

"Neither moon nor star, sir, and pit-mirk," said I. "I cannae see the bed."

"Hoot-toot, hoot-toot!" said he. "Lights in a house is a thing I dinnae agree with. I'm unco feared of fires. Good night to ye, Davie, my man." And before I had time to add a further protest, he pulled the door to, and I heard him lock me in from the outside.

I did not know whether to laugh or cry. The room was as cold as a well, and the bed, when I had found my way to it, as damp as a peat-hag; but by good fortune I had caught up my bundle and my plaid, and rolling myself in the latter, I lay down upon the floor under lee of the big bedstead, and fell speedily asleep.

Later, David's uncle tries to kill him and David realises that the old man is trying to rob him of his inheritance. Then Ebenezer contrives to have David kidnapped and taken aboard a ship, to be sold as a slave in the American colonies. One night, the ship runs down a small boat from which is rescued Alan Breck, a rebel Highlander. Alan befriends David and when the ship is wrecked, they both escape together.

It is then that Colin of Glenure, Alan's sworn enemy, is murdered and Alan is blamed for the killing. He and David are hunted across Scotland. At last, they reach Queen's Ferry where they meet Mr. Rankeillor, the Balfour family lawyer. He tells David that Uncle Ebenezer and David's father who was the elder brother, had both fallen in love with the same girl, that David's father had won her and, sorry for Ebenezer, had given up his inheritance for the younger man. David and Ebenezer come to a settlement and David helps Alan to reach safety. So ends the story.

All Things Bright and Beautiful

All things bright and beautiful,
All creatures great and small,
All things wise and wonderful,
The Lord God made them all.

Each little flower that opens,
Each little bird that sings,
He made their glowing colours,
He made their tiny wings:

The purple-headed mountain,
The river running by,
The sunset and the morning,
That brightens up the sky:

The cold wind in the winter,
The pleasant summer sun,
The ripe fruits in the garden,
He made them every one:

The tall trees in the greenwood,
The meadows for our play,
The rushes by the water
To gather every day:

He gave us eyes to see them,
And lips that we might tell
How great is God Almighty
Who has made all things well.